TIGRESS

TIGRESS

John Gilbert

"No kinde of men of any profession in the
commonwealth passe their yeres in so great
and continual hazard . . . and of so many
so few grow to grey heires."

Hakluyt

THE BODLEY HEAD
LONDON

For Marak

399477

British Library Cataloguing
in Publication Data
Gilbert, John
Tigress
I. Title
823'.914[J]   PR605.152

ISBN 0 370 31063 2

© John Gilbert 1987
Printed and bound in Great Britain
for The Bodley Head Ltd,
32 Bedford Square, London WC1B 3EL
Phototypeset by Falcon Graphic Art Ltd
Wallington, Surrey
Printed by Redwood Burn Ltd, Trowbridge
First published 1987

Contents

PART ONE

The Motive   7

PART TWO

The Voyage   76

PART THREE

The Gold   139

PART FOUR

The Homecoming   195

PART FIVE

The Enemy   249

The Motive

CHAPTER ONE

He stood among the orange stalls in the colonnade. It was dim and hot. There was dog stench. His heart thumped, but there was no way to help. Out in the square the spring sun frazzled on to the thousands who had come to watch. Soldiers with staves kept an open space in the centre, laughing and joking with the citizens. This was everyone's day. In the space they had rigged the stakes, a line of six rough-hewn poles embedded in the ground ten feet apart. They had put firewood ready and were waiting for the mayor's procession. When the mayor came it would begin. He would sit in the big chair on the platform and give the sign. Round the platform oozed the men in black, with heavy robes and shaven heads. They bobbed up and down, looking towards the town hall. Everyone was frightened of the men in black, it was best not to look at them, not to meet their eyes.

The crowd did not mind waiting. There was no work today, plenty of rough red wine in the flagon and everyone wishing to talk. No need to shout or quarrel. Just stand in the swaying, jostling throng and let the red wine bubble up into your cranium where it boiled in the sun, and burp away to whomever you were squashed up against, joke or obscenity, and enjoy the women's buttocks. A sea of cheerful, drunken babble, savage with expectation.

Tom stood against the stone wall in the sweltering shadows. He dared not risk going among the crowd. The sweat was seeping down into his shoes, and under the loose tunic he could feel the long pistol, double-barrelled. It was called "David", one of a pair. Sir Joshua, handing "David" to him, had said: "Only if you are caught. Then one bullet for the Spaniard and one for you." But he must not get caught. He must get back to the ship. He cried in his heart, "God strike the Spaniards dead."

But nothing happened.

Tom Dakyn, gentleman from the galleon *Tigress* that lay at anchor outside the harbour, twenty-four years old, red bearded, burly, with quick blue eyes.

Time: a morning in early April, fifteen hundred and eighty-seven. Place: the port of San Corda on the northern coast of Spain. Occasion: the bonfire of six English seamen.

"Good day, sir!" The black robe, the toneless voice.

"*Bon jour, Monsieur.*"

Tom had prepared himself. If he had not prepared he would have replied in English. And died. He had been sent ashore because he spoke French perfectly. The Spaniard did not. His French was book-learnt, muddy, but he tried. His eyes appeared to have no lids. He smiled with chilling humility and pinpointed his pupils toward Tom's and said in his bad French, "You are a visitor?"

"From the ship."

"*La Renarde?*"

"*L'Hirondelle,*" said Tom, smiling back.

The "*Renarde*" was a trap question. The only French ship in harbour was the *Hirondelle*. The Spaniard must have known that. What he did not know was whether Tom was a Frenchman, and for a long moment Tom's life hung on that specific ignorance.

"You have come to see our spectacle?"

Tom shrugged. "What else?"

With thin lips the man in black murmured, "They will burn not because they are English but because they are heretics." He crossed himself.

"Of course!"

From the blazing sunshine came a sudden snarling roar. The beast had seen the keeper with the food. The man in black turned his head to look, nodded, and was gone. Tom was left to watch. He did not wish to see what was going to happen, but to leave now would be suicide. San Corda desired its spectacle. Only an unbeliever would have left.

The colonnade was above the level of the square and he could see the heads of the crowd like a seething carpet. In the far corner the soldiers had cleared a narrow alleyway and the procession was moving slowly towards the centre. The soldiers carried long muskets and Tom could see the feathered caps and the muskets poking up above the carpet of heads. The mayor

8

was at the front of the line and further back, hidden by soldiers, walked the six seamen. The crowd shouted blessings to the mayor when he passed close to them and curses at the prisoners. When the procession reached the centre of the square and everyone could see them there was a mighty yell of excitement. One party of soldiers escorted the mayor and his officials to the rostrum where the men in black were waiting to fuss over them. The other soldiers took the seamen to the line of stakes.

This was not an organized *auto da fé*. There had been no trial, no formal inquisition. The victims were not wearing the fools' caps that marked those who had been tried and found obstinate. These seamen were a quartermaster and five deck-hands who had delivered bales of cloth to the harbourmaster the afternoon before. Officially, England and Spain were hostile. A Spanish invasion fleet was being assembled, but it had not yet appeared in English waters. Unofficially, the merchants still traded, and there was an arrangement between the cloth company and the harbourmaster at San Corda. A green flag hoisted by the ship asked permission to send ashore; a yellow flag on the mole said "permission granted". Sir Joshua Vine, acting for the company and as the owner and master of the *Tigress*, had accepted the yellow flag against his better judgement. What Sir Joshua with all his instinct did not know was that King Philip of Spain, seeking to please Rome, had ordered a capricious seizure of all English ships and seamen. The *Tigress* was too fast and too strong to be taken, but the ship's boat with its six seamen and three bales of cloth (a trial offering based on suspicion) had been seized by the servants of the men in black.

Night fell and the boat had not returned. The *Tigress* rode at anchor, creaking with the ship-sounds of darkness, full of unease. No one knew what had happened but everyone could guess, and Sir Joshua asked Tom Dakyn to risk his life to find out. An hour before dawn the skiff put Tom ashore a mile from the town. He would be fetched an hour after sunset.

Standing now in the hot colonnade he knew that sunset was too far away.

The nearest stallkeeper, a bull-chested brute smelling of garlic, held out an orange for the tenth time, and Tom shook his head and patted his belly regretfully, and the Spaniard grinned and kicked a scabby dog as it squatted to evacuate, and thumbed towards the sun-drenched square.

9

A burst of jeering as the first seaman was tied to his stake, then a pause of muttering, then more jeers for the second. It was impossible to see which seaman it was, only the group of muskets moving along from one stake to the next. Tom did not know all the seamen. He knew the quartermaster, Richard Myllet, a Dorset lad with a plump wife he couldn't support; and he knew John Taverner, a great boy for the rigging, son of a carpenter. The rest he did not know by name, but they were shipmates and about to die. At the sixth tumult of laughter Tom's stomach contracted. There was nothing now but to wait till the wood was ignited, what the murmuring beasts were awaiting. For one insane moment he imagined himself rushing into the crowd, shooting his way to rescue. With two bullets and a hundred yards of drunken Spaniards between him and John Taverner?

No! Get back to the ship, get back!

And suddenly a blazing crackle of faggots and a spout of woody smoke and the square shook with a belching roar of satisfaction. One gone, five to go. But who were they? Which was next? As the first smoke diluted, the second stake was lit. Long enough for each burning to make sure the citizens were satisfied but not bored. Tom was thankful he was no closer. The stakes were left standing but charred one by one. He did not wish to see what was still strapped against them. As one blaze died down there was a moment's silence before the next sprang up, as if the beast hoped for a scream of fear. But there were no screams, not an English voice crying for mercy, only the explosion of mob joy at the next licking flame.

Richard Myllet, are you still there? Or only your embers? And you, John Taverner?

Three gone! Where are you, John? Which one?

Four! And now Five! So here comes the last. The fifth fire has stopped smoking. What are they waiting for? A prayer from the last seaman? Is that what they want? Don't give it them, lad! Go like the others! They're waiting for you at the mast-head!

Then in the awful silence a voice rang out, small in the distance but clear and strong with youth. "God save the Queen!" He knew the voice. It was Taverner, so agile, like a marmoset in the shrouds. Then the spurt of flame and the obliterating crowd-yell, and as the smoke billowed up from the dried wood there was a surge of howling Spaniards from the

10

perimeter towards the centre of the square, the maddened ones who had not been able to see. The orange seller had left his stall and was barging at the outskirts of the crowd as if his life depended on getting close to the stakes. There was hysteria in the baying voices, and now the soldiers began firing over the heads to stop people being trampled to death.

Tom edged towards the crowd, moving gradually round till he was near a side exit from the square. A few stragglers, too drunk to care, were moving away and he walked slowly among them. He must not be different, not be noticed. The cobbled gutters were full of garbage. Dirty stone buildings pressed the street into a narrow alley, narrower as he walked, as if on purpose, a closing corridor of inquisition that would seize him in hot pincers if he lost his wits for an instant. What was the man in black thinking? He had been distracted. But now the spectacle was over he might remember. A foreigner? Perhaps *not* a Frenchman! Those lidless eyes! An hour perhaps to disperse the crowd. Then the order would go out. Tom was sure of it, not rationally but with a super-alertion of his senses. Now it was midday, an eternity from sunset. He must get back to the ship.

The only way was by boat from the harbour. A local fisherman? But no Spaniard today would row to the English ship without query. So it must be the French ship. He would ask to be rowed to *L'Hirondelle*, and once away from the jetty he would let "David" the pistol persuade the fisherman. It was dangerous, but all he could think of. The midday sun made an oven of the tall stinking alleyway. Most of the shops were shut. A few children played on the hot cobbles. Some took no notice of him, others shouted and got an answer in French. Now and then they would stare with their dark eyes in silence. It only needed one to make a fuss, to run for mother, to tell something to someone. In every glance he felt the warrant of death. He dared not hurry but could hardly breathe for rage. His hands hurt themselves clenching.

As he neared the harbour there were more people, the old ones who had not been in the square. At the quayside he almost lost his nerve. The harbour was not crowded but there was more traffic than he had expected. On the far side near the entrance he could see *L'Hirondelle* and along the mole a line of merchantmen, their sails furled. San Corda was a small commercial harbour and there were no Spanish vessels of war. Fishing craft clustered at moorings and small boats bustled round the ships with stores and messages. At the waterfront jetties there were many rowing boats, too many, with too many fishermen. Knots of old women were buying fish straight from the nets.

Somewhere probably there was an old man with a boat of his own. But where was he? Which one?

And then came luck. A gabble of French voices, Breton seamen by the sound, and towards him came four youths each carrying a large wicker-covered wine flagon in either hand. He greeted them in French and they shouted back cheerfully.

"From *L'Hirondelle*?" said Tom.

"That's right!" The slim figure, the quick voice. Like John Taverner!

"Do you like that stuff?"

"The captain likes it."

"Red piss!" shouted another, taller than the rest.

"Not what we get at home," said Tom.

"That's true!" The four seamen told each other how true it was. Monsieur was correct, he was a good man, their friend. They were laughing and shouting, a stores party having had a litre or two in the town. Perhaps they had not been to the square, or hearing about it had stayed away. Mariners did not like trouble ashore, they had enough trouble at sea. Tom walked with them till they stopped near the third jetty. They put down the flagons and the tall Breton said, "We must get aboard." He pointed to the boat tied to the bollard on the jetty.

"Can you take me too?"

"Sir?"

"I have a message for your captain. It is important."

"By all means. We shall take you."

Tom felt pleased with himself. He had not elaborated. The flagons were picked up and the party moved down the jetty and stowed the flagons in the small heavy boat. Three of the seaman fitted their oars and sat waiting on their thwarts. The tall seaman stood on the jetty.

"Are we ready?" asked Tom.

"The quartermaster. We must wait for him."

They stood sweating in the sun amongst the smells of the quayside, fish and tar and seaweed. "He went for the cheese," said the seaman. "He should not be long." But it seemed long, heartbeat by heartbeat. Through the angle of the harbour entrance Tom could see *Tigress* at anchor, three-masted with the high poop astern. She was not far out, but maybe too far for him. Then came the quartermaster, a small fat man panting along with a heavy sack.

"Monsieur wishes to come with us," said the seaman. "He has a message for the captain."

"What message? I will take the message."

"It is personal," said Tom. "I have been told to see him myself."

"And from whom does this personal message come?"

"From Paris. Through the mayor."

"And who are you?"

"The messenger from Paris."

Fatty did not like it but he allowed Tom to sit beside him in the stern where he clutched the tiller. The cheese sack and the flagons were stacked at their feet as the four seamen facing them pulled on their oars. The *Hirondelle* was far across the harbour.

When they were clear of the jetty Tom said, "If it is convenient I would like to be taken first to the English ship."

"She's outside! Impossible! What are you saying?"

"It is a message for both captains. It would be preferable—"

"I have no authority!"

"I will explain to your captain."

"Yes! You will ask his permission. First!" The fat man was enjoying himself. He nodded with evident pleasure. Gently Tom felt for "David" the pistol, brought it out, held it against Fatty's temple. The seamen with various shouts stopped rowing.

Tom said, "I only wish to be taken to the English ship. Pick up your oars."

"They will do what I order," said Fatty. His voice trembled.

"Then tell them to keep rowing. And steer correctly."

"If I refuse?"

"They will see the brains from your skull. It is not necessary."

The fat man nodded to the seamen and pushed the tiller over. "No one need fear," said Tom. He lowered the pistol to the man's ribs and the small boat crept towards the harbour mouth. They were passing within a hundred yards of *L'Hirondelle* and a

13

faint voice reached them from the deck. "Wave to them," said Tom, "and say it is on the orders of the mayor. Just that, nothing else." The quartermaster did as he was told. His voice cracked as he shouted back and the boat moved out of the harbour on line for the *Tigress*.

There was a slight swell and an offshore breeze as the little boat crawled over the heaving water. For two minutes no one spoke. Tom did not look behind him in case the fat quartermaster tried to be heroic. The seamen were rowing with sulky faces. Tom wished he could look back to see if there was any activity on the mole. The *Tigress* was getting nearer, and now he could see the line of heads amidships and the barrels of hand-guns. The shrouds and yards were manned with watchers. A rope ladder squirmed down the side of the ship. The fat French jelly beside him had a red face, as if on the brink of a foolish decision.

Tom said, "Go to the ladder. They will not shoot you unless I tell them."

In silence the boat came alongside. *Tigress* rose high overhead. Tom stood up and said, "Tell your captain what happened. Say that you had no alternative."

It was a long way up the unstable ladder. At the top he was grabbed and lifted on to the deck. As he turned and saw the boat pulling away a hand tapped his shoulder and Sir Joshua Vine's voice, that unmistakable rasp, said, "Dead?"

"Yes, sir."

"How?"

"The stake."

Those nearest who had heard started swearing. Sir Joshua raised his voice, but without temper, and called, "Make ready for sea."

There was a scurry of feet on the deck. Tom followed his captain into the famous cabin with its massive furniture, and on the walls weapons and ornaments from the Mediterranean, the old trophies of piracy. Tom took "David" from his waistband and gave it to Sir Joshua who stroked the barrels, ejected the two bullets, opened the leather case on the desk and eased the pistol down beside its friend "Jonathan". Beautiful steel wheellocks, their double barrels set one above the other, the breech and butt engraved with brass precisely tooled by Wasserman of Leipzig. Sir Joshua did not speak. He brought glasses and a

14

bottle of brandy, poured generously, sat opposite across the desk splaying his hands on the dark oak, the ten digits pressed down till they quivered. There was a saying afloat: "When the Sultan's hands tremble, beware." He was called Sultan because of a famous connection with the Sultan of Turkey. It was a nickname of respect among seamen, unknown to shore dwellers and never used to his face. Everyone who sailed with Joshua Vine knew the splayed hands, his trademark of anger. He sat motionless, co-ordinated, cropped black hair and trimmed beard, not tall, one hundred and forty pounds of energy, his amber eyes full of light. He said, "Tell me. Everything," and Tom told about the square, reliving it.

Sir Joshua said softly, "Not because they were English but because they were heretics? Was that it?"

"Yes, sir."

"You did well. If you had used 'David' you would not be here and we would not have been sure." He nodded as if to himself. "Now you are hungry. I will send food. When you come on deck they will all ask questions. Say little, but tell the truth."

On the wall hung a crossbow, item in the Sultan's private armoury. He lifted down the crossbow, took two bolts from a drawer, and left Tom alone. More brandy, then a plate of salt beef and onions was brought by a young seaman who asked had they all been burned, and Tom said yes, and the seaman flushed with tears in his eyes and went out. Tom could hear the anchor rope purring as it came in. He ate the food, then left the cabin, climbed up on the poop to watch the rigging parties.

The ship was rousing herself like a cat from sleep. A man climbed to the foretop with the crossbow looped on his shoulder. Sir Joshua stood by the mainmast where he could see the tiller crew. The sails were unfurled now, and Tom watched the canvas muscles swelling in the breeze. Since he was a boy he had sailed with merchant packets to Antwerp, but he had not seen sea-drill like this. He had never been on a galleon. He was here almost as a passenger because his father was Sir Joshua's friend. Now on the poop hurrying seamen kept asking about San Corda, faces Tom did not know, voices crying for news they dreaded to hear. How much had he seen? Was he sure? A Dorset voice with burning eyes shouted, "Henry Wotton? Was he there? Can you swear it?" and Tom said, "There were six," and the voice said, "He was my son."

So the *Tigress* shuddered, her sails filling gently, the soft shmollock of water round her bows as she got under way. Tom loved that sound. The cat starting to prowl. It was hardly an hour since he had stood in the square, and now he could see the masts in the harbour and behind them the white houses rising on the hill, then the buildings dwindling to a blur, the blur to a biscuit on the coastline as it sank astern. So San Corda dwindled, but not the horror. A kittiwake wailing above the mast was the piping voice of John Taverner, "Qu–e–e–e–n!"

Fifty feet above deck the foretop and maintop were crowded, heads showing all round the balustrades. When Tom asked a deck-hand why so many lookouts, the man said, "The Sultan wants a sail before sunset." The Sultan never had to say anything twice.

The ship headed north till the coast vanished in the heat haze, then westward towards Coruna and Finisterre. Tom could tell by the sun, too far on the beam for a course homeward through Biscay.

He went down to the waist, then below to the gun deck. The ports were closed for sea, but a feeble light seeped through the hatches and in the warm gloom the heavy ordnance, sakers and minions, crouched like black alligators, with falcons and falconets further aft. The crews were not at full strength, but the gunner's mate and a few swabbers were finicking about with barrels and breeches. The rest of the skeleton crews would be called if action came.

The gunner's mate said, "Did you see Myllet? Richard Myllet?"

"Yes," said Tom. "From a long way off."

"He died well?"

"They all died well. Each one."

"You could not go close? To help?"

"There were many thousand Spaniards in the square."

Five pairs of eyes forgave him, just. He climbed back to the sunlight.

So through the broiling afternoon the *Tigress*, avenger on the heaving brown-green sea, sailed west to meet whatever vessel might come up from the Azores and turn eastwards in the hope of reaching port.

16

Tom had never seen action at sea. The *Tigress* was not fully manned for combat. There were no longbowmen or musketeers, but every seaman was a soldier now, and he watched the grappling irons laid along the gunwale and groups of seamen handling their own small pieces, some with a musket or pistol, others sharpening daggers on their palms with obscenities about Spaniards. Anyone to spare on deck was looking for a Spanish sail. It was not necessary because the many eyes hoisted above would be the first to sight anything on the horizon. But every last seaman had to think that he might be the one to cry "Sail!" The Sultan knew this. He knew everything about seamen.

Between the grappling irons lay coils of rope. For what? Tom did not know. But instructions had clearly been given. There was a palpable air of purpose.

The sun was falling and the sea turned to a tranquil blue-green desert when a single voice from aloft cried, "SAIL!" and a chorus of others roared down, "Sail on the starboard bow."

From the deck he could see nothing. Changes of bearing were called down, but it was over an hour before the sail appeared low on the horizon. No flag flew from the *Tigress* mast-head. Slowly, with the amiability of strangers not yet within hail, the vessels closed. The speck on the horizon turned into a single-master, the closer she got the smaller compared with *Tigress*, and now unmistakably a trawler of about twenty tons. She would not be armed. It seemed a pity, the *Tigress* throbbing with vengeance, her guns and grappling irons and furious seamen against such a puny target.

A quarter of a mile between them. And now the *Tigress*, already losing way with sails slackening upwards, swung to starboard, and with an ear-shaking *bumph* the for'ard sakers belched their message across the trawler's bows, two spouts of foam from the sea, and at once, as if the fishermen had known what was coming, a white flag fluttered up the mast. From the *Tigress* poop Tom could see it all.

Sir Joshua was on the quarterdeck. He had given his orders. He stood silent. The mate and bosun waited in the waist with the boarding party, thirty seamen with cutlasses, daggers and the odd firearm.

Now the trawler was almost stopped, her sail bunted in loose

17

scallops to the yard. The *Tigress* made a slow curling approach, came alongside, towering above. Sir Joshua hailed in Spanish, and the answer came in throaty English from a grey-headed man: "Bilbao! Friends!"

"Then receive our friendship!"

The irons spawned down, the ladders and lines fell like snakes, and the seamen dropped aboard. At first the ten Spaniards shaped up as if to resist. One climbed on a hatch, waving an oar wildly. Before the seamen could reach him a cross-bolt, fired from the *Tigress* foretop, appeared as if by magic through his gullet. He dropped the oar, sank to his knees, motioned feebly to pluck out the offending skewer, choked and died. There was no more opposition. The nine Spanish fishermen huddled on the small deck, their hands raised, and while they were still yelling their innocence the English seamen were among them with the coils of rope, tying their hands behind their backs with a line threaded through to link them, knotted to keep them spaced. The trawler's raised sail left the mast like a maypole round which the victims were pushed into a circle facing outward, the ends of the line joined to form a necklace of jumping beans capering round the maypole. Their ankles were bound and another line threaded through. Now they could only hop and stumble. Bundles of faggots were thrown down from the *Tigress* and two barrels of tar lowered to eager hands. Faggots soaked in tar were strapped to each prisoner and rivulets of tar poured round the bottom of the mast, over the deck and down the hatches. The stumbling Spaniards were crazy with fear, slithering on the tar, howling like madmen, calling on their saints. When the seamen clambered back on the *Tigress* there was a moment of petrified silence, and the grey-head cried, "What have we done?" and the Sultan called back, "Nothing!"

"Then why this? Because we are Catholics?"

"No. Because you are the brothers of murderers."

"What riddle is that? In the name of St Christopher! Let us go! I beg you!"

On the *Tigress* seamen were coming from below with pads of tar-soaked rags aflame on the ends of their cutlasses. The ships were separate now, the grapples freed. The *Tigress* was unfurling for the breeze. On the trawler the necklace of the doomed were jostling round the mast in a frantic ring-o'-roses of escape.

18

But there was no escape. Again the old man cried, "What is our crime? Mother of Jesus! Tell us before we die!"

"St Christopher will explain," called Sir Joshua. "He is waiting for you."

With jerked forefinger he gave the sign, and the fire pads showered down on to the deck below. Seeds of flame, some glowing sulkily on plain timber, some sprouting on a tar-spot, some catching the faggots strapped to torsos, flashing red flower-tongues of death into the sky.

There was no sail in sight, only the gulls to hear the shrieks of the dying, the cheers of the avengers.

The *Tigress* stole away on velvet paws across the water, and before she was out of earshot a pillar of flame rose round the trawler's mast and there were no more shrieks, only the oily bonfire blazing merrily, receding as the sun touched the horizon, still twinkling in the dusk, prolonged like the evening star, and suddenly extinguished.

CHAPTER TWO

When the *Tigress* berthed at Lingmouth Tom Dakyn collected his horse from the inn, where the stables took lodgers, and rode up the steep track to the hills. Sir Joshua and the mate had gone to the town hall. There would be notices nailed and fury in the streets. Lingmouth would be a hornet's nest of mourning and every deck-hand would tell of the burning trawler. Tom's story of the square would only give extra pain to those who were better off without the details. So Sir Joshua had told Tom to go home.

Pola the white stallion knew the way, across the estuary bridge, then up and up till they reached the knuckle of broad fist lying clenched on the English Channel. The hills of Dorset. Along the ridge far below to the right lay Lingmouth and the grey girth of sea, to the left the valley farms of the Dakyn tenants. Tom's father Lionel was a good landlord, and as a child Tom had ridden a pony along that spectacular ridge. He rode now, slowly and thoughtfully, wondering how much to tell his mother, till he could see nestling near the cliffs the roofs of Paxcombe Hall.

It had been the Dakyn home for two centuries. In the reign of

19

Edward III a young Dutchman named William Dacquin, runaway from his merchant family, had joined an English merchant ship, fought at the battle of Sluys, and saved his captain's life hand-to-hand with a French boarding party. The captain was a friend of the king. Young William was presented at court and in the euphoria of victory given gold and a piece of Dorset where he built a modest manor, married a hot-blooded heiress from Hampshire, restored contact with his merchant family in the Netherlands, made a fortune in the trade of wool and other commodities, and changed his name to Dakyn because his hot-blooded wife thought it sounded more English. The hot blood was important. It signified a tendency in the Dakyn males. In the next two hundred years every Dakyn of Paxcombe Hall married a compulsive child-bearer. The first son always stayed to manage Paxcombe, the second went to London or Bristol to make trading money, the other sons and any daughters did as best they could by soldiering, sea-faring and prudent marriages. So the pattern was set. Pride in the home, energy in the market, bravery in battle, and always like a tonic in the bloodstream a yearning for the sea.

The family spread and blossomed. The Hundred Years' War, historically futile, proved a god-send to the lusty Dakyn adventurers. Hubert Dakyn fought with the Black Prince, and when the great French trading centre of Burgundy, feuding with her sister Orleans, joined the alliance with Flanders and England the wool merchants on both sides of the Channel, the Dacquins and the Dakyns foremost among them, rubbed their hands with justifiable delight. There were rascals, of course. Godfrey Dakyn, fourth son of Francis, reduced himself by laziness to utter poverty under Henry VII, stole a sheep, and was hanged. A few others married badly, died of smallpox or were lost at sea. But the broad pattern solidified.

Paxcombe Hall was the family home, developed and fortified by the generations and always loved. The first-born had always been a son and he always stayed at Paxcombe. Far-flung relatives, cousins of second cousins, were proud of "The Hall", and each first-born in his turn was reminded in childhood of ancestor William who had saved the king's friend at the battle of Sluys.

Lionel Dakyn, himself a first son, was encouraged by his father to visit the Dacquins across the Channel: "Get to know

20

your own people before you settle down." It would broaden
the lad's mind. When his turn came to look after Paxcombe he
would not have much time to travel. In his teens the young
Lionel made many happy trips to the Netherlands, was welcomed by widespread Dacquins in Antwerp and Delft, admired
by all their friends who included a number of Huguenot
émigrés from France. Everyone liked the English boy, so
good-looking, so warm and friendly. He already knew a little
French and quickly gained fluency. It was known that he would
one day be master of Paxcombe. The men envied his fortune
and prophesied success. The girls, unanimously backed by their
mothers, flirted openly and with intent, and Lionel enjoyed
himself. For three years he made the most of being young,
hardly of marriageable age. When a girl stopped smiling and
gazed too seriously he turned to another girl. There were plenty
of them.

But now time ran against him. The young Englishman
was twenty years old. Would he never make up his mind? The
girls were still plentiful but the mothers were getting
impatient. They spoke of responsibility and the callousness of
the English.

And then in the summer when Lionel was twenty-one the
problem was solved.

Some Huguenot friends proposed a visit to Brest. The French
naval authorities were holding a grand marine gala. Brest was a
stronghold of Protestant Huguenots, and the great Coligny,
Admiral of France, would be there. Dacquins! Huguenots!
Ships! What more could be asked? The party of twelve proceeded to Brest. There were crowds, spectacles, visits aboard,
banquets, much French wine.

And there was Gertrude Lafitte.

Daughter of a famous ship builder, himself a friend of
Admiral Coligny, Gertrude had big grey eyes, a torrent of red
hair, and laughing lips. Her pale skin glowed like satin over a
lamp. She was a life-lover. She loved food and clothes and
admiration. She was the despair of her parents for turning down
so many wealthy young men. Her mother warned her that she
was getting a bad reputation. She was already twenty years old.
Would she never make up her mind?

At a ball, held on the first floor of a magnificent residence
overlooking the harbour, Gertrude met Lionel Dakyn. It was

21

more a fusion than a meeting. He saw her through crowded swirling heads and when the dance was over he walked up behind her as she stood talking to an older man, touched her on the shoulder and, when she turned, picked up her hand and kissed it. Mechanically she smiled her famous smile. This sort of thing was always happening. Then her big eyes focused on Lionel and she stopped smiling and stared at him with a sensation she had never felt before. Lionel took two glasses of wine from a passing servant's tray. The old admirer faded into oblivion. Lionel and Gertrude as if by prearrangement walked out on to the balcony where the soft moonlit night was dreaming over the ships at their moorings. At a small table by the balustrade they sat watching the tall-masted ships motionless on the glassy water, touching fingers sometimes, and talking. Gertrude's English was as good as Lionel's French. Men came to ask for dances, received a shake of red hair. For two hours the boy and girl talked in low voices. When the last dance had finished and there was clapping from the ballroom they stood up and Lionel said, "So you agree?" and Gertrude said, "Completely", and he kissed her almost shyly, not like his usual kisses, or hers either, and they went inside.

Next morning her mother asked her to explain such behaviour—"Staying out there with some stranger we've never heard of, refusing to dance with your friends, it was an insult to your hostess"—and Gertrude said, "I was talking to the man I shall marry."

The wedding the following Easter was the talk of Brest. The Dakyn and the Lafitte parents, alarmed by the suddenness, were surprised and pleased to find how much they had in common. They exchanged visits and were mutually impressed. The dignity of Paxcombe Hall, the love of the sea, even the old hero of Sluys who had fought with the English merchants against the French. Lafitte built ships for the French navy, but the Lafittes were Protestant like the Dakyns. Admiral Coligny was a Protestant, unlike the King of France. The less said about such matters the better. One must live and let live, and in the meantime here were two fine families, two magnificent children who wanted to marry. Let them! Never mind the gossips croaking about past flirtations, or the dark prognostications of the disappointed mothers of Netherlands daughters. Let there be joy and celebration! And so there was. There had never been such a wedding. The citizens of Brest erupted in gaiety and goodwill.

Perhaps the greatest satisfaction of the Dakyn parents was the fertility of the Lafittes. Gertrude had five brothers, three older, one younger, and a twin. This surely augured well for the continuity of the Dakyn males. The twin, Georges, was as charming as his sister and as handsome. As children Georges and Gertrude had played together, conspired together, shared a mysterious communication even when apart. When they were seven Georges went for a week's holiday to his uncle in Paris. After three days Gertrude told her parents, "He is coming back," and an hour later Georges was brought home with a fever. At a picnic by the sea when Gertrude and her mother had gone for a walk Georges told his father, "She is pleased, she has found something," and when Gertrude appeared she carried a splendid crab in her bucket. Trivia, perhaps coincidence. But the children knew it was real. In their teens they saw less of each other. Georges was at the naval academy, later to take the eye of Admiral Coligny and become a member of his shore staff. Gertrude, tutored in languages and the social arts, became the darling of Brest. But the rapport remained, and the best of it was that Georges welcomed Lionel as the perfect husband for Gertrude. When Lionel took his dazzling young wife to Paxcombe Hall he felt that he had achieved a brother as well.

Two years later Tom Dakyn was born, eldest son of the new generation. Lionel was not yet master of Paxcombe, but Lionel's parents gave a feast for a hundred guests at which everyone ate and drank too much and Lionel's father Humfrey made a fateful speech which ended: "It is over two hundred years since our great ancestor William built our beloved home. The family has been blessed with fortune ever since. Tonight we celebrate the birth of our grandson Thomas, first-born of our beloved son Lionel and his dear wife Gertrude. May they all inherit the happiness which Paxcombe has always brought to its children."

This was too much for the gods who had left the Dakyns alone since the battle of Sluys.

A week later the grandparents, still celebrating their grandson, rode into Lingmouth to dine with old friends, gorged themselves on shell-fish, widgeon, prime beef washed down with quarts of Burgundy and countless toasts; and died next day

23

of food poisoning. Lionel and Gertrude, guardians of Pax-combe earlier than they had expected, stood hand in hand beside the cradle of the infant Thomas and felt the burden of lineage. The baby grunting in his sleep looked so small to be the next link in such a mighty chain. Gertrude, vibrant with animal zest in spite of her sorrow, murmured, "He shall have many brothers."

"And a sister, if you please," said Lionel, squeezing her fingers.

They should not have spoken.

When Tom was two a brother was delivered and slapped, gave his initial cry, and died. It had been a difficult birth and the physician said there must be an imbalance in the chemistry of the mother. Gertrude, he said, was a sanguine with the wrong proportions of heat and moisture. She must be careful with her child-bearing, a criticism never before imposed on a Dakyn mother. Lionel comforted her. They were still young, fond of the bed and confident in the future. But it was four years before another pregnancy. The girl was born on Christmas Eve and in her puckered features Lionel saw the advent of her mother's beauty, especially when a soft red down appeared on the wagging skull. Then on a freezing daybreak she died before she was christened.

Gertrude was now twenty-nine, still sexually superb but with dread in her eyes. Could the physician have been right? Was there something? She and Lionel prayed together in the little Paxcombe chapel, told each other that whatever their fate they had been blessed with their son Tom. He was a sturdy child, inquisitive, and adored by his uncle Georges. Each summer came Uncle Georges, appearing apocalyptically, teaching the boy to ride and fence, honing his French accent, using the advantage which an uncle has over parents.

When Tom was ten the summer was unusually hot. The flower beds and shrubberies at Paxcombe were at their best. Lionel and Georges swam in the lake with Tom, 'the little porpoise', between them. There was archery practice, a small bow for Tom. At dusk there was supper on the terrace, cheeses and luscious pears and apricots glowing in candlelight, wine in heavy glasses, the air kept warm by the surrounding walls of sun-drenched granite where the musk-roses sprawled, mingling their fragrance with the gillyflowers. Tom was never sent to bed. He could sit as long as he liked, and when he got drowsy he would lean back against the stone lion beside the lily pond and listen to the murmur of the voices. It was best when his mother and father and Uncle Georges sang together in the twilight, and later, as Tom lay in his turret room, the singing floated up through the window in the thick wall, his mother and the two men she loved.

Gertrude was very beautiful that summer, three months into a pregnancy which they all believed would bring a brother for Tom. Georges said he "knew" it. When Lionel smiled and put a finger to his lips Georges said, "Do not be afraid. I know it."

Now it was late August and time for Georges to go back to Paris. Gertrude and Lionel tried to make him stay. He had told them what Paris was like that year, a simmering stew-pot of hatred and mistrust. Catherine the Queen Mother, a fervent Catholic, despised her son the young King Charles because he was too lenient with the Protestants, in particular with Admiral Coligny, leader of the Protestants and adviser to the king.

Georges said he must return to his duties on Coligny's staff. On the last morning at Paxcombe there was breakfast on the terrace and Tom, though little was said in his presence, caught the alarm and cried at Gertrude's side when the horsemen rode away.

For ten days Paxcombe sweltered in breathless summer. Then at dawn on St Bartholomew's Day Gertrude Dakyn reared up from sleep with a long wailing shriek. "Geor–or–ges!" The piercing cry split into Lionel's dreams beside her and woke every servant in the Hall. In the room above his parents' Tom clutched the coverlet, too frightened to move.

An hour later Gertrude aborted a child. Male, as Georges had promised.

For three days she would not eat. The only words she spoke were, "Georges is dead." She would accept no comfort or contradiction. In the weeks that followed Lionel and his ten-year-old son grew closer as never before. They must help her together. News would come, good or bad, and in the meantime they must love her. The father explained and the boy, solemn and trustful, understood.

The news was weeks in coming. A handful of Huguenots in that murderous dawn had escaped on horseback and fled to London. Lionel's younger brother, a merchant in the Strand, rode down to Dorset with a confused account and no details. The massacre was certain and that was enough to make Lionel believe in Gertrude's call of agony. He had never really doubted it. Georges was dead. But in what manner?

For years there was no answer. Gradually the story of St Bartholomew's Day was assembled. Ships crossed the Channel bringing letters and tales of varying exactitude. Georges Lafitte was undoubtedly dead. "Fighting for his faith," said Gertrude, and no one denied it. How much more she knew, her husband and son were never sure. She came back to the world she had momentarily left, became again the mistress of Paxcombe. But with a wildness in her eyes.

It was not till Tom was eighteen that a German barber who had worked in Paris and become valet to Georges Lafitte appeared in Lingmouth as a deck-hand from a German merchant ship. Tavern talk brought him to Paxcombe where for a few coins Lionel learned the final truth.

When Georges came back to Paris that August there was bad news. Admiral Coligny had just survived an attempt on his life. The bullet had only grazed him. He sought an immediate audience with the king, who swore he would protect him. But the Queen Mother burst into the room and shouted at Coligny, "You shall die yet!"

Coligny warned his staff to expect trouble. Georges and two other lieutenants lived with their servants in a hostel near Coligny's apartment.

At dawn on St Bartholomew's Day the bell at the Palace of Justice tolled out, and two thousand soldiers positioned along the Seine round the homes of marked Protestants, briefed on orders from the Queen Mother, began the massacre.

Before the sun had cleared the rooftops a thousand Protestants had died. The soldiers were joined by huge numbers of grudge-filled civilians. Every Catholic knew a Protestant to kill, and the killing had the special frenzy of killers in the name of God.

Georges and his valet were wakened by gun shots and the tolling bell. The Admiral was in danger, and they must get to him. They dressed quickly, crept by a side door into the street. Georges carried a pistol and a dagger. In the eerie half-light there were shouts and shadows and footsteps round corners. It was not far to Coligny's apartment, but they were too late. As

26

they approached, an upper window was flung open. The Admiral's body hurtled to the pavement, vanished beneath a screaming mob. As Georges rushed forward a voice yelled, "Lafitte! Huguenot!" The valet, unarmed, shrank into the shadows, saw his master clubbed to the ground, sworded and hacked.

"Did you see his body?" asked Lionel.

"I saw his head—on a paling."

That beautiful head!

The German was paid to keep silent, and Lionel told Tom that which must never be revealed to Gertrude.

So Gertrude continued once a year on St Bartholomew's Day to kneel in the Paxcombe chapel and whisper, "He died fighting for his faith." And Lionel and Tom hoped she had only sensed the fact of George's death and not the manner.

As Tom turned the white stallion down towards the roofs of Paxcombe he thought about these things. How he had become his parents' only son. From above his home always looked as if it had been there for ever. The brown-tiled turrets and granite walls lay massive and reassuring in the hazy afternoon. You could not see where the tiles were broken and the walls pitted with age. Further on came the tufty line of cliff edge, and beyond that, far below, the band of grey sea so smooth, so vacant of death.

CHAPTER THREE

They had seen him riding down from the hillside and now they waited in the courtyard, Finch the groom and Jackman the head gardener and Ellen Rufoote the cook, Tom's old nurse, his favourite. Finch took Pola to the stables and Jackman showed the two rabbits he had snared, and Ellen chattered, her cheeks flushed with welcome. Then his parents appeared from the arched doorway, with no serious questions, just pleasure that he was home.

"You shall tell us later."

"Oh, let the boy have his bath!"

Ewers of hot water stood beside the hip bath in the tower, his bedroom all his life, and he bathed gratefully, looking round at the objects he remembered from childhood, the arras on the wall and the massive door lock, keeping his eyes open because if he shut them he saw the smoke and flames of San Corda. Then he went down to the dining-room, pleased at the feel of fresh linen on his skin, and found his father ready with claret in the tall glasses and a new-lit fire against the evening chill, and his mother joining them in her best green dress, tight-bodiced with shimmering sequins on the billowy skirt, and three places laid at the end of the long table, and Oschild the butler solemn at the sideboard. There was roast duck stuffed with pimentos and olives, and the tallow lamps at twilight, and his mother so smiling, so beautiful with her red hair and her green dress, and only when the table was cleared and they sat at the broad stone hearth did Lionel ask, "So what did you think of the *Tigress*?"

Tom did not answer at once, letting the hesitation prepare them. Then he told them as simply as he could. They would hear from others, but now this first time he left out some things for his mother's sake, the piping voice of John Taverner and the cross-bolt through the Spaniard's gullet. They listened in staring silence, not interrupting. When he had finished Gertrude whispered, "Thank God you are home." She turned to Lionel: "No more horrors tonight. Let us have some wine and see if we can sleep."

Next morning they sat on the terrace. The sun shone from a blue sky. The lilies in the fishpond were in bud and the stone lion was warm to touch.

"It was only three bales," said Lionel. "It is not important."

"We must try again," said Tom.

"What madness now?" said Gertrude. "Back from the brink of hell! And you talk of *again*?"

"Not to San Corda," said Lionel gently. "But perhaps—"

"Not anywhere! He is home, and that is where he shall stay."

"One hundred bales went out," said Lionel, "and ninety-seven came back. That is no great loss."

"And you will sell them fast enough. Without getting six seamen burned to death and risking the life of your son."

"We shall sell them. But perhaps not so quickly."

"Don't tell us that trade is bad!"

"It is not good."

"It never was! The first day I ever set eyes on Paxcombe you said to me, 'Look at the dovecote,' and I looked and thought how beautiful it was, and you said, 'The roof is dangerous. It won't hold up much longer.' But somehow the roof got mended. And all the other crises like the clock and the chapel, they were all solved somehow. So don't try to frighten me over a few bales of cloth." She smiled triumphantly and patted the lion's stone mane.

Lionel rubbed his chin and glanced at Tom. You did not expect sense from Gertrude about money. She had lived on passion. She had lost the brother she passionately loved and the children she passionately conceived. Since then she had given herself passionately to her husband, her son and her home. It was useless to remind her what could or could not be afforded. She saw Paxcombe as the imperishable family home, the farms with their rents and livestock and wool as an inexhaustible revenue. If you pointed out that the roofs and walls needed repair, that the farmlands had been worked to their limit, that meat prices were controlled by the crown, that the cloth trade was hampered by restriction on the ownership of looms, she would beg you not to drown her in details. Paxcombe had been the family home for two hundred years! Would it fall down today? Tomorrow? Was the family going to starve? When you explained that although there would always be a living from the farms and the cloth, nevertheless you needed from time to time a large lump of money for renovation, she would look at you with splendid scorn. Had you never heard of credit? Was the Dakyn name worth nothing any more? If you suggested that credit might one day fail even for such a home and such a name, she would put her fingers in her ears. Passionate Gertrude, so illogical, so loved.

"We will see Sir Joshua," said Lionel. "Tom and I will pay him a visit."

"Not for advice, I hope."

"We owe him for his service. We shall get our cloth back. Then we can make a new plan."

"Without Joshua Vine!"

"Whatever you may think, he is still a great seaman."

"He is a pirate," said Gertrude. "He was, is, and always will be."

"The only pirate ever to be pardoned and knighted by the Queen."

"Fame from villainy! Lingmouth's most famous son!"

"Who went away and returned to glory."

"With how much blood on his hands?"

"Not English blood. Only her enemies."

"And still a villain. Admired by my dear husband!"

"And you, dear wife, were glad enough when he paid your friend Rose Dewmark what she asked."

"For her home! Poor Rose! With no husband, no money! She was bewitched, bedevilled by that pirate!"

Lionel smiled and turned to Tom; "Your mother and I have our opinions. And now you. How, would you say, did those seamen aboard the *Tigress* rate their captain?"

"As God," said Tom.

CHAPTER FOUR

They waited three days before going to see Sir Joshua. He would be busy with the mayor of Lingmouth, comforting the bereaved, helping with money and advice.

During these days Tom and his father talked a great deal about the pirate who had knelt before the Queen. His life had been a riddle, the saga of a sea monster where fact spawned rumour and rumour bred belief. Tales were told by foreign seamen in English ports. Hearsay, exaggeration and the natural bias of those who had suffered gave a confused picture. On the broad seas there were many pirates of many nations. No government could control them. The exploits of one villain would be attributed to a dozen others, the same anecdote of terror told about ports a thousand miles apart. Reputations came and went, and the authorities ashore were not interested in the plight of another country's merchant shipping. It took Joshua Vine over twenty years to make his name as the pirate of them all.

Everyone in Lingmouth had heard tales, but Lionel Dakyn had heard more than most, for over many a bottle of wine he had listened to Joshua Vine himself, a cataract of memories from a man with an infectious belief in his own destiny.

Now Tom listened as his father spoke of what Joshua called "The four great chapters of my life."

There was childhood.

His father, Henry Vine, was a lobster fisherman in Lingmouth, seventh child of a quarryman. Henry's seventh child Joshua was born in the same year as Lionel Dakyn, heir to Paxcombe. Lionel never heard of Joshua, but Joshua as a child heard much about the great mansion along the cliff. It was a wretched childhood. At his birth his mother died. A netmaker's wife, half crazy at the death of her own baby, suckled Joshua, kept him two years in her own overcrowded tenement, then returned him to his family. In the dank waterfront cottage five boys and two girls huddled illiterate and unloved, saved from starvation by sea food but cowed by poverty, insanitary congestion, and their fearsome father. While his wife lived Henry Vine's natural violence had been held in check. Now, without his woman, he was soon brutal with alcohol. Dabs and sprats for food, lobsters for money, the money all for drink, and a length of tarred rope for the children. The infant Joshua he never forgave. When the child was three his father smashed a cockroach on the stone floor with his fist, crying, "I killed the roach! You killed your mother!" The rest of the family, the eldest a girl of twelve, fought for Joshua's safety, hid him under sacking or in some rotting cranny when their father's rages became infanticidal, bringing Joshua to be kissed goodnight when the rage had turned to the tearful howls of fuddled self-pity.

So the years passed and every twelve months the children were one year older, still unable to write their names or read a word, a brood of harbour rats, cowed in their home but outside it a band of scavengers and thieves flitting like vermin round the slimy wharves and jetties, fierce and cunning for food, their only loyalty an instinctive alliance against their father. They all got beaten, whichever happened to be within range, the rope scars wealing their backs and buttocks, but as each year passed it was Joshua, the last lethal entry, who suffered most. By the time he was ten his elder brothers were often away on manual, ill-paid work round the harbour and in the quarries. The sister who had protected him as an infant disappeared with a gipsy. Joshua was left, the target. He had heard his crime so often, been punished so often, that he came to regard himself as a boy unlike all others, not so much guilty as cursed with a deformity he could never shake off. He spoke to no one, knew no words to describe even to himself the horror that drifted in his head.

When he was eleven, one starless night without premeditation he stowed away on a Portuguese freighter bound for Rotterdam. Two days' hunger in the dark hold was enough. The captain took pity on the ravenous child dragged before him. Joshua could be his cabin boy. But with the cargo unloaded and the return voyage begun an eastern gale swept the freighter into the estuary of the Thames. The captain decided that the English boy would be better off among his own people. Joshua was put ashore in Limehouse, a fledgling among the hordes of sea-birds that surged through the docklands of Wapping, Tower, Ratcliffe, Limehouse and Rotherhithe for jobs afloat, no matter under which master or what flag.

He stood alone on the cobbles. He wanted food. There were more voices, more unknown faces, more clopping feet than he had ever imagined in all the world. In the cold wind he started to walk aimlessly, found himself in a long narrow passage lined with food shops, open-fronted, big and small, with a drain-smelling gutter down the centre. As he moved between the pushing crowd he could smell cabbage, raw meat and corn. He squeezed up to several counters, but there was always someone watching. It was not like Lingmouth where you could grab and run.

And now to this seventh child of a seventh child came a life-changing encounter.

Before him stood an immense man carrying a basket of apples and loaves. Their eyes met. Because he dared not snatch, Joshua pointed. The man gave him an apple. They walked on together, talking. The man limped and his slow voice seemed to rumble up from a deep barrel. Ten minutes later they stepped into a ground-floor room in a grimy terrace. The room was surprisingly clean. On the stove was a black tureen issuing the steam of meat stew. The tureen was being stirred by a heavy placid woman with round large eyes. The man said, "His name is Joshua. He has no home. He has come from the sea."

The woman beckoned and put her hands on Joshua's shoulders, gazing into his face. She said, "So you have come at last."

On the table lay a big book and she opened it and found a page and read it out: "Unto us a son is given." She showed the words to Joshua who shook his head.

"You cannot read?" she asked.

"No."

"Then we shall teach you."

During the next seven years Joshua, living with Brian Tebbige the sea-cook and his wife Jane, made over one hundred trips to sea, first as a cook boy or cabin boy, then, as he grew stronger, a seaman. Tebbige knew everyone in dockland. Sometimes they went on the same ship, sometimes separately. Mostly the trips were short, trawling off North Foreland, up to Yarmouth and round to the harbours of Kent, across with heavy freight or cargoes of wool and linen to the ports of the Low Countries and Flanders, now and then to Ushant and Biscay. That he should go to sea was never in doubt. There was no alternative and he had no other wish. The crafts of the sea came easily to him, as if deep instincts had only to be touched to make them blossom. Sure-footed on a heaving deck, nimble in the rigging, without fear aloft. His hands had an astonishing strength with the rope. He never complained and never quarrelled. Any master would recommend him to another. He sailed to Lisbon and the Azores and the Isles of Scilly. In his childhood the years had crawled, now they were swift. With each new experience he was greedy for the next. Discomfort he accepted, the nights on hard wood strewn with other snoring sleepers, the food that was never enough and often uneatable. These were short trips. He knew about the long voyages where your bowels went rotten and you watched the livid ulcers exploding on your abdomen and thighs. Seamen who had survived such voyages liked to tell of them. But in these seven years Joshua felt only the excitement of new places and the growth of his own strength. Coming ashore, with or without the vast limping Tebbige, he would go straight to the clean apartment in the grimy terrace. This was his home. Jane Tebbige with her moon face and loving eyes was his mother. And, as she had promised, during these seven years he learned to read. The book was the Bible.

Strictly, the Old Testament. The Tebbiges were more concerned with survival than virtue, and this treasure house of allegory and tribulation satisfied their wildest hopes and fears. For Joshua it was a beacon in the darkness of his mind. Through the enthralling pages he wandered at random, guided by Jane at first and later by choice, as he wandered at sea. When he read of God entering the soul and granting dominion from sea to sea and from the river to the ends of the land, he saw that the words were meant expressly and privately for himself.

And then there was the *Black Vulture*.

Now Joshua was eighteen, compact, confident, his first beard already trim, his amber eyes strangely alive with light. He came ashore from a small cargo ship returning from Tenerife with a load of oranges, lemons and olives. He had been away three weeks. The ship had been badly victualled, maggots in the meat and rank beer, and he hurried home. Something in the narrow streets alarmed him. There were few people about and many of the shops were shut. From an upper window came a chorus of groaning voices, lament rather than pain. Then on several doors he saw a cross daubed in crimson. He knew what that meant. From time to time mysterious outbreaks of death came to dockland, fevers that slew in hideous ways. Red eyes and vomiting, lungs that gasped and bled, stiff joints and putrid gums, the breath stifled in swollen throats. No one knew the cause, though it was noticed that when a spice ship from the eastern Mediterranean let the crew ashore there was often fever in the streets. So Joshua ran to his home.

There was the crimson cross. A plank had been nailed across the door. As he tore at the plank neighbours came to him. The Tebbiges were dead. The cart had taken them away. When he broke open the door he found his home untidy with the suddenness of death. Crumpled coverlets on the beds, small belongings in odd places, and on the dresser the Bible. The vomit and the silence. He took the Bible and went to find escape. When death came to dockland the best thing to do was to get to sea.

The tavern on the wharf was crowded but there was not much noise. Small knots of seamen talking in low voices, listening for any snatch of helpful news from another table. In the corner Joshua saw three lads he had sailed with. They were talking to an older man. He joined them. The man was lean and swarthy with a smile like the split in a mask. He spoke with an Irish brogue. He said that his ship had lost her cargo and some of the crew when a Dutch pirate caught them off Ostend. The master had sent him for replacements. He had a ketch alongside the wharf that would take the fortunate seamen to the merchantman that was lying off Sheerness.

34

Why, asked his listeners, had the merchant ship not come up the Thames? The authorities, the palaver, said the Irishman with a wink. There had been damage to the hull. The master only wanted to get back to his merchant fleet in Kinsale. They had surely heard about Bellamy of Kinsale?

They had heard of Kinsale, but not of Bellamy. It made no difference. The south coast of Ireland was an area of secrecy and enterprise. The merchants had a bad reputation and the Irish seamen when you met them in foreign ports were a dastardly collection. Joshua and his friends did not exactly believe the Irishman. Equally, they did not wish to stay in Limehouse. After a hurried whispered conference they said they would see what Master Bellamy of Kinsale had to offer. The Irishman said they would never regret it till their dying day.

The ketch beside the jetty was a poor craft. Six other young seamen were already on board, scarcely a possession between them. Joshua had a knife in his belt and the Bible in his hand. The hired crew cast off. Minutes later the ketch was threading between large moored vessels down the smelly brown water-alley of Limehouse Reach. By afternoon they passed Tilbury and at dusk came to a vessel of fifty tons riding at anchor off Sheerness.

There was something odd about her. Not as low in the water as a freighter, not as high-built and fussy as many merchant-men, not as sturdy as an English man-of-war. With no visible gun-ports. And yet in the half light there were square outlines near the dark bows that made you think of covered ports. Joshua had seen many ships. This one looked to him like something Dutch that someone had altered. She was three-masted. There was no visible damage to the hull. She lay on the still water with an air of unaccountable strength. Sometimes a sleeping man will warn you of when he wakes.

They came alongside, climbed aboard. The ketch vanished into the gloaming. From a door in the poop appeared a squat man dressed in an open singlet, breeches and buckled shoes. A man of altogether superior quality and presence to the Irish recruiter whom he addressed:

"Party complete, Mr Doyle?"

"All present, sir."

"Send them below. Feed them. I will meet them at dawn."

"Aye, aye, sir."

35

As if from nowhere a ring of hard men appeared from the shadows, holding daggers. The young seamen were nodded to the ladder in a dark hatch. Not roughly. The circle of daggers only indicated the folly of disobedience. Last to go down was Joshua, but the squat man stopped him, asking to see the book in his hand. Joshua held out the Bible and the squat man took it. There was contempt in his grasp. He opened the Bible, glowering: "Where did you get this book?"

"From my mother."

"Have you read it?"

Joshua shrugged. "I care little for it." He sensed the menace in the squat man's voice.

"Then why carry this book when you care not?"

"It was my mother's. She is dead."

"So she needs no books. And you?"

Joshua, his heart bursting, said quietly, "It is nothing to me."

The squat man glared at him: "My name is Quynne. You are aboard the *Black Vulture*. We need no scholars. You are here to sail this ship and obey my orders."

With a sudden sweep of his arm he hurled the Bible over the side. There was a moment's silence. In that moment there exploded in Joshua's mind the instantaneous inexplicable certainty that sometime, somehow he would kill this Quynne and himself be master of the *Black Vulture* on whose gritty unknown deck surrounded by hard men with daggers he now stood. A flash of knowledge too fast for thought. The moment was over. There was a soft plop as Joshua's Bible hit the salty water. He smiled and inclined his head towards the squat man as if with acknowledgment.

Thus did Joshua Vine join the pirate crew of the *Black Vulture*. There was no Bellamy of Kinsale. There was Quynne of Clonakilty and his mate the mask-faced Doyle. The truth was that a dozen misguided deck-hands had imagined they could mutiny against their tyrant master. They had been thrown overboard, their throats cut, a weight on their ankles. The problem was replacement. The Thames dockland was the obvious pool for seamen, but among that forest of ships and eyes there was a chance that the *Black Vulture* would be recognized. So Doyle had been sent to pose as a victim of his own true profession. All this Joshua learned bit by bit as he settled into his new life as crew-man to a pirate.

A hard life, but never dull and often with good reward. *Black Vulture* was, as he had guessed, of Dutch origin, built as a coastal trader. Under Quynne she had been adapted and improved. Below the waist a gun deck had been set up with ports well screened. The armament was not heavy. Two minions and two falcons were enough to stop most unarmed merchantmen in their tracks. When the vessels closed the object was to wound or kill the victim's crew, and for this Quynne trained his men with quick-firing guns, fowlers, murderers and port-pieces. When these had wrought their havoc a savage boarding party would secure the prize. Sometimes cargo ships would sail in groups. Then *Black Vulture* would hover on a parallel course, showing no concern, throwing kegs and buckets on lines astern to act as drogues if the quarry was inconveniently slow, waiting for one unsuspecting vessel to stray from the flock. Then near sunset the drogues came in, the vulture quickened, swooped, tore the heart out of the prey, and vanished into the night.

In such practices Joshua learned his part. Also, more importantly for his purpose, he learned the arts of navigation. From that first moment at Sheerness he never wavered in his preparation to kill Quynne. The preparation was slow. He had no Bible now but he clung to the stories he could remember, and as they dwindled and became confused he elaborated them. He was Daniel the mighty man of David who saw visions and slew two lionlike men who were the enemies of God. This was his mission.

It was five years before he was ready.

First he had to become accepted, a willing pirate. This was not difficult. The crew, vicious in action, were no worse as seamen than many he had sailed with.

The problem was to find favour with Quynne and Doyle. This he achieved, as so often before, by his quickness and skill about the ship. In the early months the Limehouse recruits were watched, forbidden to leave the ship in harbour. "Harbour" was any inlet or cove along southern Ireland from Forlorn Point to Fastnet Rock, especially the cluster of small islands in Roaring Water Bay and the approaches to Skibbereen. Here milled the lawless thieves of the oceans, Quynne and a hundred like him, foraging round the coasts of Britain and of Europe from Norway to Gibraltar. The better the pirate the wider his range. When Joshua had been on *Black Vulture* less than a year he made his first trip across the Atlantic. Off Greenland there were fishing fleets for the picking, and down the mainland coast many wealthy merchants were taking goods by sea because they thought they were safe. In all this Joshua was obedient and efficient. Squat Quynne and even the heartless Doyle recognized what many masters had recognized before: Joshua Vine was not like other seamen. In their own piratical way they came to trust him. If anything special had to be done, Vine would do it. Imperceptibly he gained their respect, and this he nurtured with flattery. When you are a thousand miles from land, even if you are master of a pirate ship, you feel pleased when in some boring forenoon an ignorant seaman approaches you with devoted eyes and inquires about the mysteries of the astrolabe and the cross staff. You explain. He looks bewildered. For want of anything better to do on this empty morning, you instruct him on the taking of sunsights and the value of the stars. He makes you feel like God talking to a mortal.

Thus, over many voyages and several years, Quynne and Doyle, by allowing Joshua to learn about charts and winds and the calculations of latitude, signed their own death warrant.

On a moonless night in the Caribbean *Black Vulture* lazed on an easterly course trailing a ribbon of phosphorus astern. The pickings had been good. Florida seemed to breed unwary merchants. Now it was Quynne's birthday. The quartermaster, a gaunt man from the Hook of Holland, had the watch. Quynne and Doyle were in the master's cabin astern. They had fed well and were drinking a keg of coconut firewater from Trinidad. They were old cronies and when they got drunk together they enjoyed an argument, usually about their conquests with women, for here was opportunity for what all seamen enjoy, violent assertion and dogmatic contradiction with no possibility of proof on either side.

This hot dark evening they were hard at it. If you had listened from a distance to the noise from the cabin without hearing the words you would have thought they wanted to kill each other. Abaft the cabin a platform known as the master's gallery ran round the stern. A door from the cabin led on to the gallery. When either Quynne or Doyle could stand the other's bragging not a moment longer he would step out on to the gallery

38

shouting his fury back to the drunken sot inside. These mock quarrels were famous on board. Joshua had observed them many times. On this torrid night the roaring boasts and denials were particularly violent. Quynne could stand no more. He had related his favourite story of ten women in one night, and Doyle had capped it with some fable of twenty. It was intolerable. Out on to the gallery staggered Quynne clutching his glass and belching. He had told the truth and been met with drunken lies. He called on Heaven as his witness, but he heard no sound as the shadow dropped softly from above, felt almost nothing as the hand from behind closed over his mouth, knew nothing more as in the moment of crying "Heaven" his throat was cut to the nape, his body hurled forward over the rail. What had been Quynne fell into the glittering trail astern.

The silence of death was broken a few moments later by a very rude word hissed in a coarse undertone from the gallery into the cabin. The swaying Doyle heard the insult, frowned hazily at something strange in the intonation, and stamped out on to the gallery looking for Quynne. There was no one. He hesitated. A sound like a pebble dropping by the rail made him take a step forward. The dagger was plunged beneath his left shoulder blade with extraordinary force. With a grunt no louder than a sleeping child, the dagger up to its hilt in his heart, what had been Doyle followed his master down to the phosphorus and the fishes. The shadow flitted aloft into the shrouds.

Black Vulture loitered on towards the east.

A few of the crew, flaked out on the forecastle deck, had fitfully listened to the row in the after cabin. When it stopped they thought sleepily that the drinkers were insensible. Only a fool would have gone to see.

It was dawn before the cabin was found empty. No evidence, no explanation. They were not on the ship, therefore they were overboard. As both were gone it could not have been one who pushed the other. A drunken prank? What else? They must have sat together on the rail, imagined perhaps they were on horseback, dared each other to balance without hands. The coconut firewater was famous for that sort of effect.

There were no tears. Death was a commonplace never to be mentioned once it had happened. What worried the pirates was how to get back to Clonakilty. Quynne and Doyle had been

39

their navigators for years. Who now knew the mysteries of the charts and instruments in Quynne's cabin?

It was a simple contract. Joshua Vine announced that he would get them home. He must have the cabin. They must obey his orders. If he failed they could kill him.

The journey was brilliant. He took them north past Virginia to the 50th parallel. The winds were more westerly up there. The hold was already full of liquor, hand guns, gold and saleable merchandise from the Caribbean. They paused only to take victuals from a merchantman off Nova Scotia, not even troubling to slaughter the crew. No storm hit them in the Atlantic. Quynne and Doyle would have taken at least half the booty, but when *Black Vulture* dropped anchor near Skibbereen Joshua Vine said he would take his common share with everyone else. All he asked was to be master on the next trip. He had brought them fortune once. He would do it again. Let them judge him by a single criterion.

Success.

There was Istanbul.

Now Joshua was twenty-three. For five more years he operated from this misty coastline of Cork. Pirates were above all superstitious. They believed in results, but when the first success was followed by a string of others they became imperceptibly aware that a chain of luck was being forged. This they respected. Gradually Joshua Vine, at first merely a man of the moment, became a symbol of success. His authority increased with every voyage. And equally gradually the crew of *Black Vulture*, by sickness, substitution, and the inevitable losses from victims who shot back, was transposed until the hard men of Sheerness who knew Quynne had almost disappeared, and in their place was a crew who knew only Joshua Vine. He never failed them.

He had a Bible again. Jane Tebbige had taught him to read from the Great Bible of Cranmer. Now (he heard it from a renegade priest in Waterford) wise men in Geneva had made a new Bible. He obtained a copy brass-bound. His reading as always seemed to confirm things he had felt without knowing how to express them. What else had Quynne and Doyle been but base metals cast into the midst of the furnace and melted in the fury of his vengeance? Few of his crew could read.

40

Messengers to his cabin were sometimes afraid of the silent figure with his book at the desk. But it was awe more than fear. On deck and at sea he was infallible.

And now Joshua became restless. The coves of Ireland were a good lair, but he was tired of the long winters and the poor quality of many coastal cargoes round Britain. The Caribbean was richer, but the journey was difficult and he did not fancy making it his permanent hunting ground. The Mediterranean he did not know. It was said to be swarming with juicy prey, but also with pirates. He did not fear competition, but the pirates often worked in groups based round Corsica, Sicily, Crete, Cyprus, the Aegean archipelago, and stretches of coast along south Turkey and north Africa. Between groups there were tensions and rivalries, but a single poacher would run the constant threat of concerted opposition. Apart from the pirates there were the navies of Spain, France, Italy and Turkey. Cumbersome perhaps and possible to elude, but liable to make periodic cleaning-up sweeps. Under such conditions it would be hard to operate alone, even under inspiration from the Old Testament.

Joshua decided to wait and find out all he could. He went more often to the Azores and Madeira, both Portuguese controlled, where ships of every Mediterranean country crowded the harbours on their way to or from the Straits of Gibraltar. Many facts, lies and rumours were spread in many tongues, but Portuguese, already the language of famous navigators, became the common speech, a knockabout Portuguese stripped of its grammar and injected with foreign shipwords from every coast. Joshua Vine spoke this vigorous garble like everyone else. In the main harbours he was always on his best behaviour, known as a pirate but acting like a gentleman. The officials did not object to his presence and he in return left the shipping alone. What he sought was information. And it was in Ponta Delgada, where he had wrestled with unreliable reports for a long time, that Joshua Vine received a surprising and flattering invitation.

The Sultan of Turkey, Selim the son of Suleyman, Caliph of the Faithful, Shadow of the Prophet Upon Earth, wanted his assistance.

The invitation was brought by the master of a Turkish freighter bringing cheaply dyed fabrics to compete with classy

English products in the markets of Europe. The master of the freighter was called Kepal. Joshua had known him over the years, and Kepal had told his Sultan about the famous Englishman who had taken command when his master and mate had disappeared in the night (some said by accident, some that the Devil had taken them, and others, relying on the testimony of an Irish deck-hand, that a giant sea-serpent had been observed subsiding into the ocean with Quynne between its jaws). It was not the piracy that impressed Selim the son of Suleyman, but the legend of unrivalled seamanship. Against other vessels the Englishman was a peregrine among pigeons.

The Sultan was interested. The weak son of a strong father, he had mismanaged the economy and allowed the armed services to fall into lethargy and corruption. This had been reported to the most martial character in Vatican history, Michele Ghislieri, recently installed as Pope Pius V. He advised Philip of Spain and his brother John of Austria that the infidel plum was ripe for picking. The galleys were assembled, crammed with soldiers. The fleet set out. The challenge was met by the galleys from the Bosphorus equally crammed with soldiers. At the battle of Lepanto the Turks were crushed. It was not a naval engagement but a land battle at sea, a conflict of dinosaurs with flippers. Unwieldy hulks paddled by oars ferried land armies to fight it out on each other's decks in fields of salt water. The Turks lost.

Selim, head of the Ottoman Empire, took advice. Warfare by galley was outdated. Lepanto had been all galleys, but the new Spanish ships, though carrying soldiers, were being fitted with more guns, more sail, and no oars. The English navy believed in gunfire and manoeuvre, not boarding parties. The English Queen would hardly lend her officers to guide the Sultan's demoralized navy in modern tactics. But suppose some un-attached genius could be found? The Sultan listened intently to Kepal and others who had tales of just such a man.

So began ten splendid years for Joshua. Kepal had brought to Ponta Delgada a letter signed by the Sultan and stamped with his seal. Also a bag of emeralds. After many questions Joshua made his judgement of Kepal and accepted the offer. Kepal surely was another prince of the eunuchs who would with God's help bring Joshua before the Nebuchadnezzar of Turkey. With regret he sent *Black Vulture* home under her mate, the one man he could trust, the gaunt Hollander who had been at the helm on the night of the coconut firewater. The ship would be Joshua's when he came again. His sea chest he transferred to Kepal's freighter. Then the voyage down the Mediterranean, the entry which Joshua never forgot through the Sea of Marmora, round the point into the harbour of Istanbul where the façades of the Royal Palace rose in marble magic from the sea and a forest of domes and minarets shone gold in the sunset. Sultan Selim lived with a personal opulence and power hardly imaginable in the West. The naval disaster had hurt his pride without really threatening his country.

Despotic, secretive, the envoy of Allah on earth received the Englishman with traditional magnificence. The curtained throne was a mosaic of emerald plates larded with rubies the size of ducks' eggs. Clusters of pearls dangled on cords of woven gold. One holy finger encrusted with jewels appeared through the folds. Joshua, as he had been instructed, bowed to the floor, then, glancing at the rubies, touched the finger with one of his own. So was struck an almost telepathic link as near to friendship as any Westerner had ever come with the Caliph of the Faithful. They never met face to face. Every communication Joshua made with Selim was made through the chief black eunuch, the Grand Vizier.

A strange life style for Joshua. An apartment in the palace. Fine food and wine and servants. Girls in plenty, cast-offs who had trodden the golden path to Selim's bedchamber for the last time, but still young, highly trained, and anxious to please. They gave Joshua a taste for twittering odalisques he never lost, playbirds that soothed him to sleep and were gone by morning. His real thoughts were for ships, and the sea his mistress.

It was this last irresistible passion that in the end brought about his return to England.

His work in the dockyards of Istanbul could not be done in haste. Turkish merchant seamen like Kepal could speak a version of pidgin Portuguese, but if Joshua was going to talk to designers and shipbuilders and naval officers it would have to be in their own language. He was quick to learn, but it still took many months. The process of changing the Turkish navy was a huge task and by the time a beginning had been made the Sultan Selim died and was succeeded by Murad, a man of even greater secrecy and deviousness than his predecessor. Joshua was still welcome in the palace. Had he not been he would have vanished into the dungeons and death chambers of the Grand Vizier. But ship plans hung fire. The Turks, like all Mohammedans, were basically and irretrievably suspicious. There were hidden oppositions, delays that could not be traced. Hungering for the sea, he made application through the Grand Vizier. Would the Incarnation of Allah allow his servant, when duties permitted, to seek out the enemies of Truth and bring their wicked cargoes to Istanbul?

In other words, could Joshua be a pirate again in his spare time?

This happened to be what Sultan Murad wanted to hear. The Italians had been expanding their merchant trade to the detriment of Turkey. Now they could be taught a lesson. A fast ship was provided with a crew chosen by Joshua. From the inlets of the Greek Peloponnese, an Ottoman stronghold, he could have a free hand in the Ionian Sea where the Venetian merchants debouched from the Adriatic. It was an admirable arrangement. It restored Joshua's balance of mind. It allowed the Caliph to go slow on a project which, however grand its conception, was proving more and more difficult to effect.

Over the next few years the Turkish navy struggled slowly towards new disciplines while Sultan Murad was delighted by the avalanche of Italian consumer goods brought back to Istanbul by Joshua Vine. The Sultan did not need money, but he liked the silks and the weapons and the glass and especially the discomfort of the Venetian merchantmen.

Gradually the Italians realized that their merchant torment was not from pirates in general but from one in particular. It took a long time. There were few survivors from piracy, but at last it was clear that the terror of the Ionian Sea was not a Turk but an Englishman. He was named. Protests were made to Elizabeth herself, Queen of England, and Elizabeth who for nearly thirty years had been balancing the tightrope of European power politics decided that one of her subjects, however illustrious in his field, was upsetting stability in the Mediterranean.

A message was sent that a squadron of English warships was on its way to Istanbul to bring back this Joshua Vine. If he were not released the Turkish shipping in the Aegean would suffer indiscriminate casualty.

The Sultan was not accustomed to threats from a woman. In the recesses of the seraglio such a message was a distant impertinence arriving by echo at the throne of Allah. But his advisers thought otherwise. This queen of darkness had powerful guns. Surely it would be better to lose one foreigner from the Holy Kingdom than have the waters of the Aegean and even Marmora itself stained with Mohammedan blood? This opinion, conveyed through the Grand Vizier with infinite obeisance, penetrated the swaddled skull of the Caliph.

Murad had a dilemma. For the first and last time in his life he decided to act in person.

Joshua Vine was summoned. There was an interpreter. The Sultan, turbanned, bejewelled, sat on a high dais of gold. Joshua knelt before him, but without servility. When their eyes met something occurred deeper than paraphernalia, more important than words. Somehow, with everything against them, their customs, their histories, their Gods, these two individualists, the boy from nowhere and the Shadow of the Prophet on Earth, made contact. Murad asked Joshua if he would stay. He would be wealthy, never required to turn Turk, given sanctuary till his queen should pardon him. Joshua looked straight into the Eye of Allah and said it was better to go now. In this marvellous moment they understood one another, Joshua why the offer had been made and Murad why it had been refused.

And now came the fourth and last of Joshua Vine's great chapters, his letter to the Queen.

He sailed home with the English squadron. As a parting gift, a hint of the wealth that might have been his, the Sultan Murad gave him three caskets, one of pearls, one of rubies and one of emeralds, such as most crowned heads of Europe had never seen. Joshua selected the pearls for Elizabeth because the casket itself was of spectacular design inlaid with gold and ivory. He wrote his letter:

> Give leave, I humbly beseech Your Majesty, to me your own creature. I fell not purposely but by mischance into these courses, but being in them strove to do all the service I could for this State. Nor did I ever harm or cause to suffer any of Your Majesty's subjects, but only them who served your enemies.

The Sultan of Turkey ate bread and salt and swore by his head that if I would stay with him he would bestow great wealth upon me and never urge me to turn Turk, but give me leave to depart whensoever it should please Your Majesty to pardon me.

With these considerations I beg Your Majesty to pardon such acts of mine as may have appeared contrary to your wishes and hostile to the safety of your realm, and allow me to return to my country which is yours, and thereafter remain

Your Majesty's *New* Creature.

When this letter signed by Joshua Vine was delivered with the pearls to Queen Elizabeth some of her advisers who had never been to sea told her that this man was a worthless pirate who should lose his head. Others, especially the admirals who *had* been to sea, said that Vine, although no Francis Drake, was nevertheless a remarkable mariner. He might not have circumnavigated the globe, but he had probably sailed more sea miles than any living Englishman. A pirate, yes, but not against his countrymen. A sworn patriot, and yet a brigand quite unfit for a command in the Queen's navy where discipline and pay were set out in regulations. Under Joshua Vine, according to reports, discipline and pay were mercurial elements in a savage contract adjusted to circumstances between a ruthless master who needed his crew and a brutal mob of adventurers who needed their master. Officially the admirals, hard men but inclined to law and order, could not approve. Unofficially the admirals knew that when the Spaniards came, as come they must, England would need all her sea warriors, especially one as skilled as Joshua Vine.

Elizabeth, now in her fiftieth year, had no hesitation in brushing aside the theoretical objections to this interesting pirate. In private audience she listened through a long afternoon to the romantic narrative of the boy pressed into a life of piracy, how he had saved his ship when the captain had been swept overboard in a storm, of years in the Caribbean and the last decade in Istanbul. He had been misled. He had done wrong. But never had he taken an English life, always he had yearned to return one day to his beloved queen and country.

Elizabeth was a great judge of men. She knew a romancer

when she saw one. She also knew a man of the sea. Under all her statesmanship and royalty these were the men she most loved and trusted. This man was an outstanding specimen. The pearls were breathtaking. She would wear them with her favourite auburn wig.

Joshua Vine was knighted on the deck of a warship moored at Greenwich.

With his rubies and emeralds he bought a home in the seaside town where he had been born. He commissioned the construction of a race-built galleon, to be named *Tigress*.

Lionel and Tom Dakyn left their horses at the Cockleshell Inn and hurried down the street past staring citizens who would have asked about San Corda.

At the end of the street rose the westward claw of Lingmouth harbour where perched on top, reached only by steep zig-zag steps, stood the miniature bastion of Rockways, the house that Vine had bought from Gertrude's friend, the widow Dewmark.

Tom had been inside Rockways as a child. He had known the Dewmarks, especially the daughter Alis, long before Joshua Vine came back from sea.

CHAPTER FIVE

Michael Dewmark was the wealthiest merchant in Lingmouth. His wife Rose was the greatest snob. Alis was the most desirable maiden.

Being newly rich the Dewmarks only mixed with the best people, especially those with the asset that could never be bought. Heredity. Gertrude Dakyn had married into a famous family, Rose Dewmark had not. Their friendship was finely balanced. Gertrude sometimes envied Rose the ready cash that was not always available at Paxcombe, while Rose, though she would never have admitted it, always envied Gertrude her husband's ancestors.

Between Alis Dewmark and Tom Dakyn grew an affection as between cousins. They did not often meet. In childhood, uninterested in the money and status of their parents, they played together, each enjoying the novelty of the other's home. In their teens Tom had a tutor and Alis a governess. When Alis was eighteen (and Tom a year younger) she spent a long summer in Brussels with merchant friends of her father and came back transformed, a self-possessed beauty in the height of fashion. Her father spoilt her, she could have all the clothes she fancied. She made havoc among the young men. She reminded Gertrude of her own youth. Tom could hardly believe that this costly moll was his old playmate. She was dazzling. But when he tried to take advantage of old times she opened the immaculate eyes under her exquisitely pencilled eyebrows and in the most expensively cultured voice told him to go away and not bother her. She had outgrown him.

So lived the enviable Dewmarks, father amassing the money, mother and daughter spending it on lavish entertainment and conquest without commitment. They thought, if they thought at all, that father was content with his role.

With no warning Michael Dewmark surprised them. For twenty-five years he had toiled. His wife was obsessed with possessions. His daughter he adored in his own manner. Gladly he had given her the money to make herself desirable, he was proud to have taken part in such a handiwork. And now suddenly he paid her the greatest compliment by disappearing to the Continent with a girl two years younger than Alis. Her name was Virginia. She had come to Lingmouth for the second time with a troupe of players. Michael the respected merchant sold his business for a fortune, took as much cash as he could carry and a bundle of bills of exchange, and was gone without a goodbye.

The shock to his wife and daughter was total. At first they thought some strange accident had befallen him. Then a letter came from Paris. He had lost his heart, for the first time in his life he was happy, he begged their forgiveness. He enclosed a legal document making over Rockways to Rose.

This generosity only infuriated them. How did he think they were going to live without money? They could manage for a time. There were things to sell in the house, plate and furniture which Rose had bought with such abandon. One thing they would never part with, their jewellery. But as time passed the rings and necklaces were grudgingly surrendered one by one, each like a drop of blood. The two women had never been fond of each other. Rose was too bossy for Alis, and Alis was too popular for Rose. Now, like uncongenial mariners after a shipwreck, they banded together for survival. One solution might have been a wealthy marriage. But middle-aged ladies, however prominent in the township, were not wanted without a dowry, and Alis, more desirable than ever in the bloom of her early twenties, learned the lesson that young men who swear they would die for you do not necessarily offer marriage. Secretly Rose and Alis always believed that the runaway Michael would come back to them. When they spoke of him he was an unpardonable scoundrel, but alone in their minds they waited for his return.

Then came news from the embassy in Vienna. Michael Dewmark had died of a heart attack. Too much love perhaps. The two women faced each other. Their resources were dwindling, each drop of jewel blood so desperately yielded brought an unspoken panic to their hearts. Their only real asset left was Rockways itself, their home.

At this moment of crisis Sir Joshua Vine, newly knighted, reappeared in the town he had left so long ago. His fame, greatly embroidered, had preceded him. Everyone wanted to meet him. A number of liars said they remembered him as a child. He was fêted everywhere. He heard all the news, including the tragedy of Rockways. He looked up at the stronghold and demanded to meet the unfortunate widow.

The meeting was a one-sided contest. The wealthy sea-hero acknowledged by the Queen, in his prime of strength, magnetic with his amber eyes, needing nothing, and the local widow, a year younger but past her prime, needing everything, especially a man. She showed him her home, told him her story. Alis was presented, but it was at her mother he was smiling.

When they were alone he asked if Rockways were for sale, looking at her in a way she had not been looked at for years. There was such calm, such promising kindness in his face. Over the balcony table with a bottle of wine between them hovered the notion, inexplicit but overwhelming to Rose Dewmark, that when this man had bought her home he would marry her. She asked a price that she knew would please him. He accepted. She and Alis moved out. Joshua Vine moved in.

He did not ask her to marry him.

Rose and Alis took lodgings provided by the merchant who had bought Michael's business. It was a good address near the sea front. They had money now for several years. But when that was gone?

High in his new home, Sir Joshua settled down. His father was long since drowned falling in a stupor among his lobster pots, he who had sold so many lobster meals now a meal for lobsters. Two of Joshua's brothers had died, the others gone heaven knew where. His elder sister had never returned with her gipsy. Only the other sister, Emme, appeared from the slums of Lingmouth. She was two years older than Joshua, but looked like his grandmother. She was unmarried, toothless, given to wild fits of crooning under the slimy harbour jetties when the moon was full. She scrubbed floors and lived in sheds. People told her not to show herself to her famous brother. He would be ashamed. But she came to him and he was not ashamed. He took her to be his housekeeper at Rockways.

From the western windows Joshua could look out to sea. To the east, down across the harbour, he could see the estuary of the Ling. Here Toby Tenchbury built ships. It was not a big shipyard, but along the south coast apart from the great dockyards of Elizabeth's navy small builders were encouraged. Tenchbury was a good craftsman. He had been apprentice to Matthew Baker, architect of the first *Dreadnought*, so named by the Queen in her fury after the Massacre of St Bartholomew. Her navy would dread no one and nothing. In this spirit Toby Tenchbury, now his own master, built *Tigress* for Joshua Vine. It took two years.

Vice-Admiral Lord Thomas Howard, promoter of private shipping in Dorset, approved. Vine could never be a pirate again, and it would be a shame to let his talent rust. One day his country would be glad of that talent, so Joshua was allowed to rig his ship and train his seamen. There was no lack of applicants. He was at liberty to sail up and down the Channel, attend regattas, and put the fear of God into his crews. He was a knight of the realm, and he had sworn to his Queen that his days of piracy were over.

These were years of joy, for Joshua loved *Tigress* as Apollo loved his lyre. Yet they were also years of frustration. His sea time was limited and in his citadel he was lonely. He could have filled Rockways every evening with flatterers, but with these lap-dog shore dwellers he never felt at ease. The women were worse, they all wanted to marry him. He was amazed at the varieties of their approach. He did not mind a few companions

to eat and drink, but when his loins ached he would send for the
harbour girls. Emme knew where to find them. They were no
twittering odalisques, no highly trained humming birds from
the seraglio. They were sea-sparrows, uncomplicated and without ulterior motive. There was laughter and tenderness. He
paid them well and they adored him. They were gone by
morning. Emme saw to that.

So Joshua lived with his fame and his money, and could not
believe his sea voyages were over. Among his few true friends
was Lionel Dakyn who had been the boy heir to Paxcombe
when Joshua was a harbour rat. The two men, both socially
secure, owing nothing to one another, got on well together.
When the storm clouds with Spain were gathering and Lionel
asked Joshua whether he would take the *Tigress* to deliver some
bales of cloth, Joshua agreed. There was no need to tell
Vice-Admiral Thomas Howard. This was not piracy, just a
business arrangement. Lionel asked if his son Tom could go for
the experience. Joshua Vine had no objection.

The outcome was the conflagration in San Corda.

Lionel and Tom Dakyn went to Rockways to reimburse Sir
Joshua for his expenses.

As Tom looked up at the silhouette of Rockways outlined
against puffy white clouds on this April morning when the year
was young, he felt sad that his first sea trip with Joshua Vine
had probably been his last.

Tigress had done her best, and more could not be asked. Soon
every port in Spain would be on the alert.

CHAPTER SIX

It was strange standing in the long first-floor room where he
used to play with Alis Dewmark. In those days of childhood he
had not thought of her as beautiful, that had not been the
consideration. She was his friend in league against parents. He
remembered her eighth birthday when his mother had given
him a doll to give to Alis. The doll was called Eleanor. She had
big eyes and a painted ivory face and a toy trunk full of beautiful
clothes. Alis had hardly said thank you, but she was pleased.
They dressed Eleanor up and changed her costume many times,

51

and Tom had to be Eleanor's father, son, husband, groom, gardener or whatever Alis told him to be. In those days it was Eleanor he admired, because Alis admired her. For Tom it was one game among many. Ten years later when Alis came back from Brussels and told him she had outgrown him he thought how beautiful she was, like Eleanor the doll.

Now Lionel and Tom were waiting in the long room. A servant had let them in and taken them upstairs. The master was out with his dogs. So Lionel and Tom waited.

The room was much changed. No tapestries on the walls, only maps and charts, the old ornaments replaced by impedimenta of the sea, a brass ship's bell embossed with a swooping vulture, its talons poised to strike, a vast tallow lantern suspended from the ceiling, and on the writing table a three-masted vessel six inches long hand-carved from ebony. They were admiring it when Sir Joshua came in encircled by three bull mastiffs, their heads level with his waist, tremendous animals, the chest muscles spreading like swollen iron into the forelegs, the brute jaws appallingly carnivorous, the twelve paws padding a soft tattoo on the floor. When they saw Lionel and Tom they froze. Their throats rumbled. They glanced round at their master.

"*Quieto! Quieto!*" said Sir Joshua with jovial authority. He pointed to the wall.

Two of the mastiffs relaxed, stalked to the wall and lay down, still observant. The third remained with hunched shoulders, glaring at Tom, its red-flecked eyes as lidless as the man in black.

"Japheth has a chill. He is out of temper," said Sir Joshua. Then, with a bark in his voice: "Japheth! *Quieto!*"

The massive beast retired reluctantly and lay down. Tom managed a smile. He had never met the mastiffs close to, but he had seen them in the streets. He had seen them at the pit near the estuary, ripping the life out of a malevolent black bear. An awesome sight. Everyone in Lingworth knew Shem, Ham and Japheth, sons of Noah, the bodyguards of Rockways. They were fed on the raw anatomies of English beef. Servants from Rockways said that not a trace of gristle or bone was ever left. At the Cockleshell Inn a story was told of a wild Irish stranger off a French freighter claiming drunkenly he was the brother of someone named Doyle, demanding the whereabouts of Joshua

Vine, seen climbing the zigzag steps at noon, never seen again. True or false, no one was prepared to speculate. When Joshua's sister, the silent toothless Emme, went shopping with her three escorts she was served like a duchess.

"They are fine dogs," said Tom. "Are they Portuguese?"

Sir Joshua laughed: "Only for the three words of command, I have trained them. I do not wish strangers telling them what to do. Now they are at rest. *Quieto!* If I told them to be on guard I would also say it in Portuguese."

"And the third word?"

Sir Joshua wrote with his finger in the air. K–I–L–L. "If I uttered that work in Portuguese you would die. It might be dangerous even in English. They are very wise. They listen, they think, but at least they do not spell!"

"They guard you, evidently."

"We feel safe enough. My sister would not be without her three children."

"How is the lady?" asked Lionel. "In health, I hope."

"She is not strong. And she is not at ease with strangers. You understand—" He broke off, then with a little shrug: "You were looking at the *Black Vulture.*"

"A fine piece of carving."

"By a man I trust above all others."

He motioned them to sit down, brought wine and glasses, and when they settled he said, "So you have come to pay your dues. Out of one hundred bales carried for you, I landed just three. They were taken."

"By no fault of yours," said Lionel. "We still owe you—"

Sir Joshua held up his hand.

"I do not want your money. The cost of a few days at sea? It is not important."

"I would prefer to pay," said Lionel. "I do not care for undischarged debts."

"The debts will be discharged, I hope. But in a different manner."

He stood up with his back to the unlit fire and looked down at them. Tom thought how in many ways his father and this man were alike, the same age, the same trim black beard, the same physique. And yet so different. Lionel was the big tureen in the kitchen at Paxcombe, simmering slowly with the ingredients of the past. This other man was the great kettle full of

53

spring water issuing wisps of steam, bursting with the future.

"I have a plan," said Sir Joshua. "The details can come later. What happened at San Corda was a miracle, an opportunity which with your help can make a dream come true for me, and bring us all a fortune. Let me tell you quickly, simply—"

He tapped his head as if to mark off the simple points. Then he went on: "One. There is treasure to be obtained from the Spaniards. I know where it is and how to get it. My dream has been locked away for many years. *Black Vulture* was not big enough and I could not afford better. Then fate took me to Istanbul, and Istanbul gave me *Tigress*. But I could not use her. I had made promises to the Queen. Do not mistake me. The Queen is the greatest lady on earth, but she cannot always act as she would in her heart. My plan needs official sanction, and officially, to many fools at court, I am still a pirate.

"And two. With your help, Lionel, we can get the document that will set us free. A Letter of Reprisal. You understand?"

"I know what Reprisal is," said Lionel. "But how can I help you to get it?"

"By allowing me to present your claim to Lord Howard. He is my friend. I shall tell him of your grievous loss. Not three bales but five hundred—"

"But surely—"

"It is a small lie, but it will impress the admirals. Lord Howard will persuade them. They will authorize you to recover the value of what you lost. No checks can be made. You can then engage me and my ship. There will be no charge, for without you I could not sail. You will be named as the 'owner'. You will be entitled on paper to one third of the prize."

"That is a large amount for telling a small lie," smiled Lionel. "And what will your own share be?"

"Have no fear. I shall have what I deserve."

"And I more than I deserve. If I could come with you, share the dangers—but I fear that is hardly possible."

"I agree. You have Paxcombe. And your wife."

"I would also make a bad seaman!"

"True. You have been ashore too long. So I propose a condition."

"And that is?"

"That your son sails on *Tigress*. He shall be your premium.

54

He will earn a fortune for you and your home." He turned to Tom. "You are a man after my own heart. That is not flattery, it is the truth. How say you?"

"Wait!" said Lionel. "We must consider."

"So you should. Think well."

There was a silence. Tom looked up at the brass bell and the maps on the walls. Then he looked at the mastiffs. They lay where they had been told, chins on forepaws, open eyes regarding him without sympathy. This sea-room, these dogs, their pirate master a knight of the Queen! It was no ordinary decision. Tom could feel the brink. He said, "Where is the treasure?"

"I will tell you in good time. For the present it is better that you should trust me."

"So I do. May I not have trust in return?"

Sir Joshua looked at him seriously. At last he said, "Very well. I will tell you two, but no one else till we have sailed. Words have wings. We want no reception party. I take it you give your solemn promise." He pointed to a map on the wall. "There!"

They followed him. The map showed the continents of North and South America linked by the curly isthmus of Panama. He moved his thumbnail from Panama City on the Pacific southern coastline of the isthmus up to Nombre de Dios on the Caribbean.

"Thirty miles. Up that route comes the treasure of Spain. It is brought by mules to Nombre de Dios. In the old days it was all gold and silver from the mines. Fourteen years ago there was a raid on the mule train. The gold almost sank the ship that brought it back to Plymouth. Since then there have been no raids. The Spaniards have grown confident. They have added to the treasure. Now, besides the gold, there are emeralds from Peru and Ecuador. The value is beyond calculation."

"You are well informed," said Lionel.

"Every ship that drops anchor at Lingmouth is full of information. I hear a great deal. Much of it is sea-talk, but I know what to believe. And above all there is the man who carved *Black Vulture*." He turned from the map and picked up the ebony ship from the table. "His name is Krauss. He is a Hollander. While I was in Istanbul he kept the ship safe for my return. They tried to steal *Black Vulture*. He has the scar to prove it. But when I returned to Lingmouth he brought me my ship, and much information besides. He knows the Caribbean and he knows my plan. I trust him."

"Where is he now?" asked Tom.

"In Bristol. He says he has finished with the sea. But he will come with us."

"And where is *Black Vulture*?"

"She was old and weary. Her seams had sprung a dozen times. When Toby Tenchbury built me the *Tigress* he broke up *Black Vulture* with all solemnity and respect." He paused, placing the ebony vessel gently on the table. "So there is my proposal. You have heard enough. What say you?"

Tom looked at his father. It seemed a long time since they had climbed the steps to pay their bill. There was no need for words. Tom's eyes asked several important questions, and Lionel's eyes said, "Make up your own mind."

Tom took a breath. Exhaled. He said, "I will come."

"It will be a long voyage. You know what that means?"

"I have heard."

"It will be no cross-channel holiday."

"I understand."

"And you will still come?"

"Yes," said Tom. "Though like my father I am no great seaman as yet."

"You have other talents. Your duties will be to act as my lieutenant. With you and Krauss we shall not fail. As you will see," said Sir Joshua, "it is a question of trust."

He took them down to the front entrance, the mastiffs breathing behind. At the top of the zigzag steps Lionel and Tom looked back and waved. In the doorway stood Joshua Vine, with Shem, Ham, Japheeth, and a small wizened figure in a long black skirt, her shoulders wrapped in a shawl, her eyes two black buttons on a puckered biscuit. She raised a small hand, flexing the fingers slowly. She did not smile.

CHAPTER SEVEN

Whereas we, taking into consideration and apprehending that diverse well affected people of this

Commonwealth have sustained great wrongs, losses and damages, being pillaged, spoiled, surprised by the ships and subjects of the King of Spain, and whereas LIONEL DAKYN ESQUIRE of Paxcombe Hall in the county of Dorset has sustained loss and damage by subjects of the King of Spain, we have thought fit that a Letter of Reprisal should be granted to LIONEL DAKYN to apprehend, seize and take the ships, vessels and merchandise of the King of Spain or any of his subjects until he be satisfied for all the said wrongs and damages by him sustained.

Whereof the said LIONEL DAKYN hath given bond in our court of Admiralty to commit any spoil or bulk of goods he shall take as prize to our said court of Admiralty, an inventory being taken for the approbation of the lawful prize, the court of Admiralty to keep and retain in their possession and make lawful sale as agreed (i.e. one third to Admiralty, one third to Owner, one third to Crew).

Given in the said court of Admiralty under the great seal thereof.

Signed: Doctor Julius Caesar (Judge to the court of Admiralty).

Julius Caesar, of no connection with Rome, was a colourful element in the structure of Admiralty. A young naval officer of promise, he had been forced by excruciating gout to change his profession. He took up law, but there was always brine in his blood, and by hard work over many years he took his doctorate and became chief judge at the court of Admiralty. As such it was he who executed the wishes of Their Lordships in granting Letters of Reprisal. He composed these documents with relish, imagining the consequences at sea.

Their Lordships were wholly royalist. They shared the view of those closest to the Queen, that she was in constant danger from the influences of Popery. An Act of Parliament had proclaimed that in the extreme event of her assassination no pretender would be recognized till a committee of peers and Privy Councillors, taking temporary control of government, had found the culprits. But Popery was a vague threat. Their Lordships were concerned with a single dangerous probability, invasion by a fleet from Spain. Elizabeth knew the threat, yet hesitated to declare war. She was always hesitating about something. In the meantime Spain must be challenged at sea whenever, wherever and however possible. An inner coterie at Admiralty devoted themselves to this. They called themselves "Friends of Elizabeth". Sir George Carey was one. He encouraged private sea-enterprise in Hampshire, as Lord Thomas Howard encouraged it in Dorset and Sir Walter Raleigh in Devon and Cornwall. There were Sir Richard Leveson, Sir Robert Southwell and, most powerful of all, another Howard, Charles, the Lord High Admiral of England. These were ardent men determined to fulfil the unspoken wishes of their Queen. Whatever her political hesitations, she was the true daughter of her father Henry, patron of the sea, champion of independence. Elizabeth relied on her men of the sea, even if she could not always say so. Their Lordships were sure of this. Therefore what was necessary must be done, even without the Queen's blessing. And unless things went terribly wrong the Queen would not complain. Sir George Carey summed it up when he remarked, "Her Majesty shall not need to espy the faults of those that will venture their own to do her service."

He was referring to Joshua Vine. The committee of the Friends of Elizabeth were discussing whether to issue a Letter of Reprisal on behalf of Lionel Dakyn. The admirals knew what was going on. Thomas Howard had explained. They all agreed that Lionel Dakyn was a perfect figure-head for the scheme. He had certainly sustained "loss and damage". Five hundred bales of cloth was a serious item. The murder of six seamen was unforgivable, not mitigated by Vine's act of retribution. The burning of the Spanish trawler was a closed incident. The admirals did not discuss it. There had been no survivors, no tales to be told in Spain. Dakyn, on the face of it, clearly deserved reprisal. But what about the man who would effect this?

The problem centred on Joshua Vine and his Queen. He had been knighted to keep him out of trouble. Elizabeth had said as much to George Carey. Vine had sworn to behave, not to cause complaint from abroad, and now he was aiming to take the *Tigress* on a momentous voyage. If Elizabeth knew, she would undoubtedly forbid it. So it must be done without her knowledge. If Vine were successful all would be forgiven. But if he failed? If he incurred complaint from King Philip of Spain with

58

nothing to show for it? And if Elizabeth knew that the Admiralty had sanctioned the risk?

The admirals shuddered. Men had been sent to the Tower for less. The admirals, like their Queen, hesitated.

From their hesitation came the answer.

When *Tigress* was crossing Biscay on the way back from San Corda a naval squadron of more than twenty ships had slipped out of Plymouth harbour. It was an imposing force composed of ships of the line, private galleons, three tall ships furnished by London merchants, and a dozen smaller men-of-war. The admiral in command was Sir Francis Drake. His instructions were to "impeach the purpose of the Spanish fleet and stop their meeting at Lisbon". The Queen after weeks of hesitation had given her permission, hardly given before she tried to cancel it by sending a messenger on horseback to Plymouth. But Drake was gone. His mission, loosely worded, was to find out how far the Spaniards had got with their invasion plans.

That was in early April. Joshua Vine saw Lord Thomas Howard a fortnight later. It was May before Howard made his recommendations to the admirals. In June they were still hesitating.

And now back from his mission came Francis Drake. His news was sensational.

At Cadiz, Spain's prime port near Gibraltar, he had sailed his squadron straight past the inaccurate guns on the mole into the harbour, where a confused mass of galleons and supply ships were totally surprised, half their crews ashore, the rest unbalanced. He had sunk over thirty ships without losing a man or a ship of his own.

Doubling back up the coast of Portugal (which Spain treated as hers) he had terrorized the strip round Lagos, landing a force of soldiers who captured two castles and a monastery, then withdrew. A blow to Spanish morale rather than an end in itself.

Heading north towards Lisbon he had met, maimed, sunk, burnt, robbed and generally despoiled more than one hundred small vessels, some carrying fish, others laden with wooden "hoops and pipe staves" (so ran his report) enough to construct thirty thousand tons of casks and barrels for the stowage of food and wine. These he commanded to be "consumed into smoke and ashes by fire".

Off Lisbon he had espied in the Tagus estuary the main strength of the Spanish navy, fifty galleons or more. He had sensed another Cadiz, despatched his fastest pinnace with a letter asking Elizabeth's permission, and receiving her negative (peace negotiations with Spain must not be endangered), had come home.

On the way, divine bonus, he had captured a Spanish carrack, the *San Felipe*, bringing a fortune of spices, gold and jewels from the Indian Ocean. He had put the Spanish crew ashore and brought the *San Felipe* to Dartmouth.

The details of these adventures ran to pages. The summary gave an unmistakable answer to the question mark of Spain's intention to invade.

Spain was building a vast fleet to attack England and overthrow Elizabeth.

The sinkings at Cadiz had set back the building programme. Much more important was the destruction of such a tonnage of food-casks. Invasion would depend on the army to be landed, and the army would depend on victuals that would not wreck their stomachs en route, and the victuals would depend on being properly casked.

The damage by Drake had postponed the invasion, not stopped it. On the contrary, Drake had confirmed all that Admiralty suspected.

In short:

Spain would invade.

Not this year.

But next.

The admirals hesitated no longer. The spoils of the *San Felipe* would keep Elizabeth happy. She was a great realist. If the Spaniards were coming next year everything must be done to harass them now. There was no better instrument of harassment than Joshua Vine. If he succeeded everyone would be pleased including the Queen. If he failed it would hardly be noticed in the cataclysm of invasion.

The admirals instructed Doctor Julius Caesar to compose the letter giving Lionel Dakyn Esquire permission to recover his grievous losses "till he be satisfied".

Joshua Vine prepared the *Tigress*, and Tom Dakyn prepared to go with him.

CHAPTER EIGHT

Tom stood with Alis Dewmark at the side of the dry dock. Many Lingmouth citizens were round the dock rail that afternoon. Below them like some stranded sea-beetle, her eight legs the slanting oak beams that held her upright, squatted the *Tigress*. She looked forlorn, indignant, a surprisingly fat woman caught undressed in an empty bath. She wore no canvas, no yards, no rigging, only the three masts rising bare and useless. Her decks were strewn with crates, tarpaulins and the general rubbish of a refit. Tom had only seen her afloat. Riding at sea with the water less than five feet below her gun-ports she fitted her specification, a race-built galleon of one hundred and seventy tons. She had grace and strength, not the fire-power of the Queen's great warships like *Dreadnought* and *Swiftsure*, but speed and manoeuvrability. Here in the drained oblong dock, the river end dammed up by double gates caulked with stones and clay, the underwater dimensions of *Tigress* were unflatteringly revealed. Her swollen belly was covered with barnacles and seaweed. Men on ladders and cradles were scraping them off. Her length, a hundred feet from stem to stern, seemed to have shrunk. She looked cumbersome, a waddler with an ungainly torso. There were sounds of carpentry within. Her open ports were empty, her guns in the Tenchbury yard for cleaning and replacement. Four demi-culverins for extra power. But the empty square windows still looked apologetic.

Alis touched Tom's arm, not the squeeze he would have liked, and said, "When will she be ready?"

"In two months, I believe."

"The whole town is talking of it. They say a man would walk from London for the chance to sail with Sir Joshua."

"He has a reputation."

"He will get what he wants," said Alis. "Everyone knows that."

Tom did not answer. He knew about the sale of Rockways. Rose Dewmark had told his mother often enough. But if Alis was short of money she did not show it. Here she was on this cloudy summer afternoon in a full-skirted outfit of purple linen

61

trimmed with black. She wore a velvet bonnet. Her cheeks were alabaster, her lips and eyebrows delicately drawn. She was like Eleanor the doll.

"When *Tigress* sails," said Tom "everything we have, all our friends and families, will be left behind."

"And ahead will be adventure."

"Now it's close I think of what I'll be leaving."

"Your friends? Your home? They'll all be waiting."

"If I could be sure."

"Will Paxcombe disappear? Your friends vanish?"

"Not vanish, perhaps. But some of them might forget."

"Then you will have to remind them. But that will not be necessary, I think. Who is going to forget Tom Dakyn of Paxcombe Hall?"

"You, perhaps," said Tom.

"What gratitude! After all these years! Do not talk of forgetting. Since mother and I left Rockways you have hardly spoken to me. A word or two perhaps in other people's houses. Was that the behaviour of a friend?"

She spoke with a smile, not crossly. He did not argue. In her heyday after her return from Brussels she had outgrown him. He had not competed with the beaux of Lingmouth. In the crisis after her father's disappearance and death Tom had tried to get to know her again, but she had always kept their meetings polite, unserious. It was six months since he had seen her alone. When the *Tigress* came into dock and everyone knew of the voyage (though not the destination) he had invited Alis to dine at the Cockleshell. She had come. There was the table cloth of fine linen, the fresh lobster, the white Burgundy, and Alis in her purple outfit, an ivory medallion studded with garnets round her neck, a single large ring of clustered pearls on her right forefinger, her face a faultless painting. And her eyes? There was something in them he had not seen before. A hint of readiness? When he spoke to her she looked straight back at him. He wondered whether she had come for the same reason as he had asked her.

A workman on a ladder cut his hand on the barnacles. There was a lot of swearing and rude observations about barnacles from his mates. No one looked up. From the rail Tom looked down at the belly of *Tigress*. Inside the belly was the hold. He had sailed on *Tigress* but he had not been down into the hold.

He had seen the ladders disappearing below from the orlop deck, but he had not visited the dark foetid belly below the waterline. A race-built galleon? How could she race with such a barnacled belly? No wonder they had to scrape and polish her.

"I am still your friend," said Tom.

"I hope so. Indeed."

"And more than a friend?"

"Let us not hurry," said Alis.

"It is not I that hurry. Others are hurrying me."

"Towards what? Towards questions that cannot be answered?"

"In two months I shall be away," he said. "And before I go I want to know something."

"Are you sure?"

There was a honey hardness in her voice that had always melted him. Why this woman? Why not one of the soft smiling daughters of Lingmouth? He knew several. So why this difficult moll? He looked at her long slim fingernails on his sleeve.

A fuzzy black cloud was approaching from the west. A sudden breeze brought a humming round the masts of *Tigress*. There were coarse shouts and bangings from the dock. Water was seeping through the clay-bound gates, pushing a film of muddy loops over the floor of the dock, and now the pumps clanked into action, echoing round the walls. Absurdly he had to raise his voice:

"Will you marry me? Now. Before I go."

She murmured something.

"I can't hear," he said.

She turned and looked up at him and he thought that never had he seen a face so desirable. He knew it was hopeless. The reasons were all against him. But desire had no reasons.

She said loudly, "I said thank you for asking me!"

"Is that all?"

"Yes, Tom, that is all."

There was no time. He could see himself on *Tigress* sliding from Lingmouth harbour. He said, "Do you not want to get married?"

"Very much."

"Then why have you not married by now?"

"Because the man I want has never asked me."

"And who is that man?"

"I do not know him. But he will have two most necessary qualities. One, that he pleases me."

"And the other quality?"

She patted his arm. "Money," she said.

"Should he not love you? Is not that a necessary quality?"

"I could teach him that." She said it so confidently.

"If it were me I would need no teaching."

"You are a dreamer," said Alis.

"We were children together," he said. "You have not married. I have not married. Might that not signify? Might not our stars have worked together? I have never wanted a woman as I want you. I asked you to dine today. You need not have come. But you came. It was no dream. We are standing at this rail, and down there is the ship that will take me away. I am not dreaming. I want to marry you. I have no time to tell lies."

"You flatter me," she said. "You have told me your truth. Will you listen to mine?"

"Gladly." He did not mean that.

"We were children together," said Alis. "I grew up before you did. I had a beautiful home and all that money could provide. My father spoilt me. I adored him. And suddenly there was no father, no home, only money that we must watch, my mother and I, like paupers watching a lump of cheese."

"Why cheese?" smiled Tom.

"Each day is a rat that nibbles our cheese. One day it will suddenly be gone."

"I admire your bonnet," he said. "You must be the most beautiful pauper in the world."

"I have another bonnet. Once I had a score. I had a closet of clothes and a casket of jewels. Now they are almost empty. Each morning I wonder what the rat will take next."

"If you married me I would look after you."

"You would do your best, I am sure."

"You would have a fine home. Paxcombe after all—"

"Tom!" She almost shouted. At that moment the pumps stopped clanging and an old couple along the rail turned their heads. Alis clasped her hands on the rail. She said in a low quick voice, "That ship will not sail in jest. Not for glory or adventure or because they love their Queen or country. They will go for one thing only. And you will be among them. Many will not return. Those who do will be rich or they will be poor. For that they will risk their lives. Success or failure. The town is full of strangers. They will sleep anywhere, do anything for food. They have no possessions. They do not know where the *Tigress* is going, they do not care. They have only one wish. To sail with Joshua Vine. For only one reason. It is your reason too. It is a reason I understand completely. If I were a man I would go myself, even with Joshua Vine whom I hate more than any man in the world."

Tom looked round at the knots of citizens standing at the rail, parents and friends and hopeful seamen. And other parents and wives thinking of six seamen dying by fire at San Corda.

He said, "If I come back rich, then will you marry me?"

"Who knows? It is so long, so far."

"But it is possible. You do not say 'No'."

"I say nothing. You must go on your journey, and if you come back, and if I am here, and if you are rich, and if I am not married . . ."

"What then?"

"Then you must take me to dine at the Cockleshell."

"It is a long way for a dish of lobster."

"You go for yourself, not for me."

"I had rather it were for you."

"For your own sake it is better not." She glanced up at the fuzzy cloud almost overhead. "Let us get home before the rain."

"Tell me," he said, "why did you come? You could have refused, if you care so little. At the dinner table I thought you felt something for me."

"I felt curious," said Alis. "I have heard many times about San Corda. I did not ask you to tell me again because I am sickened by such fearful things, but I felt proud to be dining with such a brave man."

It was gusting as they walked round the harbour. There were strangers in the cobbled street, young men in twos and threes standing as if they wondered what to do next. At the door of her lodgings she turned full towards him, stood very straight and smiling:

"Thank you, Tom. I enjoyed my dinner. I wish you a safe return."

"I shall see you again before—"

65

"No. See me when you come back."

"I cannot say goodbye here. Not like this."

"Then do not say it." She lifted up her face.

He bent to kiss her mouth, but she slid her cheek against his, then opened the door and was gone inside.

He collected Pola from the stables and as he rode up along the knuckle of the hill towards Paxcombe a rain-flecked wind hissed in the gorse bushes and the sea below was a flat muddy blur with no horizon.

CHAPTER NINE

August was a month of hurrying days, of hail and farewell. Hail to his future shipmates, farewell to Paxcombe. Most mornings he rode into Lingmouth to learn his duties as lieutenant to Joshua Vine. In the sunny evenings Paxcombe welcomed him back. On the farms the wheat and hay were poor, but in the gardens of Paxcombe there was an extravagance of flowers and fruit. Round the courtyard walls clumps of monkshood proliferated. There was a blaze of late roses, and on the trellises and in the orchard more plums and golden pears than he had ever seen. Paxcombe was offering him a festival before he left.

He had never felt his home so beautiful. It was like that hot August so long ago when he had swum with his father and Uncle Georges in the lake. On cloudless nights Georges had shown him the triangle of Deneb, Vega and Altair in the southern sky, and here now they hung exactly as then, bringing back things that Georges had said to him.

He became aware of his home, seeing freshly what he knew so well.

In the entrance hall there was the sun before breakfast glinting on his forebears' weird-shaped stomach-gutting lances hanging on the wall, and by the door an iron claw that had once gripped the wrist stump of his great-great-uncle, a second son who had lost his right hand at Bosworth Field fighting for the first Tudor king. In one window the stained heraldic panel of great-grandfather Dakyn impaling Pengelly (an heiress with a coat of arms). In the kitchen the chimney crane that swung the big pots over the fire, and the smell of fresh baked bread and Ellen Rufoote's sand-glass which no one but she must touch. The clock with no face whose bell had clanged every hour of his life. In the tiny chapel the Flemish triptych of the Adoration with the bearded old man whose eyes had frightened him as a child. In his parents' bedroom the four-poster where his red-haired baby sister had died and his brother been aborted. The bell-tower bats circling at twilight. On the landing the French bow-fronted court cupboard that his mother had brought when she was married. In the lamplight it glowed red-brown.

His mother surprised him. She had been told nothing till the Letter of Reprisal was granted. Lionel did not want to upset her unnecessarily. When the news came he said he would tell her privately that night, and Tom waited for morning with apprehension. He believed that marriage was exempt from promises to outsiders. Lionel would surely tell her of the gold from Panama. She would know the danger. Tom could hardly imagine her fury of protest. But at supper next day she looked from one to the other, her grey eyes wide open, and said, "I love my home and family, but I am not a child. Tom must go. It is necessary. I understand. Others have done great things for Paxcombe, and so will he."

She said no more about it till the twenty-fourth of the month, St Bartholomew's Day, the anniversary of the massacre. Tom stayed home that day. There were stairs up to the chapel from a corner of the dining-room, and waiting for dinner he heard a sob and went into the chapel and found Gertrude and sat beside her. She did not apologize or pretend. After a few moments she said, "Do you remember your uncle?"

"Very well."

"We are sea people," said Gertrude. "My father and his father built ships. Georges loved the sea. That was how he met Admiral Coligny. Your father and I met at a naval gala. He was so handsome. Irresistible! When I came to Paxcombe I thought I had finished with the sea. Now it has appeared again, to take you away. I do not complain. The sea has its own laws. I have prayed. I believe that what you do will be good for you and good for us all."

So spoke Gertrude with her feelings and insights and beliefs. As the weeks slipped away Tom felt a growing responsibility. It oppressed him. He was glad to spend the days in Lingmouth where everyone he met was busy with the *Tigress*.

He met them at Rockways where Joshua Vine was selecting

his crew. Some mornings Tom was allowed to watch the new faces appearing at the table in the long room where Sir Joshua sat with Krauss, the mate from *Black Vulture* who would soon be mate on the *Tigress*. They were the selection board. Tom felt sympathy for the seamen who waited by the dozen outside the door, and knocked, and came in to be questioned. Sir Joshua was formidable enough with his quick questions, but Krauss unnerved some applicants by saying nothing, by staring at them. The knotted scar beneath his left eye, where the dagger had pulverized the cheekbone, drew down the skin below the socket so that the eye could never close, was always circular with bloodshot hostility and apparently on the point of falling out. Tom knew that the scar was the relic of bravery when Krauss had saved *Black Vulture* from mutineers, the stigma of fidelity to his master. The older, tougher hands were immune to baleful scrutiny. They had served under grotesque masters. But some younger seamen, asked a simple question by Joshua Vine, hesitated, stammering a reply as they glanced in stupefaction at the ocular monstrosity of the other interrogator. They were dismissed.

The men were chosen for their experience and skills. A few had served in the Queen's navy. Most came from the shifting ribbon of thirteen thousand desperate mariners who swarmed in Norwich, London, along the ports of the south coast, and round Land's End to Bristol. They had heard the news. They came by sea, on foot, on the back of any donkey or nag they could scrounge. Many were ill clad, badly shod and hungry. In their faces was the uncomfortableness of seamen ashore. Some were specialists, carpenters, gun-crew, yard-men, but all were basic seamen ready for the capstan, the tiller or the shrouds. They had sailed everywhere. Many knew one another from the past and would tell any lie to help a friend or discredit a rival. All had one thing in common. They had no other trade but the sea. They were not merchants, could not build houses or breed cattle or raise crops. They could steal, for which they would be hanged, starve, for which they would be buried, or go to sea.

Sir Joshua knew this. He understood their desperation, it was the key to his choice. The crew he had taken to San Corda were locals whom he had trained in the Channel. They had done well enough, but it was one thing to sail to Spain and back, and entirely another thing to make a voyage of Reprisal lasting many months with unknown dangers and the risk of no return. The crew from San Corda had all applied, fifty-six of them. Twenty-three were rejected, but many more than twenty-three were required. At San Corda *Tigress* had been undermanned. Now she would be grossly overmanned. There would be wastage. Vine and Krauss were looking for hard, proven mariners who would risk their lives for money.

Tom watched them come to the table. He saw them interrogated, accepted, rejected. His own duties had been explained. As lieutenant of *Tigress* he would be Joshua Vine's earpiece and executor, in charge of discipline, reporting troublemakers. As he watched he tried to memorize the names and faces of those who were accepted, but there were so many and they came and went so quickly.

Wisse, Hesket, Darrell, Cheyne, Fernie, Parre, Blessington, Smolkin. Some he could recall for a day or two, then lost. Now and then someone would impinge more sharply.

There was Gostigo. Older than most. He came from Wapping and his father had sailed with Brian Tebbige the sea-cook in Limehouse. Gostigo had been fifteen years a bosun. He was a famous sail-maker. He had heavy black eyebrows and gloomy brown eyes. His cheeks were indented, as if constantly sucked from within. He sat very still and answered Sir Joshua's questions about sail-making very slowly. The grey stubble that covered his skull and spread like a fungus round his jaws and chin seemed discordant with the blackness of his eyebrows.

And there was Jabbinoth, long-boned and brawny. Over thirty but with a strange simplicity in his long-nosed, long-jawed face. His eyes had a childlike eagerness, and his big loose mouth was set in the promise of a smile that never quite broke out. He was like a boy at a picnic, ready to climb a tree or chase a rabbit or gobble anything that was offered. He did not look a man of capability or purpose, but Krauss affirmed that Jabbinoth had sailed with him in *Black Vulture* and was a first-class topman.

Newcroft, Rogers, Vaughan, Moxon, Donnimore, Twyll . . .

They were told that the voyage was for Reprisal. They asked no questions. They would sail anywhere, do anything, be paid nothing till it came to sharing the prizes. They trusted the Sultan to find the prizes, as he trusted them to man the *Tigress*.

69

Tom, looking up at the map on the wall, wondered what they would say if they knew what the real target was, the treasure of the Spanish empire, gold and emeralds, brought on the backs of mules from Panama to Nombre de Dios. What schemes, what assaults, what transportations had Sir Joshua in mind? Krauss knew the territory. Privately to Tom he had given a traveller's description . . . "The forests are like a madman's beard growing on the mountain of hell, monkeys and birds screech like the damned in the treetops, and when it rains you wait to be drowned." It was difficult sitting in the long room to imagine such a destination. Here was an atmosphere of practicality about the manning of a ship. No hint of hell, damnation or drowning. The mastiffs had been banished to the courtyard, Sir Joshua said they did not welcome strangers coming and going. Instead, by his chair, sat a new brown and black, sharp-eyed, prick-eared mongrel whom he called Sirius. The sons of Noah were too big and hungry to go to sea, and he needed a companion, he said, for his cabin.

Barlowe, Dykes, Pipkin, Waddington, Harris, Costlove . . .

On a low tide the clay-bound gates of the dry dock were opened and when the tide rose *Tigress* was warped across the estuary and brought alongside the deep-water wharf in Tenchbury's yard. Her guns were replaced. She was rigged anew. No sails yet. The tigress-head at her beak shone gilded in the autumn sun, a band of fresh tar ran above the water line, and the gun-ports and superstructure gleamed with varnish. She looked better, thought Tom, with her bowels invisible below the water. He watched the early stores going aboard. The food would come last. Now it was the crates and boxes of heavy equipment, some swung on the dockyard cranes, some suspended like flying parcels on the pulley-trolleys that plied on a cable from the shed roof to the yard-arm, some carried on the bent backs of the ant-like line of laden seamen who staggered aboard up one gangway and came erect and unladen down the other. Spare gun parts, spare blocks and rails and timbers, ropes and rigging and canvas, tools and brushes, some packed and labelled, some visible like the kedge anchor floating ponderously through the air, the duplications and replacements for *Tigress* when she was far away with no one to mend and furnish her except herself.

Tom went aboard and found the bosun Gostigo with a handful of lists shouting oathful orders to the stowage party, a more authoritative and lively Gostigo than the morose applicant in the long room. He stood with feet astride on the deck, the calf muscles bulging below his breeches. Tom asked if he might go below, and the bosun said, "They are loading the shot. You will find the surgeon on the orlop. He is a Scot by the sound of him," and Tom, not sure what the surgeon had to do with cannon balls, went below.

They were handling shot on the ladders and he squeezed past, down to the gun-deck, then down to the orlop where the lanterns were feeble and there was a smell of tallow. Handlers stripped to the waist were passing the shot and there was a metal-clanking as they stowed it in the racks. Tom called out, "Is the surgeon there?" and a voice unmistakably Highland said softly, "I am heeer!" and a canvas flap was drawn aside and Tom stepped into a barely-lit wooden cubicle and met Robert Seaton, aged twenty-seven, member of the Fellowship of Surgeons, pupil and apprentice to surgeon William Clowes, recommended to Joshua Vine by Robert's godfather, Lord Thomas Howard. This much was murmured in a lilt from the Cairngorms with his face in shadow in exchange for Tom's own synopsis.

"And how do you like my wee den?" asked Robert.

"Is this the best they can offer you?"

"It is only for the battle. Till the guns have stopped."

"I had forgotten!"

Whoever else was killed in action it must not be the surgeon. He would be wanted afterwards for the wounded. Tom knew that. He had never pictured where the surgeon would be hidden. Now it was obvious. Well below the flight of cannon balls. Surely *Tigress* would not invite battle on her way to the Caribbean, but she might have battle forced upon her.

The hatch down to the hold was jammed with crates, and they climbed up to the daylight, and Robert's face was shown to be pale with a straight nose and chestnut hair. When Tom suggested a meal at the Cockleshell Robert said he must get back to Southampton before nightfall. They would meet again. In the meantime it was another glimpse cut short. There were many. Tom felt as if he were being shown a picture book by someone who turned the pages too quickly.

71

At the butts near the prison ten seamen in line abreast listened to the caustic sergeant. Another forty behind them waited their turn. The sergeant was on loan from the Lingmouth militia already under training against the threat of invasion. The sergeant, a professional bowman in his youth, had a low opinion of seamen. Sir Joshua Vine was a great man, no doubt. A word from Sir Joshua and he, the sergeant, had been seconded to instruct this rabble. They would never make archers. Most of them had never had a bow in their hands before. And why now? The longbow was dead. They called it the "country weapon". The trained bands being assembled along the Channel coast were armed with muskets. Out of four thousand reserves only eight hundred were archers. The caustic sergeant and many others like him despised these old-fashioned arrowmen. To have a crowd of seamen required to handle a longbow for the first time put the sergeant in a very bad temper.

His emotions were reciprocated. Soldiers at sea were bad enough. They ate too much, sculled around on deck, were sick at the first heave on sloping spumy water. In a sea fight soldiers manned the tops and waist. That was their only purpose. If the Sultan needed soldiers why did he not hire them? The seamen lined up grimly at their targets. They had been told that any man who did not pass muster with the sergeant would lose his place on *Tigress*.

Tom watched the bad-tempered lesson, admiring Sir Joshua's foresight. The men had been chosen for the strength in their chest and shoulders. They suffered the sergeant's sarcasm with cold eyes, not answering back. Goaded by their silence he picked on every fault. The feet were too far apart, too near together. Why stick the neck out? Were they hens pecking at worms? Would they frighten the enemy with their rolling eyes, their protruding tongues, their pouts and grimaces? Were they Frenchmen, holding the bow at arm's length like a girl, drawing the shaft back with the right hand? Keep the right steady! Bend the body weight into the horns! Don't draw to the pap! Slow! To the right ear! *Imbeciles!*

The ten seamen gave way to ten others. Tom joined them. He had been brought up to shoot, but was out of practice. The sergeant gave him no favours. He was cursed like the rest of them, the more for faults which he well knew, the too tense grip, the hold too long, the loosing of the arrow too snatchy when it should be soft and gentle. The target was only fifty paces away. He scored better than the others, but nothing to be proud of. Next to him stood the brawny long-boned Jabbinoth. The same childlike beginnings of a smile, the concentration, the delight in what he was doing.

Jabbinoth did not know why or when he would have to be a bowman. But Tom knew. Sir Joshua had said to him, "When the time comes you will command half these men. So learn this. First, I would sooner teach seamen to shoot than soldiers to sail. And second. When we take the mule train, the less noise the better. Gunfire carries."

Each morning for five weeks the fifty seamen came to the butts. Slowly the sergeant's sarcasm dried up. He remembered his early days with the bow. Out of date, maybe, but still a beautiful weapon. These seamen were a wild crew, but they applied themselves and listened to what he told them, he had to admit that. At first there were many aching back muscles and raw fingers, but gradually a semblance of rhythm began to appear. They were standing better, with an easier swivel, letting the torso do the work. Each morning he repeated the litany, "Shoot straight and keep a length," hammering it into their brains. He inspected their gloves and bracers, showed them the pride of equipment. Each man had his own bow (provided by Joshua Vine), tagged and kept for safety in the butts store. The sergeant taught each man to feel and know his bow, and the seamen understood because it was the same with a knife. They would take their bows on *Tigress*, and they knew it was important.

Tom watched them shoot better day by day and wondered how it would be. *The less noise the better. Gunfire carries.* At dawn perhaps? *The beard of a madman on the mountains of hell?* The guards with muskets slung on their backs? And how many mules? Fifty? A hundred? He could not picture it. But he trusted Sir Joshua.

Now August was gone and in a week or two *Tigress* would sail, and suddenly there were only three days left. The canvases were furled on the yards, the hard stores all shipped, only the victuals to come. Some of the crew were already sleeping on board. The

73

Lingmouth men were loosening the ties of home. The strangers who had no home were getting restless in the great room at the Cockleshell, sometimes hired out for banquets or balls, but now rented by Joshua Vine as a dormitory for his new mariners. A mattress and one good meal a day. For the rest they could forage. There was a general impatience that now they had finished with the land and the land with them.

Paxcombe was bathed in September sunlight. In the little chapel the whole staff gathered, Ellen Rufoote and Finch the groom and Jackman the head gardener and Oschild the butler and the kitchen maids and the house maids and the gardener's boys and stable lads. Tom sat in the front with his mother, and Lionel stood at the lectern and read from the 107th Psalm. Then he asked for silent prayer, each to appeal in their own way. There was hardly a rustle in the silence. The sun through the high small windows made patterns on the wall. Then Lionel spoke the family prayer written by William Dacquin's son when his own sons went to sea. Not the first-born in those days. Lionel had a fine voice for reading, and Tom closed his eyes and felt strange to be having a prayer said for him.

"Almighty God, keep safe our beloved Thomas this day and hereafter on the stormy waters. Guard him against sickness and the assaults of his enemies. Attend him if he calls. Strengthen him always to serve his Queen, his country, his companions and his home."

Afterwards Tom stood at the door and the men shook hands with him and the women touched his hand and curtsied. One of the maids was crying, and Tom held her hand and smiled and shook his head, and she went away still crying, but more cheerfully.

He rode to Lingmouth with his parents. The sea chest that Joshua Vine had allowed him was already on board. They rode slowly and talked without being too serious.

The *Tigress* had been moved from the wharf and lay at anchor in the harbour. The foretop and maintop sails were swelling in a light breeze, the others furled. The decks were crowded, and boatloads of well-wishers circled round shouting last messages. The whole arc of the harbour was lined with waving flags and hands. Lingmouth was saying goodbye. The embarkation jetty was solid with families and friends. An eight-oared harbour cutter was ferrying out the last embarkees, and when it returned to the jetty Tom kissed his mother and father, and Gertrude said, "God bless you," and Lionel said, "Take care of yourself," and Tom said, "Take care of each other" and got into the boat with Robert Seaton and five others he recognized from the long room without remembering their names, and the boat was rowed out to *Tigress*.

On deck there seemed enough mariners to sink the ship. Everyone was shouting to someone in a boat below. For another hour the cutter went to and fro. Then the anchor came in and the big sails were unfurled and *Tigress* glided gently out of harbour, the flags and faces dwindling quickly, the sky cloudless, the sun dazzling on the paint and the varnish and the so-white sails, as if she were slipping southwards on the easiest of all possible voyages.

PART TWO

The Voyage

CHAPTER TEN

At sunset Lingmouth harbour was still in sight twelve miles astern, a smudge on the low line of white cliff. *Tigress* was making four knots in a fair breeze, her head kept steady by the spritsail at the bows. On the fore and main masts the square-rigged sails swelled without stress and on the mizzen the big triangle of the lateen canvas billowed to larboard.

The upper decks were thick with seamen, most with nothing to do, pieces of scattered jigsaw waiting to be fitted in. Each man had left his bedding-roll somewhere in the forecastle or below decks, wherever he judged best. The quartermaster had given instructions where they should sleep, but some had not listened and others had not obeyed. It was a question of what you could find and whether you could keep it. The normal company on *Tigress* would have numbered about eighty. Now there were two hundred and fifteen all told. Later they would go below for their supper and secure their billets. For the moment they were content to have the last of the fresh air before night. On the western horizon a bloodstain oozed magnificently up the sky and a track of golden fire shimmered from the sun to *Tigress*, a low sun, no longer the dazzling high disc too bright to be looked at, but a much larger crimson ball that did not hurt the eyes and was about to plunge and vanish, the monster sky-king saying goodnight to his subjects, perhaps his victims.

Over the decks of *Tigress* hung an awe-filled silence of private thoughts.

Gideon Jabbinoth was afraid of the sun. He could not understand it. As a child he had seen it disappear at bedtime into a wood near the Bristol docks, only to reappear next morning climbing up from behind the caravans. He had asked his mother about the sun, but she could not understand it either. She had never been to school and nor had he, and they could not ask Gideon's father because he had only visited the caravan briefly one evening about nine months before Gideon was born. The gipsies said that the sun went to hell at night and that one morning perhaps, if Gideon did not stop making faces at the girls, the Devil would keep the sun for himself and there would be darkness over the earth and everyone would die and it would be Gideon's fault. The girls were another of Gideon's problems. He made faces at them because he could not understand them. Once when he was fourteen a gipsy girl had said she would give him a kiss if he would bring her a piglet, and he had taken the piglet from market and been caught. They whipped him and put him for a whole long day in the stocks, and the girls came and laughed at him, and the girl with the kiss poured a bucket of slop over his head and everyone laughed a lot more. His mother told him he was better off without girls, and he agreed. His mother said that if she had money she would buy a caravan that did not leak and two dappled horses to pull it, and she and Gideon would find a new home far away.

So Gideon went to sea to get money. He was strong and willing and when they explained about blocks and tackles and ropes he understood something useful for the first time in his life. After many years at sea he joined *Black Vulture* and sailed under Mr Krauss who taught him a great deal and did not laugh at him. Gideon did not get enough money to buy horses, but he found a new life at sea where Mr Krauss was his father to be obeyed utterly, and when he came home he gave his money to his mother.

At the gipsy encampment he was known as "Neptune's Fool", but he did not care. He liked ships because he knew what to do. But he still had fears. The sun that might not rise. The girls who laughed but never kissed. And the invisible wind that came and went for no reason, filling the belly of a sail, then suddenly leaving the belly sagging like an empty sack, the wind that could not be summoned or dismissed, not even by Mr Krauss.

Gideon was leaning on the rail. He was in the maintop party and the sail bulged high overhead above the maincourse. Unless the wind rose unexpectedly he would not be wanted again till morning. He gazed at the crimson sun and his big mouth

77

formed into the beginning of a smile as he thought about the two dappled horses.

Behind the mainmast Tom Dakyn stood with Sir Joshua and Krauss. The mongrel Sirius sat whining at the sky.

"Don't worry, boy! You'll get 'em! They're down in the hold waiting for you, be sure of that!" said Sir Joshua cheerfully, adding to Krauss, "He's a great ratter. He'd better be. I paid good money for that."

Through the grating hatch they could see down to the tiller crew, eight seamen, four either side of the long massive beam that turned the rudder that would keep *Tigress* on course south by south-west on the two-thousand-mile run to the Cape Verde Islands off the bulge of Africa, then due west another two thousand on the fifteenth parallel across to Martinique and into the Caribbean.

The isthmus of Panama was too far to be reached without taking on fresh food and liquid. Most ships crossing the Atlantic would first put in at one of the European islands. The Canaries were normally a favourite, but this was no normal voyage. Spain was preparing an invasion, there was frenzied marine activity in all Spanish ports. The Canaries belonged to Spain and an English vessel would not be welcome. The Azores and Madeira were officially under the flag of Portugal, but the Spaniards were there too. Admiral Howard had informed Sir Joshua of Francis Drake's assessment and Sir Joshua had talked with Krauss. The Cape Verde islands were Portuguese. They were a long way south, but once there the currents of the Equator would favour a western course on a steady parallel, and the Spanish ships were less likely to be on guard duty so far from home.

Of all the islands Santa Antao was famous for its springs of fresh water, so it was towards Santa Antao that *Tigress* was being aimed, and the aim would be accomplished by compass headings shouted down from the mainmast position to the helmsman below. The compass in its box was set in the wooden plinth at the mainmast. The helmsman also had a compass and from his orders the eight seamen swung the long tiller slowly with strength-sapping obedience. When the sea got rough there were tackles on the tiller to help take the strain. Now there was no strain, just the crimson sunset and the Sultan and Krauss with his horrible left eye. The waist was milling with seamen crammed round the capstan and between the small boats, but a respectful space was kept round the compass and if anyone came too close he was richly bawled out by Krauss. Sir Joshua stood calm and content. Often at Rockways he had seemed fretful, thought Tom, a shepherd stuck indoors without his flock. There was no fret now. He was out in the salty pastures with Krauss his sheepdog and the long tiller his crook and the sheep-pen of Santa Antao waiting two thousand miles south.

"And what," asked Sir Joshua, "is Mr Dakyn dreaming about?"

"Nothing of importance," smiled Tom.

"You have stowed your gear?"

"Yes, sir."

"You have no cares?"

"None, sir."

"We are well trimmed?"

"I believe so."

The Sultan looked skywards, his head craning, his eyes screwed up towards the so distant mast top where the flag rippled stiffly in the breeze. Then he glanced at Krauss who winked with his good right eye. The Sultan said to Tom, "Tell me, Mr Dakyn. When did you last go aloft?"

"Never, sir."

"Jabbinoth!" shouted the Sultan. And when the long seaman ambled over—"Take Mr Dakyn to the topyard. Show him your perch." And to Tom, "Hold the shrouds! Tread the ratlines! And don't look down!"

Jabbinoth swung out into the main rigging and Tom followed. He had no time to think or be afraid. When you climbed a ladder you grasped the uprights and trod on the cross pieces. Only now it was a network of rope ladders joined side by side, and the uprights were shrouds and the cross pieces were ratlines. He knew that much. He also knew that he did not want to get left behind, so he clawed tightly at the rough rope that rasped his palms and felt with his feet for the next ratline, and each time he put his weight on the foot the ratline sagged before it gave support, and he kept his head back and his eyes up, looking at the soles of the shoes at the ends of the stockinged calves above him, and now and then, when he paused because

79

his hands hurt or his foot had slipped, the shoe-soles also paused and he felt grateful.

Past the climbing calves he could see the underneath of the fighting top half-way up the mast. He concentrated on getting there. It seemed a great distance.

He glanced left at the concave wall of ballooning canvas which was the mainsail. His biceps ached and his fingers were sore, but now he was level with the mainyard and it was only a few feet to the fighting top. The tall taper of rigging came together round the mast and to get on to the fighting top it was necessary to use the last length of angled shrouds that stretched from the mast out and up to the edge of the circular platform. Very slowly he manoeuvred himself up the outside of the trembling spidery cone and when his feet were slanted in too far to be of any further use he kicked them free and hoisted on his arms alone, and an almost grinning face appeared over the balustrade, and a hand gripped his wrist, and a moment later he was slouched on the platform with his back against the mast.

He said, "Thank you, Jabbinoth." He meant it.

"It's not so easy in a high wind," said Jabbinoth.

Tom got to his feet and looked astern. The sky and the sea seemed to have grown. Past the slant of the lateen sail he could still see the smudge of Lingmouth and the pencil of cliffs too low to catch the sunset. Then he looked over the rail. He did not mind looking down now. He expected to see the deck, but the ship was heeling in the breeze and from fifty feet up he was looking perpendicularly down at the white-horsed waves.

From below rose the Sultan's roar: "Mr Dakyn! I said the topyard! Get aloft!"

Again Jabbinoth went first. The topmast rigging was narrower, only the width of two ladders, and to Tom following slowly upwards the swaying ropes seemed a most flimsy way of reaching the yardarm above. There was still no view for'ard because now the bellying topsail was in the way. The breeze was stronger up here, he could feel it on his body. He did not look down, but he thought about the waves getting further and further away as he climbed. He could see Jabbinoth already astride the yard above him, and he imagined sitting beside him, and suddenly, with a last knee-knocking scramble it was true.

They were face to face with the mast between and a stay to hang on to. He found himself laughing breathlessly, unable to speak. The sky was so enormous, so red, so empty.

"Mr Dakyn!" The voice below was still clear, but fainter. "Don't sit there! Touch the flag!"

It was the Dorset admiral's flag designed by Lord Howard himself, a red St George's cross imposed on a background of diagonal blue and white stripes. The mast-head was only ten feet of pole. By standing on the yard he could almost touch the flag. He wrapped his hands round the pole and pincered himself up with his knees and touched the fluttering flag and slipped down to rejoin Jabbinoth on his perch.

Tom swivelled to let his eyes follow round the huge circumference. The only objects in sight were a few gulls planing to and fro. He felt like a gull himself, suspended and calm. To north there was nothing to see except the thin dark hairline of Dorset, to east there was nothing, to south there was nothing, to west there was nothing but the stained red mackerel sky and half the crimson sun sinking into the horizon. The sails were all below him now and although the foresails ahead and the lateen astern hid the ends of *Tigress* he could see the seamen dotted about like small coins on the waist and half decks. *Tigress* from this height was a pale chip of timber floating on the limitless darkening pond whose far rim seemed to support the bowl of nothingness overhead. He closed his eyes and thought about Alis Dewmark and her slim fingers. And at Paxcombe they would be sitting down to supper without him and his chair would be—

"Is it true, sir—"

"What!" The voice had startled him. He was back astride the yard with the weird Jabbinoth.

"There is an island, sir, and the palace is made of gold."

"Is that what they say?"

"The floor is gold and there are sacks of gold everywhere." The words tumbled out of the big loose mouth.

"Where is this island?"

"They say you know, they say he tells you everything."

"They say false," said Tom. "I know no more than you."

Jabbinoth did not believe it. There was a twitch in his clumsy face, but he said nothing and when the next shudder of twilight touched them they climbed down from the aerial perch, Jabbinoth going first, guiding Tom's feet into the inward-sloping footholds of rope beneath the fighting top.

At deck level they swung inboard and as they did so a shrill pipe and "Hands to supper" sounded below. The milling seamen, Jabbinoth among them, disappeared jostling down the hatchways. The decks looked empty with hardly a dozen hands left on duty. The dog Sirius was scratching himself plaintively. Tom joined Sir Joshua and Krauss at the mast.

"So now he has been aloft," said the Sultan.

"And the better for it," said Krauss.

"We'll make a seaman of him yet!"

The sun was gone and with it the path of golden fire. Still a redness in the western sky but elsewhere the light draining and the last trace of Dorset vanished astern. Tom bent back to look at the topyard, a finger of shadow in the dusk. Had he really sat up there?

"This Jabbinoth," said the Sultan. "He's quick in the rigging."

"He's a good hand," said Krauss, "for all his thick wits."

"And you, Tom. What did you make of him? Did he talk up there among the gulls?"

"He thinks we are heading for an island with a palace made of gold. He asked me where it was."

"You said nothing—of Panama?"

"Not a word."

"Mariners!" said the Sultan. "When they're not drinking or whoring they dream of gold. If it's not there they'll invent it. A golden palace, eh? That was the bowmen no doubt. *Why the longbow?* they say to each other. *Why not muskets?* They don't know, so they work it out. They've heard tales of cities across the sea. They know seamen can fight ashore. They're still puzzled about the bows and muskets, but they must have their dream. So it's flying arrows and bags of gold, and an armful of women, I shouldn't wonder."

"When will you tell them about Panama?" said Krauss.

"When we've left Santa Antao. When there's no one to listen to their speculations. When there's nothing between us and the Caribbean but salt water." He laughed and tapped the deck with his heel. "They're at it now. They're spinning dreams of gold. Can't you hear it?"

From the deck where the mess tables were set between the guns rose a parley of voices, no words distinct but a throbbing vigour. The Sultan nodded towards the hatchway.

82

"Keep it up, lads. While you still have the strength."

"Aye, let 'em talk," growled Krauss. "If it stops at that."

"And why not?"

Krauss narrowed his bloodshot eye, "Because you cannot lay two hundred bodies where there is not space for one hundred."

"Hasn't the quartermaster—"

"He told them. But half of them are going to be packed down below the waterline with filthy air and no light. On the first night they'll risk a broken head to get a good billet."

"Have you made arrangements?"

"I have."

The Sultan smiled. He took a piece of broken biscuit from his pocket and gave it to the begging Sirius, and Sirius wagged his tail. The Sultan told Tom to lay aft for his supper.

In the sterncastle were two cabins. The upper was for the Sultan, an apartment under the poop with separate bedroom and access to the quarterdeck. As in *Black Vulture* a gallery ran round the stern. The lower cabin was for all other officers. Here they would sleep and eat and suffer proximity. Toby Tenchbury had done his best to give space. The bunks were fixed along the sides and across the bulkhead, and each bunk could take a sea chest stowed beneath. There were chairs and a central table all bolted to the deck, and curtained portholes. It would have been fine for two officers, but there were six.

That first evening they met warily. Sir Joshua had stayed on watch, telling Krauss to muster the officers, and Krauss had followed Tom into the cabin. Supper would be served when the crew had finished theirs, and when the officers had finished the Sultan would be relieved on watch and would eat alone in his cabin. He would not be lonely, he would be enjoying the privacy which he alone could ever enjoy.

When Tom and Krauss came into the big lantern-lit cabin they found the pale-faced surgeon Robert Seaton holding something which he put behind his back, and Krauss asked him what he was holding and Robert shyly produced a flute, and Krauss said, "Do not be ashamed. We shall need music as well as food." The Krauss eye still glared down from the fearful cicatrix, but the voice sounded amiable. Robert put the flute into the sea chest and a moment later Gostigo the gloomy bosun came in, and after him the two remaining officers: Viccars the master gunner whom Tom remembered from the San Corda trip, black-bearded, a Lingmouth man unshakably courteous except with his gun crews; and the purser Fernie, glimpsed in the long room, an obvious food lover with a big stomach and a carnal expression.

A steward appeared with wine and Krauss bade everyone be seated and there was a wary politeness all round. Mr Gostigo inquired about the new brass cannon and Mr Viccars said he was well pleased. Mr Fernie reminded Mr Gostigo that on their last voyage together a storm had ripped the foretop to shreds, and Mr Viccars complimented Mr Fernie on the stowage of the food bales. They reminisced of ships. Tom and Robert Seaton sat silent, conscious of their lack of sea time. Then Mr Krauss proposed a health, "To our young comrades", and the older men raised their glasses. Other toasts followed.

"Fair winds and calm seas!" by Fernie.

"Perish our enemies!" by Viccars.

"The *Tigress*!" by Krauss.

To which Gostigo added in a loud voice, "Not forgetting our captain!"

"That is hardly possible, Mr Gostigo," snapped Krauss. And after a moment's pause: "The Sultan!"

"The Sultan!" said everyone together, then several times in pairs to and fro. The repeated name brought a calm. Glasses were emptied and refilled.

Supper was served. Rich beef stew hot from the cookroom, a basket of fresh fruit and a piled cheese board. The cheese and fruit would not be fresh for long. It was a last-of-shore feast and they made the most of it, the conversation dwindling, the munching silence finally broken by a rumbling burp from the purser which spoke for them all.

There was a knock at the door, Krauss shouted, "Enter!" and a square-shouldered man stood in the doorway.

"Was I right, marshal?" said Krauss. He rose without hurry.

"Yes, sir. You can hear them."

Somewhere for'ard there was shouting muffled through the bulkheads.

"Where's the trouble?"

"On the gun deck, sir."

"Mr Viccars. Mr Gostigo. And Mr Dakyn."

84

They stood up. So did Robert Seaton, but Krauss said, "Stay here, surgeon. Your work comes later."

It was all done quietly and in order.

The quartermaster was waiting outside. He issued a baton to each officer. The batons had wrist thongs so that they could not be knocked out of the hand. The marshal and Krauss led the way, down a ladder to gun deck level, through a dim compartment stacked with bows in racks, into the long gun deck itself.

Here was hubbub, an inferno of flailing fists, murderous obscenities and overturned tables between the guns. Krauss yelled, "SILENCE!" but there was no silence. To the officers he shouted, "Go for the knives!" Viccars moved in bawling like a bull with Tom behind him. He had a chaotic impression of a long low cavern crammed with tumbling bodies, the deck strewn with rolls of bedding. It was no time for inquiry. If you saw a knife you aimed at the wrist. If a throat was being grasped you hit the grasper. Tom ducked an elbow, stumbled over a gun rope and plied into the loudest mêlée. He saw Viccars crack two heads together and Gostigo slam someone backwards over a gun barrel.

It did not take long. The flailing subsided and the shouting stopped. Krauss did not have to yell. He said, "Pay attention" but at that moment the figure of Sir Joshua appeared down the hatchway ladder. Krauss pushed through to where he stood.

"What is the trouble, Mr Krauss?"

"The billets, sir. It appears that some of the ship's company—"

The Sultan held up his hand. He said quietly, "The billets have been assigned. Let the quartermaster read them out once more. If any man refuses his billet or causes disturbance hereafter he will be put ashore at Santa Antao."

He turned to the ladder and was gone.

Later in the big cabin Tom stretched in his bunk and closed his eyes. He had not had to fight for a place to sleep. Robert Seaton had been busy for an hour with blood and bruises, but there had been no serious damage. No one had been killed.

CHAPTER ELEVEN

So *Tigress* began the long days down the Atlantic, a solitary traveller in the watery desert taking short steps towards some distant oasis. The Sultan was taking them to fortune, everyone believed that. No other thought was possible. The only thing the Sultan could not do was to take them quickly.

Each morning after breakfast all off-duty seamen mustered on the upper decks and the Sultan stood on the edge of the half deck above the waist so that some men were in front of him and some behind. He carried a small Bible (not the heavy brass-bound volume from his cabin) and a Book of Common Prayer. First he read a short passage from the Old Testament on each of three themes: valour in battle, courage in adversity, and GOLD. The passages were read in a commanding voice without comment. The battles and tribulations were received with unsmiling silence, but when they heard about the river Pison encompassing the land of gold, or when the voice rang out, "Be strong, O Zerubbabel . . . I will shake all nations . . . the silver is mine and the gold is mine," a satisfied murmur sighed through the audience. Sir Joshua intoned the words of the Lord as if they were his own. Next, from the prayer book, came the appeal of St Chrysostom reminding God of His promise that when two or three were gathered in His name He would grant their requests, and asking Him to fulfil the desires and petitions of His servants "as might be most expedient to them". Then everyone joined in the Lord's Prayer.

It was the first ritual of the day and Tom, standing behind the Sultan, looked down at all the upturned faces and saw attention and response. The Sultan's voice gave everyone confidence, including Tom. Ritual was important. It gave you purpose and made you share. Meals were rituals, so were the daily exercises that filled the forenoon.

Tom's exercise was with the bowmen. Each morning after prayers the quartermaster issued bows to the fifty seamen, calling out the names on the tags. The practice took place on the gun deck between the mainmast and the foremast. The gunners did not like it because they had to clear the mess tables and stow their bedding and go where they were not wanted, on the upper deck where they were cursed by the watchkeepers and sail parties, or down on the stuffy lamp-lit orlop where Gostigo was exercising other hands in the maintenance of spare sails and ropes. The gunners had not forgiven the archers for trying to steal their sleeping billets, and the archers thought the gunners were unfairly favoured, being allowed to sleep in the most airy conditions just because their guns happened to be there.

The guns were secured with their barrels jutting through the open ports. This left an avenue fifteen foot wide and forty foot long from mast to mast. Hardly space for the flight of an arrow, but this was not the object. Tom's orders were firstly to keep the muscles in trim after the training at Lingmouth and secondly to instil care of the weapons and awareness of the dangers. The sergeant at the butts had briefed him well.

Five at a time the archers lined up and strung their bows, easing the looped ends of the strings gently into the nocks at the bowtips. The practice arrows were padded at the head, aimed at a loose curtain of thick netting rigged across the foremast, but not released during the muscles exercise. The right hand held the arrow steady against the right ear, the silk thread snug in the nock of the shaft. Then the left gauntleted hand holding the bow was thrust slowly out with the strength of the chest. The arrowhead was drawn back to the gauntlet, held for a count of three, gently relaxed to its starting point. Now and then fingers would slip and the arrow would fly into the netting, but not often. This was the best part of the bowmen's day and they were grimly serious. Tom made them take it slowly, increasing the number of stretches day by day. When the muscles could stand no more he let them rest. Then targets were set up, five wooden torsos with heads (pride of the carpenters) hung from a line across the netting. Each man had three shots and Tom would call out "Head" or "Chest". At forty feet it was no great test and after a few days the shafts were thudding into the swinging Spaniards with flattering regularity. No one was deceived, but the archers loved it. From the ten groups of five there was a daily winner and bets were laid in beer.

Then came the care of equipment.

In the armoury were stacked two hundred bows in woollen cases, four for each man. The bows were all of fine-grained yew as free from warts and blemishes as the eye could detect. The nocks at either end were cut into the wood itself, not fashioned from horn and glued into position (like some hunting bows in England) because glue might weaken in the hot forests of

Panama. The bows had been chosen to suit the size and strength of the men, and each owner used his bows in rotation and rubbed in wax to keep the wood supple.

The arrow shafts were of seasoned ash cut precisely along the grain, the steel heads narrow and sharp for maximum penetration, the nock long and deep to hold the string surely, and the feathers of young goose, the best for short-range attack. Ten thousand arrows lay in boxes beneath the bow racks, the shafts in slots to keep the feathers apart. Each bowman was allowed five practice arrows, and when the feathers got rubbed it did not matter. Once a week the boxes were opened and the shafts rubbed with wax or oil.

Lastly the dangers, the several ways in which a bow might break.

If the string were too short the bow itself was under pressure and could snap at any moment, the end fragment hurtling into the face or groin.

If the string snapped at the stretch the bow with nothing to arrest its recoil would be shattered at the belly as the ends whipped back.

If the arrow were drawn back too far, either because it was too long or because the gauntlet hand was wrongly positioned, the bowtips again might fly. This was the commonest cause of breakage. To make it less likely the arrows chosen were shorter than usual, the loss of range being unimportant for the task ahead.

Thus the main dangers from shooting. Yet the yew wood itself, scrutinized though it had been, might be hiding frets and cankers that would make the bow break however carefully handled. So the Sultan had ordered the spare bows and the ten thousand short arrows. He had conferred with the sergeant at the butts, and the sergeant had told Tom how impressed he had been with Sir Joshua Vine's knowledge of archery and insistence on details.

Tom was not surprised. The Sultan did not interfere with his officers at sea, but he knew their problems and foresaw their troubles.

Sometimes a stranger power seemed to be at work. Luck perhaps. But mariners considered luck to be a personal asset as reliable as wealth, strength or a handsome face. There was the Sultan's luck over the gunnery practice.

When Tom had finished with the bowmen in the forenoon Viccars took over with his gunners. Tom would have liked to stay, but this was not favoured, so he went up to the poop and watched. With the old armament whose performance was known it was a question of gun-drill and handling. But with the four new demi-culverin there was need for practice. They had been fired on shore, but there had been no time to test them at sea. Splendid brass guns, muzzle-loading, firing a nine-pound shot with accuracy at a quarter of a mile and with menace but less accuracy up to two miles.

The problem was what to use for a target. In the past over shorter ranges Viccars had used buoys supporting a pole with a piece of canvas fluttering as marker. The canvas could not be hit directly, but you could see the splashes and adjust the errors reasonably well. With the demi-culverin the extra range made the splashes hard to see except in very calm water. A week out from Lingmouth the sunny spell changed to overcast, the wind got up, and the sea though not rough became a heaving plateau of spumy green. The master gunner complained jokingly to the Sultan, "Can't you find me a better target? An old wreck perhaps?"

"The markers do not serve?"

"We need bulk to fire at for a correct assessment."

"I shall arrange it," said the Sultan.

That evening at supper in the great cabin Viccars recounted this conversation and Gostigo said sceptically, "Do not expect too much even from the Sultan."

"I have faith in him."

"Faith," said Gostigo, contracting his black eyebrows in a furious scowl at no one in particular, "is like a piece of money."

"Because it has powers of purchase?" asked Krauss sharply.

"No. Because it may be counterfeit. It should be tried by the touchstone before it can be ascertained to be right."

"What touchstone is that?"

"The event that follows," said Gostigo.

Viccars was not an argumentative man. Fernie's only response to any opinionated remark was a well-fed grimace. Robert Seaton smiled at Tom because they had agreed several times about Gostigo. His head seemed full of provocative statements. But Krauss, though clearly irritated, was having no more of it. His own rule in the cabin was no altercation between officers, and now he called the steward for more wine and the nature of faith was not pursued.

Next day the wind backed and strengthened. The waves were not high but the sea heaved in long green undulations as if stirred by some mighty horizontal arm in the depths. *Tigress* was a wholesome ship but running before the wind she pitched like any other, so now she was kept on a course of long zigzags to keep her on a broad reach with all sails full. The ports on the gun deck were closed and there was no gunnery or archery practice. There was rain, not heavy but depressingly persistent. The upper decks were still crowded, since it was better to get wet in the air than stifle below, but visibility was poor and you felt trapped in the veil of wetness and with nothing to see there was little to talk about and *Tigress* seemed like an infant toddling to nowhere. The Sultan, who had the watch, told Tom that they were running between Portugal and the Azores. The low visibility pleased the Sultan who wanted no sightings, only to make Santa Antao in good time, but it bored the mariners. By dusk the rain was diminishing and at supper time you could see across the still heaving water a horizon with sky above it.

But no sign of a hulk for Viccars to fire at.

At the supper table, with Krauss himself away on deck, Gostigo asked what anyone now thought of the Sultan's assurance to the master gunner, and Viccars said he regarded it as a jest more than a promise. Gostigo said, "A word spoken is like an arrow flying in the air. It cannot be recalled. It is well, therefore, to weigh the consequences of our words before we let them fly."

He glared round, but no one answered him and Tom thought no more about a target for the demi-culverins and was unprepared for the visitation next morning.

Coming on deck he found a mysterious transformation. The wind had dropped and was now a light breath on the beam. The sea was flat grey and the sails hardly alive. Moisture in the air, visibility less than a mile, and as *Tigress* floated in the gentle cocoon an eerie sound came from out of sight somewhere ahead, a faint chorus of high-pitched voices unrecognizable but somehow conveying the idea of multitude, the falsetto chatter of a thousand souls. This and a faint background purr like shore waves on shingle. Tom was on the quarterdeck and could see others below him craning their heads, and a voice called from the foretopyard, "Object on the starboard bow!"

Very slowly, heard before it could be seen from deck level, the object came into sight, the carcass of a black whale almost as long as *Tigress* herself, bloated with decomposition, bulging high out of the water, now being furiously pecked to pieces by an obscuring horde of gannets, kittiwakes, terns, and gulls of every marking, their wings rustling like the wheeze of death as they rose and pounced, twittering and screaming with gluttony.

As Viccars joined Tom a voice behind said, "Your target, Mr Viccars."

For the next three hours the Sultan working the lateen sail kept *Tigress* on a slow to-and-fro beat four hundred yards from the whale, a triumph of ship-handling in the stillness, presenting first one beam and then the other while Viccars, taking the demi-culverins in turn, bullied the gun crews who were keen enough but still raw as a team. Priming, loading, pointing, firing, sponging. Four shots from each gun was the best they could achieve. Sixteen times a cracking blast sent the nine pounds of iron on its journey. Ten harmless splashes left the birds still gobbling. Only six times when the shot sank into the rotting blubber did a cloud of clattering scavengers rise up, hover shapelessly, and settle back to their grisly consumption.

Then the breeze returned and *Tigress* proceeded south leaving the black corpse, so like a stricken mastless ship, to its indignity.

How could the Sultan have known? Perhaps from his vast sea-knowledge he had dredged some microscopic intimation that whales were about. But surely not such a carcase at such a moment? It was strange. And the aftermath even stranger.

As the whale fell astern, while the screeching could still be heard, a single bird appeared suddenly high overhead, lurching in loops above the mainmast as if wishing to perch yet doubtful. As it came lower the crew could see the sturdy grey-barred wings almost a yard in span, the pale belly, the long black neck and the snow-white face. All along the ship there were pointing arms and shouting: "The goose!" "The barnacle!" "*Barnacle!*"

Tom, standing beside the Sultan, felt a chill curiosity as he looked up. He had never seen a barnacle goose but he knew the stories from childhood. How by the Irish sea grew a tree whence gourds fell into the water, clung to rotting timber, were heated by the sun, and disgorged the geese called barnacle. Wild solitary fowl preferring Arctic regions, returning in hard winters to the shores of their origin. At Paxcombe there was a nursery book where Uncle Georges in that last fateful summer had drawn the barnacle in black and white chalk, and beneath it the lines that Lionel had heard somewhere:

> First a green tree,
> Then a broken hull,
> Lately a mushroom,
> Now a flying gull.

Mariners, said Georges, feared the barnacle, a bird without parents issuing from the slime of some sunken keel, a bad omen for any honest ship. From childhood Tom remembered the white face and the contemptuous round eyes, and now here was this bad stranger wobbling hardly higher than the maintop.

"He's sick," said the Sultan. "He's come to die."

At that moment the barnacle flopped on to the maintop rail and clung awkwardly as if the feet could hardly uphold the fat body. There were more shouts along the deck. "Kill him!" Three seamen swarmed up the rigging and the first was up the outward cone and heaving himself on to the platform when the bird turned its head, took a step forward, and sank cumbrously down to the deck, its wings just strong enough to break the fall. It crouched. A seaman with a drawn knife ran forward but the Sultan shouted, "Stop!", walked over, picked up the unstruggling barnacle, brought it back to the compass.

"Look! His eye!"

There was only one eye. The other had been gouged into a clot of dried blood. The open eye looked sideways with no fear or contempt, just resignation. The Sultan held him gently and spoke as if he were alone with a dying friend: "What did they do to you? Your strength's gone. You're way off course. Lost your compass. You wanted no whale meat, did you? You wanted some grass, a good bowl of seaweed. Is that it?"

The barnacle did not move or blink, and the Sultan shifted his hands up the long neck, tightened, gave the sudden merciful wrench.

That evening the Sultan joined his officers for supper. It was a calm sea and the quartermaster took the watch. The boiled goose was served with a pudding of crushed biscuit, apple and onion soaked in brandy. The plums and peaches were finished, but there was still cheese and plenty of wine. There were no comments on the appearance of the whale or the arrival of the barnacle. Whatever your private thoughts you did not challenge the Sultan to his face. No explanations were suggested, not even by Mr Gostigo.

When the plates were cleared the Sultan inquired, "Music, Mr Krauss?" and Krauss said, "The surgeon has a flute," and Robert Seaton, producing his flute from the chest with some diffidence, showed himself a musician. They had the tunes everyone knew. "Dusty My Dear", "Nobody's Jig", the Scottish "Leaves Green", and an Irish air "Killala Bay" sung by purser Fernie in a drunken carnal voice.

Later, when the Sultan had turned in, Viccars was gone on watch, Gostigo was complaining to unresponsive Krauss about Fernie snoring already, Tom and Robert went on the quarter-deck. It was a gentle night with a young moon. On the sloping half deck below them they could make out the shadowy outlines of sleeping mariners. Along the waist and up on the forecastle there would be others. The billets below were still proscribed, but now the nights were getting warmer and the men slept anywhere they could find except on the quarterdeck and poop, huddled shapes dreaming of gold under the stars.

"Are you married?" said Robert.

"We're waiting till I get home." It made Tom feel better to put it that way. He wondered how to describe Alis, but he was not asked.

Robert said, "I met a girl at the hospital. I had no money to get married."

In silence each thought about his girl.

High ahead in the sky hung the big square of Pegasus, so unlike a horse, more like a tureen with a curved handle. But you could not follow the imagination of the ancient Greeks. North-wards astern lay the smaller skillypan which the Greeks had called a Great Bear. At last: "The trouble being the surgeon," said Robert, "is that I only know the men when they're sick or dead. You're lucky. You know the bowmen at least."

"That's only a quarter," said Tom. "That leaves a hundred and fifty. I don't know the gunners, or half the seamen."

"Do you know Nils and Henrik? In the cookroom?"

93

"The Norwegians?"

"Yes. The big ones."

Tom had seen them on rounds. Marshal Smolkin had pointed them out. They had surnames no one could pronounce. They were the biggest men on board, neckless shaven heads sunken on musclebound shoulders, brutal hands and thick legs that waddled under the weight.

"They are my friends," said Robert. "That's what Krauss called them when he brought them to see me. 'The Carver's friends,' he said. 'They're good hands. They don't know two words of English, but they know what to do.' "

"The Carver!" said Tom. "I don't like the name. It has a grim sound."

"Grim but necessary," said Robert. "Rotten flesh and splintered bones must be carved away."

"But why friends? Is it a time for friendship?"

"If ever I have to carve a limb from you," said Robert in his quiet Highland voice, "someone must hold you down."

It was said so softly, a whisper of unimaginable pain.

The moon was gone now. In the deep ebony sky Aldebaran glowed like the eye of Jehovah, and above it glistened the tear-drops of the Pleiades.

CHAPTER TWELVE

So the routines and rituals welded the long days together. In the forenoons the men were kept busy. The longbow practice, the gunnery drill, the scrubbing of decks, the sail exercises, the inspection of ropes and rigging, and for the cooks the preparation of dinner, the day's climax. For every task to be done there were three men who could do it. Krauss had organized a loose system of watches, but there was still triplication, worst during waking hours. Hesket the carpenter, Newcroft the cook, Costlove the gunner's mate, each had to ring the changes, two men idle for one at work. Gostigo and Viccars did their best, inventing labours of splicing and polishing and swabbing which the men welcomed rather than be bored. This was not the Queen's navy. There was no book of discipline. But the ancient rule of the sea said that between breakfast and dinner you were busy. *Tigress* was overmanned, and everyone knew why, but

94

no one wished to think about it, so no one complained about the forenoons.

In the afternoons there was no gun-drill or bow practice. The gun deck was thoroughly scrubbed down after dinner and the tables reset for supper and any empty food or beer barrels restowed in the hold according to a plan devised by Gostigo to please the purser. The plan involved moving full barrels to a position of readiness and pushing the empties into the vacant spaces in such a pattern that the overall weight would remain constant and keep *Tigress* on an even keel, but as some barrels were stowed horizontally and others vertically, and as the weight of full barrels varied with their contents (biscuit or beer or salted meat), and the hold being ill-lit and the handling parties often clumsy or careless (believing that *Tigress* was not going to capsize from the misplacement of a couple of barrels) the plan was not always accomplished to Gostigo's satisfaction, and his powerful oaths resounded up the hatches to the orlop.

The men mimicked the rages of Gostigo, but if they joked about the empty barrels they did not joke about the full ones. The daily food ration for each man was one pound of biscuit or pea-and-lentil hash, with salt meat, fish or cheeses every second day. The liquid ration was one gallon of beer or wine. Ten twenty-gallon barrels were emptied each day. The men preferred beer, the strong Dorset ale they knew, to wine, a fancy drink at the best of times, liable to loosen your bowels in hot weather, and now on *Tigress* a peculiar wine not always made from grapes.

Surgeon Robert Seaton had unpopular ideas about wine. He believed that while grape wine made you happy, wine fermented from fresh fruits like oranges and lemons, blackberries and gooseberries and apples was a medicine against scurvy. He had learned this from his famous mentor, William Clowes. Onions and watercress, said Clowes, were also good. Some ships with normal complements carried many strings of onions together with wooden pans of soil in which to grow watercress at sea. But *Tigress* had no space for such luxuries. Seamen had enough trouble finding space to lie down at night without falling over earth pans in messdecks festooned with onions. So Robert Seaton had got permission from Sir Joshua Vine to take on board a number of twenty-gallon barrels containing the medicine-wine. The officers in the great cabin accepted their daily tot. There was still plenty of real wine to wash it down. But to the mariners this inferior fruit juice was a bad substitute for beer. They drank it if Marshal Smolkin was watching them, but much medicine was thrown through the ports on principle.

Mariners had ideas of their own. They knew that at sea death came in three ways: enemy action, storms, and sickness. And the greatest peril by far was sickness. At least half the crew had suffered themselves and seen others die. There was scurvy with its swellings and ulcers and asphyxia. There was dysentery when your arse felt like a rusty drain flowing with acid. There were unnamed fevers with frightening symptoms. There was the calenture which you picked up in hot latitudes and your head became full of boiling nightmares and you were lucky to recover. Some of your messmates had not recovered, and you had seen them in their last hours go mad, babbling of green pastures, imagining the azure water to be the verdant fields of their childhood, thinking if only they could get down to the emerald lawns they would be safe and happy, and in the end diving overboard to the sharks.

A few mariners had learned the medical jargon, but most had not. Scurvy was known as 'the Knobs' because of the swelling. Dysentery was 'the Flux' because of the acid flowing in your drain. The calenture they called the 'Idiot's Death'. The mariners knew, they had seen it, that more would die from sickness than from cannonballs or the swallowing waves.

Yet sickness was not the first concern of mariners. At sea they were accustomed to bad food and they believed that if you contracted the Knobs, the Flux or the Idiot's Death, it was because you had not been fed on beef and beer, but palmed off with biscuit like wood shavings and barrels of griping black-berry juice.

So the mariners did not joke about the contents of Gostigo's full barrels. They regarded them with devoted seriousness. Food and drink were the mariners' number one consideration.

And yet.

The great dread among mariners was not of sickness. Your messmates got sick, not you. Nor of drowning by storm. That only happened to those who could not handle their ship. Not you. What the mariners feared above all was the bloody bone-splintered wound that ended in amputation. Hence their respect for surgeons. The surgeon could staunch your blood, extract the metal from your flesh. In the extreme, if your life itself depended on losing the smashed remnants of your leg, only the surgeon could save you. Some crews refused to put to sea without a surgeon, but Joshua Vine had forestalled this by recruiting Robert Seaton.

The mariners trusted Robert to guard their blood and bones. When he prescribed medicine wine, they threw it into the sea. Mariners were not interested in preventive medicine.

Tom tried to know and understand the mariners, not from any libertarian motive but because as Sir Joshua Vine's lieutenant he was the lowest officer in the chain of command. In case of crime or complaint the first to know would be Marshal Smolkin. He had been at sea all his adult life, he slept in the forecastle, he rumbled seamen in every way. If he could not settle some problem himself (with common sense or the end of a rope) he would report the offender to Tom Dakyn. Tom did not use the rope's end, but he was empowered to order minor punishments like an hour's deck-scrubbing or the loss of half a day's beer ration. If Tom felt the problem too big he could report it to Krauss. A frightening enlargement of the situation. It would be no joke whatever for any miscreant to be brought before Krauss. That bloodshot eye had seen too much, the sea-weary brain behind it had come to the end of mercy or compromise. The Sultan, explaining the process of discipline to Tom, had said, "Don't take them before Krauss if you can help it. He has a partiality for flogging."

And flogging was not wanted on *Tigress*. It would miss the point. As a seaman in the Queen's navy you had regular pay and your ship was one unit among many. The fleet was your essential reality, it guarded your country and your Queen, and was your livelihood. The fleet could only operate with discipline. If the admiral wanted something to happen, every man on every ship had to do what he was told. If you did not obey orders you could be flogged. A drunk could be flogged with the cat-o'-nine-tails. A thief could be flogged with a cat bristling with iron claws. A deserter or a man who struck an officer could be flogged round the fleet. You were rowed round the fleet in a boat. Abreast of each ship in turn you received twelve lashes or more. There were twenty ships or more. You usually died. Rightly. In the Queen's navy you must have discipline.

But *Tigress* was not a fleet on some national mission. *Tigress* was a hundred-foot hunk of timber carrying two hundred men on a mission of their own. She was not in company. Discipline on *Tigress* did not mean the enforcement of fleet orders. It meant ensuring that this crew of savage seamen would work together, would not disrupt each other by quarrels and animosities, would be comrades for the fortune across the sea. Such discipline would not be achieved by flogging, and perhaps the Sultan had exaggerated about Krauss's partiality. What the Sultan meant was that neither he nor Krauss wished to be bothered with humdrum misdemeanours. These would be filtered by Tom, with Marshal Smolkin to help him. Serious offences would go before Krauss. Only the most vital matters would need a decision by the Sultan.

"They respect you, Tom," said the Sultan. "Those who were at San Corda have told the others. Make use of that. Get to know them."

The bowmen were a start. He met them each morning for their practice. Their names he already knew from the Lingmouth butts, and now he tried to judge them by their behaviour and application. They did not talk much about themselves. He had to judge them by what he could observe. The younger ones were quicker, more impetuous, like Dykes and Pipkin who had wagers with each other when they aimed at the swinging torsos. "A pint for his head! And one for his belly! There's another bastard gone to hell!" And there were older men more deliberate, with great purpose in their eyes. Like Wotton with his Dorset voice whose son Henry had been burned at San Corda. Hard-muscled father Wotton, his fingers deliberate on the bowstring, his face implacable. And there was always Gideon Jabbinoth, silent with his mates, smiling to himself with his big mouth as he waxed his shafts or leaned his weight into the bow. Tom gave no favours, but he felt something for Jabbinoth because they had been aloft together.

Some men he knew by sight, watching them at exercise. From the poop he could watch the sail parties shortening canvas, maintop and foretop competing for speed, sometimes even the main and forecourse, though these took too long for frequent practice. He could see Jabbinoth high overhead in the line of seamen who balanced on the footrope beneath the yard, and the sail bunted up as if by magic against the blue sky, and the seamen like marionettes leaning over the yard, their arms dangling as they waited, and the canvas crinkling as it came up, and caught at last by reaching fingers, and furled tight round the yard, and loosened again. In silence, no words of command, only the blasts of the whistle from below. A voice could have been lost in the breeze, blanketed by flapping canvas, but the whistle blast could always be heard punching out the code of shorts or longs, singulars or plurals, that the seamen knew so well.

As Tom watched the beautiful white garment crinkle up, pause provocatively, rustle as it fell, he pictured Alis with a nightgown.

The gunners he never saw because Viccars did not allow spectators. The cooks he saw when he went with Smolkin on rounds, among them the Norwegians in whose immense hands the knives and ladles were toylike. He saw men coiling the hawsers and anchor rope that had shifted in a heavy sea. He saw carpenters fashioning spare rudders for the small boats, and Gostigo's men making cradles for the painters.

Official rounds came after forenoon exercises and before dinner. He met Smolkin outside the great cabin, proceeded down the ladder, through the vestibule of the armoury, along the gun deck into the forecastle, round the carpentry stores, down to the brick-floored cookroom at orlop level, and back through the canvas and rope stores, past the shot racks and powder barrels, through sleeping spaces and the surgeon's den, emerging up two stern ladders to where they had started. Men not at work were supposed to stand beside their bedding rolls, but the overcrowding made nonsense of such exactitude. Tom and Smolkin were not inspecting orderly messdecks, they were threading through equipment-packed compartments bursting with bodies that had nowhere else to go.

So Tom became acquainted with the mariners, some by name and conversation, others as men at work or standing shoulder to shoulder in the smelly confines of the orlop.

There were few occasions for punishment. Sometimes men complained about one another and were sorted out by Smolkin's violent vocabulary. Often men complained about the food, asking for more meat, and were told to be thankful for what they got. On the way to Santa Antao there were only two

99

incidents where higher authority was needed. Tom passed both cases on to Krauss, and in each case was surprised. The first, which Tom thought difficult but not too important, was taken straight to the Sultan. The second, which made Tom shudder, was dealt with by Krauss as if it hardly mattered.

First, the red-faced Mulfroy, a swabber in one of the saker crews. Mulfroy was brought before Tom by Marshal Smolkin, with the gunner's mate Costlove as witness. The charge was that Mulfroy had been upsetting his messmates by Popish practices, namely the ostentatious fingering of rosaries and the defiant recital of Hail Marys when his mates wanted to sleep. Costlove had rude words for all this but the fact was clear. Mulfroy the swabber was a Catholic.

Tom was unprepared for this problem. He had assumed that the seamen on *Tigress*, so far as they were anything, were Protestant. At sea, he thought, it was not much of a problem. At morning prayers there was no communion or ritual and for the rest of the day you did your work without worrying about the next man's faith.

He would have dismissed the case, except that Smolkin was looking very serious and Costlove very indignant and Mulfroy remarkably obstinate.

"Passed to Mr Krauss," said Tom, not relishing what Krauss would say to him.

"Mr Krauss!" said Smolkin with evident approval.

But when Krauss heard the case he did not complain to Tom. Instead, with no questions to anyone, with hardly a flicker of his bloodshot eye, he said, "Sir Joshua."

So it was before the Sultan in his cabin that Tom stood beside the dark oak desk with Marshal Smolkin and the two seamen.

The charges were repeated. There was silence. The Sultan sat very still, then placed his hands on the desk, the fingers open but not pressed down with the trembling fury that mariners dreaded, just resting motionless and firm with the indubitable message that what he was about to say had better be hoisted in.

"Mulfroy!"

"Sir!"

"Do you think yourself superior to your comrades?"

"No, sir."

"Then do not disturb them when they wish to sleep. Do not look so aggrieved, Mulfroy. Say all the Hail Marys your soul

100

requires, but go aloft to do it. Find yourself a piece of yard-arm. Understood?"

"Yes, sir."

"And you, Costlove. Have you ever in all your life said a Hail Mary?"

"No, sir!"

"Then do not judge another man's need by your own. Mulfroy may believe what he pleases. So may you. But let there be no argument or provocation. The matter is finished. You will not mention it again, neither of you, to each other or anyone else. Forget your opinions. Remember the common purposes we share, I and you and every man on this ship."

He nodded to Smolkin who took the seamen away. As Tom was following them the Sultan said, "Wait!" When the door closed he pointed to a chair. Tom sat down and the Sultan said, "I'll have no dispute about the Son of God on this ship. On land they kill each other for that. You have seen it yourself."

Tom nodded, thinking of the smouldering stakes.

"At sea," said the Sultan, "it is the Father we need to look after us. There were storms and sickness on the waters before ever God sent His Son to earth."

On the desk lay the big brass-bound Bible, and the Sultan twisted the book round and pushed it towards Tom and said, "Open the Old Testament and close your eyes and put your finger on the page."

Tom did as he was told, and the Sultan said, "Read it," and Tom looked under his finger and, startled, read out, "And the flowers and the lamps and the tongs made he of gold, and that perfect gold."

"You think it strange that the book knows our secret thoughts? The gold in our hearts? It is always so, providing we have trust. Try again. And have no fear."

Tom opened another page blind and read, "Better a living dog than a dead lion."

"And better a living seaman than a dead Spaniard," roared the Sultan, crashing his fist on the desk. "Tell that to the purser and the surgeon. Tell them to nourish the rascals as best they can. Give me the men in Panama and I will give them all the gold they dream of!"

He looked up, his amber eyes gleaming, the trim black beard framing the face where doubt was absent. Tom smiled back, convinced against reason. Suppose his finger had come to rest on one of those verses about who begat whom? Would that have brought a message to the heart? Were there not ten thousand verses without meaning or relevance to *Tigress*? Yet whatever might have happened, his finger had in fact twice pointed significantly.

He remembered what Sir Joshua had said to him at Rockways: "You will see, it is a matter of trust."

Sirius the mongrel rat-catcher had been promised rats, and he was not disappointed. *Tigress* in dry dock had a hold free of vermin. When the food barrels were loaded on at the wharf there was daily inspection. No rats. At night sentries with lanterns guarded the loading ramps and ladders. No rats. The hawsers tying *Tigress* alongside had anti-rat discs. If at the moment *Tigress* left the wharf you had gone into the hold you would have found no rats. There would have been utter silence in the barrel-filled belly, no patter of scraping feet.

Yet now at sea there were rats. Only a fool from shoreside would have been surprised. The mariners knew that when you went to sea, especially on a long voyage, there was a rodent population (implanted by the Devil perhaps) based in the hold, consuming instantly any meat, cheese or biscuit carelessly spilled when the big barrels were emptied into baskets to be taken up to the messdecks, agile at following the food up ladders to compete with the mariners at mealtimes, endowed with razor teeth to tear up canvas and tallow and rope or even the barrels themselves (seasoned English oak though they were) if the slightest crack released the odour of its contents (salt beef greatly preferred to liquids). At first perhaps a few dedicated rats whose burning instinct, second only to feeding, was procreation. A rapid cycle. In a three-month voyage the few would have become a devouring horde.

The favourite time for hunting rats was after supper and before lights-out, those dangerous hours when the day's work was done and your beer ration was getting low and you were not ready for sleep. You could argue about simple things that would never be decided, the meanest fighting cock, the lustiest woman, the worst storm. You could sing, sentimentally or bawdily. You could gamble. But there were restrictions. Cards and dice were permitted, but no man must gamble with his clothes or his knife or any personal weapon. Some men had a cutlass or a pistol of their own, and these were kept marked in the armoury cupboards. So the gambling was mostly for beer, though sometimes notches were cut on a stick showing what one seaman owed another of the wealth they were going to collect at the rainbow's end. Disputes were settled by arm-wrestling or fisticuffs and if the fights got lethal the warriors were parted by their mates. No one wished to be put ashore at Santa Antao. Tedious violent hours, bad enough on the gun deck hunched in bays between the firing pieces (even with closed ports there was air through the upper hatches), but worse on the orlop, crouched against the shot-racks or leaning back on the mound of tar-nifty anchor cable; beer-swilling knots of cavemen, arguing, cursing, wagering their hopes on the cut of a card or the roll of a single dice, their throaty cantatas shouted down from further along the tallow-reeking cavern, and always someone's knee in your back, never a moment alone, always the others.

The rat parties were popular. Six men from a roster, Smolkin or Costlove in charge. Each man with a cudgel. Seven men and Sirius the mongrel. Down to the hold, and a strong lamp hung overhead, and a chunk of raw meat tied to a bolt in the deckplate. Then the cudgellers positioned in the shadows, and no speaking, and Sirius held quivering with rat-lust, and the black beast suddenly beside the meat, and Sirius released, and the plunging pounce, and sometimes the death (if Sirius got the head one shake was enough), and if he missed, it was up to the cudgels. The rats came singly or in twos or threes and they were very quick. Between each skirmish there was a long wait till the rats' greed overcame their fright. On a good evening there might be three corpses but often there were none.

It was important to get the rats before they multiplied. Some already pregnant might have come aboard, but from scratch a healthy mother could deliver eight babies six weeks later. Once the families appeared the increase rate would rocket upwards.

One evening Tom joined the rat party, leaned against the root of the mainmast, his cudgel ready, waited in the silence. There were no leaks in *Tigress* but the ship sides oozed and glistened in the tomb-like mustiness and there was a sensation of being deep deep down in an immensity of crushing water. There was a phalanx of barrels at either end of the hold and

103

amidships a many-folded pile of new canvas. Fingering his cudgel Tom fancied himself, imagined the crunch as he hit the rat, hoped Sirius would miss. But it was a bad evening. Sirius scored one, the cudgels none. The party went up the ladder taking the remains of the meat, leaving the dead rat to the rats.

Smolkin led the way carrying Sirius under his arm, lifting the mongrel ahead of him on to the orlop deck. As the others followed a sudden hubbub broke out above them, angry voices, and a pause, and a single voice yelling "NO!", and a moment later the single voice, now unmistakably Jabbinoth's, erupting into a sobbing howl of pain, and a loud yelp from Sirius, and the general uproar continued.

By the time Tom joined Smolkin on the orlop Jabbinoth had been taken aft to the surgeon, there was blood on the deck, and no sign of Sirius. The shouting had stopped, and although Jabbinoth was not there to defend himself there seemed little doubt what had happened. Jabbinoth had been caught stealing a seaman's knife from the bedding-roll of a foretopman named Harris. When challenged Jabbinoth could not deny it. He was dragged before a summary jury of his mates and instantly sentenced. His hand was held hard against an oak stanchion and foretopman Rogers, assigned as executioner of the sentence, placed the heavy blade just above the first joint of Jabbinoth's little finger on his right hand and delivered the blow that severed the pink tip immediately. The tip fell in front of Sirius who swallowed it, was kicked by the desperate Jabbinoth wanting his finger back, and scuttled aft.

The surgeon bound up the finger. Jabbinoth was questioned and in extenuation could only plead that he had lost his own knife to a gunner who had cheated him at dice, but as such a gamble was forbidden in the first place and in any case did not excuse theft, he was advised simply to plead guilty of theft when taken before Krauss.

This Jabbinoth did, standing in front of the man who had taught him all he knew of the sea. It made Tom think of a son with the father he admired. In Jabbinoth's loose face there was an acceptance of whatever was going to be said or done to him, a trust in his eyes. Krauss looked up at him for several impassive seconds, the right eye half closed, the left a livid marble, then said gruffly, "Next time it will be your hand. Case dismissed."

In Jabbinoth's countenance there was desolation.

CHAPTER THIRTEEN

They were going to be late reaching Santa Antao. At the fair average of one hundred miles a day the journey would have taken about three weeks, but the winds had been erratic. South of Biscay there had been five days' battling against a strong southwester and later, when they had passed Madeira, a sudden lull had cut their speed for two days to something less than three knots. In addition they had to make sure of approaching the island from the west. On arrival at the correct latitude, fifteen degrees north of the Equator, if they were then not sure whether Santa Antao was to the east or the west they might turn the wrong way and find themselves off the bulge of Africa where there was no fresh citrus fruit and fresh water ashore, only fever and cannibals.

Tom learned about latitude and longitude from the Sultan. Each day at noon, except when the sun was overcast, the Sultan and Krauss went up to the poop to take a sunsight. The principle was simple. If you drew a line from the horizon to your eye and another line from your eye to the sun, then the angle between these two lines would, with minor adjustments, show the altitude of the sun, and from this could be calculated your latitude, the lines of latitude being imaginary hoops round the surface of the world parallel with the Equator.

The only line that could be drawn was the line of sight. So you needed an instrument that would let you look first at the horizon and then at the sun, and would record the angle between these two sightings.

On *Tigress* there were two such instruments. The astrolabe and the cross staff.

The astrolabe, a heavy circle of brass, had a cross bar for lining up on the horizon and a slim pointer rotating on the centre of the circle. You held up your hand with the astrolabe suspended from your thumb on a brass ring, and sighted the sun along the pointer, and read the angle on the scale.

The cross staff was a beautiful rod of polished pear wood marked with a scale of degrees and minutes. A cross piece holed in the centre could be moved along the rod. You held the butt of the rod against your cheekbone and slid the cross piece away from you until the horizon was just visible beneath the bottom edge of the cross piece and the sun appearing just to touch the top edge. Where the cross piece rested the figures on the rod showed the sun's altitude.

In the first week out from Lingmouth Tom had asked to watch the ceremony at noon, and the Sultan had said, "I learned from the master of *Black Vulture*. You shall learn from me." He glanced at Krauss and they both laughed. They did not explain the joke.

The theory of sight-taking was simple, but in practice the astrolabe swivelled on the thumb, and when the sun was bright the cross staff needed an eye shade, and the rolling *Tigress* made the horizon jiggle, and when it was cloudy at noon you waited till night and took the altitude of the Pole Star instead. When Krauss and the Sultan took sights with different instruments their readings hardly varied, but when Tom tried he was usually a long way out. Afterwards in the Sultan's cabin there were sums to translate altitude into latitude that Tom could not follow, but one thing he understood.

Your latitude, how far north or south of the Equator, you could discover from the sun and stars. Your longitude, how far east or west you were along a line of latitude, you could not discover. You had to make estimates with the log-line and sand-glass, and the estimates could be very rough.

So far it had not greatly mattered. They had come south-west to somewhere west of Madeira, turning due south till they should reach the latitude of Santa Antao. "When we start across the Atlantic," said the Sultan, "then you will see the difference."

Tom enjoyed playing with the astrolabe and cross staff. He could imagine his mother polishing that smooth pear wood. He remembered when his head was no higher than the kitchen table and he stood beside the warm black oven and smelt the dough baking, and his nurse Ellen Rufoote let him play with a long wooden ladle, and how he loved her.

He also enjoyed being with Krauss and the Sultan. Something between them gave heart to the whole ship. Not a big ship compared to the monsters of the Queen's navy, but still your home, your refuge, perhaps your prison or your tomb. Whatever it was, still yours. And you had better love it because there was nothing else. In the early morning when there was dew on the deck it seemed hardly credible that in the enormous watery disc stretching to the perimeter of the horizon there was no sail to be seen, only the shimmering expanse grey-green before the sun rose, and *Tigress* the only vessel. There had been occasional sightings, but the Sultan did not alter course.

He was not chasing Spanish trawlers. *Tigress* was on her own with a life of her own, a temporary city obedient only to herself, and her laws not the laws of land dwellers. Ashore there was rancour and the prolongation of dispute. If your neighbour did you wrong you remembered and plotted revenge. Even if he was punished you still remembered, the tracks of hostility did not disappear from your mind. But at sea it was different. Each day was complete and tomorrow there were no tracks. The ship's wake vanished in the night and in the morning there was no yesterday. Gideon Jabbinoth stole a knife. His finger tip was cut off and swallowed by Sirius the mongrel. But there was no rancour from the mariners. At archery practice there were no scowls or hard words for Gideon. His little finger was bound up, but he could still hold the bowstring in the nock of the shaft and bend his strength into the bow. In the gun deck hung the notion: "You did it. You paid for it. Finish."

But to Tom Dakyn, watching the slack lips and the blank eyes, it seemed that perhaps it was not quite finished.

They would be late at Santa Antao, said the Sultan, seven days or more. Now each noon the sun was higher and hotter, and with the heat came the maggots, the cockroaches, the bad food, the rancid beer, and finally the sickness.

The ship's biscuit was served in several ways. In broken pieces the length of a long finger, to be dipped in broth or smeared with cheese, or pounded with fruit into a hot pudding, or mixed with lentil and suet into dumplings that were dropped with all honesty into the cookroom stew but appeared at the dinner table in the great cabin as a glutinous disintegration of frogspawn. Complaints only brought surly messages of poor materials. Krauss did not care what he ate, Viccars preferred the biscuit disguised, but Fernie insisted on a pannier of broken pieces with every meal. He said the mastication helped him to digest his meals, and he was encouraged to masticate because the Fernie belches were an annoyance to everyone.

One stifling evening, with the cabin door ajar and the

107

curtains motionless across the open ports, Fernie reached for another biscuit, broke it, and waved it over his head shouting, "Welcome, my friends! What kept you?"

He showed the biscuit. Three sleek white maggots with black heads were writhing half out of their holes. The purser opened his mouth and with a wink at Gostigo snapped his jaws over the morsel, munched happily, and when he had swallowed enough to speak, pointed at the frowning surgeon and said, "They're good food. Not much taste, but meaty. These gentlemen only take the biscuit when it is fresh. When the biscuit dries up the maggots leave and the weevils come. They are no gentlemen, sir. Weevils are bitter on the tongue. The bosun agrees?"

"So you have always told me," said Gostigo, smiling. He never smiled except to Fernie. They had been young together, serving before the mast.

The pannier had other maggoty pieces. Tom did not try one. Viccars picked up a piece without a glance and ate the visitors. There was no more to be said. The black-bearded master gunner was a sanction of his own.

The cockroaches were no gentlemen of any sort. Just shiny brown stenchy beetles. Like the maggots they appeared without warning, but they did not confine themselves like gentlemen to the biscuit. They were everywhere for food, vegetable or animal, living or dead, boiled or raw. In the cookroom at cook times and the messes at mealtimes, clinging to the undersides of tables till the humans were seated and the plates set down, then appearing with insolent unconcern waving their slow feelers in the air, moving towards the food as if they owned it. It was easy to kill one cockroach. The Sultan, dining in the great cabin, had a strange look on his face as he crushed them with the flat of his palm, saying, "That's how my father killed the roaches. Like that! And that! And *that*!" But there was always another and another. They observed no hours of wake and sleep. By day between meals they lay under bedding-rolls and at night they were ready to slither down the weary outstretched legs, rubbing their oily backs against the shins and calves before settling to gnaw the soles of the tired shoeless feet. Insects ashore would bite you anywhere they landed, even bed bugs which had not yet appeared on *Tigress* would take blood from any pulpy region, but the cockroaches seemed to prefer the hard flaking grimy skin you never thought about, your basic undermat, bloodless and unappetizing. It was an insult to decency. There was something mysterious about the cockroach, an inexcusable loathsomeness. The rats could be hunted, the maggots could be eaten, but the cockroaches were too many to kill and too foul to swallow. Fernie the purser never munched a cockroach, and cockroach soup was never on the menu. When at morning prayers the Sultan read in booming tones from the book of Joel, "And I will restore to you the years that the grasshopper hath eaten, the cankerworm and the caterpillar and the palmer-worm," he was telling the ship's company that he shared their suffering.

The fruit and vegetables were finished. There was no more cheese and the fish with all its brine had gone putrid in the barrels. The purser swore he would cut the liver out of Jacob Biscombe the Lingmouth victualler, but it was probably not Jacob's fault. Fish never kept as long as the meat, and no Lingmouth victualler would have dared do less than his best for Joshua Vine. The sun was to blame, not Jacob Biscombe.

So now the meals had a terrible sameness. The beef was good, but it was always salted and always stewed or boiled. Roasting ovens got too hot and were dangerous in a storm. Apart from the steam, ships had been gutted by fire from roasting ovens. The cooks tried hard. They cut the beef into lumps of different size, and sometimes the dried peas and lentils were served separately and sometimes they were mashed up with the biscuit and doused with the salty beef water. Whether these delicacies were better washed down with beer or wine was a matter of taste. The choice came to an end on the morning when the day's first beer barrel proved rancid. A second barrel was opened, and a third. There was no doubt. From now on it was wine for the mariners. At dinner Smolkin reported the bad news and there was a hullabaloo of obscenities and a banging on mess tables with spoons that could be well heard aft in the great cabin.

But there was nothing to be done.

A gloom settled over the ship. That night the Sultan supped with his officers. He told them it was not long now to Santa Antao. He called for wine and music, and Robert Seaton played his flute with confidence, and Viccars surprised everyone by singing "Dusty My Dear" in a tuneless baritone, and Gostigo, though he would not sing, contributed by beating an inaccurate tattoo on the table for "Nobody's Jig". Then the Sultan called for his favourite, "Killala Bay", and Fernie, who had been drinking heavily, sang the haunting little air with surprising sweetness:

> *There's a tree beside the waters of Killala,*
> *And there I kissed a maid with golden hair.*
> *It was springtime when she left me on the hillside,*
> *She promised she'd be back to love me there.*
> *She said 'Today's a sad time,*
> *'Tomorrow is a glad time:*
> *'We shall love each other through*
> *'The longest summer day.'*
> *And I'm waiting by the waters of Killala,*
> *And the trees are bare beside Killala Bay.*

Later in the sweltering darkness Tom lay in his bunk and rubbed roach liniment into the soles of his feet. It was Viccars's own invention, a mixture of gunpowder and the juice of aloes. A paste, said Viccars, was useless because any kind of grease or tallow would be food for the cockroaches, whereas the aloe juice and the gunpowder would scare them away. He had tried it on the route to India where the cockroaches grew especially plump and foetid. So Tom rubbed in the liniment and smelt his acrid finger and heard the song still in his head, the pure notes of the flute beneath the strange sweetness in Fernie's voice. Had Fernie once lost a girl? It was hot and dark in the cabin. No one spoke but you could feel the others awake.

So *Tigress* moved towards Santa Antao, and with the gloom came a peculiar lassitude. Tom saw it at bow practice. Several times archers put down their bow and shook their heads as if wondering where their strength had gone. It was only momentary. Under ridicule they soon picked up their bows. But Tom saw it again in the steerage doing rounds with Smolkin. Eight seamen on the long tiller, four either side, and one suddenly slouching forwards banging his forehead on the oak, and sitting up with a grin as if it was an accident. Viccars reported the same with the gun crews, men falling on their knees as they ran out the guns. There was less firing practice now, but still the daily exercise in handling.

With the ebbing of strength there was less talk everywhere and a general hope that Santa Antao was not far off. Krauss said they would get some good victuals at Santa Antao and Robert Seaton said he wanted plenty of lemons and oranges to double the men's ration of citrus fruit juice. There was no beer in the Cape Verde Islands, but mess-deck rumour said that the local wine was fit for seamen because the islands were a supply post on the route to India. So the men talked of the food and drink at Santa Antao and not about the weakness in their arms and legs. In the great cabin the daily incidents were mentioned but not discussed. At sea it is unlucky to speak of disaster till it happens. The limb weakness was an early symptom that many of the ship's company had seen before, but perhaps this time they were mistaken. In any case no one wished to put a name to it. Whether you called it scurvy or the Knobs it was better left unsaid. The victuals at Santa Antao would surely put the strength back.

Santa Antao was not what Tom expected. Remembering San Corda he pictured danger and hostility. When the smudge appeared on the horizon he wondered where they would anchor and what the reception would be.

It was not like San Corda. In full sunshine *Tigress* made a slow approach with shortened canvas. It was a natural open harbour with two low claws of land giving partial shelter to the bay. There were no masts of Spanish men-of-war to be seen. A mile out *Tigress* ran up a blue and white quartered flag, the international request for stores, and received the green pennant that meant affirmative. Half an hour later, with ports open and all guns ready and loaded, she slid through the wide pincer mouth. On each claw an ancient iron cannon pointed out to sea. Men with wide-brimmed straw hats were sitting on the cannon waving to *Tigress*.

Gently, with only her topsails puffed in the breeze, she moved like a swan to the centre of the harbour, turned into wind, came to rest, dropped anchor. There were several bulky merchantmen and a swarm of fishing boats. A small single-masted cutter was already bobbing out towards *Tigress*. The harbourmaster came aboard, agile up the rope ladder, presenting the compliments of the governor. The ship had been recognized as English from her style and the flag bearing the cross of St George. The governor requested her master's name, destination and purpose. The answer—"Sir Joshua Vine: Cal-

111

cutta: the procurement of charts for the Queen of England"—
brought smiles of respect from the harbourmaster. He went
ashore and returned that afternoon with the governor himself
who gave assurance that all facilities would be granted.

It was as the Sultan and Krauss had calculated. Portugal
herself was the unwilling neighbour of Spain. Allies ashore, still
rivals at sea. Here, over a thousand miles south, the spirit of the
old Portuguese seamen flourished defiantly. The governor's
name was Gabriel Diaz, great-grandson of the immortal Bartholomew who had been the first man in the world to round the
"Cape of Storms" before it became the "Cape of Good Hope".
Before him, Prince Henry the Navigator had had an English
mother. After him, Vasco da Gama had used Bartholomew's
experience to reach India. What Spaniard had ever done such
things? Spaniards were not seamen, they were soldiers in
floating fortresses. They went to sea only to plunder gold and
jewels from the natives in the New World. He, Gabriel Diaz,
spat on Spaniards.

The Sultan and Krauss gave the talkative governor as good a
supper as *Tigress* could still offer. In the cabin under the poop
the wine flowed till midnight. Gabriel knew all about the great
Sir Joshua! He was proud to welcome such a brother of the sea.
A chart-making voyage of discovery? How admirable! A toast
to Portugal and England! To all true seamen! Governor Diaz
was getting drunk. Another toast, to Joshua Vine the famous
navigator! How much the governor really knew, how much he
had chosen to forget, whether he guessed the true destination of
Tigress, or cared, never became clear.

Tigress would be provisioned. Costing could be left to the
stores officials. The English guns would not be needed in Santa
Antao. He, Gabriel Diaz, guaranteed satisfaction.

For three days the whole ship's company toiled under a fierce
sun. No one was exempt. The Sultan, stripped to the waist,
insisted that all his gentlemen worked with the mariners. There
were two hundred empty wine and beer barrels. Then the
water, used mostly for cooking on the way out. The remaining
water barrels were emptied because the water was getting
brackish. Then the food empties, the fish barrels scoured of
their stinking remains, the beef barrels scoured ready to receive
the salt pork that was the island's best meat, the biscuit and

112

lentil barrels to be replenished with flour and maize.

It was a back-breaking task. The harbour had two deep-water jetties for loading, but all berths were full. There would be a vacancy in two days. The Sultan politely declined. He did not mistrust Governor Diaz, but an aberration was possible, and *Tigress* tied alongside would be a target for muskets. So she stayed in mid-harbour with her guns ready, and the barrels were brought to and from the quay in small boats, her own and a dozen others lent by the harbourmaster. Some boats had a sail and could carry ten barrels, but most carried two or three and were rowed. The big side hatches in the gun deck were opened and the barrels were lowered and lifted on a block and tackle. From the gun deck they were manhandled down the ladders to the hold. The bare torsos had a certain levelling effect, Fernie with his plump hairless chest looking no more of a gentleman than most of the mariners, and Gostigo, whose black mat not only covered his chest down to the navel but also sprouted between his shoulder blades, a good deal less. Slowly the belly of *Tigress* filled up again. The wine was tasted and approved. The water was fresh from the springs. The surgeon got his oranges and lemons in quantity and when the final barrel of food had been stowed in the hold a load of fresh fruit in baskets was somehow squeezed into the deck space round the cook-room. Last of all, a gift from the thoughtful governor, a huge open vat of live shrimps and sprats squirming in salt water was hoisted on to the forecastle and lashed to the mast.

The victualling bill was paid in gold coin. Governor Diaz came aboard for a few last toasts and when he had gone *Tigress* weighed anchor.

Tom watched the tired men on the capstan, two men to each bar, the endless messenger rope coiling slowly round. The heavy anchor cable was coming in at gun deck level, nipped to the messenger rope. When a length of cable had been dragged clear through the hawsehole the nippers were taken off and the messenger rope nipped on to the cable further back towards the hawsehole. So the wet sea-smelling cable was drawn aboard, passed down to the orlop level, and coiled away. The men on the capstan were very tired. It was a burning hot evening with a red sunset waiting on the horizon. Tom felt tired himself, and he had only been humping barrels all day and was not required on the capstan.

Now the mainsails were swollen gently and *Tigress* moved out of harbour towards the sunset. Tom watched the handling party as they swayed on the footrope beneath the mainyard. The sky was cloudless and he could feel the breeze like a blessing on his cheek.

Suddenly there was a shout from above, a stabbing yell of despair. Tom looked up just as the arm-waving body left the yard, plummeted fifty feet, thudded on deck, lay sprawling. Tom ran to him, but the starfish did not move. Hurrying feet and crowding faces. Seaman Kettel, said his mates, had complained of the weakness for days. He was a first-class yard man. He fell off because he could not hold on. Tom had known him by sight, but not his name.

Seaman Kettel was wrapped in canvas with his possessions, his knife and his shoes, the shroud weighted with shot. *Tigress* was five miles out of harbour when the Sultan read from the Ninetieth Psalm, "So teach us to number our days . . ." and the parcel of seaman David Kettel slipped down the angled wooden shelf into the sea.

Tom felt somehow guilty, not knowing his name.

CHAPTER FOURTEEN

By breakfast the wind was steady on the starboard quarter and *Tigress*, who on the approach to Santa Antao had struggled slowly into this same wind, was now under a blue sky being blown westwards the way she wanted to go.

At morning prayers there was an unusual silence. Tom, standing beside the Sultan at the rail of the half deck, felt the tension in the upturned faces below. They were waiting for the word, though what it would be no one could guess. Death had come to *Tigress*, and something must be said. Tom, feeling the stillness, wondered where in the book he knew so well the Sultan would find some morsel of comfort or encouragement. Tom did not know the Old Testament very well, but he thought of phrases by childhood preachers like "the bread of adversity and the water of affliction", and hoped that they would not be used now. The seamen crowded in the waist did not want to be told that their peril was somehow a blessing. And complaint would be no better. The whinings of Job would not help the mariners who had come on *Tigress* knowing the danger, knowing now that they were on the brink of scurvy, knowing they had been packed like pigs in a slaughterhouse so that when some died, as they must, those left would be enough. So what would the Sultan have to say?

Sir Joshua held the Bible and the prayer book, but he did not open them. He turned slowly to look at the men behind him. When he was facing for'ard again he said, "Next time we go ashore we shall be on the isthmus of Panama. The Spaniards bring their treasure from the south up to the north where their ships wait. They bring it on the backs of mules. Emeralds and gold—and more gold. We shall take that treasure. The gold will be ours. Every man who by the grace of God is alive will take his full share. Let that be your strength and your courage."

There was a murmur round the decks like a hallelujah of bees. When it died down the Sultan began the Lord's Prayer. The response was whole-hearted. Not because of the words. Trespasses, Temptations and Delivery from Evil were not part of life on *Tigress*. But the prayer was the one they all knew best, their ritual.

The mariners dispersed and with Krauss left on watch the Sultan took the officers into his cabin and told them about the ruttier of Claud Robyns.

The facts were simple. When Joshua Vine was planning for Panama he knew that to capture the mule train on its northward journey he must land on some unfrequented stretch of coast and strike down through the jungle, taking the mules well before they reached the port of Nombre de Dios. West of Nombre lay other Spanish settlements, some fortified and all with garrisons. The coastline was open and ill suited to secret landings. East of Nombre, before the coast dipped down into the Gulf of Darien, the sealine was more rugged, more desolate, and less charted. A mass of small islands, mostly uninhabited, dozed like sheep along the shore. These islands, so convenient for surprise and concealment, presented a threatening network of reefs, shoals and banks with currents and soundings unrecorded by the navigators from Europe. Sir Joshua knew the area. As a youth in *Black Vulture* he had waylaid merchantmen off Nombre and her neighbour Porto Bello. But he had no detailed knowledge of the island approaches. It was for this he waited in his early years at Rockways, listening in the harbour taverns, patient with any drunken mariner, steering the likely talkers up the zigzag path for further questioning.

The reward of his fanatical patience was an English carpenter named Erasmus Chyne who had come off a Dutch vessel holed outside Lingmouth in a fog collision. The repairs would be lengthy. Those wishing to leave the ship were paid off. That night in the tavern Joshua Vine noticed two things about the lanky seaman at the corner table. One, that the group of Lingmouth locals round him appeared agog for his next drunken joke, applauding whatever he said. This could only mean he was buying their drinks. And two, that between his legs rested a dirty bulging canvas sack which he patted now and then in a fuddled protective manner. Joshua joined the table, learned that two Dutch vessels carrying pearl traders and accompanied by a warship had been in the Caribbean to raid the pearl beds off Cartagena, the Spanish stronghold guarding the eastern tip of the Darien Gulf. An unknown vessel intruded, was fired on, ran up the white flag. A boarding party was sent over including Erasmus Chyne. There was blood on the decks and many casualties, some still alive. In the captain's cabin lay a dead man, his head shattered. At this point in his narrative Erasmus became blearily taciturn, as if the thought of the cabin somehow frightened him. The ship's crew, he said, were put in their boats, given a bearing for Cartagena. The ship was scuttled. The traders, after some satisfactory pearl-snatching, returned across the Atlantic. More he would not say.

When the tavern closed Sir Joshua took Erasmus up the zigzag path, gave him food and a lot more ale, and with Shem, Ham and Japheth couchant beside the log fire heard why Erasmus was afraid.

Alone in the cabin he had searched the dead man's pockets, found nothing. Looked in the desk drawer, found a small linen bag containing pearls. These he now produced from his sack, a dozen pearls of medium quality. And there was something else. From beneath the waistband of his breeches he took a pocketed leather belt that had lain next to his skin. In one pocket were ten emeralds. By now Erasmus was feeling what many had felt, an utter trust and admiration for the man with those fire-lit amber eyes sitting motionless except for the hand that stroked the head of the mastiff beside the chair. Erasmus knew that the stones would fetch money, but he also knew that merchants ashore were no friends of mariners. The merchants cheated you, and if you were lucky enough to get a good price there was still every possibility of having your throat cut in the backstreets of any port. Disposing of the valuables for which you had suffered at sea was difficult for a friendless mariner who could neither read nor write. Erasmus was afraid not simply of being cheated or killed but because if he were asked how he came by the pearls and emeralds he had no answer. "They"—the enemies of all seamen—would find out and he would be hanged for thieving. Erasmus holding his wobbling ale-pot beside the fire was full of stupefied self-pity.

Joshua Vine calmed him, promised that he personally would speak to a merchant who could be trusted. Erasmus need fear no more.

It was then that Joshua picked up the leather belt, opened the second pocket and found the many-folded sheets of paper that was the ruttier, the private sea-diary of Admiral Claud Robyns.

Next day Joshua made good his promise to Erasmus Chyne. Together they took one emerald to a merchant who was honest with Joshua Vine if with no one else. Erasmus was given as many gold pieces as would fill the pockets of his belt. When that was spent, said Joshua, he could come back for more. The pearls and emeralds would be safe at Rockways.

And so they would. The fact that Erasmus Chyne went back to the tavern that evening, again drank too much, picked up a gipsy girl with her man waiting outside, was found at dawn with his throat cut beside a slimy jetty, all this was no fault of Joshua Vine who had no interest in cheating a seaman out of a few pearls and emeralds, but every interest in the record of Claud Robyns.

It was an old scandal but still talked about. Admiral Robyns of the Queen's navy, taking as his mistress the wife of another admiral, begged her to run away. The lady refused, and Robyns, on an expedition to the Gulf of Mexico, disappeared at a port in Florida. One morning in harbour there was no skiff and no admiral. No explanation. In Florida, said rumour, there were serpents with three heads and four legs. It was a place of mystery. But the mystery of how the love-sick admiral had found his way from Florida down round the horn of Cuba into the Caribbean, how he had lighted on the isthmus of Panama, what his business was or the name of the vessel carrying him when it intruded years later on the Dutch pearl seekers, this was never explained.

To Joshua Vine the ruttier seemed a confirmation of his destiny. The diary described a landing on the coast west of Darien, the latitude given as 09° 17' N., the longitude shown in bearings and distances in sea miles taken from the Rock of Sharks as a starting point. The approach to shore, threading through the islands, was shown in detail. Claud Robyns had named his landing place "Elizabeth Bay". He described the natives as "a tribe of Cuna Indians, lazy in temperament, gentle in habit, with the surprising characteristic that they use no money and despise gold as being a metal of corruption". There was more about the natives, though nothing as to why the admiral had landed among them. Last came a description of their chief—"an unusual personage whose name I could not pronounce. He speaks English of a sort which he claims to have learned in Jamaica. He is treated with complete awe and obedience by the tribe. I called him Gentleman Jack."

Joshua knew the Rock of Sharks. He felt that he had been guided in all his plans for Panama culminating in this ruttier delivered to him by the hand of a drunken carpenter off a ship holed in fog. "There shall not a man be able to withstand thee," said the Book of Joshua, "all the days of thy life."

Joshua Vine agreed.

On *Tigress* that hot morning he did not tell his officers the whole story of the ruttier. Simply that he had acquired it in his preparations.

On the desk he spread two charts, one of his own showing the whole isthmus lying east–west with Panama in the centre of the south side, the other a creased paper on a much larger scale showing ten miles of northern coastline with several islands and a dotted track through from the open sea to Elizabeth Bay, the soundings marked in fathoms, the reefs and shoals and currents labelled alphabetically with plentiful notes below. The ruttier was signed in a firm flowing hand and dated two years previously. Only the Sultan and Viccars had heard of Admiral Robyns, but each officer felt a new excitement as he looked at the record of someone who had been where they were going now. An actual destination made everything seem possible.

118

Gostigo, more cadaverous than ever after the long hot weeks, asked sombrely, "These Indians, if they have no trust in gold, will it please them when we go hunting for it?"

"We shall make them our friends. The Admiral says that will not be difficult."

"Does he say how?"

"Hunting knives and hatchets for the men. Ornaments and cooking utensils for the women. It's all here." The Sultan patted the folded pages.

"And have we brought these bargaining materials?"

"Some of those crates marked 'sundry equipment'. You stowed them yourself with the purser's help." Then with a smile, as if not wishing to put the bosun in a bad light: "I did not want to bother you with every detail."

"And the admiral himself. Did he part willingly with—"

"The admiral died at sea. I obtained the ruttier from a man who had no use for it."

He spoke in a quiet tone of finality, but Gostigo persisted: "It was a great piece of fortune that you came upon this remarkable chart."

"I allowed fortune every opportunity over many years," said the Sultan.

That was true and everyone in the cabin knew it. The Sultan had thought and planned for them all. He had made himself lucky by foresight and perseverance.

Only Viccars seemed dejected, murmuring what use would his guns ever be if the treasure was to be taken on land. But the Sultan put his hand on Viccars's shoulder and said firmly, "No one knows. Do you think I would take *Tigress* to sea without her claws?"

In the mornings there were piles of fleecy white cloud on the horizon. The sky was clear blue and the sea a darker blue with small waves sparkling as they played together. The stem of *Tigress* cut into the dark water carving up pillows of hissing foam round the bows, and astern trailed the long white ribbon beneath the planing gulls. The days stretched out amiably with the sunshine and the following breeze, and by afternoon the white wool had cleared from the horizon, and the sunset was a crimson banner of welcome, and the night sky powdered with stars.

119

It was ideal weather for sailing. For *Tigress* it was a passage of death.

Citrus fruits had been taken on board at Santa Antao. The squeezed juice was presented on the messdecks as an alternative to the unpopular tots of Seaton's medicine-wine. Re-doubled orders were issued that the mariners must drink. The orders were not posted up in writing because most of the mariners could not read. The orders were shouted out at dinner time by Marshal Smolkin in a glowering voice: "Physic Down!"

He was obeyed, but doubt remained. On the messdecks they said that David Kettel had always drunk the fruit wine, yet he had fallen and was dead. Others had drunk, yet now felt the ache in their joints which they were afraid to admit to. Some had not drunk and were still healthy. Perhaps the fruits of Santa Antao were a help, perhaps not. Whatever the truth, the mariners knew that scurvy was among them, and day by day they were proved right.

In the next two weeks all gunnery and bow practice was cancelled and *Tigress* became a hospital ship. On the gun deck the guns were made fast as close to the sides as possible, leaving an avenue for the mess tables. The armoury became the first sick-room with other spaces for'ard taken over as the numbers increased. As long as the men could stand up they stayed in their own messes. When they could no longer stand they were brought with their bedding-rolls to the armoury. As Tom Dakyn had no forenoon duties he became chief orderly and assistant to Robert Seaton. Robert had learned what he could about scurvy from his teachers, but he had never seen a case. He kept a book with a page for each patient, and in the evenings he and Tom wrote up the symptoms, comparing one case with another, trying to establish a routine of treatment. It was a crude register. Some men sickened quicker than others. There were partial recoveries, sudden lapses, treatments that some-times worked and sometimes did not. As the days went on the details of the separate case-pages were written up into a survey constantly changing but slowly taking shape.

Scurvy

Warning symptoms: Pallor. Complaint of dizziness. Short-
ness of breath. Slowness in obeying orders (reported by
Viccars and Gostigo). Weakness in hands and legs. No loss
of appetite.

Onset: 1st stage: The gums become itchy and swollen. Later bleed. Dryness of skin especially at roots of hair. Mild haemorrhages. Spots (at first red, then blue turning to black) appear on thighs, arms and trunk. Swollen legs. Breath foetid. Appetite worsens.

2nd stage: Fever. General swelling including trunk and abdomen. Spots turning to deep ulcers. Loss of the use of limbs. Contraction of tendons with cramp and extreme pain in joints. Sleeplessness and much hardness of breathing. Vomiting after fish and meat.

3rd stage: Skin bursts on swollen thighs. Total degeneration of ulcers. Putrefaction of the abdomen. Rotten evacuation of blood. Melancholy. Constraint of the chest. Respiration impossible.

Treatment: No fish or meat. Fruit best. Biscuit or maize pudding with broth to give strength. Responses vary. Some hold their food, others vomit at once. Sea water calms the stomach but does not cure. Purges help some, but weaken others to death.

These notes were deliberately impersonal, intended to form a general picture of the disease and how, if at all, it could be stemmed. When Tom read through the notes he remembered words and faces and things not recorded.

The bowmen Pipkin and Dykes were friends. Both from Lingmouth, they slept next to each other, on deck if they could find space, if not, on the stuffy orlop. They had beer bets at archery practice. Both had drunk the surgeon's wine. Yet Pipkin got scurvy but Dykes did not. Tom remembered Pipkin in the early stage, the blood on the dry scalp where he had scratched himself, and Pipkin saying all he needed was some ale to pour over his head. And later the ulcerous bog on Pipkin's left thigh, and Pipkin saying, "I won't die, will I?" His bewildered green-tinged eyes as he looked at his leg, the putrid bulging mess that surely did not belong to *him*. And one morning going round with the surgeon and finding Dykes sitting beside the open-eyed corpse. Dykes was frowning but he would not speak.

And deep in dreams one night being woken by a pulsating scream as if from the bottom of the sea, and leaping out of the bunk and going down with Robert Seaton to the steerage where

121

Latham, one of the tiller hands, had fallen from the bench and was lying on his back with his legs bunched up like a foetus. From fear he had somehow concealed the onset, not complaining about his itching gums and the growing ulcers, but now when he was carried screaming to the armoury and his breeches were cut away because he could not endure their being pulled down, the tendons behind his knees were like iron cords showing black through the skin, the calves bent tight against the thighs. Sea water relieved the immediate contraction. He was purged and his ulcers bound up. Of all the sick he was the most melancholy. As a rule they started with false hopes and a determination not to die, losing heart only towards the end, but Latham was steeped in pessimism from the first moments of his agony at the tiller. When he stopped screaming his first words were, "I'll be gone by morning." It took him eight days to die, complaining all the time, saying each morning that he would be gone by nightfall. When he looked at you his brown eyes were full of a sadness too big for one man. You felt he was suffering for all the rest, and when he groaned it was a reproach to the whole world. He died with a hideous abdomen and spouting blood.

One of the worst was Blessington, the bosun's mate, an expert with canvas and cables. The mariners were divided roughly into seamen, gunners, and others. Gostigo controlled the seamen and others, who included carpenters, cooks and Tom's bowmen. Viccars controlled the gunners. Blessington was to Gostigo what Costlove was to Viccars, a trusted executive. Tom only knew Blessington as a surly oak of a man who would hardly say good-day. He was a Gostigo man, one of the majority on *Tigress*, and he died at Tom's side.

There was the usual progression. Reporting to Robert with a stiff knee and a smile as if it did not matter. Then the gums, the mild fever, the swellings all over, the ulcers spreading through the spectrum from red to livid purple, and finally the annihilation of breath. The armoury and the forecastle spaces were all full now, so a new sick-room was prepared in a compartment next to the surgeon's den. Below the waterline there was no vent of fresh air. Normally you breathed in the stale leftover oozing down from the gun deck, a distillation of body sweat, but now in the sweltering nights this somewhat pure intake was clouded with the odour of rotten flesh. Your taste buds were revolted, yet you had to breathe. The lungs collapsing seemed momentarily soothed by this tepid lava, foul though it was. But in the end the lungs cried out for the fresh air that was to kill them.

On their morning visit Robert and Tom found Blessington on his hands and knees, his chest shaken by quick spasms. His mouth was wide open but the breathing was pitiful. They held him erect but he was limp and kept whispering "Air! Air!" He pointed feebly upwards. Somehow they lifted him up the gun deck ladder, but again he pointed up to the hatchway with its square of blue sky. Two seamen came to help and at last Blessington was sitting propped by Tom's hands against the mainmast with a heavenful of fresh air above him. For a moment the head lolled sideways, the cracked lips sagging open in a ghastly smile of gratitude. Then in a final paroxysm the head was flung back with a huge intaking sigh, as if even now on the brink of annihilation the poor bellows could be filled with life. But it was death that came, the strong salt air swamping like a tidal wave into the frail cavities.

This hard man killed by a breath of air.

As Tom read through the notes he remembered such deaths and many like them. Two weeks out from Santa Antao thirty-one men had died. They were parcelled into the sea with honour and reverence, except for their knives and shoes. David Kettel had been wrapped in canvas with his knife and shoes, but now, with the sun-scorched decks hostile to bare feet, and shoes wearing out, it was a senseless waste to lose the shoes with the corpse. Gostigo's men could cobble up shoes of a sort, rope soles with canvas uppers, but why throw good leather shoes from Lingmouth into the ocean? The armourers could fashion a blade with a handle but it would not be well tempered. So the Sultan ordered that the knives and shoes be stored for replacements. At sea burials he now read from the Book of Job: "Naked I came from my mother's womb and naked I shall return thither." It was an unpopular order. Mariners had few possessions, and if a man had to make his last journey to the bottom of the sea he liked to take with him what he had prized most dearly. And for those left alive what luck could come from stepping into a dead man's shoes? The Sultan understood this, but he knew that apart from scorching decks there was a forest ahead in Panama.

It did not seem a very important matter. A mariner in the last stages of scurvy did not protest about the ritual of his burial.

Tigress carved on through the blue Atlantic, the breeze steady, sun by day and stars at night, and always the expectation of death. After morning prayers there was a roll-call of fitness, the men filing past Smolkin and Robert Seaton, each man required to say if he felt fit to go aloft, the surgeon on the lookout for early symptoms. There was no shame in staying on deck. It would help no one for more to die like Kettel, and Tom, looking up to the dizzy maintop and the flag he had so perilously touched, could imagine the terror of being on a topyard with the sudden weakness in the hands. Yet men went aloft freely even when there was no work overhead, not to the topyards but at least to the mainyards and fighting tops. To be alone. *Tigress* in health was bad enough. Always the others, never silence, not a moment that was privately yours. When death spread through the ship, with the ulcers, the groans and the burials, men had to escape. You could see them low in the rigging or perched on the yard-arms like sparrows in the trees that grew high above the slum where they were trapped.

In the great cabin there was no sickness yet, but a creeping despondency. Viccars brooded about the men he had lost that day. Fernie munched his maggots without making jokes. No one asked him to sing because no one wanted songs mingled with the voices of dying men. The armoury sick-room was below, and the sound wavered up into the cabin. Most gloomy of the officers was Gostigo, hardly speaking except to inquire of the bulkhead at intervals "How much longer?", brushing the cockroaches lethargically from his plate as if he hardly cared. Robert Seaton was exhausted. Tom helped as much as he could, but it was Robert who examined each sick man twice a day, applied the purges, dealt with the contractions and vomitings, left his food to hurry to the latest victim, worked again and again through his notes seeking a remedy for what he did not understand. He was trained as a surgeon and could only do what the physicians had told him. The physicians themselves knew no cure, only the possibility of prevention through a diet of fruits. And the fresh fruits of Santa Antao were running out. There was dejection in the cabin. Even Krauss, whose scarred face with its ever-glaring eye gave no hint of his thoughts, had

124

no words of help. Like his master in the cabin above, Krauss did not believe in false encouragement.

The Sultan himself set the example. At morning prayer there was no more recital of valiant deeds from the Old Testament. Gold was not mentioned. If your messmates were dying below deck, and you might be next, it was no time for the poetry of dreams. The Lord's Prayer and the appeal of St Chrysostom, then to the day's tasks of sailing the ship and caring for the sick. The Sultan was tireless. Each morning he conferred with the surgeon and the purser about the fitness list, the sick list, and the diet of the day; then with Krauss and Gostigo about the ship-handling parties. After that, when he was not navigating, he was on constant rounds, listening, advising, using his life's knowledge to help men, whatever their task or state of sorriness, to save their energy against the scurvy, the rats, the cockroaches and the heat.

The dysentery first showed itself when the anchor cable got doused by a gunner who could not reach the privy platform in time. No one blamed the gunner. He was running for'ard toward the bows and at the moment when his arse exploded like boiling soup he happened to be passing the anchor cable coiled on the orlop.

Normally on *Tigress* the privy routine was straightforward and satisfactory. The Sultan had a privy stool of his own and the officers shared another curtained off outside the great cabin. These were emptied by stewards. For the ship's company there was the crescent-shaped platform built out from the bows and reached from the forecastle by climbing down over the bow rail. Lengths of planed oak had been formed into a lattice with the apertures nine inches square so that when after breakfast before prayers you sat down with your knees hunched, surrounded by your messmates, you were safe but your gifts would fall into the morning waves. It was a moment of comradeship and the exchange of pleasant vulgarity. The platform (known as the Bosun's Roost) had space for twenty backsides, and each mess was allowed five minutes before Marshal Smolkin standing in good humour at the bow rail would call out "Cockerels! Show me your eggs!" After breakfast was the appointed time, but nature could not be totally regulated. At Lingmouth regattas when the mayor's party with its ladies had been invited to dinner on *Tigress*, the ferrying boat would be directed to the stern because if it passed under the bows the visitors might receive an unwelcome welcome. The Bosun's Roost was a work of considerable carpentry and Toby Tenchbury had been proud of it, and the Sultan, who knew the importance of comradeship at sea, had encouraged Toby to do his best, even to rounding off the sharp edges of the timbers.

Now this pleasant morning ceremony was upset. The healthy cockerels could still lay their eggs but with the new bowel sickness there were accidents everywhere, uncontrollable. Men not wishing to foul their bedding tried to reach the scuppers or some corner where it would not matter. But everywhere mattered. From end to end *Tigress* became a stench of diarrhoea that all the scrubbings and sluicings could not dispel.

Dysentery was not so dramatically frightening as scurvy. There were no ulcers rotting your swollen body as you watched, no black sinews or the white hot flame of contraction. Instead there were abdominal pains piercing and irregular, the rectum awash with hot tar, the innards (*your* innards which you had never seen and always taken for granted) swilling about with a subterranean laxity that you could not understand or prevent.

Robert kept no daily survey this time. The course of dysentery was known in the hospitals. He had seen cases. Initially the bowel flux accompanied by headache and skin pallor, then a growing ulceration of the intestines with deep fatigue, then a chill and high fever leading to complete prostration and abdominal collapse. Death was common but not certain. The best treatment was rest and good water to replace the loss of body liquid. No raw vegetables, fresh fruits or alcohol. There was a puzzle here, because these were the very intakes that were supposed to discourage scurvy. Clowes had said that you could only treat one disease at a time and Robert tried to obey this advice and hoped that one would not lead to the other. New spaces were prepared for the dysentery patients with a diet of lightly boiled lentil or maize and as much of the crystal spring water from Santa Antao as could be spared.

Above all it was the smell. Sluicing parties with buckets of salt water moved constantly through the sick-rooms, but the smell filled the bowels of *Tigress* as the bowels of her mariners, and even the upper decks, scrubbed though they were, reeked like a sewer. Many were caught running to reach the Bosun's Roost. Later they lay on their bedding in the sick-rooms too weak from fever and flux to move. Gostigo improvised canvas bedpans. Buckets of salt water stood along the scuppers. But there was no answer to the irresistible ignominy. No one blamed the sufferers but no one could tolerate their smell. Those who died did their own nostrils a favour. Marshal Smolkin conducted the healthy cockerels at their morning roost, but he forbade the early dysentery cases because they stained the woodwork. Who wanted liquid eggs?

The mizzenmast rigging started below the quarterdeck and you could reach it from the rail. That was how Tom went up one moonlit night. You could not perch on the lateen yard-arm because it was on the slant, but Tom did not want to perch. He was no mariner. He had not been aloft since that first evening and now he did not fancy going up alone, to the fighting top for instance with that outward spidery cone. At the beginning you had to prove things. The Sultan and Krauss had to see what you could do. It was different now. There was no more trial and speculation, there was too much death. All Tom wanted was to raise himself a yard or two above *Tigress*, away from the heat, the bodies, the jostle, the smell of other people's bowels, and in the great cabin the complaints of Gostigo and the groaning and belching of Fernie the purser.

Fernie was sick with the flux, not badly sick so far but very sorry for himself. There was no reason to put him on bedding in a sick-room when he had his bunk in the cabin, so he stayed with his fellow officers and was a test of patience. Fernie with plenty of wine, salt beef, biscuit with or without maggot, was a cheerful, carnal companion who made you feel that the only sensible aim in life was pleasure, and if there were no women around there was always food and wine and a song. Fernie on a diet of maize and water, with gripe in his entrails, was a sack of misery. Fernie in health was a fair-haired sensualist with the sparkle of life in his blue eyes. Fernie in sickness was a groaning windbag with pallid dank hair and an awful smell.

Tom climbed twenty feet into the moonlight on the sagging ratlines. Then he threaded his arms past the shrouds and clasped his hands. He was safe, not elegant or seamanlike, but safe. He would not fall off. He was for'ard of the lateen sail and below him on the half-deck he could see the sleepers jammed like dominoes on a wooden tray, and beyond them the luminous concave mainsail, and overhead the circle of the smiling moon that filled the endless nothingness with a haze so bright that no star could be seen. *Tigress* rocked slowly from side to side on the swell, the flag on her mainmast a black, silhouetted bird flapping to and fro across the moon. Sixteen men had died since the dysentery began and another twelve from scurvy. The scurvy seemed to be tailing off, from the citrus physic perhaps, or because most of those destined to die had already done so. Forty-three from scurvy and sixteen from dysentery made a total of fifty-nine mariners who would never get their gold.

Only twenty feet up, but what stillness, what clean air, and the murmur of voices from the drowsy dominoes but no words distinct. In the soft moonlight he listened to the gentle creaking of the yards and stays and the inward thumps and thuds of *Tigress* on her way west. He thought of Santa Antao, so far astern, and the fresh fruits that were going to prevent the scurvy, and the big open vat of shrimps and sprats that had been lashed to the foremast. The cooks had been told they could have the sprats for their stews but the shrimps must be left to be eaten live by passing mariners. The Sultan had eaten live shrimps on *Black Vulture*. The ship's company enjoyed the shrimps, some pulling off the heads and tails and others crunching them whole. Nils and Henrik, the massive friends of the Carver, went further, plucking out the sprats as well from the seething vat. They held the sprat by its tail and you could tell Nils from Henrik because Nils bit off the head and spat it into the scuppers before eating the rest, while Henrik ate the head also. Both threw away the tail and neither had contracted scurvy or dysentery. Newcroft the cook told Robert Seaton about the fish-eating Norwegians, but they were not quoted as an example for others and the vat was emptied within a week.

Tom, suspended in the moonlight, thought about these things. He thought of Paxcombe, but it was like recalling a dream clearly remembered but hard to believe. He could see the stone lion and the belfry tower and his mother arranging the autumn flowers and his father riding back from the farms. It was unfair that he could picture them. They surely could not picture him. And there was Alis Dewmark at the dockside in her purple dress. "That ship will not sail in jest." But Alis even with her ivory face and slim fingers seemed less real than his parents. He could not picture what she was doing now and he preferred not to imagine. One day he would see her again. And then!

He felt the shrouds move. He looked up. A dark shape was coming down from above and when it came alongside it was Gideon Jabbinoth. The shrouds were narrow here but there was room for two.

Since the bow practices had stopped they had not met as regularly as in the early days. Tom had been busy with the sick, but now and then he had seen the long bony figure aloft. Now alone in the night it was like meeting an old friend.

"I thought you would come," said Jabbinoth.

"It's hot down there," said Tom.

"The mainyard is better. There's a crowd tonight."

"This is good enough."

Jabbinoth smiled broadly. His eyes were dark blots on the pale moonlit face. He stood casually, his left hand holding the ratline by his chest. He lifted his right hand and showed the little finger with no top joint. A gesture of pride?

"It's well healed," said Tom.

"Mr Krauss said next time it would be my hand."

"I know. I was there."

"He had to say that because of the others. But he gave me a new knife."

"Of course!"

Jabbinoth nodded. He seemed about to speak, then frowned and was silent. After a while he asked, "How far is it?"

"I don't know. We are more than half way."

"How many days?"

"Do not think of the days," said Tom. "Think of the gold."

From below came the sound of Robert's flute. No one was singing and the flute notes rose like a crystal fountain. Jabbinoth said, "I think of the mules with gold on their backs. Have you ever seen a mule?"

"No, never."

"I saw mules in Madeira. They are like dirty ponies with long ears. Not like horses. But I could drive a mule, I expect."

"And shoot a bow. You're going to be very useful."

"When I get the gold—" he paused.

"What will you do with it? Have you a wife?"

129

Jabbinoth shook his head.

"Don't you want one?"

"Not me. I don't like girls."

They spoke very quietly and the words were like thistledown in the night.

"Then what will you buy with your gold?"

"Two horses," said Jabbinoth. "Big dappled horses."

Robert with his flute had been playing a lively reel. Now he played "Killala Bay", and Jabbinoth went on down the rigging, and Tom stayed in the moonlight listening to Fernie's song without Fernie's voice.

CHAPTER FIFTEEN

Three days later at noon, when the sunsights had been taken on the poopdeck and Tom was waiting to follow the Sultan and Krauss down to the Sultan's cabin, there was a sudden strangeness as if *Tigress* had sailed into an oven. Since Santa Antao it had always been hot on the upper decks, the sun roasting forearms and the tar-lined wood blistering any naked feet, but this was different. Suddenly the sun was closer and the air sluggish with no salt. For a moment the three men stood still with surprise. The sea itself, just now a deep blue fizzing with tiny white horses, was matt and lustreless. The Sultan looked aloft and pointed at the sails. They had lost their ballooning bellies and drooped from the yard-arms barely fluttering. *Tigress* moved slowly forward on her own impetus, but it would not be for long. When she stopped she would be at a standstill under the burning sky with death in her bowels.

There was no wind.

They went down to the cabin where the charts were spread on the desk. Krauss said, "How far are we from Martinique?" and the Sultan said, "I don't know. Two days, perhaps six."

It was as he had explained to Tom. Travelling north or south you could measure a day's journey by the change in latitude. Going east or west on a certain latitude to reach a certain destination you could only work on time and distance. How far had you gone in one hour? The sand-glass would give you the time, but the distance could only be reckoned from the logline, a primitive apparatus for such a momentous task.

A line of woven cotton little thicker than a curtain cord was spooled round a reel that could be held between outstretched hands. At the free end of the line was attached a triangular board of wood called the log. When the log was hurled from the stern of a ship and hit the water it stayed where it was, bobbing about like a buoy while the reel unwound and the line flew over the stern rail. The log was given time to settle. Then a piece of red bunting tied round the line slipped over the stern rail, and at that moment the thirty-second sand-glass was upturned.

After the red bunting each fifty-foot length of line was marked by a knot. Fifty feet in thirty seconds meant a hundred feet in a minute. In one hour you would travel six thousand feet. One sea mile. Two hundred feet in thirty seconds would mean four sea miles an hour, with appropriate adjustments for fractions of knotted line and heights of sand in the waisted glass.

These dubious calculations were used on the traverse board, a circular plot marked with the compass points, where your ship was always at the centre and your progress was registered by sticking pegs into holes in the plot to show your bearing in a given half-hour, always supposing that the ship's compass was working properly, that the wind had not varied, that the helmsman had kept the rudder on the bearing he had been ordered, that the log had not been pushed about by a dolphin or swayed by a tide.

Periods of half an hour on a given course at a rate suggested by the logline would be plotted as distance on the chart. The distance covered in twenty-four hours was a matter of multiplication and judgement. An experienced master was not for ever throwing the log over the stern. He judged variations of speed from the bow wave, from the wind on his cheek, from the aspect of the ocean, most of all from the countless memory traces, inaccessible but potent, of his life at sea.

When Joshua Vine said, "Two days, perhaps six", he was being truthfully vague. In a journey of two thousand miles no one could predict the day of arrival. There was no need for Joshua to pretend, least of all to Krauss.

Tom had learned a little in theory about the logline, the sand-glass and the traverse board, but on that ovenlike morning in the Sultan's cabin he understood the figures translated into fact. *Tigress* had come to a halt in a stifling flat ocean. The horizon was blurred with haze. Men were dying of scurvy and

131

dysentery. No other ship, friend or foe, could approach because there was no wind.

The next two days seemed unreal, as if *Tigress* had entered some Stygian half-world where the living, hardly able to move or speak in the airless catacomb, were beckoned by the dead. The carpenters made canvas fans and on the gun deck, with all ports open, the men with strength formed relays of sweating fanners, but there was no coolness, only a slow flux of hot air. Down on the orlop it was worse, the sick lying helpless in the churning density of diarrhoetic vapour. Cooking was cut to a minimum because the cooks were fainting beside their fires, but no one had much appetite. At the mess tables between the guns cockroaches feasted on food pushed aside. No one had the interest or energy to crush them. In the great cabin meals were still served but, with Fernie on his bunk tended by Gostigo, Krauss often up with the Sultan, Robert and Tom tired after their rounds fancying little except some lentil or dumpling hash, only the calm Viccars ate his dinner without comment. It was too hot to speak, too hot to think, too hot to worry. The one item everyone wanted was water, and here the toll of death had brought a grim benefit, since the ration from the Santa Antao barrels could now be increased. Tepid water no longer fresh, but precious, swilled in the mouth, gargled in the throat, grudgingly allowed to seep down into the stomach. On deck there was no breeze, not the smallest puff to move the sails. *Tigress* lay immobile under the sun. There was nothing to do but wait. And how long could she wait? Till she became a hundred feet of lifeless timber?

On the third night came an unexpected and repulsive climax.

Since the onset of scurvy and dysentery the rat-hunting parties had become less frequent. Each morning the food and drink were fetched up in baskets and flagons. Some days after leaving Santa Antao it had been noticed that there seemed to be fewer rats scurrying among the barrels. On several evenings when men waited with their cudgels there were no customers for the meat lashed to the deckplate. One explanation was that the rats had all been killed, but this was unlikely. More probably they had gnawed their way into some food barrel, but if so it must be hidden deep behind the others. There was no trace on the ballast plates, and to shift the whole phalanx was

132

reckoned a waste of time when there was so much else to do, sick-rooms to be cleaned, sufferers to be treated, watches to be reorganized. As long as the rats did not appear let them solve their own problems.

On this third Stygian night Marshal Smolkin came to the great cabin to report the smell from the hold. Supper was over. Krauss and Viccars were on deck. Fernie was groaning in a feverish sleep. Gostigo was sitting beside him with a flask of water and a wet cloth. Tom and Robert were at the table with a bottle of wine. Gostigo said what was Smolkin doing to mention a smell when the whole ship was nothing but smell, and Smolkin said that this was not like the smell of the sick-rooms, it was a special smell, and everyone on the orlop was complaining.

Gostigo stayed with Fernie, and Tom and Robert went down to the orlop. From the dark hole of the afterhatch came a pungent animal stench of foul flesh. Six of Smolkin's seamen were standing back from the hole. They carried lanterns. Smolkin led the way down. Robert asked where Sirius was and Smolkin said he had left him topsides because if they found poisonous flesh he did not want the dog to touch it. And Smolkin was right.

The stench came from behind the barrels in the stern. These were meat barrels still in place since Lingmouth. They were stacked horizontally, each one resting on the two beneath. Some barrels had gone from the top, but the wall was still six barrels high and four barrels deep and they had to shift over fifty barrels to reach the beef barrel with the broken end. It lay at the bottom of the pile, and round the barrel and inside the opening among a mess of rotting meat and in the crevices under adjacent barrels lay the corpses of rats, at first trodden on before they were noticed, and then in the dim lantern flicker seen to be big rats and some smaller and some very small, not always whole rats but some with their innards chewed out, and here and there the head of a very small rat or a tail in the dust.

No sign of anything alive except, when a foot turned over a bulbous corpse, the squirming of maggots in the open belly.

Two seamen fetched a sack and shovels from the cookroom. The beef barrel was dragged clear. Then in the heat-dizzy gloom the refuse was scooped into the sack. The outline of the story was clear. The first new families from *Tigress* pregnancies

133

had begun to appear some time after Santa Antao. With many new mouths to feed there must have been consternation among rat parents. The cudgel parties with Sirius and the guards on the hatch ladders made it hard for bread-winners to reach the mess tables or cookroom. When the barrel came open, either torn by desperate mothers or because it had been badly coopered, there was respite. Here was a common larder for weeks ahead. But something went wrong. Perhaps the meat was already bad, perhaps it putrefied in the rising temperature of the hold. But why had parents turned on children? Cannibalism was the first instinct of a rat without food, but some of the children were well grown. So perhaps the beef came first, then the families, then the deadly fermentation. And in the end when *Tigress* slid to a halt the ovenlike prison, far hotter than the orlop, had finished off what hunger and cannibalism and bad meat had begun. The last surviving rats, those not poisoned or devoured, were baked to death.

It was impossible to make a total clearance. Each barrel that was moved revealed hideous pieces of rat. But the centre of the stench was the half-empty barrel, and this was hoisted up through the orlop and gun deck on to the waist, and with it the sackful of rat remains, and all tipped overboard. When the barrels in the hold were restacked there was still a smell but nothing to complain of. After two hours in the hold the upper deck seemed almost cool, and Tom and Robert thanked Smolkin for his work party, and went down to the great cabin to get some wine and sleep.

They had the wine but not the sleep, because Fernie was dying.

When they came in Gostigo got up from the stool and turned to Robert with a wild look on his face, blinking as if he wanted to cry but had no moisture left behind his eyes. He waved his hand towards the figure on the bunk, and Robert sat on the stool and felt Fernie's forehead and pulse, but there was no need to look for symptoms. There was death in the cabin and everyone knew it. Perhaps Fernie knew it too, but he said nothing. He lay in feverish sleep. His eyes were shut. For moments he would lie still, then his breath began rasping in his throat and his arms flailed from side to side, the fingers opening and shutting as if to catch something they had lost.

Some men recovered from the dysentery fever, but Fernie

134

was not going to recover. Viccars came in, and later Krauss. No one tried to sleep. They sat on their bunks or passing wine at the table and kept an unspoken vigil for Fernie. Only Gostigo did not sit down, but wandered about or stood at the bunk asking Robert what was to be done. Robert let him fetch sponging cloths or hold Fernie's head while they tried to give him water, but these were only gestures of respect before the departure.

As the night went on the cabin seemed to get hotter. Little was said they waited. Tom told Krauss about the rats but Krauss showed no surprise, grunting impatiently, as if this was a common experience at sea. At intervals Krauss or Viccars would go on deck to check the lookouts, but no officer stood the watch that night, for there were no sail or helm orders to be given on a motionless ship which none other could approach. Through the small hours they waited and as the first moment of dawn fluttered at the open porthole Fernie's breathing grew faster, more in spasms and Robert got up and whispered to Krauss, and Krauss left the cabin and came back with the Sultan.

Now the light was coming fast up the sky. When the sun flooded into the cabin the overhead lamp lost its authority, and Tom reached up to put the lamp out and there was a smell of tallow.

Gostigo was wiping Fernie's cheek with the damp cloth, and at that moment Fernie died. For an hour he had been restless with the breath sounding in his throat, and suddenly there was a violent splutter and the sound stopped and he lay still. Gostigo snatched away the cloth and stood back as if he could not believe what Fernie had done. Robert bent to look at the eyes and feel the heart, and the Sultan said, "He is dead," and Robert said, "Yes."

"No!" cried Gostigo. He was sitting at the table, and now he beat his fist on the wood and shook his head madly like a dog shaking a rat, and cried again, "No! No! *No!*"

"Mr Gostigo!" The Sultan put a hand on his shoulder. "That is no way to say farewell to your friend."

Gostigo shuddered and calmed himself. Then he said quietly, "More than my friend. He was to be my brother."

"Your brother? How so?"

"I was to marry his sister. When we returned."

"And so you shall," said the Sultan.

135

"When I tell her!"

"You have no blame."

"Except that I persuaded him. It was I that brought him to this hell ship."

The Sultan was not pleased. There was more than displeasure in his amber eyes as he turned away from Gostigo and said to Krauss, "The burial at morning prayers." As he passed the porthole he shaded his eyes with his hand and said, "There is cloud. The wind will not be long."

He walked towards the door in silence. Tom, looking at Gostigo's sunken brooding face, wondered what charms Fernie's sister had found in this explosive man. And what a night to hear Gostigo's secret. You learned your brother officers' behaviour but not their secrets.

As the Sultan was at the open door Gostigo leaped up like a spring uncoiling and yelled, "We must go back! To our homes! Before it is too late!"

"Go *back*?" The Sultan froze.

"While we can!"

"For your sake, Mr Gostigo?"

"For the sake of the dead! Before we join them, all of us!"

"That is enough!"

It was an icy command, but Gostigo only shouted, "The mariners are at the end of their strength. They have no heart to go on. They do not believe any more in your dreams and promises. They want to live, not to die."

For a frightening moment the Sultan stood like a statue. Then he pointed his finger at the bosun and said slowly and with a tremor in his voice that Tom had never heard, "If the day should ever come when the mariners do not trust me, I will hear it from them. Not from you."

He closed the door behind him and the *Tigress* prepared for another day.

At morning prayer there was still no wind. The sun beat fiercely from a cobalt sky, but far to the east hung the ribbon of woolly flecks that the Sultan had seen.

Fernie in his weighted shroud was slipped into the sea, and after him a carpenter who had died of scurvy. "So teach us to number our days . . ." Better two deaths than one. To see a single white parcel falling and hear the plop and watch the waters close always brought a stab of pity. Two parcels together even in those vast depths would keep each other company.

Before the seamen disappeared the Sultan addressed them: "There will be wind before nightfall. The next land we sight will be Martinique. We shall then be in the Caribbean, where with God's will we shall sail directly to our destination on the isthmus of Panama."

It happened as the Sultan said.

The wind reached *Tigress* before supper and when the sails began to writhe there was cheering along the decks and in the sick-rooms below there was hope. The dysentery and scurvy did not immediately cease because the Sultan had spoken of destination, but there was a renewal of belief which saved many who might have died. For three days *Tigress* had been becalmed in an inferno of heat climaxing in the night of the rats and the death of Fernie and the carpenter. Now that climax was past and in men's minds was the thought, however vague, of land and rest and healing food.

Martinique appeared two days later as a smudge to the south at sunset.

From then on the wind strengthened, as if the gods who had punished the Dakyns of Paxcombe for being too complacent were now favouring the mariners of *Tigress* because they had suffered enough.

In the three weeks between Martinique and Elizabeth Bay only eighteen more men died: scurvy five, dysentery thirteen. A total now of seventy-nine. Of the two hundred and fifteen souls who had sailed from Lingmouth there were one hundred and thirty-six when *Tigress* slid down the latitudes till the Rock of Sharks was sighted. The decks were crowded on the day when Joshua Vine edged his ship, with shortened sail and the soundings called every minute, through the reefs and shoals so accurately recorded on the chart of the Admiral Robyns. The sun was low when *Tigress* crept through the narrow opening in the claw of wooded land higher than her mainmast into the haven where she came to anchor in twelve fathoms of lucid water.

The skiff was lowered and two seamen rowed the Sultan and Krauss and Tom Dakyn towards the shore. There was no *Tigress* smell, only the sweet air tanged with salt. The Sultan and Krauss sat in the stern with a sack of gifts between them. Tom stood in the bows holding up a boathook that bore a grommet of white-painted rope, the colour of peace.

On the beach three hundred yards away stood perhaps fifty brown-skinned men. They were waving clusters of white flowers.

The beach was a ribbon of clean sand, and behind it towered a precipitous shelving wall of deep green forest. Tom looked astern, then ahead. The *Tigress* was growing smaller and the arc of forest was growing wider and higher and altogether more immense moment by moment, till it hung over them threatful and silent, a monstrous curtain to an unimaginable journey.

PART THREE

The Gold

CHAPTER SIXTEEN

As the skiff from *Tigress* drew close on a low tide the Cunas threw their garlands into the water and Tom tossed the white grommet among the flowers. Some Cunas held short spears, but these they now put behind their backs, beckoning with their free hand, smiling and wobbling their heads like children. They were naked except for a deerskin apron reaching half-way to their knees. When they turned away their buttocks were bare. They waded into the water and when the skiff grounded they dragged it up the beach till the visitors could step on to dry sand.

The two seamen were left with the skiff. The others were led by the Cunas across the sand to the hem of the forest, a belt of thorn bushes and low shrubs blazing in the sunlight with scarlet and purple flowers. Here a long mat had been laid. At one end sat four Cuna leaders and at the other sat a man of middle age with a fine head poised on a straight back, naked except for the deerskin apron, his legs crossed with a suppleness not possible to Europeans. His ebony black beard was trimmed short, his jowls shaved, his ebony hair twisted into a single plait drawn up over the crown of his head. From each earlobe hung five slim spillikins of copper that matched his cheeks. Round his temples he wore a narrow fillet of burnished copper clustered with threaded pearls. His thick lips were confident. His wide-set brown eyes were calm. They appeared never to have witnessed in other men's eyes anything but obedience. The Cunas who had met the skiff stood in a semicircle twenty feet from their chief.

He motioned his guests to sit beside him. To Tom Dakyn squatting with aching knees he looked, apart from the lips and hair style, remarkably like a walnut-stained Joshua Vine.

As soon as they were seated he pointed to the *Tigress* out on the blue water and said, "Robyn? Amral?"

139

"Admiral Robyns . . . dead!" said Joshua. He pillowed his cheek on his hands, then stabbed a finger into the sand.

"Ahh!" The brown man shook his clenched fist sadly. "You! Friend?"

"Big friend!"

"Me! Friend!" But he still looked puzzled.

Joshua took from his belt pocket the folded approach chart from the Robyns ruttier, opened it out, indicated with gestures towards *Tigress* and himself, with finger-tracing on the chart, with solemn repetition of the name Robyns, that everything had been done in peace, that the new visitors were as friendly as the old.

The brown man understood. He made smiling signs of welcome, tapping first his own forehead, then reaching out to tap the foreheads of Joshua, Krauss and Tom, then patting his own chest and afterwards theirs. Then a roly-poly of the hands to show that they were all friends.

"Me chief. Chucunaquiok," he said. "Robyn say—Jelman Jack."

"Chucunaquiok," said Joshua firmly. "Me Admiral Vine. Here Admiral Krauss. Here—" he dug Tom's arm—"my son Tom."

The chief was pleased. He glanced at Krauss's revolting left eye and made dagger motions and asked, "Battle?"

"For me!" Joshua shadow-boxed how Krauss had protected him.

The chief shook Krauss by the hand, then pointed with query from Joshua's hair to Tom's, and Joshua said, "Mother red—him red," and Chucunaquiok nodded graciously and observed, "Me black—daughter black."

Now he leaned forward and prodded the sack of gifts and Krauss held the sack open and Joshua reached inside and brought out a hunting knife in a leather sheath which he presented with a little salute. Chucunaquiok was delighted. He tested the blade with his thumb and held up the knife for the men at the end of the mat to see. They nodded admiringly, exchanging a gabble of whispers. It was clear that no one must speak loudly in the presence of Chucunaquiok. When he lifted the knife for the semicircle behind him to see they wagged their heads and flapped their hands in absolute silence, and by now the chief was looking for his next present. This was a small

140

hatchet engraved with the Scorpion of Istanbul, followed by a bottle of French claret, a stonemason's hammer and tool from Lingmouth, a belt of filigree silver, a brass lobster, and other reminiscences of Joshua Vine's life and travels.

Each gift was welcomed with pleasure quickly evaporating into expectation. Of all the things he saw what pleased the chief most was a bright tin dish designed for sweetmeats at an English dinner table. The dish had handles at both ends. Joshua began the difficult task of explaining in simple monosyllables what the dish was for but Chucunaquiok, not listening, waved the words aside and put his finger through the handle and held the dish against his chest, making signs that he would hang the dish round his neck as a protection against arrows or daggers.

When he stretched out his hands once more Joshua produced two ornamented tortoiseshell combs which he put down on the mat saying "Wife! Wife!" Then a bunch of ivory bracelets and strings of coloured beads—"Wife! Daughter!" Chucunaquiok smiled, but with less interest, and when a brass stewpan appeared ("Servant! Cook!") he nodded politely, got to his feet and clapped his hands. The men standing leaped forward. He gave orders in a quiet clear voice. The gifts were put back in the sack. The men from the mat were beckoned and introduced— "Me chief. Here big Cuna." They tapped their foreheads and beat their breasts with both hands. The Englishmen did the same. Then the procession formed up. A vanguard with the sack-bearers, Chucunaquiok with Joshua Vine, behind them two Cunas carrying long fly whisks with bamboo handles, Krauss and Tom similarly protected, then the four leaders from the mat, and the rest of the Cunas darting up and down on the beam like ceremonial scouts.

So they proceeded out of the sunshine of the beach, through a gap in the flowery bushes, along fifty paces of narrow pathway between thorny scrub zinging with insects, and then, where the ground rose sharply, into the dim cathedral of the forest.

As a child Tom had heard stories of the tropical rain forests, but he was unprepared for the sudden army of tree trunks reaching a hundred feet above his head, for the total canopy of high foliage except for ragged holes where some monster tree had been struck by lightning, for the orchestra of insect and bird sounds, for such abundance of growth. At first there was light from behind, but soon only a green dimness with small torn

141

patches of sky here and there in the roof. He tried to notice what he saw but there was so much so quickly. Thick fibrous cables twined round the trees festooning themselves from bough to bough, from trunk to trunk, high and low, moss-covered, looped in endless chains vanishing into darkness, and where the cables reached the vaulted ceiling they fell dangling almost to the ground where they hung with split ends like the jaws of snakes trying desperately to lick the soil. On the leafless branches long queues of shapes like cabbages made of rotting mushroom, and grotesque ferns, and orchids everywhere. Bright butterflies as big as his hand. Birds mostly too high to see, flashes of colour screaming in the treetops. Insects round his face, his neck and nostrils bitten, the zinging in his ears, the fly whisk brushing his head. Beside the path an anthill as tall as a four-poster bed seething with black bodies as big as wasps.

And above all the smell of decay. Lichens and fungi smothering the corpses of trees that had once reached the sunlight but now lay barkless and crumbling with the infestation of parasites. Mounds of mouldy leaves steaming like a compost heap. A patch of green slime with a frog's head appearing from the stagnant pond beneath.

For weeks Tom had seen nothing but sky and sea and *Tigress*, so familiar, had smelt nothing but rotten flesh. Now what he saw was too extravagant to comprehend, yet the plant stench of the forest was not unlike the body stench of *Tigress*, except that no new mariners sprang from the corpses of scurvy, while here every tree that fell decomposed into life for another.

Such was Tom's first acquaintance with the forest. He walked beside Krauss up the steep path and Krauss, slapping his neck and cheeks against the insects, was not talkative. Tom asked whether this was the part of the isthmus that Krauss knew, and Krauss said, "No, further west," and they walked on in silence, the forest crowding round them as if it would never end, till suddenly there was daylight ahead and they came to where the gradient flattened out and the forest had been cleared into a circle three hundred yards in diameter. There were cedar-wood thatched huts and a central compound of larger huts enclosed with a mud wall. There were no women in sight, only Cuna men seen from a distance who disappeared into huts as the procession approached.

This was the village called Macaweo because of the macaw

142

trees bearing nuts with scented oil and because of the long-tailed parrot-like birds that lived in them.

The chief's hut was the biggest in the compound, a long low building of red cedar with an upper storey. A doorway led into the main room, and the doorway and the four windows were hung with loose rush curtains soaked in some acrid insect-repelling substance. A ladder near the wall went up through a hole in the ceiling. The floor was hard trodden earth swept clean and sprinkled with a sweet-smelling essence of flowers. There were coloured floor mats and a line of low stools and in the centre a large low round table of polished cedar. The room had an air of importance and hospitality.

At the doorway Chucunaquiok dismissed his retinue and took his visitors inside. They sat on the stools, and he called out, and a woman came in from the adjacent room. He presented her as "Wife!" and she gave a shy smile and put her fingers to her forehead. She wore a short skirt and a bolero of deerskin covering her breasts. Round her ebony hair rested a broad bandeau of white coral. Her hair bunched on both sides fell to her hips, from each ear there hung three small bracelets of pearls, and five pearl necklaces reached her waist. When the guests were introduced by name she bowed and at a sign from her husband called back to the room she had come from, and three servant girls brought bowls of water and cloths and a jug. The girls wore only skirts and their brown dark-nippled breasts looked firm and young. They set down the bowls without raising their eyes and glided out with a smooth animal grace, treading the earth with their bare feet. Then the wife knelt in front of Joshua Vine and unlaced his shoes and drew off his stockings and lifted his feet into the water. Nothing was said. This was a traveller's welcome which Vine understood. He watched gravely as she poured the jug of oil into the water and washed his feet and calves up to where the breeches ended. There was nothing menial in her action. She was still the chief's wife, kneeling before her guest with great dignity. When she had dried his skin with the cloth she stood up, and Joshua put on his stockings and shoes.

Krauss was next, but as she poured the oil into his bowl Chucunaquiok rose and beckoned Joshua and at that moment another girl came in. Chucunaquiok announced, "Daughter!" and when he had made introductions once more he led Joshua out into the compound, and the wife knelt before Krauss and the daughter knelt before Tom.

He sat very still while she reached for the jug and poured the oil, mixing it into the water with a leisurely paddle of her brown hand. No haste, just ceremony without guile. She wore a coral bandeau like her mother, and the bracelets in her ears, but no necklace and no bolero. She was more than a child and not quite a woman. About sixteen, he thought. Her lips were full and innocent. She did not raise her head or look at him but he could see the brown satin of her unlined cheeks and the lashes of her wide-set eyes. She took off his shoes and pulled down the stockings. One was held in the breeches and when he released it their fingers touched and he put his hands on his lap and felt them tremble. Then unhurriedly the soles of his feet and his ankles and the muscles in his calves were stroked by the soft brown oily fingers massaging the dust away. Her breasts were like ripe passion fruit and if he had stretched out his hand he could have touched the dark big-circled nipples. He sat as still as he could.

Next morning at prayers on the *Tigress* half deck Tom thought about the welcome in Chucunaquiok's home. Cool fruit drinks in earthenware jars, and when the chief returned with Joshua Vine the sack emptied and the mother and daughter receiving their combs and beads and utensils with smiling shyness, and a meal of stewed venison served on wooden platters at the round table. When it was time to go Chucunaquiok did not come with them but sent guides and Cunas with the fly whisks. On the way down the forest path Joshua said how he had seen round the village, met three more daughters with husbands and six sons with wives. He had arranged with the chief that the crew of the *Tigress* could use Macaweo as a rest camp and the sick be looked after. The operation in the isthmus had not been mentioned. That would come later when trust had been established.

"I admire these Cunas," said Joshua.

"They are simple people," said Krauss.

"We must not betray them. Or offend them," he added.

"Will you warn the men?"

"Assuredly. We know what mariners are like, especially when they are far from home."

"Even when their hearts are bursting for gold?"

"They have been at sea. It is not their hearts that frighten me."

Tom thought of these words as he stood behind the Sultan on the half deck. When prayers were finished the Sultan told the ship's company about Macaweo and their good fortune in having a place to rest and regain their strength. Huts were being prepared. The first batch from *Tigress* would be sent ashore in two days' time.

"A warning before you go. Pay attention," he said. "No man shall force a native woman, on pain of instant death."

CHAPTER SEVENTEEN

From the village nestling on the north slope of the forest you could hear the midnight thunder beyond the mountain ridge. It was not a high mountain, less than two thousand feet, but the north slope was steep and the thunder sounded as if someone was trying to knock the world to pieces with booming blows, muffled yet awesome. Now and then the darkness was ripped by lightning. Macaweo lay at the bottom of a deep barrel of trees and from the hut window you could look up and see the flashes high above in the opening of the barrel. At first it was just the jagged instant of light, then a count of seven, then the boom. The seven count became five, and now there was wind in the trees, a rustling that changed to a sudden burst of crackles and wood-groans as the wind rose, and when the storm came over the ridge it was as if the curtain had parted on a war pageant of the gods of night. The lightning stabbed your eyes and with hardly a pause the thunderclap hit your ears like a cannon blast ricocheting through the tree trunks. The wind was a gigantic owl that hooted in the blackness of tearing foliage and splintering wood. Then as the lightning and thunder moved seaward came the rain, at first rattling like a downpour in England but soon increasing to a deafening roll of kettledrums as the massed millions of water rods smashed on to the surrounding forest and deluged the village in the barrel.

It rained for five hours, then stopped as suddenly as it had begun. Through the hut window came the gurgle of water in the deep-cut village drains and from the forest an eerie multi-throated chorus of croaking frogs.

It was Tom's first night ashore. He and Robert Seaton were Chucunaquiok's guests and at dawn they stepped outside the hut half expecting to find the village washed away. The ground was damp and the drains were swirling with muddy water, but the huts were still there, so was the mud wall reinforced with strong stakes that poked up to form a barricade along the top. By isthmus standards it had been a small friendly storm. No trees had fallen from the sides of the barrel. The treetops were motionless and the morning light grew in the circle of sky. The frogs were still croaking their lungs out and in the air hung a smell of sulphur.

"Krauss told me it would smell after the rain," said Robert. He sounded excited, a true Scot, always greedy for knowledge. "There's a natural sulphur in the earth, and the rains bring it out. The mountain paths are like bogs for days after."

"Could we bring the mules—"

"Never! But the mules will not leave Panama till the rains are finished."

"When is that?"

"He says it varies. Not later than January."

"So we have time to prepare."

"Yes," nodded Robert. "Because Krauss has been here before, and because long ago when they were planning it all the Sultan listened to Krauss. The Sultan listens to everything. He attends to everything, plans everything. I have never met such a man."

Nor had Tom.

Tigress had anchored in the bay. There had been the first meeting with Chucunaquiok. Next morning the Sultan had given his warning about the Cuna women, but this was soon forgotten in the excitement of that first glorious day.

The tide had risen but you could still see the sand and seashells in the crystal water. Long canoes brought out meat, fresh fruit and vegetables. Lookouts were posted on the sea cliff. The sick, three dozen, were brought on to the upper decks. Robert Seaton supervised in the cookroom. A light-boiled hash of plantain and beans for the dysentery cases, and for the scurvy sufferers (the early victims were dead and this was a new outbreak since Martinique) pineapple and big black cherries and fruit the size of oranges but with the life-saving citrus pulp of the lemon. The sick-rooms on the gun deck and orlop were scrubbed out. The hold, a day's work in itself, was left till tomorrow. In the afternoon the two boats were sent to fish in the bay, returning crammed with tarpon and cavally. Swimmers (a minority of the seamen) were allowed to swim ashore but not to take the forest path alone. They came aboard like children, insect-bitten, cheerful, carrying shells and sea-weed and telling each other what it was like to tread on sand again. *Tigress* that day was like a fortress when armistice is declared after a long siege. The alacrity, the smiles, the obedience! The Sultan had promised to bring them to the land of gold!

They were here!

How far was the gold? When would they get it? Soon?

The Sultan allowed them their day of rejoicing. Then he brought them back to reality, explaining the plan in outline to the seamen and some particulars to the officers.

To the assembled company he listed what must be done. The sick must be made healthy. They would be the first to go to Macaweo, together with the bowmen who would need all the practice they could get for the coming operation. Everyone would have their turn ashore, but it was the sick and the bowmen first. Let no man complain. *Tigress* had but one goal and when that was achieved each man would receive his fair share. *Tigress* herself needed cleansing and recuperation. Masts and yards to be scraped, decks to be oiled, standing rigging to be treated with tar and tallow, running rigging to be over-hauled. A new set of sails for the homeward journey when the winds would be stronger in higher latitudes. The hull to be cleared of weed and barnacles, especially the barnacles. No one wanted ill omens on the way back. Lastly there was the rain. The Sultan did not elaborate. He said, "There is a time to every purpose under heaven. Your time will be when the rains have finished. By God's grace that will be in the new year. Then we shall take our gold. Let every man prepare. Let no man think himself more important than another. We shall do what we came to do. Together!"

To the officers he read a curious passage from the ruttier of Claud Robyns. It was headed CUNAS—GOD—ENGLISHMEN—GUNS. To save space it had been jotted down with abbreviations, but the Sultan turned it into plain language.

The Cunas, it seemed, believed that God first made the earth with its fruits and flowers and animals. Then He made the sun and moon and stars, and to manipulate these wonders He created from nothing a family of sons who held up the sun every day, and at night the moon and stars sometimes and sometimes not. There were other sons of God who blew the wind and dragged the clouds and clapped the thunder and dropped the rain and lifted the waters up the beach. Lastly God made a woman and put her on earth. Then He visited her himself and so began humans.

These beliefs, noted Robyns, except for the distasteful notion of God mating with a woman (surely inferior to the inspired truth that woman had come from the rib of man), were not unlike the Book of Genesis. But the Cunas had stayed where they were in awareness of the world, while the English had developed. The Cunas could not write or read. Their medicine was primitive. They knew nothing of science. Simple objects like a magnet or a magnifying glass were beyond their understanding. When they saw iron filings cluster to a lodestone or a small beetle suddenly appear large under the glass they cried out and put their hands over their eyes, believing that such magic must be the work of gods. So the Englishmen were either gods themselves or at least their intimate friends.

But of all such objects the two which most amazed the Cunas were the Bible and the gun.

Here was a box, and inside it many white leaves covered with marks like the footprints of a mad spider. The Englishman said that the box contained the word of God. Why should he lie? But if it were true they wanted to know what God was saying. The Englishman said he could tell by looking at the crazy marks. So he could hear through his eyes. The Cunas could not. They begged to touch the box, to kiss it, to clasp it against their breast and place it on their head, to stroke it over their body so that they might absorb the word of God.

The gun too was magic. The Englishman pointed it at a tethered deer twenty paces away. There was a flash and a bang and the deer was dead. In its heart was a bullet which the Englishman said came from the gun. No one had seen the bullet pass, but there it was in the deer's heart.

Such miracles could only come from God through one of His sons. The Englishman said he was not a son of God, but the Cunas were not sure. They determined not to offend him or any of his followers who came in the big ship.

Such was the information in the ruttier of Claud Robyns. It did not explain how the admiral had acquired his ship and his crew or with what exact purpose he had edged his way through the shoals to Elizabeth Bay. The Sultan had never told his officers about the statements of Erasmus Chyne. He did not tell them now. The past was unimportant. What mattered was to make use of the ruttier in handling the Cunas. On his walk through the village with Chucunaquiok the Sultan had come to certain conclusions. These he outlined to the officers, summing up, "The Cunas believe that we have the power of gods. Let us give them no cause for doubt. Let us treat them well in all things.

"Chucunaquiok being son of the river holds himself as related to the gods. Nevertheless he cannot read and he has never possessed a firearm. So the Bible and the gun will be our weapons of persuasion.

"We need his help and his blessing. Without his guides we cannot take the mule train. Without his permission we cannot bring the mules and their gold back to Macaweo.

"Are we clear in our purpose?" He looked round the cabin. "Yes, Mr Gostigo?"

"If the chief is slow to grant what you ask," said Gostigo gloomily, "is it wise to threaten him?"

The Sultan smiled: "The gun will be a gift, not a threat."

It was the last day of November when *Tigress* reached Elizabeth Bay. Two nights later came the storm which Tom and Robert witnessed from the hut. The rains were coming to an end. There were other storms, but each less violent and with longer intervals. By mid January the dry season had arrived.

During these six weeks the Sultan prepared his men for the raid on the mule train. The sick made wonderful recovery in Macaweo. Good diet, rest, and fresh water from springs further up the mountain. Dysentery seemed to respond more quickly, perhaps because the visible symptoms were less dramatic. But it seemed almost a miracle, said Robert, taking notes as the scurvy victims (none beyond the second stage) were brought back to health, their swollen gums subsiding, the livid spots fading on their arms and thighs, their tendons freed of cramp.

Of Tom's fifty bowmen nine had died. The rest resumed the forenoon practice they had given up at Santa Antao. Targets were rigged at the edge of the forest with netting curtains and the padded arrow-tips, as it had been on *Tigress*. It was hard work at first. Their muscles were flabby. The Cunas watched with curiosity, shaking their heads at the netting practice but clapping when the steel arrowheads, their pads now removed, transfixed the swinging torsos. The Cuna arrows had hard-wood tips.

The men from *Tigress* were quartered in the outlying huts. Only the officers stayed with Chucunaquiok in the compound, a recognition of the hierarchy natural to the Cunas. The Sultan and the chief became inseparable. Chucunaquiok was invited aboard *Tigress* to dine alone with the Sultan. The magic box of God was shown and admired. They talked for hours. After two weeks of comradeship and mutual flattery Joshua Vine explained the purpose of his voyage. He put it in a way that Chucunaquiok would appreciate. The God-Queen in England was beset with enemies. She had commanded him, Joshua, to find her the gold to pay her armies. It was a regrettable fact that the daughter of God should need this base element. In that respect the English could learn from the Cunas. Her servants in ships had brought the news of the gold train from Panama.

At first the chief hesitated. He knew the Spaniards in Nombre were not good men. They had used the Cimarrones, the black slaves from the East, without scruple. Many Cimarrones had escaped and now roamed the forest. But the Spanish had never harmed the Cunas. Joshua was very careful. He praised the Cunas. They were good people living where God had put them in the ways He intended. God did not allow men to come in ships and build cities and make slaves. He would send a great fire to burn these wicked men. It was all in the sacred book. Joshua opened the Bible on his desk and showed Chucunaquiok the spider marks he could not read. Slave-owners would burn for a thousand years! The Bible said so!

Chucunaquiok was impressed. But he still hesitated. Joshua said no more. But the next day he brought to Macaweo the pistol "David" that Tom had carried in San Corda. Two Pecary hogs were tethered. From five paces Joshua fired one barrel.

One hog died. Chucunaquiok, his aim guided by Joshua, fired the other barrel. The second hog, to Joshua's relief, was dead. The miracle was watched in fearful silence by a hundred Cunas. Afterwards in private Joshua presented "David" to the chief. If he would give his help in the service of the English God-Queen, he would receive "David's" brother "Jonathan".

There was no more hesitation.

December was passing and there was much to arrange. There was a track beyond the ridge that led towards Panama, but it was not often used and would need clearing. A working party was brought from *Tigress*, leaving the village each morning with Krauss and Cuna guides. Chucunaquiok agreed to send two of his trusted leaders to find out when the next big mule train was planned. The bowmen would be supported by gunners with muskets for emergency. Provisions must be organized. There was rehearsal and practice in forest paths.

Through all these weeks the crew of *Tigress* came to Macaweo in turn. Many could read and write no more than the Cunas. There is no better behaved man ashore than a seaman when he wants to be. The mariners from *Tigress* had suffered enough trouble lately. They had escaped death, they were within strike of the treasure they dreamed of. They took an instant liking to the Cunas. There was sign language and the exchange of noun-noises. There was trust and laughter.

While the mariners grew healthy and were drilled for the coming action, the *Tigress* officers ashore pieced together a detailed picture of the Cuna people and how they lived, from the ruttier, events in the village, talks with Chucunaquiok. Robert Seaton, trained in the hospital to observe and record, was the official chronicler.

The Cunas, it seemed, believed in God. But they said no prayers, built no temples, had no priests to reiterate man-made scriptures. The Cuna God was the Creator, the Beginning and the End. His existence was obvious, since the world they lived in with its beauty and danger could not have invented itself, but they did not seek to know the unknowable. God did not interfere in their daily life. Their customs were ancestral, maintained by leaders obedient to their chief, Chucunaquiok, son of the mighty river beyond the mountain ridge. Other tribes had kings, but to the Cunas the only king was God and

151

His representative was their chief. The Chucunaque flowed south, dropping through deep gorges to the Gulf of Panama. God had made the Chucunaque and the chiefs passed on their sacred name generation by generation for ever.

The Cunas were not, as Claud Robyns had reported, lazy. They were sensible. Life in the forest had its dangers. Huge falling trees split by lightning, deluges of rain washing homes away, skin torment from many insects, crocodiles that sobbed like a woman and if you went close from curiosity snapped you to a bloody dismemberment in the river swamps. There was death from fever or the poisoned thorn or the juice of the manchineel, from the tusks of the Warree hog, from the river worm entering the feet of fishermen, from childbirth. But not from lions or tigers, for there were none, and not from the jaguar (who had food enough with monkeys and deer and never attacked a Cuna), not from the Spaniards of Nombre and Porto Bello because the Cuna forest had no gold or emeralds, and not from probing European settlers by sea because the island approach was too intricate.

On the whole the Cunas had a life which they enjoyed. They enjoyed the seasons. In the sun months they hunted and feasted and taught their children about the forest. When the rains came they kept to their huts living off salted meat and making ready their arrows and fish-hooks and canoes. The hunting was good. Juicy red deer, short-legged black sweet-tasting Pecary hogs, bearded succulent monkeys, fat poultry with feathered legs, pink fish like roach caught in riverbank holes, the white-fleshed tarpon and cavally swarming in the little bay. Plantains, marsh potatoes, pineapples, prickly-pears, cherries, bananas, tamarinds with pulpy pods, the indigestible calabash gourd to be sucked and spat out, and honeycomb from the wild bees.

The Cunas were not greedy or envious. They used no money—Robyns had been right about that—because there was nothing to buy. They were surrounded by all they needed. They had no desire for ownership or accumulation. So they hunted for food, built huts for comfort, married for pleasure (which the gentle laughing Cuna women understood so well), brewed wine for feast days, expending the energy required for these things, but no more.

This was not laziness. It was common sense.

The Cunas loved life but they did not fear death because

152

death was the glorious re-enactment of life. You would continue in heaven as you had achieved on earth. The good fisherman would continue to catch, the good bowman to shoot, the good voice to sing, the swift to run and the prolific to multiply. Whatever you did on earth it paid you to do well because after you passed through the shadowy gate you would do this same thing for eternity.

The chiefs, the Chucunaquioks, were born blameless. All other Cunas were equal in rights but not in ability. So it was important they should develop the qualities they lacked. And here they were assisted by three great concepts from antiquity:

Niga. Kurgin. And *Purba.*

Niga was courage, the ability to conquer. The enemies were pain, sickness, and death. The Cunas had dignity. They taught their children how to suffer without tears or complaint because God never answered complaints and blubbering never cured a bruise. The Cunas did not explain why courage was necessary. They just knew. If a boy found it hard to be brave he should hold a jaguar's tooth in his left hand while he slept. A girl should wear a necklace of jaguar's teeth. The Cunas respected the jaguar. They caught him in baited pits but only killed enough for a supply of teeth. No one wished the jaguar to die out.

Kurgin was intelligence, the power in the head. To plait the roof, to smoulder out the canoe from red cedar, to sing well at feasts, to bemuse the river fish from their holes with a torch at the correct angle, to take the wild bees' honey, these things must be learned, easily or with difficulty, and it was *Kurgin* that made the difference. In childhood and adolescence sons looked to their fathers and daughters to their mothers to help the *Kurgin* grow.

Purba, perhaps the most important, was hard to describe. The Cunas had no words for mystical ideas like "soul" or "essence", but they said that the heat of a fire was that fire's *Purba*, that a man's reflection in water or a mirror was his *Purba*, and so was his shadow. If the bad spirits of the forest stole your *Purba* you would sicken, and if your *Purba* could be found and persuaded to return you would be well. The leaders knew that certain drum beats, potions and rhythms of feet round aromatic fires had power of persuasion. As you could not do without your own *Purba*, so you could improve yourself by borrowing others, like the tarpon's *Purba* to help you swim, or the *Purba* of a singing bird to give you a good voice.

These habits and beliefs of the Cuna people were learned slowly by the *Tigress* visitors over many weeks in the forest, especially by the Sultan who became blood-brother to Chucunaquiok, and by Robert Seaton whose training in observation now proved such an unexpected benefit. Some things could be understood without words. The strength of the mud-built village wall, the height of the red cedars, the beauty of the Cuna women. When questions had to be asked sign language was often enough. A plump bird flew from a prickly-pear. You pointed first at the bird and then down your opened mouth with query in your eyebrows, and your Cuna friend, either smiling and patting his stomach or shaking his head with a frown, would tell you if the bird was good to eat.

If sign language was not enough there was Chucunaquiok himself who, as Claud Robyns had said, spoke "English of a sort". As a young man he had been sent by a wise father to the great island across the sea where, it was reputed, strange men with white skins had come in ships from another world.

These white strangers in fact were firstly Spanish settlers who had not yet been brutalized by orders from the inquisitors of Madrid, and secondly some English escapees from Florida. The Frenchman Laudonnière had established a successful colony in Florida where he received and looked after the crew of an English pinnace that had been separated from her parent ship and wrecked in a storm off the coast. For a time the Englishmen were safe, but when the Floridian Indians (a violent tribe of cannibals) began to attack the colony in earnest the English saw no reason to risk their lives defending a French colony, so they stole a barque, avoided Cuba because of Frenchmen who might recognize the barque, and came to Jamaica where they made lives for themselves in the Spanish community.

It was here (arriving in a Spanish trader from Nombre) that the young Chucunaquiok acquired enough words from both languages to claim that he could speak with the white men's tongues. Syntax he never mastered, but he could produce like coloured marbles from a pouch a surprising number of English word sounds, a feat made possible because he had brought with him in a cage a parrot whose *Purba* he respectfully borrowed.

* * *

154

Now the rains were dying out and the people of Macaweo welcomed their visitors. The danger at which the Sultan had hinted seemed remote.

Coming ashore in a foreign port you wanted a drink and a woman. The big ports of western Europe, the Netherlands, France and southern England, were full of taverns where a mariner could drink as much as he could afford and find a woman if not for bed at least for a kiss or two. Sometimes there were too few women, or the mariners drank too much and got rough. Then it was up to the woman. If she couldn't handle a man she had better have kept away from taverns. If she came off worst no one cared. Tavern women had no claim on virginity. It was a brawling market and the rules were understood by both parties. In the Mediterranean it was much the same except that in the ports of north Africa and the eastern islands of Islam the girls were much younger. They did not talk or drink with you, they were installed for only one purpose. You went to the sheds with them, or you didn't. If you went, and then haggled over the price, or if they started caterwauling, there were men with knives in the darkness and you would be lucky to get back to the ship. There were variations in the rules, but on the whole the customs of the Old World east of the Atlantic were established, the results predictable.

Among the Cunas of the rain forest there was an unpredictable innocence. They only drank alcohol on feast days. They had no taverns, nor any idea how to cater for mariners after a long sea voyage. Even the Sultan in all his travels had never met such people. Perhaps he misjudged his mariners in hinting that the Cuna women might be at risk. Perhaps Krauss had been right. With the end of the rainbow so close, surely no mariner would bother with women, not even the lithe, brown, satin-skinned, bare-breasted women of Macaweo. In any case the women all slept in the compound and the men from *Tigress* hardly saw them except in groups carrying fruit baskets or playing with their children. Only once a day did the Cuna women disturb the mariners, and then without intention.

Early each forenoon when the sun was not high enough to be directly visible from the village a line of forty women would leave the compound with large earthenware jars strapped to their backs and disappear up a path opposite the path from the beach. They were going to fetch water from the springs. An

155

hour later when the sun had reached the circle of sky and bathed the village with colour the women returned bearing the water jars on their heads. They walked slow and sure-footed, one hand on hip, the other lifted to steady the jar. They wore necklets and bracelets of red and white coral. Their firm breasts bounced a little with their footsteps. They passed the bowmen at practice as naturally as you would pass strangers in a street, their eyes lowered to watch where they were treading, their taut brown limbs glowing in the sun. The bowmen put down their arrows and watched admiringly. There was no misbehaviour but the admiration was intense. The bowmen relieved their feelings by picking on Gideon Jabbinoth. He had talked on the long voyage. They knew about Gideon and the girls. "Hey, Gideon, look at number three!" "*She* won't laugh at you, Gideon!" "Laugh! She'd pour slop over his head!" "Gideon wants his crumble!" "Gideon can't have his crumble!" But it was all cheerful. Gideon Jabbinoth smiled his big smile and turned back to the target. The waterbearers, not understanding the cries of the white men, glided on with ancestral innocence into the compound. Tom Dakyn called the bowmen to order.

But he sympathized with them.

He felt the same in the presence of Chucunaquiok's daughter. He did not see much of her. She and her parents slept in the upper storey, while *Tigress* officers slept on rush matting in an end room on the ground floor.

But at midday dinner Tom sat at the low table with other *Tigress* officers and the Chucunaquiok family. The wife was named Assumpa, the Cuna word for Shedir the bright star in Cassiopeia pointed out by Chucunaquiok. Assumpa was gracious and her husband knew it. The daughter who had washed Tom's feet and calves was named Rakiocka, the tree of sweet wood which rivalled the red cedar for the making of canoes. Rakiocka, the canoe girl, thought Tom. She did not come to breakfast or supper. Her father explained that she spent much time with her married sisters and their children. She was training for marriage. A year from now there would be a stern competition among the sons of Cuna leaders, tests of strength and courage and the skills of forest living. The victor would win Rakiocka. In the meantime, from the way her father looked at her and touched her shoulder and passed her the bowls of food and smiled when she spoke, it was clear what he felt. Chucunaquiok was proud of his women, and rightly. Lucky son of a leader, thought Tom. It was not a serious thought, or at least not practical. He could not talk to Rakiocka. Sometimes at dinner he sat next to her and was aware of her brown soft-muscled forearm on the table and the petal-fragrance of her skin. He liked it best when she sat opposite, naked above the line of the table. She never looked at him in a personal way, and when sometimes in the middle of a mouthful she raised her eyes her glances were without meaning or inquiry. She was a young tawny doe from the forest, her liquid eyes exquisite with the savour of what she was chewing. He could not talk to her, and if he could have talked there was nothing to say. There were too many ifs between them. But if he had been born the son of a Cuna leader, and not the heir of Paxcombe, if he and Rakiocka had met at this very table, he would have made sure to win that competition. Her beauty made him smile to himself, as you smile at a melody or a sunrise.

So the day of departure for the gold strike approached. The reports said that a big mule train was being prepared. The Cuna leaders had mixed with the polyglot workers in the dockland slums of Panama. There was waterfront language. Gold and emeralds were already in the guarded storesheds. More was coming in ships from the south. The mules could carry a heavier load in the cool of night, so the train would travel at the first full moon in the New Year.

The Cunas had no calendar. They did not know about Christmas, but three days before that date they celebrated the Festival of the Seed when nature died to be reborn by the mystery of God. Chucunaquiok told the Sultan that it would be the first full moon after the Seed Festival, which the Sultan could calculate as the sixteenth day of January.

Now time was hurrying for *Tigress* and every morning each man thought "One day nearer".

The Sultan asked to see the route himself. He and Krauss climbed with guides through the abrupt north face of the forest, over the ridge, down the gentle southern slope till the forest flattened out into grassy pampas land where the Chucunaque flowed into the Pacific, and beyond the Chucunaque another river, the Chepo, and then the environs of Panama. They were away a week. They found the ideal spot to take the mule train, said the Sultan. The journey was thirty or forty miles each way. The Sultan seemed very pleased with himself.

For *Tigress* lying in the bay the preparations were more for the homeward voyage than the gold strike. When the gold came aboard, the ship must be instantly ready to weigh anchor. The two most responsible were Viccars and Gostigo. Both had vital duties and both, though they stretched their legs ashore and walked the forest path to Macaweo and back, refused for their own reasons to spend a night away from *Tigress*.

Viccars would not leave his guns, the claws of *Tigress*. There was no practice firing even without shot, lest the sound carried to ears along the coast. The Spaniards from Nombre had never come through the dense forest of the northern ridge, but the risk could not be taken. Joshua Vine had shown the guns to Chucunaquiok and when it was explained that the magic bullets as big as a child's head could be hurled invisibly many thousands of paces through the air the chief had observed with great seriousness, "Cuna good people. Cuna love God-Queen," and Joshua, understanding the logic, had given his oath on behalf of the God-Queen that no bullets would fall from the sky on Macaweo. Viccars had been presented as master of the guns and friend of the Cunas. He had been flattered by Joshua Vine and admired by Chucunaquiok. But the master gunner had his problem. Of all the ship's components, the sails, the rigging, the rudder, the compass, the guns, the ovens and the food barrels, the least often required were the guns. Yet when required, they were essential. On a long voyage the guns might never be required—or only once. But if once, that occasion might decide the fate of the ship and all her crew.

An occasion was unlikely to occur in Elizabeth Bay. If by some rare coincidence an enemy ship had learned the intricacy of the island approach she would be seen hours in advance by the lookouts on the cliff. Should this happen, Viccars would fire three cracking sakers with blank charges. Those ashore would return on board at the run. *Tigress* would be out to sea in plenty of time. So Viccars went on with his masterful painstaking exercises. The guns cut loose and levelled, the tompions removed. The guns run out and pointed, the breeching ropes and wedges adjusted. Everything except the insertion of powder and shot and the final ignition. Viccars insisted on precise rehearsal. Not for now. But in case, just in case.

Gunnery practice did not take all Viccars's time. He helped Gostigo whose tasks were more immediate. There were three.

First, the preparation of *Tigress* for her journey home, the new sails and the clean hull. Second, the food and drink for her crew. Third, the rafts.

The sails were straightforward. There was spare canvas in the hold, and the men who could work it. For the hull he would have liked to beach the ship on a high tide, shore her up with timber, clean and refloat. But the tides were not high enough and the slope of beach was too gentle, so the scraping was done by a few underwater swimmers from *Tigress* with several dozen Cunas to help them. The Cunas were magnificent. Provided with scrapers from the stores they dived round the keel of *Tigress* like the tarpon whose *Purba* they believed themselves to have borrowed.

The victualling was on the same plan as at Antao, but much more varied. Barrels scoured for new contents, then taken ashore by ship's boats and canoes. Barrels entirely of salt now broken open to pack the homeward meat. The unwitting meat, Pecary hogs and small red deer and jabbering bearded monkeys and fat pheasant-like quams and the turkeys called carroson, were caught and penned ready for slaughter. Barrels were counted and numbered for fish. There were barrels for plantains and beans and maize. Barrels for fruit. Barrels for fresh water and the feast-wine of Macaweo as yet untasted on *Tigress*. The mariners might be short of alcohol going home—but who would care? A vast organization of victuals, ordered by the Sultan, surpervised by Krauss, checked by Robert Seaton and executed by Gostigo and Viccars. The food to get home.

Lastly, the rafts. The mules, said the Sultan, would carry packs. It was no terrain for wagons. Loads varied with the quality of the mule and the greed of the traders. A good average load per mule would be two hundred pounds. The trains from Panama to Nombre were known to be as large as one hundred and fifty mules. Around fifteen tons of precious metal and stone was too much for canoes and ship's boats. It had to be rafts, and these would be constructed from planks of cedar and rakiocka wood lashed to empty barrels for buoyancy. *Tigress*, with fewer mouths to feed, had plenty of spare barrels. The rafts must be of

159

manageable size to be towed out to the ship. The Sultan and Krauss calculated that eight rafts would be enough to carry the expected load. They ordered twelve.

In all these preparations on *Tigress* Viccars and Gostigo worked together, but with a difference. Tom noticed this when he came aboard. He did not always sleep in Macaweo. Sometimes he was back checking equipment with his bowmen. Since their first spell ashore they returned in batches to give other seamen a chance to rest and build up their strength in the village. On these visits to *Tigress* Tom noticed that while Viccars was always calm when you passed him with his gunners or a work party, always hungry at meals in the great cabin, always ready to talk, Gostigo was remarkably the opposite. There was something stifled and disturbed about Gostigo. He had lost his friend Fernie, yes. But the seventy-eight others who had died had each left a messmate. To each survivor his grief, but as the Sultan had said, let no man think himself more important than another. The men understood this. They had been to sea before, and death at sea is more communal than ashore. Father Wotton did not imagine himself unique because his son had been burned at San Corda. Dykes did not moon over Pipkin. The messmates of Blessington, whoever they were, had no claim to special behaviour. But Gostigo seemed sunk in private gloom. He was bad-tempered with the seamen, swearing at them for nothing, and at the cabin table would eat in silence, glaring down at his food as if he were doing a penance to swallow it.

For Tom the days passed quickly. Now the Sultan came to the shooting practices, insisting on greater and greater accuracy, especially at a distance of fifty paces from the target. Accuracy and rate of fire. The men responded, catching the Sultan's urgency. Now the moment was almost at hand and on *Tigress* and in Macaweo each man, whatever his job, felt the excitement of climax.

Suddenly it was the last evening. The bowmen and the musket party were ready in the village. Viccars would be left in command of *Tigress* with Gostigo (moody indeed but still a very experienced bosun) in support. It had been a hard decision whether to take Krauss to Panama or leave him with the ship. In the end the Sultan had said to him, "*Tigress* needs you, but I need you more." Robert Seaton was going with his surgeon's knife and a satchel of medicines. Tom was going with the bowmen.

It was a hot sunny evening. Tomorrow there would be the forest, the tryst with the mules, the end of the rainbow.

Tom felt the moment. Everyone on *Tigress* had his own destiny and Tom's destiny was with Paxcombe, his parents, and the girl he planned to marry.

He was standing outside the hut in Macaweo. Overhead the circle of sky was golden with the hidden sunset. He was standing beside the Sultan and out of the silence the Sultan said, "So. Are you ready for tomorrow?"

"Yes, sir."

"There will be little time for converse. Before we go, there is something I had better pass on to you."

Tom waited.

"A compliment," said the Sultan.

"From whom?"

"From Chucunaquiok chief of all the Cunas."

Tom waited again.

"He would like you to marry his daughter. She is a very beautiful girl. Do you not agree?"

"Yes! But—"

"He asked my permission because he thinks you are my son. He said that you may stay in Macaweo and receive his blessing and the obedience of all his people. I told him, as gently as I knew how, that such a union would not be allowed by our God-Queen. I made clear that we, you and I, are most sensible of the honour he suggests."

"Indeed!"

The Sultan glanced at him sharply. "Dreams may be very pleasant. But we must not take them seriously."

"By no means," said Tom.

CHAPTER EIGHTEEN

Dawn was in the sky over Macaweo when the column moved into the forest up the steep track towards the ridge. There was little talking. They were thinking of the encounter ahead.

Forty-one archers, thirty musketeers, a dozen Cuna guides including two leaders, and the four *Tigress* officers. Each archer

161

carried his two best bows, oiled and tested, and fifty arrows in quivers. Some musketeers, besides their weapons, carried a hatchet for undergrowth, others a bundle of four-foot staves, torches on bamboo poles, a mallet or a coil of thin strong rope. Every man except the Cunas carried a knife, a short-handled fly whisk, a sack of rations for the march, cooked meat, fruit and a deerskin carafe of water. Those who needed new shoes had been fitted from the dead men's store. "They died for you," said the Sultan. "Be worthy of them."

The Cunas walked barefoot and had their own ways of feeding off the forest. Strange berries, doubtful-looking fungi, and nuts.

For the first three hours the path was familiar from practice ascents. At the top they halted. From here they had always turned back. Now ahead the main path led south to the right bank of the Chucunaque. They rested after the climb, then started westwards, led and flanked by the Cunas down a glade of hardly trodden earth. Now they were crossing the gentle gradient that sloped south. They marched for another three hours without hurry, two abreast, step by step through the lonely green gloom.

Still high above the rivers, too far from the sea for fishing, this length of forest was easy for marching because it had never been the home of man. Where men had cleared the big trees to make villages like Macaweo and later, perhaps centuries later, moved away, there sprang up a density of shrubs and softwood trees proliferated by the sunlight, fast-growing, unsplendid, impenetrable. But here the primeval giants, replacing themselves one by one over thousands of years, had created an immense vault where never more than a handful of sun came through some torn hole in the canopy. It was a sinister enlargement of the walk from the beach to Macaweo. The same looping lichen-covered cables, but higher. The same twining orchids, but fewer. The same colossal trees, but now even taller, of greater girth and more spaced out, a countless army of titanic sentinels rooted to the earth, with endless glades disappearing into darkness on every side. There was no recognizable path. Without the guides how could anyone find a way back? Suppose, thought Tom, the Cunas ran away? But the brown, bare-bottomed men did not run away, and the long column wound on, the Sultan and Krauss at the head, Tom and

Robert in the middle of the bowmen line, and behind them Marshal Smolkin with the musketeers.

Now the sun must be getting high. There was cavernous heat, but no sight of the sun through the canopy, nothing to indicate direction. Did the Cunas really know where they were going?

Questions were not easy. Noun-noises had been exchanged, but the only words of value available to both sides were *Good* and *Bad*. They could be used for food, weather, or anything else. So now when Tom wanted to inquire about the route he waved to the nearest Cuna, pointed forwards in a general motion, stabbing his finger out and rotating both hands in large circles to indicate concern for the future in all its aspects, and called out:

"Good?"

"Good! Good!" shouted the brown man, wobbling his head with smiles.

"Good! Good! Good!" called little voices further down the line. They did want to please.

Not conclusive perhaps, but reassuring. So the column marched on, and in the ovenlike cathedral whose roof was a tangle of leaf-darkness and whose walls were a multiplicity of dim glades vanishing into nothing, the silence was broken by the chatter of bearded monkeys overhead, the flashing bird-squawks in treetops, and the zinging of insects everywhere. Large animals were never seen. Sometimes there was a distant shape, a movement or a crackle. The Cunas would point and shout, but whatever it was, jaguar, deer or Warree hog, it never appeared in view—instinct of the hunted perhaps.

The insects had no such qualms. Never in their lives, probably never in the millenial history of all their ancestors since the forest began, had such a long intrusive defenceless target of appetizing blood-juicy flesh been presented to them. They attacked it with an uninhibited frenzy of anger and greed.

From the ground, from the air, biting and stinging, piercing ankles and calves through stockings, not bothering with shirt-covered arms, content to pilfer the naked hands and wrists and necks and cheeks and scalps. The trodden paths round Macaweo had been rid of some of the worst insects. The nests of wasps and fighting bees had been smoked and burned away. Ants had been cleared at least from immediate tracks. Perhaps through the ages the insects of Macaweo had tired of Cuna blood and did not waste their time with strangers. Whatever the explanation, Tom and the other walkers round Macaweo had been well served with fly whisks and had not suffered too much from the odd bite on neck or nostril.

Now it was different. No palate had been dulled, no stomach sated.

The onslaught was tireless, the humming like the massed bands of successive armies waiting to attack. The noise pitch varied with the insect. Every hundred yards or so seemed to be dominated by a different tormentor, but it was only a choice of miseries. The whisks were soon thrown away. You needed both hands to crush the aggressor and scratch the inflammation.

Somehow it reminded Tom of the gardens at Paxcombe, but with nightmare exaggeration. There were wasps, but twice the size and purple-striped, bees vast and more rotund, hideously daubed with orange, glimpsed for a second as you slashed at your wrist. Next a spear of pain beneath your eye, and the clonk of your palm, and the miniature black bee flattened in your hand. But too late. And the black ants, gross like the four-poster pile near the beach, but in such numbers. A short halt, and Gideon Jabbinoth chewing a lump of meat and throwing the gristly bone aside, and at once from nowhere a throbbing inundation of red ants, and seconds later the redness gone and the polished white bone lying in ultimate uselessness. Suppose a dead bowman had fallen beside the path?

But there were other marauders, unseen or unfamiliar. A vitriolic agony under your fingernail, your shinbone drenched with prickly pain and when you tore down your stocking no sign of whatever had burrowed, your earlobe drained of blood by something gone before you could smash it. And the unfamiliarity. Flying beetles weirdly shaped, squat jumping globules never seen at Paxcombe, and worst of all the bulbous hairy slug (or was it a slimy caterpillar?) that fell from above on to Robert Seaton's neck exuding an irritation that made him scream out with Gaelic profanities incomprehensible to the Sassenach bowmen.

There was no sun check, but from the increasing oven heat it must be around midday. The Sultan ordered a halt. Another four hours would take them on the slanting course down to the

164

edge of the forest. That would end the day's march. Let the sun decline a little. It was unnecessary to risk exhaustion by marching at the zenith.

So they halted. It would have been pleasant to sit down, but there was nowhere to sit. Three bowmen tried a prostrate tree trunk. Hardly seated, they bent down swearing and slapping at the black ants around their ankles. Then, lifting their feet to escape, were too heavy for the worm-eaten bole and fell backwards into a colony of humming predators that clouded up from the intestinal fungus. Comrades seized the bowmen's outstretched arms, yanked them to safety. The bowmen, bitten through their breeches, clutched their buttocks.

It was better to move slowly than not at all. Calf muscles needed rest, but the long queue ambled on at half pace, eating as they went, munching whatever winged enemy came in with the food. The territorial divisions were more apparent at half speed. Now it was the ants, the black hills larger but the red swifter to deploy their myriads. Now it was the bees, the ebony pea-sizers homing in to eyelids from nests clustered like dark melons in the forks of trees, the huge orange-bottomed giants sweeping down from citadels that hung from high branches, shadowy geometrical absurdities as big as wheat sacks with jagged corners. There were no honey bees that the Cunas loved. Now it was the purple-striped wasps arriving in small forays from unseen garrisons, diving for fruit in the food sacks, venomous if thwarted. Now some acid mandible on your scalp, and when you clawed into your hair you found between your finger and thumb the unexpected carcass of a black ant with wings. At one scary moment Tom caught sight of a dangling thread before him, felt something on the back of his hand, raised his hand to look, saw spreadeagled, covering the whole space of pink skin between the roots of the fingers and the wristbone, a motionless spider, like a furry crab, the thick hirsute legs disappearing underneath to tickle his palm. Wildly he slashed the monster to the ground, trampled it. A thin Cuna walking beside him cried out, "No bad! No bad!" There was sympathy in the brown face for the harmless spider, but Tom was only half convinced.

Only the butterflies were truly inoffensive, gaudy pageant flowers floating over the battle scene. The Cunas would bang an orchid-covered tree with their sticks, and a posy of multicoloured blossoms, patterns of crimson, yellow and black, would flutter up, and the Cunas would clap their hands and jabber encouragements to the sweating mariners.

There was a hollow in the hill at Paxcombe where small gentle-coloured butterflies drifted in sunshine.

So the column slanted on through the loneliness of the green shadows. You were not alone. You were one of nearly a hundred. But sometimes for a moment when the cursing stopped and there was no sound of human voice you were aware of the size, the age and the indifference of the forest. You were lonely.

Some time that afternoon they trod through a dank rivulet oozing in a mossy channel and the Cuna leaders cried "Chepo! Chepo!" and made signs with their fingers showing many small things joining into something big, and the Sultan said that this was an early tributary of the river that flowed down between the Chucunaque and Panama. Much later, when the oven seemed less hot, the green gloom even dimmer and the drone of insects not quite so insistent, they came suddenly as at Macaweo to the edge of the forest and emerged footsore and thankful into an enormous vista of shrubby hillocks and tall pampas grass waving in soft breeze, the late sun poised over a distant wooded horizon.

Here they would camp. Tomorrow they would rest all day gathering strength for the coming night when there would be no rest. At dusk they would march the last few miles to the point of rendezvous with the gold train. So far the forest had given them protection. These last miles were more open, but the Spaniards did not patrol the waste land of the isthmus, and when darkness fell and the moon was up, the time when the mules started from Panama, the men from *Tigress* would be waiting at the chosen place some ten miles north of the city. They would wait well in advance in case the mules started early. The Sultan explained this to the mariners sitting round him.

"The mule track leads along a dried-up river bed," said the Sultan. "There is cover. Everything we could wish for. We shall take the gold."

He spoke for half an hour telling each section precisely what they had to do. Then they prepared for the night.

It was strictly a camp. There were no palisades, no fires. They crouched in a stony hollow, sheltered by the tall grasses.

166

They could not have been seen from fifty yards. They ate their supper and refilled their water bottles from a stream without sparkle but better than the brown leaf slush of the infant Chepo. The Cunas sat apart, chattering and smiling among themselves.

In the last minutes of sunlight a swarm of gnats appeared, tiny specks like everyone knew from their gardens at home. The small familiar gnats went for necks and cheeks, inflicting almost friendly bites. Krauss observed that the Spaniards had a special name for these harmless gnats. In Spain, said Krauss, gnats were called *musketas*. They bit you, but it was of no consequence. Their puny lacerations were insignificant compared with the maddening wounds of the ants, wasps and bees of the forest.

Tom agreed. He had a gnat bite on his wrist. He smiled. It seemed so little.

The sunset came and went, but now instead of darkness there was the moonlight that made them talk softly. No one was listening, but it was impossible to shout under the moon. Everyone had been bitten or stung by a forest insect in some tender location, and they whispered, each claiming fiercely that his particular injury was the most painful, and Robert Seaton produced ointments from his satchel that gave some alleviation but not much, and lanced an alarming bulge on the neck of one of Smolkin's party.

Now pale moonlight filled the sky. The oven heat from the forest had gone and there was almost a chill in the air, not cold but a relief from the heat of noon.

Robert and Tom were sitting together. Robert said, "I only know surgery. I wish I knew more of medicine."

"Why?" said Tom. "You know what you were taught."

"It's the calenture," said Robert. "Sometimes it brings fever. No one knows why. I can cut your leg off, but I do not understand why the evening breeze brings fever and madness."

"Is that what they taught you?"

"They do not know. They can only say what they have observed. Sometimes I wish I were less of a surgeon and more of a physician."

With the Cunas already silent the mariners settled down to sleep for the last time before the encounter. They rubbed their *musketa* bites cheerfully.

Dawn brought the final anticipation. Last night the Sultan

had told them what to do when they reached the dried river bed. Now after breakfast he told them about mules. He chose this moment to concentrate their attention and so their energies.

The mule, said the Sultan, was the offspring of a male ass and a female horse. The Spaniards brought jack-asses from Catalonia and La Mancha to cover the isthmus horse mares, especially mares from Mexico. The Mexican mustang wombs produced hardy offspring responsive to training and the Spanish jack-asses contributed long tireless legs to the foals. Only male foals were used as pack-bearers, first because they could carry more and second because a man mule wanted a woman mule. So, said the Sultan, for a few days before each trek a white mule mare would be turned among the stallion pack-mules. On the journey a handler would lead the mare, now with bells round her withers, and the stallions would follow her however precipitous the track. The close followers could see and smell her, and those further behind were reminded by the bells. "Like a mariner after a woman," said the Sultan. The mariners understood that. Bawdily.

The mule was a strange mixture. Stubborn yet sensitive. If annoyed he could kick dangerously or lie down obstinately. Food he would take if he fancied it, but what he fancied was a mystery. Some said that a mule would only eat something if convinced he was not supposed to have it. He might refuse an oilcake and devour a pile of sacks. Yet for his regular handler he could develop an affection like a dog for his master, recognizing the voice. He hated being shouted at. *Talk to a horse, whisper to a mule*.

The mares were less stubborn, more affectionate towards their handler. The man leading the white mare must continue to lead her to Macaweo. The train must be got quickly on the move along an unfamiliar track. No moonlight penetrated the forest, so for the first twenty miles they would be moving east through the stony pampas land of the south isthmus. When dawn broke they would turn north into the forest towards Macaweo.

The Sultan ended with a simple image: "Think of the mules at Macaweo. Think of the gold. Think of *Tigress*."

The men thought of these things. All that day they waited in the long grass hardly talking, each wrapped in golden dreams.

168

At dusk the Cunas led them the last few miles to the dried river bed which the Sultan had chosen.

They waited in the silence of the moonlight, straining their ears for the sound of mule bells. They crouched behind boulders and in the tall grasses that grew to the edges of the river bed. No man would be more than forty paces from his target. Two lines of hidden men spaced out down three hundred yards on both sides of the track. Behind them the staves had been driven into the ground and the thin strong rope stretched to form the outline of a long alley closed at the north end. The length of the mule train coming from the south was not certain, but behind the white mare the mules would come two abreast. The rope trap had been calculated for two hundred mules. When the leading animals came near the north end of the trap the Sultan would be waiting for them. He would blow a whistle. At once this would be echoed by three other whistles from those in charge on the east and west flanks and at the south end of the trap. The mule train would be halted, the guards not knowing what to expect from whistles on all sides.

In that moment of confusion the archers would release their arrows at the guards, aiming at the chest.

Some guards would be on foot, others on horseback. The mounted guards were the prime target. If a guard did not fall from his horse at the first arrow other shafts would quickly arrive. In speed trials, the quiver at the hip for access, an average despatch had been five arrows in half a minute. If a rider reached for his musket he must be shot again. If he turned his horse towards the archers he must be shot as he came. If the horse charged through the line of archers it would stumble on the rope hidden in the grass. Smolkin's men would be waiting. If a rider was not dead they would knife him. If a horse were riderless it must be caught. In the last emergency if a horse broke loose it must be shot by musket. The sound of one shot was a more acceptable risk than a loose horse galloping back to Panama.

The second target was the foot guards. They too if they carried a musket must not be allowed to fire it. If they ran it could only be towards the archers.

Reports said there might be twenty guards, perhaps less. The only enemies of the Spaniards on the isthmus were the Cimarrones, the runaway black slaves who were glad enough to be free living off the forest. They had no firearms. They might steal food from a Spanish outpost but they would never attack a gold train. They would almost certainly be killed in the attempt, and if by some overwhelming onslaught they took the gold it would be of no use to them. The Indians despised gold, and if a Cimarrone appeared with gold in Panama or Nombre he would be beaten to death by Spaniards. The guards did not fear the Cimarrones. The chief duty of the guards was to ginger up the mule handlers.

For each guard on horseback or on foot there would be at least two archers firing ten arrows in the first minute. There would be the tripping rope and the knives. The surprise. Above all the will of seventy-five men from *Tigress* who had come a long way.

For dealing with the guards there was a single order: *No survivors.* For the handlers the orders were: *Take alive the man with the white mare. Spare the others unless they run.*

The mariners waited in the moonlight and behind them the audience of silent Cunas. The Sultan was at the north end with his whistle and half a dozen archers. Robert Seaton waited with them. Krauss was in charge on the eastern flank of the river bed, Tom on the west. Smolkin would close the south end. These three each carried a whistle. They waited with their men. No one spoke. They waited and listened. And waited.

There was a light breeze from the north and the bell jangle was only heard just before the mules appeared. They came like phantoms from nowhere under the full disc of the cloudless moon. They were led by a snow-white mare picking her way precisely and delicately along the track. There was no hurry. A man holding the halter walked beside her but you could not see the halter, only the man's hand. The mare looked like a white queen leading a procession of grey followers.

The bells and the clopping hoofs were music. She nodded her head slowly and rhythmically like a woman nodding to the music of a funeral march.

Tom was half-way down his line of archers. Stooping at a chink between two boulders he watched the white mare pass and behind her the pairs of grey mules carrying their lumpy packs.

Four mounted guards, two on each side of the train, rode beside the mules. The guards wore pale shirts and dark jerkins. They had muskets slung on their backs. Others with muskets were on foot. Tom watched the mules ambling along at a man's pace, slow and measured. The horses were being reined in to stay with them. The riders' pale shirts in the moonlight were a perfect target. And how many mules so far? Perhaps sixty mules, thought Tom, about thirty pairs. Maybe more. The white mare was out of sight now, and suddenly there was a gap in the moving line and along came another white mare leading a second group. Another handler, more horsemen and walking guards.

Tom held the bow in his left hand. The whistle was in his right hand, the cord round his neck. On the ground beside him lay the first arrow. He hoped the archers next to him had their first arrow already slotted on the string, the bow not yet bent. He glanced each way to make sure. Both men had the arrow poised. They were both crouching, their torsos braced, ready to leap up. He felt his mouth dry and a stiffness in his jaw. He thought of San Corda and how he had stood helpless among the orange stalls. He was not helpless now. The mules were still passing.

Away to his left the Sultan's whistle blew a scream into the night. Krauss was next, then Tom, then Smolkin, three short stabbing blasts. Tom dropped his whistle, grabbed his arrow, slid the knock on to the string, exhaled to steady himself.

Voices! Shouts from Spaniards up and down the river bed. Questions barked. Orders yelled. Bewildered oaths. Horses rearing up as their heads were wrenched round. Men standing in their saddles. A cessation of progress by the mules as the stoppage at the front came shuddering down the line. From their boulders and grasses the archers were rising up, forty-two bows bent now in earnest. Forty-two arrow feathers nestling against cheekbones, forty-two shafts aligned on the pale-shirted targets, only awaiting release till the eye was satisfied. *No panic. You have been trained. Shoot when you are ready.*

Then in that vulnerable static moment so accurately foreseen, so exactly fulfilled, a hissing like geese as the arrows flew.

Massacre swift and total. Surprise complete. No opposition but voices hoarse with alarm. A second and third volley of arrows followed the first. Less shouting now, more screams.

The mules started to lie down. Men stumbled, tugged at the shaft in their chest, half rose, fell transfixed again. Men ran and never reached the boulders. Riders plunged from their saddles. One rider swivelled his horse, came straight towards Tom. The man had arrows sticking out of him. Tom aimed, held, released. The man twisted suddenly, throwing up his arms, crumpled to the fast-moving earth, his ankle held in the stirrup. When they caught the horse the dead guard still hung by the foot like a bedraggled pincushion bristling with five splintered arrows. And more arrows in flight. No musket was fired. No guard lived long enough. Three riderless horses were stopped at the trip rope. Six more were taken by Smolkin's men running through to the train when the archers stopped firing. Dying guards were knifed. No shouting now. Not a Spaniard to be heard. Visibility strong and luminous but colours vanished, everything white and grey and black, an etching of death over the river bed. The mules lay like a long double string of lumpy beads, a head raised here and there, hardly participant. No mule had been touched by an arrow. The Spaniards lay with no head raised, beyond participation.

Only one Spaniard lived, the handler of the first white mare, saved by the Sultan as an excited archer lifted his bow. The handler with the second mare had been killed in the confusion when he dropped his halter and ran. On the count, eighteen guards with muskets and seven unarmed handlers lay dead. Ten horses unhurt. One hundred and seventy-four mules.

The first thirty mules in the train carried provisions for the others, sacks of oats, straw and oilcake. Ten of these mules behind their white mare were separated for their journey with Krauss.

Half-way from Panama to Nombre lay the stronghold of Venta Cruz on the river Chagres. In the dry season the mule cargo would be taken on by boat. Now in January the river would still be swollen, so the mules would be expected by road at Nombre. From this moment in the river bed it would be at least two days, allowing for food and rest, before they would be missed. Krauss, with a small party of guides, archers and musketeers, would take his ten mules north along their usual track. South of Venta Cruz he would stop at some point where the ground was soft and the grass long enough to show signs of transit. The Cunas briefed by Chucunaquiok knew where to

172

choose. Here empty food sacks and scatterings of hay would be left and a new track made branching right towards the forest, the diversion to be well trampled. Long before any search party came Krauss and his mules would be high in the forest on the northern ridge, a route parallel to the way they had come. Cimarrones were known to congregate in this area. They would be found, and presented with the mules. Chucunaquiok insisted that no evidence should ever be found in Macaweo. By the time that searching Spaniards, perplexed no doubt, were following the trail left for them, Krauss and his men would be on gold-filled *Tigress* far out to sea.

Now the wooden staves were pulled up, the rope coiled, the bodies hidden in a deep gulley a hundred yards away, the arrows left in the bodies, the muskets beside the bodies.

The food mules stood in two groups. The living handler, shaking with fright, was getting the main section of pack animals to their feet. The Sultan knew enough Spanish to give orders and the handler obeyed with the alacrity of a doomed man who still hopes, yelling in a cracked voice at the grey mules who rose one by one with a pantomime of reluctance. After patient manoeuvre and many oaths the two convoys were lined up. Krauss would take the handler because the first white mare, leader of his mules, would respond to no one else. The second mare stood at the head of twelve dozen pack mules now in single file with the remaining food mules tacked on astern. With her own handler dead the crisis of who should lead her was solved when Gideon Jabbinoth pushed past the jabbering Spaniard and cupped his hands over the mare's nostrils and breathed gently into them and whispered gipsy words, and the mare unstiffened herself and gave an abrasive whinny.

The Sultan standing beside Jabbinoth handed him the halter and moved away.

"Before you go, Mr Krauss." The Sultan's calm voice carried in the clear air.

He walked slowly down the line of mules, inspecting the packs, opening a flap here and there, feeling, peering. At the end he turned back to the centre where some thirty mules stood strung with polished panniers neater and more elegant than the packs of other mules. From one pannier he took an object. It was flat, a foot long, half the width of his hand, the colour of the moon.

He lifted it high above his head. The moon baton glowed in the pale light.

"Stand where you are," he called. "Every man shall touch the gold."

First to Krauss, then with Tom and the surgeon slowly down the rows of mariners. Each man in turn held the ingot, passed it on. Some kissed it. Some rubbed it against their beard, drew it between their fingers as if to be imbued with the precious stain. They hardly spoke. An incredulous awe hung in the silence. Tom held the ingot last before it was put back in the pannier. The bar of gold, heavy for its length. A sensation on the skin, the caress of cool metal, the burning triumph. And thirty mules with polished leather panniers.

"There is much besides," said the Sultan. "Necklaces, coins, caskets of gems, silver. But the gold alone would be enough for us all."

He shook hands with Krauss and the convoys parted, Krauss northwards with the decoy and the Sultan eastwards, walking beside Gideon Jabbinoth at the head of the treasure train.

The stony river bed bore no trace of their departure.

CHAPTER NINETEEN

The mules walked in line ahead because instead of the well-trodden track to Nombre the path now was what the Cunas chose through the stony marshy pampas land. Some Cunas went in front, others walked beside the mules, taking a halter now and then to steady a straggler, but the white mare conveyed her presence down the long line and the mules needed little guidance. The horses were still nervous, better led than ridden. Smolkin's men led the horses. The Sultan said that anyone tired or footsore could have a ride later, but no one was tired yet. They felt as if they could walk for ever. The clatter of the mule bells was the music of a victory march.

Sometimes the grass was head high, sometimes in hummocks with the path a slim ribbon through patches of spongy ground. Such space, so much light, and yet a distant perimeter of blackness as if the moon were a beadle's lamp following a band of happy burglars. Surely you would be seen or heard under such vast exposure? The moon seemed to grow bigger, more powerful, a total authority overhead. Was it God Himself up there? If so, He was smiling, albeit vaguely.

The train moved on, each mile further from the route to Nombre.

They came to the Chepo, now a broad shallow river approaching the Pacific. The ford was easy. The horses stopped to drink the churned water. The mules stopped but would not drink till clear water from upstream had been fetched in the buckets carried by each tenth mule.

Through the moonlit night the column moved east, further from danger, nearer to *Tigress*. Tom and Robert walking together passed up and down the lines of mariners on either side of the train. Robert was worried about some of the bites and stings from the forest. Worst had been the eyelids punctured by the small black bees. Nils and Henrik, the muscle-bound friends of the surgeon, both in Smolkin's party, had suffered. Henrik's left eye was closed with a livid bulge, Nils's lip looked like a purple damson. They had complained savagely last night in the dell, but they were not complaining now. They took Robert's ointment of alum and mercury with a smile. So did archer Dykes, bitten through his breeches yesterday when he fell into the rotten log. It was the same everywhere, men's sores and lacerations no longer vexatious, as if joy had filled their veins with some magic antidote.

At dawn they breakfasted and fed the mules who in the absence of forbidden materials accepted their oats and straw with grudging amiability. The moon had gone and the early sun painted the etching of night with colours. Grasses green, sky pale blue turning to cobalt, mules not all grey but shades of brown, their bulging packs bright with yellow and red canvas, the leather panniers now a shining sepia. It was easier to believe in the daylight. As if you had dreamed of treasure and woke to find the dream true.

The men were told to rest. They sat down, but no one could rest. "We shall rest on *Tigress*," said someone, and he spoke for them all. Instead of slanting north towards the forest the Sultan decided to continue east across the open country till they reached the Chucunaque directly south of Macaweo. The mules seemed content with the stony track. Let them be saved from the forest as long as possible.

The train moved on.

175

Three hours later, the sun already hot, they came to the basin of the Chucunaque and saw the sacred river glinting a mile away down the gentle valley, a majestic broad road of smooth water. Now they started north with the forest in sight and the ground rising gradually. Once in the forest there would only be a few hours' easy climb, then the last steep descent to Macaweo. Marching with the Chucunaque in view gave a sense of homecoming. A pair of slow-flapping herons soared over the column, circled as if on inspection, drifted away. A mob of cumbrous pelicans trundled low above the river towards the sea. So this was the Chucunaque whose secret springs had once given birth to the first Chucunaquiok. Near the mountain ridge from a cave, whose narrow entrance was forbidden to all but the descendant chiefs, gushed the first visible cataract, so superior to the squelchy beginnings of the Chepo. The Cuna people had always lived over the ridge down beside the bay of sea food, but here to the south flowed the river of their god.

From the boggy margins a sound like sobbing women floated up to the mule train. The Cuna guides put their wrists together and made crocodile jaws with their hands. "Kaka-kaka-boom!" laughed the Cunas, snapping their teeth. Chucunaquiok had spoken of the crocodiles and Robert shouted "Kaka-boom!" and the mariners who understood explained to those who did not. They marched on singing and joking, the sun hot on their necks. As the ground rose the river disappeared into a gorge, and before noon they reached the forest.

On the edge they rested and fed for the last time. The mules were on short rations because of the decoy food-loss, but they would be rewarded at Macaweo.

From the sunshine into the dim vault. This was a regular Cuna track, firm and clear of bees' nests. Insects came, but not the fierce hordes of the outward journey. There was forest on the Nombre route and the mules seemed unconcerned, though they were walking more slowly. They had been carrying two hundred pounds on their backs for more than twelve hours. From Panama to Nombre they would have rested more often. This was a forced march. Would they weaken? Or revolt? The Sultan called Tom to the front. Gideon Jabbinoth, his bony face creased with an inward smile, was still holding the white mare's halter. "As long as she leads," said the Sultan, "they will

176

follow. But we must not pause again. She must not lie down."
So the column crept on under the giant trees and in the opaque
greenness there were orchids and lichen-covered cables and
butterflies and flying ants and airborne stabbing beetles and the
stink of decay, but there was an unimportance about these
things because every man knew that Macaweo was only over
the hill and down the other side. As long as the mules did not
collapse. The Spaniards could not come now. Surely there was
nothing? Yet after all that had happened since Lingmouth they
dared not quite believe.

The track ran near the gorge and they could hear the muffled
rumble of a waterfall. The men were tiring now, though none
would admit it. The horses were not ridden because who would
risk his horse bolting into the labyrinth? The singing had
stopped. They needed their breath.

So the treasure train came to the ridge top and passed slowly
safely down the steep incline. The sound of the mule bells
carried forward and there was cheering from below, and when
they came into the clearing of hard earth the whole village was
there in welcome, Cuna warriors shouting, waving, crowding
round, three hundred or more. Cuna wives and children
coming from the compound. The Cuna guides who held mule
halters steered batches of mules to break the long line, the train
became a loose formation halting one by one till they stood like
a flock of porters waiting for permission to dump their luggage.
They craned their necks and pawed their feet.

Chucunaquiok came with Krauss, and there were greetings,
hugs, handshakes, Chucunaquiok pointing at the mules, clapping, saying, "Big fight! Big fight!" Krauss and his men had
arrived before noon. They had found the Cimarrones, presented the mules, made a torchlit dash through the forest. "And
the handler?" asked the Sultan.

Krauss answered, "I sent him with the Cimarrones."

"If he reaches Nombre he will have a tale to tell."

"If he reaches Nombre," said Krauss.

But it was no time to speculate on what the Cimarrones
might do with a Spaniard. Macaweo was about to celebrate.
The bows and muskets were stacked, with Smolkin's seamen
forming a rota of guards in case the Cunas could not restrain
themselves. The horses were led away to feed. Between the
huts carcasses hung spit-roasting over open fires. Smoky

succulent aromas drifted over the ground. In the compound stood rows of big wine vats. The feast was ready.

It had been agreed. The Cunas would say goodbye to their friends from *Tigress*. Chucunaquiok insisted. The mules would be unloaded here in the village. They would be fed, then taken with the horses up into the forest by Cunas and handed over to the Cimarrones. There must be no delay. No one knew what the furious Spaniards might do, how quickly they might come searching. When Macaweo had toasted *Tigress* Cunas would help carry the mule packs down to the beach. Long poles lay in bundles for the bearers.

Chucunaquiok, splendid with a ceremonial fillet and earrings and massive bicep bangles all of copper encrusted with pearls, stood with his guests. He shouted an order and running Cunas surrounded the mules.

The Sultan asked Krauss, "Has Viccars sent word?"

"Yes. The men are ready at the beach."

"The rafts?"

"Rafts, canoes. Everything is prepared."

"And *Tigress* victualled?"

"It is all aboard."

The packs came off the mules like packages off carts. The sacks and panniers were set aside in piles. The remains of the food sacks were taken to a line of troughs where a mash of maize and beans had been prepared. The mules were free. Brown men took the halters to lead them to their feeding place.

Then the mules made a collective decision. They lay down, rolling on their backs, whinnying with the delight of no burden, thrashing their legs in the air. For several minutes they rolled and kicked, rubbing their backs on the earth. With a final wriggle they flopped on to their sides, their eyes shut, their long legs motionless. They were exhausted.

Chucunaquiok gave another order and the Cunas began pulling at the halters and yelling at the mules to get up, but the mules did not like being yelled at. They lay still with their eyes shut. Chucunaquiok was frowning.

The Sultan told Gideon Jabbinoth, "Show us how. The Chief wants them fed and away."

Jabbinoth went to the white mare, knelt, spoke to her, patting her withers. She raised her head, paused, rose stiffly. The Cunas stopped yelling and watched Jabbinoth. He went to the next mule, had no response. The mule lay as if dead. He stooped, slid his hand under the mule's neck murmuring gipsy talk, and in a few moments the mule shook itself and struggled up and stood glaring at nothing. Jabbinoth went to the mule next astern.

Again he bent down, but there was not enough room, and he put his hand on the rump of the standing grey mule, not roughly or rudely, but too much for the mule who had wanted to rest. The lightning flash of a hoof. Jabbinoth sprawling with a scream of pain, clutching his left thigh.

Robert Seaton ran to him. Tom came and they lifted him up. He could put his foot to the ground but his thigh was agony. With his hands round their necks they took him limping into the compound. Chucunaquiok led them to his hut. Assumpa his wife appeared and he spoke to her and she hurried indoors. He took them into the end room where Tom and Robert had slept. Jabbinoth was laid on a low rush-covered trestle. His breeches were loosened at the left knee and drawn up. Robert examined him. The thigh bone was not broken but the muscle was gashed and swollen. Assumpa brought water and Robert bathed and bound the wound. The Sultan said Jabbinoth was lucky not to have been killed and Jabbinoth said he had been a fool to go behind the mule. A servant girl brought a bowl of steaming meat and a jar of wine. Jabbinoth was told to rest. They left him leaning on one elbow, smiling, the jar in his hand. Chucunaquiok led them through the rooms of the long hut to the big room where they had first been entertained.

The polished cedarwood table was laid with wooden bowls and spoons. The floor smelt fragrant. Two bare-breasted girls poured wine from a black cask carved with leaping jaguars. Krauss came in. The mules were feeding now. When the white mare's bells sounded they had followed her to the troughs. He had been to see Jabbinoth.

"And the men?" said Joshua.

"Well cared for. Enough wine to drown them."

"They deserve it."

Now all the jars were filled and Chucunaquiok put his arm round Assumpa's shoulder and raised his jar and boomed, "Amral Vine! Amral Krauss! Amral Tom! Amral Robert! My friends!"

So the drinking began. Many toasts, many affirmations of

179

friendship, many smiles and handshakes. No sentences, just graphic words darting to and fro like carrier pigeons.

"Big ship! Hurrah!"

"Macaweo! Hurrah!"

"Gold! Gold! You like! Much good!"

"Thanks, Chucunaquiok! Thanks, Assumpa!"

"Aaaaah! Spain men dead! Good, good!"

Then from a hole in the ceiling appeared two long brown legs and down the ladder came Rakiocka. She ran to her father. He kissed her hair, held her wrist, turned her to face Tom.

"Rakiocka chief daughter. Tom chief son. Tom stay."

Tom looked at her. She was standing quite still, her smooth arms straight and loose. Rakiocka the canoe girl in her deerskin skirt, her brown body moulded with grace, a coral bandeau in the black hair that fell to her waist, her eyes wide open, meeting his without challenge or provocation or fear. The daughter of the sacred river waiting for her destiny.

He smiled at her as he had often smiled across the table. Then he shook his head and said quietly to Chucunaquiok, "I am proud to have met your daughter. But I must go."

"You stay. You my son."

"The God-Queen has need of him," said Joshua Vine. "Tom big warrior. God-Queen need him against her enemies."

For a moment Chucunaquiok Chief of the River gazed at Joshua Chief of the *Tigress*. Then he smote his forehead with the palm of his hand, as if to brush away any unhostlike thoughts, and called for the wine and took his guests to the table.

The feast was brought. Boiled tarpon, tender fowl with herbs, steaks of venison and the Pecary hog, thick gravy with maize and plantain; pineapples, pears and tamarinds, sauces and sweetmeats, biscuits and pie-cakes larded with honey; the bowls passed and filled and renewed and changed, the wine jars never empty. Smooth tawny wine tasting of wheat with the tang of cherry. Assumpa spoke to a girl who took a large jar and left the room, and Tom thought of Gideon drinking alone.

Sitting opposite Rakiocka and her mother Tom felt the warm fumes rising into his head, but his stomach was full and his thoughts, though increasingly affable, were still clear. Round the whole table hung a sense of well-wishing and though conversation grew less the faces, especially the eyes, showed the feeling in their hearts. Even Krauss's bloodshot eye seemed less horrible when you caught the contented dreaminess of the other.

Outside in the compound there was Cuna singing and *Tigress* singing and the thump of many feet.

When the table was cleared Joshua Vine reached under his jerkin and drew out of the holster on his belt the second pistol, "Jonathan" brother of "David", and presented it to Chucunaquiok together with a pouch of fifty bullets from his food sack on the floor. "Jonathan" had not been used at the river bed. Now Joshua kept his promise.

The result was spectacular. The Chief gave a roar of joy, grasped the pistol, stroked it with a muttered stream of Cuna gratitudes, gave it to his wife and daughter to touch, took it back. Then he laid "Jonathan" on the table and pronounced, "Amral Vine! Chief Chucunaquiok! Brothers! Blood! Good! Good!"

From his own belt he drew the knife Joshua had given him, took Joshua's forearm, poised the knife an inch from the skin, stared at Joshua with regal inquiry. Joshua Vine understood. He nodded gravely without flinching and said, "Good!" The nicks were made, the forearms locked together, steadied by the free hands, the blood mingled in the veins. "Brother!" said Chucunaquiok. "Brother!" replied Joshua. The arms were freed and washed and Robert bound them up.

Outside the singing and dancing went on, and in the big room the girls poured wine from the cask of the jaguars. Assumpa drew another large jar from the cask and smiled at Tom, raising the jar and pointing down through the hut towards the room where Jabbinoth lay alone. Tom nodded, and Assumpa handed the jar to Rakiocka, and Rakiocka glided out holding the jar with both hands like a libation.

Gideon Jabbinoth looked into the empty jar. He tipped up the jar into his open mouth in case there was any left. A few drops crawled down on to his tongue. He put the jar on the floor and lay back on the trestle, his hands behind his neck. His leg throbbed and there was a pleasant muzziness in his head. The room was hot and dim. There was an outside door strung with a rush curtain. A small window the same. Behind him was the inner door where the girl had appeared with his second jar of wine. A fine girl wearing nothing but a skirt. The gipsy girls were not like that. They laughed at you and made hurtful remarks and poured slop over your head. His mother was right. You were better off without them. This girl was different. She said nothing, did not even look at you, stood beside you like a brown dolly half dressed, her long breasts swinging like pears in a soft breeze, gave you the jar, took the empty, was gone.

He wondered whether she would bring another. It was good wine, not like ale of course, not so tasty and without the immediate warmth in the belly, but good all the same. He lay listening to the singing and dancing. The English and Cuna songs mingled together sounded like a monkey carnival. He was content to lie here. His leg hurt and it would be no pleasure to go outside. He had no mates on *Tigress*. They had cheated him out of his knife and when he took another they had chopped his finger off. He was as good a seaman as any, not afraid of the topyard, but he had no mates. Mr Dakyn spoke to you, but it was not the same with an officer. The mariners were as bad as the gipsies in Bristol. The gipsies called him Neptune's fool and the mariners called him a gipsy fool. He did not care. He could not talk and argue like some of them, but he knew things they did not know. He had led the white mare. Who else could have done that? The wine tasted harmless but after a while it sent fumes up your throat, past the back of your nose, way up into your head. He closed his eyes and saw the caravan, the two dappled horses, his mother sitting beside him holding the reins. It would not be long now. Soon he would be back on *Tigress*. His whole body seemed bathed in tingling comfort. They couldn't go without him. They wouldn't forget him, would they? Someone would ask "Where's Jabbinoth?" He stretched out on the brink of sleep.

A hand touched his shoulder. He opened his eyes.

For a moment he thought it was the girl from before, but this was a different girl. She was taller than the other one. She had coral in her hair. She held out a big jar. He took a long drink, put the jar on the floor.

She was saying something he could not understand. She pointed at his bandage, frowning, shaking her head. He said cheerfully, "No bad! Leg strong!" She reached down and rubbed his leg gently below the bandage, her big eyes worried, her mouth half open, the pink tongue passing with slow concentration to and fro along the heavy lips.

He caught her arm above the elbow, closing his fingers on the muscle. She drew back with a little grunt, like a dog when you have hurt his paw but he knows you did not mean to. He still held her arm. Somehow he could not let go. A violent impulse surged through his body. He reached up, grabbed her other arm, pulled her down to his side. She stumbled to her knees on the floor with a volley of Cuna words, but quietly, as if to say, "No, please! Let me go! Please!" Her lips were so close, he could not let her go. He wanted to kiss her. He was on fire for that wonderful tongue-stroked mouth only inches from his. He swung her round like a child. Her face was upturned. He smelt the sweetness in her breath as his mouth crushed against hers. She wrenched away, cried out, pushed at his chest with her hands. Suddenly he panicked. She was frightened. If she called louder they would hear. She must not call out! Must not! He snatched her long hair with one hand, put the other over her mouth, twisted her beneath him, pressed his mouth furiously on her lips. She was mewing, writhing, kicking, her head still pinioned by the hair. Now madness. He fondled the sheen of her breasts and belly, ripped off her skirt, thrust his hands between her thighs. Then a fearful pain in his lower lip, like a dagger. His mouth filled with blood. He tore his lip away, glimpsed her teeth red with his blood, heard the head-splitting squeal that pierced the hot room, reverberating through his skull like the death cry from a porcine abattoir.

He let go of her. As she sprang up, the room was full of brown jabbering men.

CHAPTER TWENTY

In the big room they had their jars raised for yet another toast. Everyone was shouting "Macaweo!" The penetrating scream cut off the voices in mid shout, brought the jars crashing on to the table. Assumpa was first through the inner door. The others leaped to their feet. As Chucunaquiok went to follow his wife she returned with her arm round Rakiocka, sobbing beside her. Chucunaquiok barked a question. Assumpa shouted back. Chucunaquiok bellowed. Utter silence. An answer from Rakiocka standing with splendid dignity naked among the white men, her throat still choked with tears, telling her father the truth. No one could doubt that. She walked to the ladder, climbed slowly, her long legs last to disappear. Assumpa followed.

At the outer doorway two Cuna leaders were shouting and beckoning. Chucunaquiok strode out, the others after him.

Gideon Jabbinoth stood held by Cunas, many brown hands round his arms and wrists, a mixture of outrage and alarm in the brown faces as if they half expected this wicked relative of God either to slay them by some mysterious exhalation or else vanish from their grasp. Gideon did not struggle, he stood with his left stocking rumpled round his ankle, the breeches caught above the bandage on his thigh, his lip bleeding into his beard. Cadaverous and abject.

Chucunaquiok stared at him and cried in his deep voice, "Shame! Shame!"

The whole village was crowding round, hundreds in a thickening circle. A low murmur swelled up, ominous and hostile.

Joshua Vine asked, "What do they say?"

The chief flipped his hand impatiently, "White man bad! Gold bad! No gold! No carry!"

"This man will be punished," said Joshua. "Do not punish us all."

"No carry! Curse gold!"

Joshua stepped up to Jabbinoth, "You know what you have done?"

There was no answer. A fuddled hopelessness in the bony face.

"You know the punishment!"

A mumble from the bleeding mouth.

"What are you saying?" shouted Joshua.

"I only wanted . . ." The long head bowed, the eyes lowered.

"Wanted! You stupid lecher!"

Joshua beckoned Krauss. They turned away, spoke hurriedly in low voices. An endless minute, then Joshua pointed at a red cedar tree. Krauss hurried off.

The cedar stood at the entrance to the beach path. Thirty feet up, reached by a ladder on the trunk, was a platform between two clefts. Here the Cunas kept a line of wooden hives to tempt the honey bees. The end of the platform stuck out and above it stretched a strong lateral.

184

Gideon saw the pointing hand and looked up at the platform. A terrible thought came into his head. He would have liked to speak to Mr Krauss, but Mr Krauss was hurrying away calling for Marshal Smolkin. The Sultan was strolling after him. Gideon waited, clutched by the Cunas, his wine-sodden thoughts paralysed by fear. He saw Smolkin coming with two seamen. The Cunas stood back. One of the seamen was the red-faced Mulfroy who said Hail Marys in the rigging. Mulfroy was afraid of heights. He never went higher than the mainyard. Gideon had often chased him from some perch he fancied for himself. Now Mulfroy held a coil of rope. Smolkin cut a length. Gideon felt his hands being tied behind his back. He could see Mr Krauss and several seamen climbing the ladder. Gideon knew what was going to happen but somehow he did not believe it. He was dreaming. Sometimes dreams were like that. You said to yourself *This is impossible, I shall wake up.* Mulfroy was going off with the big coil. Gideon was pushed towards the red cedar.

At the trunk his ankles were bound. A long rope fell from above and was passed under his armpits. He felt the jerk as he was hoisted off the ground. He saw the Sultan starting up the ladder. It was strange to find yourself floating up into the sky. What was happening? It was a dream. Now he was standing on the platform. The Sultan came up and there was Mr Krauss and Smolkin and a lot of seamen. All for him! Smolkin was looping the rope into a bunch which he threw up at the bough above. The rope fell back. The third time the rope passed over the bough and Smolkin caught the end as it came down. Now they put the rope's end round Gideon's neck. He felt the bowline draw tight, but he could still breathe. This was not really happening. His head swam with wine fumes. Wild images of terror filled his brain. He called out, "No! No! No!" but no one paid attention. Smolkin bent down. There was more than enough rope to reach from the bough down to the platform, but Smolkin did not cut it, he coiled it into a neat snaky pile, securing the end to a stanchion. Now Gideon was pushed along to the very end of the platform. He looked below. Carcasses were still roasting over red fires. The mules had gone. There was a long pile of saddle bags and panniers. Many faces looking up at him. It was a long way to the ground. If he jumped perhaps his head would slip through the noose. He would wake

185

up. It would all be a dream. He was harnessing the two dappled horses. He heard the Sultan say, "God rest your soul." He felt a prod in his back.

Tom standing with Robert Seaton looked up at the figure poised on the end of the platform. It had happened so quickly. Minutes ago wine at the table, then the scream, then Rakiocka, now the lonely figure, bound, motionless, the rope from his neck leading up over the bough, back to the platform. Silence from the massed Cunas, silence in the trees, a greyness in the circle of sky. A pair of macaws, chunky bodies, stubby wings, long spiky tails, glided from nowhere into a high hole in the cedar.

The figure fell forward, plummeted, blocked to a thudding stop ten feet from the ground, hung by its neck, inert. A rumbling murmur from Cuna throats, but not loud. They did not move. They seemed to be waiting for something. A leader called out, "Chucu!" and at once every man, woman and child took up the cry:

"Chucu! Chucu! Chucu!"

The chief had been standing with folded arms. Now he walked majestically towards the cedar. The Cunas streamed after him, still calling his name, but in the wild, mass voice there was a sinister expectation as if they knew their master would protect them against the still evil stranger dangling from the tree.

Chucunaquiok came to the target, halted, was surrounded by a ring of chanting Cunas. "Chucu! Chucu! Chucu!"

He stood with his legs apart, drew out "Jonathan" the pistol, raised it with both hands.

Bang!

Bang!

A flurry of birds overhead scared by the detonations. A frenzied roar of satisfaction. "Chucooo! Chucooo!" The corpse gyrating slowly from the impact. The Englishmen climbing down off the ladder. Chucunaquiok marching back ahead of them, shouting orders. Cunas breaking from the clamorous circle of audience, running to the lines of poles and mule packs. The Sultan and Krauss coming sternfaced and frowning to where Tom and Robert waited. No comments, no explanations. Dreadful death for one because the alternative was failure

186

for all. The treasure would never reach *Tigress* unless the Cunas helped carry it to the beach.

The packs and panniers were split up into manageable weights, slung on to the poles with two men to each pole, Cunas and mariners. Krauss would go with the leading guides, then the line of pole-bearers, Cunas nearer three hundred than two, weary mariners with a bow or musket on the back and a pole end on the shoulder, then the Sultan, Tom and Robert. So the preparations were quickly made. The exodus from Macaweo began. No farewells, no last handshakes, all celebration obliterated by the sight and significance of the body hanging at the red cedar. Beneath it still squatted the circle of women and children. The Cuna warriors almost to a man were disappearing down the beach path with the laden poles on their shoulders.

Robert Seaton said, "We can't leave him like that."

"We have no choice," said the Sultan.

"We can bury him. Surely?"

"He will not be buried. Look!" He pointed across the clearing. Bundles of wood were being stacked round one of the fires. "They need his ashes. Then his body cannot rise to persecute them."

"Savages!" cried Robert. "It cannot be allowed!"

"It cannot be stopped," said the Sultan. "Would you have every man on *Tigress* lose all he came for?"

"Has the man not paid his penalty?"

"We cannot teach the Cunas their loyalties. There has been vast affront. The girl is a daughter of the gods. Would you suffer your Queen to be defiled by some drunken Spaniard? We are lucky her father allows us to take the treasure. He has not yet forgiven us by the look of him."

Chucunaquiok was approaching. The Sultan held out his hand, but the chief did not take it. He said harshly, "Big ship! Go! Go quick!"

"The gold is on its way," said the Sultan. "I thank you from the bottom of my heart—for all of us."

Chucunaquiok shook his head, "Gold! Curse to Macaweo!"

"You will not see the gold again."

"Curse! Curse!" The dark eyes burned with contempt. He clapped his temples as if wounded by unspeakable distress.

"Let us part friends," said the Sultan. "We are brothers."

187

The Chief's face was a mask of impregnable gravity. He answered:

"Rakiocka my daughter!"

That was how they left him.

The forest was very hot and quiet and dim, a relief after the daylight horror of execution, yet still with its own fungoid stench of death. The tail of the column was all mariners, and Tom, walking behind with Robert and the Sultan, noticed how they trudged stiff-footed after the long march, stumbling now and then from the weight on their poles. They were not talking. Neither was Tom. Sometimes his mind flashed to Paxcombe and his parents and Alis Dewmark, but they were all so distant, hardly real. His ankles ached. His brain was as tired as his legs. He rubbed the *musketa* bites on his neck. He did not feel good. Probably too little sleep and too much wine. It did not matter, nothing mattered now. His thought, as far as he could think or wanted to think, was simply that in spite of Jabbinoth's misfortune the rest of them had done it, all of them together, they had got what they came for.

As they walked out of the forest he looked down over the last fifty yards of thorny scrub and saw *Tigress* waiting in the bay. She looked clean and ready under the grey sky. The big side hatches on the gun deck were open, the derricks rigged above them in the waist, the top canvases curving in a gentle off-shore breeze, the mainsails still furled waiting for the anchor to be raised. She was beautiful.

The tide was up and the loading had begun. The mule packs as they arrived were being stacked on the narrow sand. A few yards from shore a line of twelve rafts bobbed about held by Cunas up to their waists in water. Viccars had brought a party from the ship. He and Krauss were shouting at the seamen of whom some were passing out the packs from hand to hand, holding them high out of water, while others stood at the rafts with the Cunas ready to lash down the sacks and panniers with criss-cross ropes secured to ringbolts. The empty barrels giving buoyancy to the rafts were visible round the edges. As the weight of cargo increased the rafts sank a little, but they still held the packs clear of the water. The carpenters had done well. On the sand lay a heap of tarpaulins to cover the rafts as a final security. Further along the shore a fleet of long canoes were drawn up ready to ferry the mariners and tow the rafts.

The mariners who had carried the poles dropped their burden on the sand and like the mules sprawled down tired but happy. The Sultan told them they had done enough. They would be ferried to *Tigress* while the loading went on. He called to a Cuna leader, pointing to the canoes, and the canoes were pushed into the water and manned by Cuna paddlers. No smiles or wobbling heads now. Serious brown faces, yet with a strange hint of some private triumph. The mariners started to shuffle along to the canoes. One was fumbling at his belt and the Sultan shouted what had he got there. It was a gold ingot. The Sultan was not too hard with him. He took the ingot and said in a voice for all to hear, "The gold will be shared when we land at Lingmouth. You will be searched as you go aboard. Any man hiding gold in his breeches will find himself in the sea."

Three more ingots were put back in the panniers and the mariners went off in the long canoes. Robert Seaton went with them. Some looked as if they might need him. The loading was completed, the tarpaulins stretched and secured. The party from *Tigress* was ferried back. The canoes returned and now they lined up on the tow ropes, three canoes to each raft, all paddlers now, ten to each canoe. One last canoe waited for the Sultan, Krauss and Tom. The Sultan picked up three seashells and said, "For a keepsake," and Krauss and Tom took the shells and stepped into the canoe where four unsmiling Cunas sat with their paddles. As the Sultan took his seat a dark figure came from the scrub and stood on the margin of sand. A throng of Cunas who had not been needed for the rafts were gathering up the poles. He called to them and they dropped the poles and clustered along the water's edge looking out towards *Tigress* as they had looked that first evening, but now they carried no spears and threw no white flowers into the sea. Behind them their chief stood hands on hips, a statue in walnut.

"He has come to wish us good riddance," said Krauss.

"Farewell, Chucunaquiok!" said the Sultan softly. "Farewell, my brother!"

The canoe moved out through the slow-moving rafts. The towing canoes were paddling with care, edging the precious heavy cargo towards the ship. When the three officers climbed aboard *Tigress* and stood at the waist rail watching the solitary canoe going back, the rafts were no more than half-way out. On *Tigress* the derricks were ready with the big nets. The rafts were too heavy to be hoisted intact, so when they came alongside seamen would be lowered to take off the tarpaulins and lift the panniers into the nets. When the treasure was safe on board the rafts would be left as a parting gift to the Cunas. At the gun deck hatches, along all the starboard rails, on the yards and in the rigging the voyagers watched the twelve creeping platforms. There was a sticky heat in the air, the sun hidden behind a veil of grey cloud.

Then it happened.

Chucunaquiok, small in the distance, still standing apart, raised his arm. There was a flash, only one barrel this time, a cracking blast that echoed up into the forest and rippled out over the bay.

The canoes stopped with back-paddling froth, turned, sped to the rafts. Plopping puddles as brown men dived into the water. Heads bobbing like coconuts round the rafts. The canoes—two paddlers left in each, the tow ropes cast off— sliding towards the beach. From the beach a rush of Cunas surging out like porpoises to join their comrades.

On *Tigress* a moment of stupefaction, then a chorus of frantic obscenities, the voice of the Sultan yelling, "Bowmen! Musketeers!" the voice of Krauss yelling down to Viccars, "The guns! The guns!", voices from everywhere to anywhere yelling with fury, men coming down from the rigging and others seizing their weapons from wherever they lay, the rattle of muskets and a rain of arrows, and the Sultan yelling, "The boats, Mr Smolkin!" And even then only a partial realization. The rafts had stopped. They floated like a pattern of tarpaulins a hundred and fifty yards from the ship. The Cunas were massing round them. What next?

The bobbing heads vanished. The heads coming from the beach kept dipping under water. The fusilade from the ship died down because there was hardly a target visible. Krauss and the Sultan were shouting for the boats and the guns, but there was no time for either. The boats were lashed for sea and the guns would take ten minutes to lay out and train. Long before that the Cunas had obeyed their orders.

First a single barrel appearing beside a raft. Then two more from other rafts. Brown heads coming up for a gulp of air, here and there a raised brown arm with a knife in its hand, then only the smooth sea and barrels appearing everywhere as the cords

190

were cut beneath. Now the tarpaulins were low in the water, now one by one as the buoyancy was stripped away the black squares settled under their impossible burden, paused half awash, were gone. The Cunas were gone, scattering under water, momentarily on view, soon beyond reach. Chucuna-quiok was gone. Only the barrels were left, swollen legless pigs floating in disarray.

Tigress lay in a vacuum of disbelief. All over the ship men were waiting, dazed by fury, bewildered by shock. As if, like children rushing to a door marked *Happiness*, they had pulled it open to find a brick wall. They waited for an order. Even Krauss waited. Tom watched the Sultan's face as he looked at the aimless floating barrels.

"Lower the boats! Smolkin! Fall in the boat parties! A grapple and line for each boat! Two men to haul!"

The bellowing orders jerked the ship out of her paralysis. The two boats were already unlashed and lying on deck. When the rafts sank the hands had stopped their work. Now they leaped to obey. The boats were manhandled to the derricks, hooked up, swung out, lowered gently. Rope ladders fell.

"Mr Krauss, take the skiff! Mr Dakyn—with me!"

Viccars came up from the gun deck. Normally so calm, he looked weary and uncertain. "The guns, sir? Shall we carry on?"

"Too late!"

The Sultan pointed to the shore. The last Cuna had reached the sand. The long canoes miniaturized in the distance were being carried up into the scrub, black sticks lifted by small brown men into the curtain of forest.

"If I could lay one salvo!" said Viccars.

"The Cunas are no matter now. It is the gold that needs our attention."

"In twelve fathoms of water?"

"We must go fishing, Mr Viccars."

The master gunner stared at him. "From the boats? With grapples?"

"The breeze is against us. We cannot move inshore."

"But the weight! There's tons of it!"

"And it is lashed down, Mr Viccars. But perhaps the tarpaulin has come adrift here and there. A few panniers would be enough."

"Is there time?"

"We must clear the island by sunset. By dawn the coast may be crawling with Spanish sail. We must do what we can."

The boat parties were going down the ladders, and Viccars said, "Good luck!" and the Sultan said, "You would never forgive me if we did not try," and swung his leg over the rail.

In the bows of the cutter Tom stood with Dykes and another seaman. The oars were manned, the Sultan on the tiller. Tom had never seen the cutter afloat. Compared with the skiff it was cumbrous, but steady in the water. When they came among the barrels, now widely scattered, the Sultan gave the order and Tom flung out the grapple with the line attached.

The two seamen paid out the line slowly, the end secured to a thwart. The same from the skiff twenty yards away. Oars were shipped while the grapples sank. Depth unknown. The boats were half-way from *Tigress* to the shore. Probably the sea floor was shelving. There might be less than twelve fathoms now. But the tide was high. Somewhere down there lay the panniers, last night mule-borne under the moon—how the ingot had glowed!—now buried in a million tons of water.

While the grapple sank the line stayed taut. Tom watched the coil of rope shrinking beside his feet. When the line slackened the grapple had found a resting place.

The boats rowed slowly to and fro twenty yards apart. He pictured the iron claw dragging on the sea-bed, bumping on a rock, slowed by sand, catching now and then on something unseen, checking the line for a moment, sending a shudder of hope to the surface, ungrappling what had been grappled, stumbling forward on the blind chance of a catch.

There was no chance. The Sultan knew that. The tarpaulins had been well secured. No flapping edge would reveal a pannier, and if the claw caught timber the weight of a laden raft would be as much as the cutter itself. To and fro went the boats, and every man knew why they were fishing for the impossible. It was as the Sultan had said. They must try, lest they spent their lives in a delusion of regret.

The sky was still light but the sun had dipped beneath the cliff line. The oarsmen rowed slowly with sullen defiance, pausing when the line shuddered, edging on as it went free, turning back between the bobbing barrels.

At last the Sultan stood up and ordered: "That is enough!"

192

And raising his voice across the water: "Mr Krauss! Haul in the grapple! Return aboard!"

The oarsmen backed on their blades, and when the boats stood still Tom nodded to the two seamen and watched the line coming in, dropped with scowls into an untidy pile in the bows. It came up easily, clearly without weight attached.

Dykes was hauling the rope with desperation in his face. When the grapple appeared and Tom reached down and brought it over the gunwale Dykes suddenly cried, "No!" and jumped aside and stooped and tore off his shoes, then his stockings, his breeches, his shirt, till he stood naked with his knife in his hand: "I'll go down! I can find it!"

A roar from the Sultan: "Stand fast, that man!"

But Dykes shouted, "I'll get the tarpaulin! I can swim! I'll pull the line to come up!" And seized the grapple, took a prodigious breath, and leaped, and was gone beneath the blue water.

Tom snatched the line as it ran out, letting it graze through his fingers. The rippling circle of entry widened and died on the surface.

In the stern the Sultan stood silent. He could have told them to hoist Dykes back, but he stood motionless and his silence spoke for everyone. If Dykes could reach the bottom, if he found a raft, if he could slash the tarpaulin, free a pannier, plant the grapple, tug the line, if he had breath to do all this and then be hauled up, what a prize he would deliver. Not the whole treasure. That could never be raised. But a single pannier of golden ingots would seem like a sign from God that He was not entirely wrathful.

As Tom paid out the line he could feel the others praying Dykes to succeed. Tom took a deep breath himself, held it, willed it down to the sea-bed. The line ran on. He felt a hovering emptiness in his lungs, his skull tightened, he started counting how long he could last. A little longer. He could not—but he must.

Then the line was tugged. A choke in the water. Someone cried, "He's got it!" Hands grabbed the line. The Sultan shouted, "Steady!" As Tom hauled on the wet section he could feel the weight. Now a dizzinesss as he still held breath. His head would explode. He could stand no more. Guiltily he

193

inhaled. The lungs that were rising from below could not inhale. But soon. Surely.

When the iron grapple broke surface there was a gasping cheer from the boat, stifled by the appearance of the human head. Then the torso. The grapple had caught under the armpit. As the head lolled forward in the water Tom reached down, grasped the bicep with one hand, the shank with the other, freed the jagged metal from the flesh. A few weak drops of blood splashed into Elizabeth Bay. No treasure on the claw, only a drowned man. Tom passed the grapple into the boat and with his free hand clutched the other bicep. The body came higher out of the water, the lolling head fell back, the boat lurched, and Tom was jerked down to rub noses with the dank face whose fish eyes stared into his own.

His fingers fell loose from the flabby bicep. Seaman Dykes, trained archer, friend of Pipkin, sank waterlogged for ever.

The boats returned, were hoisted aboard, the derricks stowed, the lateen unfurled, the anchor taken up. Tom watched it happen, listened to the familiar sounds, felt the shudder as *Tigress* started to move, saw the high jaws of rock on either side when she slid into the open sea, heard the soundings called from the forecastle as she slipped along the island channels. The veil of cloud was clearing and when sunset came the sky astern was ablaze.

Tom stood beside the Sultan at the mainmast compass. Seamen passed with stony faces. What desperate thoughts? What conceivable hopes?

Sirius, the only crew member who had not been ashore, was whining round the deck. Because there were no rat smells? Or did he feel the turmoil?

The Sultan, in a rasping matter-of-fact voice, as if it were the most obvious truth, said, "God has brought us this far. He will not send us home empty-handed."

PART FOUR

The Homecoming

CHAPTER TWENTY-ONE

Tigress was not the same.

Tom saw it that evening at supper in the great cabin. They spoke, but not their thoughts. Mostly food talk with simmering politeness. The fish was fresh, was it not? The vegetables went well with the fish. Was Mr Gostigo satisfied with the stowage of victuals? Steward! More wine! Mr Dakyn was looking pale. Had Mr Viccars ever tasted better fish? In the surgeon's opinion had the mariners been tried by their long walk? Mr Krauss said it was a treat to have supper without cockroaches. He complimented Mr Gostigo on the scouring of the ship. Mr Viccars said the roaches would be back, but perhaps not the rats. The hold had been swept of all corpses. No sign of living rats, so the voyage home should be rat-free.

"Unless," said Gostigo with a twisted grin, "the Devil has given them a hiding place."

"We'll have no Devil on *Tigress*," said Krauss. The left eye was still less hideous than usual, the voice mellowed by the wine cups of Macaweo.

"Some say he is here already," muttered Gostigo. He had not been drinking. His voice was irritatingly distinct.

A flicker of rage in Krauss's bloodshot enormity. Then with ominous restraint, "Not in this cabin, I trust?"

"Surely not."

"Then where?"

Gostigo did not answer. He sat staring dark-eyed at the table as if he could see through the timber into the depths of the sea.

"Mr *Gostigo*?" The cabin filled with threat.

The bosun gave a gasp, clapped his hand over his mouth as if to stifle the escape of a violent prisoner.

Krauss stiffened in his chair, asked in the loud formal voice he used to offenders brought before him, "If the Devil is on this ship and he is not in this cabin, then where may he be? I require an answer, sir. At once!"

Gostigo's arm shot up, his hand stabbed at the bulkhead: "Out there! At the compass! With the dog beside him!"

Krauss had his glass in mid air. He slammed it down, caught the edge of the platter. The crash of splintered glass, the white fish flakes sprayed over the table, the steward rushing to clear up. All without words. When the food and wine had been restored and the steward had gone to fetch fruit Krauss took a long drink, set down his glass with emphatic deliberation and said, "The bosun made a foolish jest. We shall not remember it. If we took him in earnest he would be hanged for mutinous lies!"

The meal finished without further jest. Marshal Smolkin appeared at the door. On this first evening Krauss had ordered rounds before lights-out. He would take them himself with Tom and the marshal.

On the familiar journey Tom again saw the new *Tigress* where every face seemed a mask for thoughts too terrible to be voiced.

On rounds you were met at each mess by the hand in charge. He reported if all was well. You inspected the bedding. He stated any complaints or requests. If a seaman looked talkative you had a word with him.

That was how it had always been. It was different now.

On the gun deck Smolkin called, "Stand for rounds!" and the party walked along an avenue of dummies. At each mess Krauss was met by the gunner, inquired of complaints or requests, was told none. No man moved, no man spoke. Tom knew most of the gunners by name, but he had not worked with them and did not know them as he knew the archers. Standing by their guns they looked an ugly lot. Between the culverins stood two men from Yarmouth, Skelling and Cage. They were hard-boned East Englanders of the same physique as Blessington who had died of scurvy. Tom knew their names because on the outward journey they had been brought before him for brawling on the messdeck. As both had presented equally bloody cheeks, with no animosity towards each other, he had dismissed the case with a caution. Now, as Krauss was speaking to the messman, Tom stopped beside these two bony apes who regarded him morosely. Skelling stood rigid, but Cage slowly wiped the back of his hand to and fro beneath his nose, puffing down his nostrils to expel the snot. A clear message to authority. *We have lost the gold. What can we do now? If you are our superior tell us what to do.*

The same in the cookroom. Nils's damson lip looked better, but Henrik's eye was a slit in the poisoned bulge. Tom's inquiry brought two surly grunts. Further along the orlop more signs of baffled fury and disquietude. In the mess where Dykes had lived men scrambled to their feet, the bedding unkempt, a heel kicking away a tankard, in the eyes a desperate protest. *What now?*

When rounds were over Krauss said he would relieve the Sultan on watch and Tom went up to the quarterdeck.

The moon was still almost full, no stars visible. The narrow island channels were astern and all sails set. Beyond the lateen yard he could see the maintop bellying in a breeze from the south. Many times he had felt the beauty of *Tigress* on a warm night. The pale lustre of the sea, the purposeful tremble of the ship that even with death aboard was taking the living towards the gold. Now there was no purpose and the beauty was sterile.

He paced slowly from side to side of the gently rocking deck, nine steps between the rails. He had a stiff neck and the deck felt hard through his shoes. The forest path had been softer but the brine in his nostrils was better than the stench of fungus. He heard no other footsteps and was surprised by the Sultan's voice: "Have you found your answer?"

The compact figure approaching in the moonlight, black beard trim, eyes shadowed in their sockets, the dog Sirius jumping alongside.

"No, sir."

"Come."

In the quiet cabin the Sultan poured brandy and they sat at the dark oak desk. Sirius was restless and the Sultan gave him broken biscuit saying, "Calm yourself, I am back," and the dog went to his corner. The Sultan sipped the brandy, tapped his fist on the brass-bound Bible, and said, "Well, Tom Dakyn, what now? Would to God we had been content and dwelt on the other side of Jordan? Is that it?"

"Sir?"

"Joshua and his men displeased the Lord and were punished. They wished they had stayed at home on the other side of

197

Jordan. You might say at Paxcombe on the other side of the Atlantic. Then Joshua grovelled, and the Lord did not like that. He told Joshua to get up. 'Wherefore liest thou upon thy face?' And Joshua rose and the Lord said, 'Sanctify yourselves against tomorrow!' "

Tom thought of Rockways, and Sir Joshua Vine a steaming kettle of conviction. Now it was the same Sir Joshua.

"They put failure behind them. They triumphed. The man who had caused their misery was hanged upon a tree till eventide. Joshua and his men became rich and victorious. And so shall we!" He thumped the Bible. "Fortune will come to us. We must never doubt that. You understand?"

Tom did not understand. But he believed. Against the evidence, the searing images of Jabbinoth on the rope, and the empty barrels, and the drowned face of Dykes, these living amber-lit eyes gave him an inexplicable sensation of trust.

Joshua Vine smiled grimly and said, "On the way out they were sustained by the thought of gold. They believed me when I said it was waiting. I was right. Now I must make them believe a second time. It will not be easy. There will be some who doubt. Krauss tells me there is one already who speaks of the Devil."

Later in the darkness of the great cabin Tom lay on the hard bunk and felt the others awake. Dawn with the mules seemed a lifetime ago. His head ached and there were pains in his muscles.

It was not only Gostigo who doubted, but Gostigo might be the one who mattered most.

CHAPTER TWENTY-TWO

Tom woke with nausea and at breakfast suddenly felt the hot cabin grow cold. Icy shudders rippled through his chest, his arms were trembling. When he stood up his legs buckled and Robert helped him on to the bunk where he lay shivering with the coverlet drawn round his neck while the others went to morning prayers.

They seemed to be away a long time. Robert came back and sat on the bunk and told him what the Sultan had told the ship's company.

"It is quite simple," said Robert with hilarity in his Highland voice. "We go across the Caribbean. We pass Jamaica and go through between Cuba and Hispaniola. There will be many merchantmen. We shall take only the best. Then we shall go north to find the strong west winds that will take us home."

"And the gold?" said Tom.

"That was a test. Fate was against us. Now we discover what kind of men we are."

"How did the mariners take that?"

"Without a word. In the most awful silence. Those that were there."

"Not a full muster?"

"About half of them."

"Marshal Smolkin must be losing his authority."

Robert shook his head: "It is not Smolkin's fault. Think of yesterday morning. We had breakfast with the mules! And now today! The men are desperate. Can you blame them?"

"Don't shout," said Tom. "My head feels like an eggshell. Nobody blames anybody."

A convulsive chill swept through his body. He saw his fingers. The nails were tinged with blue. He held out his hand, showing Robert the nails, and Robert took the wrist between finger and thumb and looked at Tom in a friendly personal way and said quietly, "I've been on the messdecks. You are not the only one, I'm afraid."

"How many?"

"Fifteen. They are all shivering like you. There will be more." He dropped Tom's hand and stood up.

"Is it the calenture?" asked Tom. He tried to make it sound casual.

"So they all tell me. I have not seen it before."

"But you know about it."

"In theory," smiled Robert.

"The cool wind, you said. Why this cool wind and not others?"

"I do not know."

"And the madness?" said Tom lightly.

"Oh! That was seamen's talk. Some of them down there have had it. And survived."

Tom smiled back: "What cure have you got for us?"

Robert counted on his fingers. "Rest. No meat. Plenty of fruit and water. No wine."

He took a jug of water from the table and put it beside the bunk. As he went towards the door a steward named Pulmar came in with a bucket and mop.

Robert waved back to Tom: "Learn what you can. Then you can doctor me if I succumb."

He was gone, and Pulmar started to clean the deck. Officers were not usually lying down after breakfast, and Tom waited for an inquiry, but Pulmar dipped the mop without a word. Tom had had many chats with Pulmar but today they had nothing to say to each other. Pulmar sluiced the deck, then fell on his knees to scrub. His heaving back was a reproach to heaven. Pulmar like gunner Cage with his snotty hand had only one question, to which Tom had no answer.

Pulmar finished and went out and the forenoon began to seem long. Tom had taken off his shoes but not his breeches. Something was nicking his thigh and he felt in his pocket and brought out the seashell the Sultan had given him as a keepsake. It was a cowrie shell and it smelt of salt. He shook it, and sand came out, and he threw the shell across the deck. He needed no keepsake to remind him of Macaweo.

Now the cabin just as suddenly as it had felt cold felt chokingly hot. His throat was dry, a tide of warm blood flooded up his neck and his head seemed to swell with burning vapour. He flung back the coverlet, gulped some water, lay down propping his head gently against the bolster. His head cleared and his throat had saliva. For a while he lay still, more annoyed than frightened. Then the hot tide swept through him again as if someone had opened a tap of firewater into his veins.

So the forenoon went on and the fever grew. Slowly, with less respite between the surges. It was annoying just to lie and wait. The sun shone through the porthole. He imagined the white topsails pouting against the blue sky. Perhaps a breath of salt air. But when he stood up he swayed dizzily and sank stretching his weak legs on the bunk. How long to dinner? He was not hungry. But where was everyone? Had no one been told? Viccars and Gostigo in turn came in to fetch something and seemed surprised to see him. They were solicitous but with an air of preoccupation. Then he dozed and when he opened his eyes the Sultan was standing beside him.

"You were asleep," said the Sultan. "Do you feel hot or cold?"

"Very hot," said Tom.

"And before that? Earlier?"

"Very cold."

"It is the calenture," said the Sultan abruptly. He looked down with a kindly exasperation. "Your fever has begun. It is not yet bad. When it is bad you will have wild thoughts and see strange things. There will be a madness in your head. You must prepare for this. There must be an image in your mind that you can hold on to. Not a person. You will not see people as you see them now. Something you believe in. Your home perhaps. Think of Paxcombe Hall. Think of it now. Say 'Paxcombe Hall'."

"Paxcombe Hall," said Tom.

The Sultan smacked his fist on his palm and said, "When I was your age I had the calenture. I had no home, so I believed in the ship I would have one day. I did not die. But I saw others lose their wits and perish."

"The Idiot's Death?" said Tom.

"Because idiots die of it. I did not die. Nor must you."

He went out and Tom was left with his fever. By dinner time he was in a flood of heat. He watched the others come in and sit down to their food. He wanted none himself, only a mouthful of soup and a few sips of salt water which Robert explained was not from the sea but fresh spring water salted from the barrel. Tom asked no questions. Already he felt cut off in a stupor of his own. They all looked so cool sitting at the table. He heard them talking but could not follow what they said. He dozed. The cabin was empty. He thought of Paxcombe Hall, seeing the round tower and his bedroom window. There was no difficulty. Pigeons flew above the line of gables. His cheeks and neck were pulsing with hot blood. He got up and stumbled across for another carafe from the rack. On the bulkhead hung the polished bronze mirror they shared to trim their beards. He saw the scarlet frowning face with dry lips parted, the tousled hair and short beard, their redness muddied in the bronze. What a sight, Tom Dakyn! He flopped back on the bunk and the afternoon collapsed into a haze of surging heat and floating images that became dreams.

He woke with Robert's hand on his shoulder. The overhead lamp was burning. There was a smell of tallow.

"They will not hurt you," said Robert.

"Hurt me? Who?"

"The mastiffs. You were shouting about mastiffs. What were they doing to you?"

Tom shook his head. The dream had gone. So had the fever. Supper was finished. The others were at table with their wine. The dry skin-hotness had left him. Instead he was draped in sodden clothing. On his belly he felt a puddle of sweat. All day he had lain in his shirt and breeches. Now they clung like a soaking shroud. Robert helped him take them off, brought a pile of towels to absorb the rivulets that welled from his whole body. For what seemed hours, while the others talked and drank and got ready for bed, he lay exuding moisture in frightening amounts. Surely there was none left? But there was. What became of a body when the last drop oozed away? A heap of dry death? He never discovered. Late that night when the others slept he felt a stillness in his limbs and a pleasant warmth in his skin, but the sweating had ceased.

Had the calenture come and gone?

In the morning he felt empty and weak but not ill. He went on deck, enjoyed the sun, soon tired, ate some fruit and drank the salted water, spoke when anyone spoke to him, rested and slept, saw the sunset, lay in the dark cabin wondering what dawn would bring.

It brought the calenture. The same cycle. An hour or two of shuddering chilliness, a day of dry burning stupor with nausea and headache, an evening of towel-soaking sweat.

Tigress took sixteen days to cross the Caribbean and for Tom it was a double life, days of increasing fever when he lay helpless unable to think or believe in anything but his own peril, alternating with days when he could watch and listen to ship life without much strength to take part. There was little for him to do. Archery practice was over. The bows were packed away. He went on rounds with Smolkin, but on the messdecks there was only sullen apathy and Smolkin brought him no defaulters. They had no spirit to misbehave. Robert Seaton had reported fifteen sufferers from the calenture. As the days went on the numbers grew. Each man had his own day-on day-off cycle, but some were on the opposite curve so that he saw them

202

stretched out with fever, while others he met tottered about like himself. Not all those who had marched to Panama were stricken by the fever of the cool wind. Uncertainty bred fear. In the evenings, when once the cheerful shouts and songs of brawling mariners on the messdecks could be heard in the great cabin, there was now a threatful silence broken sometimes by a flurry of angry voices soon dying away, bursts of gathering thunder.

In the cabin nothing was the same. On the outward journey in spite of the long boring days down the Atlantic and the heat that brought maggots and cockroaches and bad food and rancid beer, and after Santa Antao the deaths from scurvy and dysentery climaxing in the night of rats and the death of Fernie, in spite of these trials there had always been a unity because everyone deep in his mind had held the same vision. Somehow, somewhere the gold would be won. No one had foreseen the loss.

Now the unity had gone because there was no vision to share. Tom looked at his fellow officers and saw four men with nothing in common but misfortune. Each had joined ship for his own reason. Hope had made them brothers. In disappointment they were strangers again.

Krauss did his best to preserve civility at table, but when he addressed you the glaring eye negated the courtesy of his inquiry. Viccars, once so impassive, now developed an almost slovenly gloom. There was still gun-drill, but no firing till *Tigress* was clear of listeners on the coast. The master gunner seemed wrapt in private dejection. His beard, once rounded and kempt, now daily grew into an irregular spade which he tugged and scratched between mouthfuls. Robert Seaton was busy with the sick in their early stages of fever. When he was not on the messdecks or in the cookroom he sat for hours in his den working through his notes and journals. His flute he never volunteered and it was not requested. Gostigo made no more rash outbursts, but the news he brought from the workshops and storerooms in the forecastle was disquieting. Wild stories were going round. Someone had seen a cloud at sunset shaped like a wolf with slavering jaws. Violent hammering had been heard in the paint store, but when someone went in the space was empty. Three separate men on the same night had dreamed of a crocodile dragging a tiger cub into a swamp. Mariners'

203

chatter no doubt. Gostigo could not give names. It was always someone who had heard from someone else. All nonsense, of course. But it was Gostigo's duty, was it not, to report such things? Krauss thanked the bosun with an icy calm. So the unrest of the ship percolated aft into the great cabin like the smell from a hidden drain.

On his lucid days Tom watched and listened to the life on *Tigress* but now on the ship he had grown to love he felt an interloper. He was no seaman. It was all a pretence. He heard deck-hands using shipwords he did not understand. They all knew their tasks, he knew nothing. He could not furl a sail or splice a rope, and the scraps of navigation he had picked up would never stand a practical test. If it were up to him to bring *Tigress* home she would be lost for ever in the ocean desert. Six hundred miles to Hispaniola, they said. As he gazed round the perimeter of empty water stretching to the limits of vision it might as well have been six million.

At noon the Sultan and Krauss still met to take sunsights. Tom did not join them. He had no heart to play with the astrolabe and cross staff. Besides, his legs ached and there were steep ladders up to the poop. From the half deck he could see the two men with their instruments standing against the blue sky. The breeze was favourable. The sea was laughing with white foam. Krauss and the Sultan, the two in charge, were the decision-makers. The rest only carried out orders. But were the decisions good? How were they reached? Were there really merchant ships waiting to be plundered? And if the chance came would *Tigress* be fit to take it? Her entrails had been ripped by scurvy and dysentery. Death in terrible ways, but at least known to come from bad food and drink. Now again there was sickness, not yet death, but a mystery fever, wafted into your body by a gentle wind that at the time had seemed pleasant as you sat in the long grass after the insect-lacerations of the forest. As Tom watched the two friends high up together on the poop, isolated in their authority, he thought of the apprehension that was brewing on the messdecks. Suppose no merchantmen ever appeared?

There were none in sight now. Not a sail in the whole circumference of sunny water.

The only fellow travellers were sharks, an incessant convoy, the black triangular fins sliding to and fro past *Tigress*, grouping and regrouping.

On fever days he lost awareness of time. Somewhere after breakfast the shivering chilliness gave way to the fierce dry heat that fried his brains, and when the heat changed to sopping perspiration there was lamplight and his cabinmates finishing their supper or preparing for sleep.

He did not know the moment, but during these lonely days he had a new experience. The fear of death. He had always known about death. As a child, the death of farm animals. As a boy of ten, his father's story of the death of Uncle Georges. The head on the paling, the awful truth shared by the boy to protect his mother. Death by flame at San Corda, death ulcerous and smelly at sea, death by rope, death hoisted on a grapple, all these he had watched and shared, with pity, with horror, with the secret relief that the lucky feels in the presence of the unlucky. But now for the first time in his life he feared for himself.

Waiting for the fever he was frightened. The fever was a stranger bearing strange thoughts, entering his body unasked and once inside taking control so that Tom was a guest in his own house, helpless beside the rampant new owner, and worse, because the moment always came when they changed places and Tom was master again, but now feverish with the approach of his death, not knowing himself, half hearing a weak voice somewhere in the cabin whispering, "Paxcombe Hall", and an image of turreted roofs on a hillside, but the image distant and useless, swept aside by the fear that he was dying. Men were already dead from the calenture. Ten days out from Elizabeth Bay he had watched two white canvas parcels falling into the sea and he remarked to Robert, "So it has begun," and Robert said, "It began yesterday." Tom had not been told on his fever day that three of his archers had died. Now in the stifling cabin when the small voice said "Paxcombe Hall" he felt impatient with such folly when his head was dizzy with hot fumes and his limbs weak as if the strength in the bones had boiled away. He clenched his hands but the grip was infantile. He said aloud, "God, help me," but even as he spoke he knew that help was not coming from the sky, only from himself. Not from his home, not from gratitude or expectation, but simply because

205

Tom Dakyn would not die as long as Tom Dakyn forbade it. He said aloud, "I will not! I will *not!*" Then a sickening heat filled his skull and he lay back and watched the lamp swinging overhead.

Not only death but the manner of it. One evening as he was beginning to sweat after the fever a cackle of violent laughter burst through the timbers. Someone for'ard had a joke fit for hell. Suddenly the insane staccato was cut off. Suspended moments. A fearful angry voice shouting indistinguishable protests drowned by a chorus of anti-voices. Silence. Thuds in the silence. Muffled groans. Gagged, they sounded. What had the man said? What were they doing to him?

When Robert came in Tom asked about the rumpus and Robert hesitated and said, "I heard nothing."

"You must have heard it. He was laughing like a lunatic."

"Oh, that one," said Robert. "He was in the carpenters' mess up for'ard. I'm surprised you could hear."

"I heard very well."

"One of Hesket's men," said Robert.

Tom waited. Robert handed him a sweat towel from the hook above the bunk and said he hoped it would not be fish again for supper tonight.

Tom said, "Why was he making that noise. I want to know."

Robert pursed his lips, "They have a delirium. Their wits are astray. We do what we can."

"By restraint?"

"What?"

"That man was being held down. What was he trying to do? Kill someone?"

"Only himself, perhaps."

"Has anyone done that?"

Robert hesitated as if he had a problem with his answer, but when it came it was quite simple, "Three men have gone overboard. They were seen. One was shouting he would climb the hill. The other two were calling for home."

They looked at each other in silence.

A steward came in to lay the table and Robert glanced at him with relief. But Tom had not been going to ask more questions. He understood Robert's reluctance. Robert's eyes said plainly, "Men are going mad. You are not mad, not yet. It may not come, but if it does I shall be helpless. So I will not alarm you."

But Tom had been alarmed since the Sultan had told him he "*must*" not die. As if he had a choice. But was this true? "I will not! I will *not!*" He could believe in himself as long as his mind was in charge. But suppose the mind gave way? Suppose he looked overboard and saw the gardens of Paxcombe and decided to take a stroll? Would *Tigress* stop to pick him up?

She would not. There would be no time. The sharks would not waste a moment.

He had better save his wits. But how? So far he had always been aware when the stranger entered the house. They recognized each other. Sometimes it was Tom-from-Paxcombe waiting for the wild hot man to come through the door, and sometimes it was Lord-fever-Dakyn aware of death and contemptuous of the lamb's voice bleating about Paxcombe. But it had always been a performance, two Toms both played by himself. Suppose the recognition stopped? Suppose Lord Madness took full charge? Would honest Tom still have a say?

He dabbed his sopping stomach with the towel and lay back ready for the evening of rivulets. He did not mind them now. He knew he would not disappear in his own puddle. The others came in for supper. Next morning he woke for his rest day. His legs were unusually weak. He sat in the sunshine by the scuppers on the quarterdeck and watched the shark fins looping to and fro beside the ship like insignia on the caps of submarine demons engaged in some peripatetic ritual of sacrifice. He had little appetite for the plantain mash at dinner time. He drank his salted water and two tankards of fresh. In the evening he dozed, not listening to the cabin talk.

He woke to fever day. But something was different. At breakfast Krauss said he looked better, and Tom said he felt better. But it was not true. He felt weak like a drowning child clinging to a twig. When the others went out to their forenoon business he felt an absurd panic. He wanted someone to stay, but could not ask.

He waited for the chilliness in his body, and when it came he hoped it would last because he was frightened of what would follow.

Much later, lying alone, he saw his cold finger tips change from blue to tingling warm pink. In the chimney of his throat a blast of hot air as if a furnace had been lit below. In the leafy glade beside the strawberry bed he saw his nurse Ellen Rufoote waving to him.

She was calling but he could not hear her words. She wore her pale blue dress with white cuffs, his earliest memory, and over it her apron. She must have come from the kitchen. He could smell the crusty loaf on the table. He reached up and poked the loaf with his finger, and she laughed and lifted the loaf. He could smell the yeast. The table was covered with loaves fresh from the oven. From the window he could see her down by the strawberry bed waving to him. She held both hands high in the air, beckoning. He was standing at the round window in the turret bedroom, he might have squeezed through the window and floated down to where she stood, that would have been easy with his strong legs, but unfortunately his head was so big it would get stuck, so he decided to run down and join Ellen by the strawberry bed. He waved back, jerking his thumb to show he was coming down, and turned to the white mule beside the bedroom door. She was eating a coiled pile of rope. She gazed up at him with her brown liquid eyes and said, "Will you marry me?" and he said, "I love you" and she gave a long whinny and went on chewing up the rope till the iron grapple attached to the end was hanging below her chin. She could not swallow the grapple, so she bit through the rope and the grapple fell on the deck with a clang, and she nodded her head gracefully like a woman nodding to music. He picked up her halter but she stood on her long brown legs and held his hand and he marched towards the door, proud to have her beside him, and she squeezed his bicep with her soft oily fingers and he could smell her skin. There was lightning overhead and from the huge trees the massive rope plummeted down and thudded to a halt in front of his face and an object as big as a barrel terrified him, but the naked brown girl said, "No bad! No bad!" and he brushed away the spider with the staring eyes and opened the door because he wanted to show Ellen Rufoote the tall brown sweet-smelling girl he was going to marry.

As he stepped through the door his arms were gripped by strong hands. The girl was not beside him. She had disappeared. His biceps were being held tightly by two men he knew very well. Their names were Skelling and Cage, they were labourers on the farm, insolent men who Uncle Georges had always said would cause trouble. Cage had a filthy habit of wiping the snot off his nose with the back of his hand. He was doing it now. Tom shouted, "Let go of me! I'll have you strung from the yard-arm!" but the two apes lifted him off his feet and dragged him back to the four-poster where they flung him down. Skelling was calling for someone and a face without a name appeared holding something against Tom's lips and saying, "Drink! Drink!" and Tom did not wish to drink because he knew it was poison, but iron fingers squeezed his jaw and his mouth was forced open and he drank because there were too many of them, there were a thousand Spaniards in the hot square and if he did not drink he would be torn to pieces.

He was alive, so it was not poison. He wanted to get up and carry the brown girl down to the strawberry bed, but whenever he tried he was held back. At first he struggled and cursed but in the end he saw it was useless. The turret room was bakingly hot. They would not let him go. He could not remember why he was here or what he was doing or who were all these hands and voices. Only the jar pressed against his lips and the liquid and the muffled realization somewhere distant inside him that he wanted this liquid. He waited, and sipped, and waited again.

For hours? For days? He did not know.

There was sunlight and lamplight and darkness, but always the sweltering heat. He could not escape from the four-poster because of the hands all round him. He did not seriously wish to escape, only to find the girl, to see her, that was all, with her dark-nippled breasts making a double-U on the line of the table. Whenever he thought he would slip away there were hands holding him and the voices saying things he could not understand. He said, "I will only take her to the strawberry bed, I will come back, I give my word." But no one listened. He had never been so hot. His eyes scorched in their sockets, his throat was a sandy desert, his veins throbbed with boiling blood.

Where was the liquid? Why so long? Without it he would die, he was sure of that. It had not cooled him, but in some deep recess of his mind he believed that the only way to reach the soft-fingered girl he loved so much was to keep drinking what they brought him. It had a strange woody taste. He shouted for it, kicked out, swung his fists, was overpowered. When the jar came he took long gulps, lay down weak with despair. It was too late. There was something he had to do, but now he could not remember what. He must save his strength. Someone he must fight for. There would be one last chance, only one.

Dark hours. Or was it years? He was growing old, he could not see in the darkness, his bowels were burning to death. Was the liquid a cure? Or another of God's false promises?

Suddenly he saw the girl. She had come down the ladder and was standing naked at the end of the four-poster, smiling with her big doe eyes, saying "Yes" to the question that filled his heart.

Nothing could stop him now.

As he reared up hands clutched his shoulders. He glimpsed brutal strangers, cursed them, fought them, yelled one last galvanic command to his outnumbered fists—"Now! Now!" But there was no response. His strength had deserted him like a runaway coward. Somehow he got to his knees. She was standing almost within reach, her brown satin breasts so close. Then he was lifted up, flung to the ceiling of the turret bedroom. His mind exploded. There was no girl to love. She had gone, like his strength. There was only darkness and certainty.

He was going to die. No more resistance. So this was how death arrived.

When he opened his eyes he saw Robert Seaton standing beside the bunk. The others were eating at table. There was sunshine through the porthole.

Robert was looking at him intently, and Tom said, "Why didn't you wake me?"

"Would you like some breakfast?"

"If I may! I'm hungry."

Krauss from the table said, "He is better. Thank God!"

Tom's recovery was not instantaneous. His strength came slowly. It was several days before he could clench his hand tight. He still had the bouts of cold and heat and sweat, but each day less violent. He could remember when the fever had started, but somewhere there was a gap, a half memory of unformulated terror. No details, but the dread still echoing.

A nightmare?

Three times a day Robert brought him a draught of woody liquid. When he asked what it was Robert told him about the tree beside Chucunaquiok's house in Macaweo.

210

Robert strolling the village with Chucunaquiok had come upon a man filling buckets from a vat of water. The buckets were half full of red-brown tree bark. When the water reached the top and pieces of bark floated up, the Cuna dunked them down till they were sodden. Chucunaquiok explained: "Man hot!" A sipping motion. "No die! Good! Good!" So this was a remedy for fever. Robert, pointing at the slosh in the bucket, inquired, "How long?" The chief, smiling with encouragement though short in vocabulary, said, "Big moon . . . big moon!" From one full moon to the next, in cold water. Robert, always inquisitive about the ailments and remedies of the Cunas, took a small sack of the bark back to *Tigress*. This was a week before they started on the march for gold. There was no fever on *Tigress*. The sack of bark was stowed in Robert's den.

Now, with the calenture aboard, there was no time to brew tree bark for a month in cold water. Fever had many forms. No way to tell what Chucunaquiok had meant. But Robert, desperate for any chance, had tried to accelerate the recipe by starting the bark in a bin of boiling water, pressing, swilling, and hoping. After six days he had tried the woody filtration on Tom Dakyn.

Tom believed that without it he would not have lived. The facts were confusing. Of the seventy-five men from the gold march fifty-three suffered the calenture. Nine plunged overboard to the sharks. Of another seven who were restrained four died howling with visions. Thirteen deaths in all. Of the survivors only twenty had been given the wood bark potion. There had not been enough to go round. Robert admitted this, swearing Tom to secrecy, but it was not Robert's fault. He was lucky to have brought even one sack of the mysterious bark. No man who took the liquid died, but another twenty who had not taken it survived.

Tom did not remember the hours of his crisis but he knew that he had escaped from the brink of a deadly danger. Because Tom had forbidden Tom's death? Or might it have been the prayer at Paxcombe? *Keep safe our beloved son.* Had destiny shown Robert Seaton the buckets in Macaweo?

So *Tigress* crossed the Caribbean, passed between Cuba and Hispaniola, headed north towards the west winds that would take her home.

This was the area where the Sultan had promised merchant

shipping, spoils to make up for the disaster at Elizabeth Bay. That was twenty-one days ago. The calenture was over. The skies should be sunny. White sails of unsuspecting victims should be appearing on the horizon.

None appeared. Instead, as the ship climbed the latitudes in the Tropic of Cancer, the sea and sky themselves became strangely transformed. Daily there seemed to be less glare in the sun, as if some invisible veil was somehow diminishing the heat and subduing the light. The great circular lawn of water looked as Tom had never seen it look before. He had seen the sunset bloodstains, the long green undulations, the seahorses prancing so far below the fighting top, the flat grey disc pitted with rain, the smooth grey disc supporting the whale carcass, more seahorses sparkling on indigo with Santa Antao astern, the stifling blur of distance on the days before Fernie died. But now something new. The sky drab ochre, the sun veiled but still sickeningly hot, the sea a lifeless grey-green and the wind coming in puffs and pauses, now sweeping a length of ruffled carpet towards *Tigress*, now dropping to a whisper and the ruffles gone flat, and this performance repeated erratically from different southern bearings as the wind veered and backed through the day. There was something ominous. The wind was not violent, but it was not supposed to dodge about like this. As a child of three at Paxcombe Tom, playing hide-and-seek with his father, had been surprised, then alarmed and at last frightened by the "Coo-ee" that emanated from behind the summerhouse, then the holly bush, then the arch of roses. He could not see his father passing from one hiding place to another, and what began as a game ended by Tom bursting into tears because he thought his father had become invisible.

Standing now beside the Sultan at the mainmast Tom remembered the inexplicable voice and felt the same fear. Perhaps he was influenced by the serious expression on the Sultan's face as he looked round the horizon.

Gostigo was passing and the Sultan stopped him and asked, "All secure, bosun?"

"Sir?"

"The canvases and rigging."

"Tested and tarred at Macaweo. Spars and canvas, all checked." He paused. "Has something been overlooked?"

"I trust not, Mr Gostigo. There are storms around us. It

212

would seem the merchantmen have all run for safety."

"They are surely not in sight." A cadaverous glance across the sea.

"If they are in harbour, how could they be here?" And when the bosun glowered and dropped his eyes: "Is my logic faulty?"

"No, sir."

"Then why the blame, Mr Gostigo?" Steely wrath in the voice. "If merchant captains are afraid, what am I to do?"

A plethoric flush in the ravines of Gostigo's cheeks. Then the reckless outburst: "You must tell the mariners! They were promised gold! It was taken away! They were promised merchandise! It is not here! What do they hope for now? What did they die for? What purpose? They need to know!"

He got no answer.

The ship suddenly bucked like a man hit on the back of the neck. A slapping rattle of halyards, the mainsail bloated from the shock wind astern. Jarring groans of yards jerked against their masts, the thump of lines and rigging tugged by a monster impulse.

The Sultan half stumbled, grabbed the compass plinth, steadied himself, roared the command that rang through *Tigress* like a call to arms: "Storm stations! Sail parties on deck! Furl the main canvases!"

Gostigo started forward, thrust on his way by the flat palm against his shoulder. From the gun deck the voice of Viccars: "Close all ports! Party for the hold muster on the orlop!" Aft by the lateen mast Krauss yelling a repeat: "Sail parties on deck!"

Mariners appeared like rabbits blasted from their burrows. The sea trembled and from the south-west a long line of green-brown water was advancing like a low bolster fluttering with white spume.

CHAPTER TWENTY-THREE

Often Tom had watched the sail crews at work, in forenoon practice, entering or leaving harbour, the canvases growing or dwindling with a leisurely exactitude to the accompaniment of whistle calls, as if *Tigress* were a seabird making her own decisions how to manage her wings.

213

There was no leisure now.

The wind was squalling gusts of air like cannon blasts from a blank charge. First priority were the mainsails. The wind puffs, however ferocious, were only a prelude to something worse. In the sea and sky was a palpable warning which every man on *Tigress* could sense. Long undulations on the now muddy water, the bolster approaching as if with personal animosity, the sun drained of its blood suspended like an enormous biscuit-coloured moon behind the ochre-ish veil domed over the entire sky. Violence was on its way, wind that could rip the extended footage of a mainsail into oblivion, the yard-arm and maybe the mast itself vanishing like the twigs and tissue paper of a child's boat struck by grandfather's bellows. It was essential to furl the canvases, wrapping the huge sheets into spindles, so the wind could scream past the poles and through the rigging without the leverage that might splinter the superstructure to fragments.

Seamen were moving up the rigging and along the footropes below the yards. In an ordinary breeze they would have climbed quickly, sure-footed, almost careless. Now there was caution, the feet testing each sagging ratline, the fingers making sure of their grasp before the body lift, but also a frenzied speed. Marionettes clutching to save themselves, hurrying to save the ship.

The Sultan said, "The main hatch, Tom."

It was a small duty, to check that the hatch fitted snug over the hatchway opening. He had done it for exercise on the outward journey. Already the boats were being lashed down and a dozen seamen were dragging the heavy cover back to the hatchway. He watched them slide the lid over the opening, bang in wedges to keep it tight against the hatch coamings. They could do it without supervision, but the check was important. If the wedges were not driven home and the hatch worked loose and blew away, a heavy sea could pour enough water down the gaping mouth to send *Tigress* and all her crew to the bottom.

From the half deck Krauss bellowed, "Seas astern!" and the hatch party in the waist started banging their wedges furiously. One seaman hit askew and the wedge flew into the air, and at that moment the bolster caught up with *Tigress* and jolted her stern and a lump of sea crashed on to the upper decks. Not a big

214

lump but enough to make Tom stagger and to send two of the crouching seamen into the scuppers.

Now the fore and mainsails were bunted up to the yards, furled and lashed. The spritsail was already inboard, the lateen furled and secure. The wind was rising but still erratic, puffing and pausing as if in doubt. The ship, driven only by her topsails, lost momentum and began to roll through the shallow diagonal troughs that followed in the wake of the bolster. As long as *Tigress* could run before the wind she could be kept on a course fore and aft to the swelling seas that mounted from the south-west. Without canvas she might swing broadside, and no one wanted that.

Tom regained his balance and slithered round the oblong hatchway, bending over the seamen with their mallets, testing the wedges. There was no good foothold on the wet deck if a big sea came, he thought. As if in answer the lifeline party appeared on the edge of the forecastle above him. They had rigged a line from the bows to a stanchion aft of the capstan. Now they brought down from the forecastle a second line at shoulder height from a ringbolt on the forecastle front along over the main hatch, past the Sultan at the mast, securing the line to another ringbolt beside the door under the half deck. Then up the ladder, and a third line stretched up the slope past the lateen mast, across the now closed afterhatch, up over the quarterdeck rail, and so through to the doorway from the Sultan's cabin.

From the lines hung long grommets of supple rope. In a heavy sea you would loop a grommet through your belt and not be carried overboard. To Tom, the landsman taking passage, a heightened admiration for the preparedness, the sea-rules evolved to make safe this hundred-foot hulk of timber waiting her peril.

He reported to the Sultan, "Main hatch secure." The Sultan nodded. Krauss had come from the lateen. They were looking up at the topsails, two white squares flapping wildly like swans chained to their perch. The Sultan pointed a finger at the horizon astern. Sulphurous clouds had swirled up from no-where. Swivelling he called to the forecastle—"Mr Gostigo! Furl your topsail!"—then raising his whistle blew the staccato blasts to the seamen in the main rigging.

Echoing whistle blasts from Gostigo. Overhead the mainsails

were now tight round their yards, marionettes moving up the narrowed rigging to the topyards, clinging for a moment as the wind hiccuped in the shrouds, creeping on skywards. Tom glanced up, identified, felt his hands clammy. That gentle sunset up there with Jabbinoth. "Not so easy in a high wind." Now *Tigress* began to roll and the beetle seamen were wafted to and fro in long dizzy arcs as they took up the last shreds of catchment. Without sails there would be no power of direction, only resignation to the sea. As the beetles swung out so high, so far from side to side, their footholds flimsy, their hands rasped on the tarred hemp, they would see below not friendly white horses on a blue pond but swollen acres of choppy brown water ploughed into eddying furrows.

Now the sun was gone and the wind stronger. And suddenly the rain came, hard pellets smacked laterally like a handful of gravel against your cheek. A rattle of waterbullets on timber, a shriek of airblast in the rigging. And the voice of Krauss yelling, "The hatch!"

It was still there, but it trembled. At one corner the wedges were jerking and groaning.

Now everything was rapid.

Krauss ran forward, Tom behind him. Some hatchparty seamen had gone below. The rest turned back, flung themselves on the flapping lid, hammered again at the wedges. They all knew what to do. The lid must not lift. One big gulp through the main hatchway and *Tigress* would drown. The sea was swelling and falling in a long powerful rhythm. Now the stern bumped again and another thick slice of water swilled over the waist and the mariners appeared like dolls with no legs beneath their knees. Then the water sloshed away and Krauss shouted, "Hatchcord!" and two seamen stumbled towards the forecastle doorway, and the Sultan roared from the compass, "Secure to the lifelines!"

It was not difficult. You opened your buckle, slid your belt through the nearest rope grommet, fastened the buckle. Now you could run free ten foot either side of the lifeline like curtain rings sliding on the rod, limited but safe. As long as you made the buckle fast.

Krauss was furthest for'ard, then Tom, then the seamen. They fixed the grommets through their belts, and the coil of hatchcord was brought, and they started to wind the cord

216

round the coamings, turn after turn, frapping the wedges tight. Now the sea was running harder. They were on their hands and knees, and when the water washed over the deck it knocked them sideways, flooding into their ears. Now the troughs were much wider and deeper. One moment you were on the ridge with a long view of the white-crested rollers chasing up from astern, the next moment you were down in the ravine with no view but a hundred feet of foaming water angled up on either side, and a fearful sucking noise like some sea titan slurping before he swallowed an oyster. In the next heaving metamorphosis the slanting walls fell away and the ravine-bed rose, layer after layer of ocean swilling across the deck. Bodies were swept and tugged by irresistible water, but the grommets held, and when the water gurgled through the scuppers many hands strained fiercely on the cord that bound the wedges that saved the hatch.

Then it was done. Krauss was satisfied. He stood up, one hand bloody from the biting cord. He shouted, "Enough. Get below!"

He stood defiantly, sodden to the skin, his legs apart, his lidless eye bulging with triumph above the hideous gouge in the cheek.

Again *Tigress* was lifted on the dromedary mound of water. Her tall bare masts swung slowly and with dreadful rhythm. The topsails were furled, the yards and rigging clear of mariners. The wind was a fury of water capsules. Krauss winked his right eye at Tom and growled, "Let the Devil come! He will not sink her now!"

Then *Tigress* shuddered, and turning they saw the wave.

An arrowshot away, coming fast towards them. It was not possible, there could not be such a protuberance of such dimensions. But it was true. As high as the mainmast. The ocean was convulsed but still roughly horizontal, a tumultuous counterpane of brown and purple with a sheen like satin pitted with rain holes. So what or who had generated this bulge, this knuckle, this vertical nightmare shape?

It was upon them, poised above, seventy feet of dark gleaming destruction crowned with froth.

In the instant of terror Tom saw the waist of *Tigress* like a frozen cameo flashed on to his brain. The lifeline stretched taut with the grommets hanging like loops in a butcher's shop, and

217

every grommet slid through a man's belt, the Sultan furthest away by the half deck, and every man motionless, every head raised in helpless expectation.

schschsch schsch-schLOMP!

The whole watery cliff fell upon *Tigress* and for long moments Tom thought *"Death!"* He was submerged. No time to take breath. His eyes registering far above him through an infinity of fragmented water some dim greenish glow that might have been daylight in some unattainable portion of space.

His feet went numb. He could not feel the deck he was standing on. He was moving through the water, his body carried like the carcass of a mouse on the impetus of ocean. Then, as he knew he must breathe in, be it water to kill him, the light glared stronger and his head came into open air, and he thrashed his arms fearing his legs were paralysed, and sucked in the salty sweetness through his nostrils. And saw the impossible.

Three bare masts were sticking up out of the sea about thirty feet away. It was absurd. You could not have masts without a ship. But as he looked the sea fell away and *Tigress* rose up broadside level with him, the high sterncastle bucking like a cart hitting a stone, and figures scrambling in the waist, and a length of line dangling over the rail. He could hear no voices in the wind, and now suddenly he was raised and saw the tilted deck at the bottom of a boiling green slope.

So the lifeline had been torn from the forecastle and he had been whipped off the end. He was not paralysed. His feet felt no deck because there was no deck beneath.

He wanted *Tigress*. Wildly he tried to plough towards her. It was useless. A leaf in a gale could have done as much. And as he hung powerless, windmilling his arms in a frenzy of longing without hope, he remembered Krauss hooked on to the line ahead of him. If he was here in the sea, so must be Krauss. Others behind them perhaps, but without question Krauss first off the rope.

But no Krauss now. No head to be seen in the few visible yards of rain-lashed foam. Only Tom Dakyn who wanted *Tigress*.

Then he was plucked even higher on the curling wavetop, precipitated like a sodden fledgeling towards the ship. In the moments since the rope had snapped *Tigress* had rocked for-

218

ward the distance between the forecastle and the mainmast. Now he had a glimpse of the upright pole as his body hurtled past, a sensation of being clawed in a net as he hit the rigging. Himself thumping on the deck. Voices, hands. Then blackness.

In the cabin Joshua Vine and Robert Seaton were crouching beside him. The bunk was rearing up and down. They were holding on to the side, unable to stand. Everything shook. There was a shattering din of wind and rain.

Tom did not ask about Krauss. The Sultan's face gave the answer.

CHAPTER TWENTY-FOUR

Tigress was a sealed box, every storm port and hatch battened fast, the tiller lashed fore and aft, no crack of daylight, only a funereal glimmer from overhead tallow lamps now corded to the deck else the plunging and rolling would have smashed them against the bulkheads. In the hold the phalanx of food barrels was already festooned with storm ropes. The weight of stationary barrels would add a modicum of stability to the ballast beneath the bottom plates. If the barrels broke loose their random bulk flying from side to side would make probable the strong possibility that *Tigress* might capsize. Viccars had acted instantaneously to the Sultan's command with the guns too. The heavy ordnance was lashed firm to the sides. Next the lesser weights, the racks of shot on the orlop, the coiled anchor rope, the piles of spare spars, the folded banks of new sail, all secured. Then the remainder of movable objects, benches and pots and pans and bedding and instruments and things in cupboards, all tied and jammed and wedged as best they could be wherever they lay. If *Tigress* was to be flung at all angles, let there be no missiles.

That left the humans. They could not be lashed and battened, for how would they move to feed?

The humans were all alike now, from the Sultan who knew much to the last mariner who knew only his seamanship and his fear, all free to move not always in the direction they planned, free to swallow providing the stomach was still below the gullet, free to shout and sing and swear at the tops of their voices against the storm, free to catch a hurtling messmate, to grip hands, to form human chains where the links if left to themselves would have ricocheted like fir cones in a wind-blasted wood, free to survive as long as their ship was afloat. But not free to exert the smallest influence on whether the flotation would continue. No sails, no rudder, no visibility, no means whatever of counteracting the wind and sea. If *Tigress* floated upright they would live. If she capsized but still floated they would die suffocated in the tomb. If her bottom were ripped out or the hatches gave way she would fill and sink with all aboard, masts up or keel up. It was debatable.

Hardly humans any more. Insects within a cork being tossed in a universe of raging water.

There was motion.

When she pitched you could be flung face down on a bulkhead, the deck rising steep behind, or on to your back with the far bulkhead almost a ceiling above. When she rolled the ship sides became floors and ceilings and in the great cabin you saw now and then the mushroom table still clamped to the deck but protruding like a wall bracket above your head.

If any of the superstructure got carried away it would be the high sterncastle. So the officers moved down to the gun deck and orlop, but also to be with the men. The Sultan, wedged against a demi-culverin with Sirius between his legs, did not have to explain. When he yelled down the gun deck, "What have we for dinner, Mr Newcroft?" and the cook yelled back, "Biscuit, sir!" and the Sultan shouted, "Pass the biscuit!" he was announcing that now he had become a plain member of the crew, no longer master, for there was nothing to be master about. No superiority, therefore no privilege. Whatever happened to them would happen to him. The biscuit was passed in broken pieces from hand to hand down the long space and the Sultan passed on the pieces till everyone astern had been supplied and it was his turn to hang on to his share of the bitter rock-hard cereal. Fernie's forecast had come true. The maggots had perished for lack of moisture. In their place were the weevils. No more wriggling pulpy visitors, instead an infestation of pin-head acrid bodies, some alive some dead, all bitter to taste. No cooking, for fires must not be lit. Pecary hog meat and tarpon flesh in the raw would be revoltingly unpalatable. So just two weevil-owned barrels of Lingmouth biscuit and two barrels of Macaweo now-tepid water were brought up from the hold and strapped in the cookroom. The chimney packed with wadding braced by wood-blocks lest the chimney became a spout for the inrush of aperture-seeking ocean. No wheat wine. No drunks needed in this confrontation.

The Sultan and Tom were on the gun deck, Gostigo and Viccars below on the orlop, the surgeon up and down the ladder, edging his way to help those bruised or terrified in the jolting maelstrom.

Tigress, designed for horizontal travel, now pitching almost to the vertical, now on her hind legs, now on her head, the bows and stern switching from top to bottom of the clock face but not yet passing the zenith, not yet completing the somersault from which no ship returns.

Not yet.

There was noise from above.

Some of it was identifiable. The wind screeching in the rigging like a choir of demented seagulls, the rain catapulting the upper decks, the juddering groan of yards against masts, the squelching thud of huge weights of water, cliff waves as high or higher than the monster that had snapped the lifeline, fists from heaven banging on your cottage roof, then a slooshing hiss as the liquid drained over the decks and through the scuppers.

Some unidentified.

A rending sound somewhere aft of midships, a metallic scraping and bouncing crash on the forecastle, a twanging and snapping like breaking bowstrings on the waist, then the massive drawl of wood dragged on wood. These to a general orchestration of wheezes and creaks and rumbles and bangs, some close overhead, some seeming to penetrate from the sky, and always at intervals the worst noise blanketing all others, delivering each time the threat of finality, the enormous thump of another water cliff falling on *Tigress*.

There was fear.

Not the crowd panic you get ashore. Then if you are quick you can be first away, grab the only horse. On *Tigress* there was no exit, no one to get the better of.

On the orlop men felt trapped, already deep in the gurgling throat. On the gun deck it was worse. They could see the main

221

hatch above them. They knew about Krauss and the hatch party. They knew that Krauss had been taken and Tom Dakyn flung back. No others had been snatched, only Krauss and Tom. In the feeble tallow-glimmer eyes stared at Tom as if at some portent of nature. Nothing was said. You could not shout questions and answers in such a din. It was worst when the Sultan looked at him. Then Tom cried in his heart, *I am sorry, it was no fault of mine, I made no covenant with the Devil.*

But mostly men stared at the hatch. If it blew away their lives would end. The slightest creak or quiver chilled them with dread.

Above the screaming wind a voice yelled, "We are sinking! God help us!" and the Sultan yelled back, "What fool said that? If we hear the wind we are not below the sea! Thank God for the sound of wind!"

There was time.

On shore you had clocks. You had day and night with their events. At sea there were no clocks, but still the daylight and darkness and especially the moment of the sun's zenith when it was noon. You had sand-glasses to measure the hours and minutes.

Now on bouncing hermetic *Tigress* the glasses were useless and there was no light of day. At first no one thought of time. You listened to the storm and were flung about like beans in a bag and wondered when it would end. Tom did not worry about time till he suddenly felt hungry and could not tell how long it was since he had eaten the biscuit. The ship was buffeting like a sledge being dragged through deep snow. How long? Hours certainly, but how many? Did it matter? Only when you started to worry. It was unpleasant not being able to tell. He felt a strange slipping in his mind. He thought of mad Molly in Lingmouth, said to be the only friend of Joshua Vine's sister Emme. Molly lived in sheds and alleys. She had been a suspect for witchcraft. When she did not confess they screwed her thumbs. When she still did not confess they put her in an underground dungeon and no one spoke to her for a year. When they let her out she became a ragged joke scurrying round the wharves and jetties. People shouted to her, "What time, Molly?" and she always cried, "Three of the clock!" "Is it

222

night or day, Molly?" "Night! Night! Night!" Even when the sun shone at noon.

Once Tom had remembered mad Molly he could not stop thinking about her.

What was time if you could not measure it? He was hungry, but when would he eat again? Who knew when to bring more biscuit? In one convulsive shudder the three tallow lamps were shaken out and there was darkness. A slow match had been kept alive in the cookroom and while a taper was being fetched, a slow process of bumps and oaths, you could feel the leg next to you but see nothing. Men stopped talking. The storm without voices was unbearable, as if the wind and rain had conquered. Men began swearing. A few high-pitched voices gabbled prayers, shouted down by stronger lungs. Your own fear was enough. You did not want it stoked by another's cowardice. A bawdy song was cut short by obscenities, started again because someone, somehow, had to compete with the deafening roars and screams of the enemy above. In the darkness Tom thought of mad Molly and her year alone below ground. How long before her wits had departed?

At last the lamps were relit. An improvement, but now the air began to smell foul and the singing stopped and the voices dropped to a drone of expletive. They swore for comfort, but softly because the air was running out. Once gone, no need for the sea to swallow them. They would be breathless corpses.

Why me? thought Tom. Ejected with Krauss, instated when Krauss was lost. But for what? To be sunk in a thousand fathoms? What purpose?

So each man on *Tigress*, all survivors till now, thought *Why spare me for this?* as if the storm were an attack by some power malevolent to them in person. Why had the Moon God smiled at them that night? As a taunt?

When the knocking started in the hold it seemed like a clap of thunder from the bottom of the sea. Barrels had broken loose. First one, then many. Now giants were slashing sledge hammers against the ship's echoing belly. Nothing to do but listen and wait and register each blow jarring into your body. No man could be sent below. A single stationary barrel could be manoeuvred. Many hurtling barrels would be certain death.

As Tom listened to the barrels he felt a sudden exhaustion. His eyes ached and he wanted to sleep. But that was impossible.

He had jammed himself in the gun-mounting opposite the Sultan. The ship was rolling to extremity. When Tom lay on his back he saw the Sultan across the deck perching high up with his knees straining for hold and his arm through a lashing. The line of guns were tilting almost to the vertical. Mariners wrapped their arms and legs round the sakers and minions, monkeys clinging to the branches overhead. Then the monkeys sank and Tom was lifted till he had to find an armhold and brace his knees and see the Sultan looking up from below.

Now the air was hot and nauseous. Tom closed his eyes. He did not sleep but there was a dazement. Eyelid darkness, bone-jolting seesaws, the ears baffled by the clamour of the barrels and the screams and thuds of the storm. No plans, no hopes, no wishes. Not a man any more. A trembling deafened object with vomit in its throat enclosed in timeless fury.

Not all at once. First the scream in the shrouds dying away. Still wind and rain and the suck of water in the scuppers. Then no rain patter, the wind no longer shrill. She still rolled, but no more pitch and toss. A few more dragging thumps from the hold, then silence.

Now only the gentle sway, a slow pendulum getting slower. You could hear men coughing.

Respite? Survival? What was happening?

Slowly men uncoiled themselves from their nooks. Still gloom and foul air, but the lamps almost steady.

Tom opened his eyes. For a moment he thought they were sinking because there was no sound of wind. Then he saw the Sultan beside a gun-port. Two gunners were helping him unfasten the storm cover.

When the big square cover came off a shaft of sweet air and light prodded into the gun deck. There were yells. Men scrambled up from the orlop. On the starboard horizon the dawn sun was half out of the sea. A sheet of pink and amber grew up the sky. Across the measureless, grey, friendly water a dazzling avenue stretched towards *Tigress*.

Dolphins, long-snouted, dark and elegant, rose and plunged in their joyful parabolas.

CHAPTER TWENTY-FIVE

Toby Tenchbury would have been proud of his hull. In the hold there was a gurgling slosh of fruit, meat, wine and shattered barrels. Fifteen in all, but luckily the water barrels were intact. The ballast had not shifted, the plates had not buckled, there were no leaks. The wine puddles were cleared by the bilge pumps and the food mess hauled up in buckets. By dinner time there was order.

On the orlop and gundeck, cupboards and racks had been broken, utensils and sailing gear flung about, men strained and bruised by their various catapultings. But no deaths. Smiles and bravado in the morning sunshine. "What's up with Mycroft? Looks like he swallowed a bad egg." "Banged his head maybe." "He should look where he goes." At sea you never speak of danger before it comes or dwell on it afterwards.

The real damage was on the upper decks.

The two boats had gone and with them half the waist rail. There was no cookroom chimney poking up beside the capstan. The lateen yard was still angled on the mast, but the tight-furled sail had been torn away. The top section of the foremast had snapped off and the shrouds to the main fighting top were in tatters. The mainsail still clung, but now in loose scallops with a shirt-tail of canvas hanging at one end.

For three days Tom watched *Tigress* being restored. The new sails, intended for the strong winds at a higher latitude, had not been fitted. They were fitted now. Blocks and tackle, spars and stanchions, lengths of line and rigging appeared from the store spaces. The mariner ants swarmed on deck and aloft to repair their home. Tom was busy himself checking the bows and arrows in their boxes and helping with inventories, but he had time to watch the renewal. He passed the main hatch now open to the sun. The closing of it had cost Krauss's life and, but for the sea's whim, Tom's life. It was eerie to stand in sunshine on the spot where the water had seized them. There was no lifeline now, no shiny wet mountain poised overhead. And no boats. As if the storm had left its card of warning. But *Tigress* would soon be ready to sail on. She had survived. She was seaworthy. She could go where she pleased.

Where was that?

"What do they hope for now? What did they die for?"

The question that Gostigo had asked before the storm had not been answered. For a moment, finding themselves alive, men had been thankful. Now, putting the ship to rights under a warm blue sky, edging northwards with a lull in the wind, their doubts and anger returned. They waited for the word. No merchantmen topped the horizon. The Sultan seemed lost in calculations of his own. He roamed the deck all day and far into the night, handing over to Viccars for a few hours' sleep, appearing at dawn, snapping orders to the work parties, silent to the seamen who passed him, causing even the undemanding Sirius to whine at not being spoken to. But his master moved like a creature separate from all others. In mourning for Krauss? Conceding defeat? Searching his brains for another golden rainbow?

On the fourth morning, when the sullen scowling cockerels had squatted in their turns on the Bosun's Roost, a pipe was made: "All hands on deck." In the first days of shock after Macaweo the attendance at morning prayers had dwindled. No compulsory order had been made. Now at last, after the long days of fever in the Caribbean and the terror of the storm, the mariners knew why they were being summoned.

They crowded the waist and the lower shrouds. The Sultan stood on the half deck holding the small Bible. He waited till the shuffling and muttering had stopped. Then in a clear voice, pausing between each sentence, he announced, "We found the gold I promised you.

"It was taken away through no fault of yours.

"We have suffered sickness and storm together, and our prizes have escaped us."

Now a long pause and slow scrutiny, as if he would look into each man's eyes. Then:

"We must return to the seas round Santa Antao where Indiamen will be bringing rich cargoes for the Spaniards.

"The King of Spain is planning to invade our country. He needs vast money. Though we lost the gold of Panama, we struck a famous blow for England, and now God will reward us by delivering laden vessels with which our enemies seek to pay for their wicked enterprise.

226

"Let us take courage from the words of the Psalmist who has aided mariners for a thousand years."

He opened the Bible and read with enormous resonance:

"They are tossed to and fro, and stagger like a drunken man, and all their cunning is gone. Then they cry unto the Lord in their trouble, and he bringeth them out of their distress. He turneth the storm to calm, so that the waves thereof are still. When they are quieted, they are glad, and he bringeth them unto the haven where they would be."

He closed the Bible and held up his hand as if on oath: "That ship is waiting for us. I know it. For your own sakes you must believe me."

He led the Lord's Prayer, and the crew dispersed in silence. No complaint, no acclaim. A silence heavy with the future.

At noon came the first answer.

The ship was under full sail on course east by south-east. Tom was helping the Sultan unroll the chart on the big desk. The Sultan had taken the sunsights and Tom had stood beside him because there was no Krauss.

A knock on the door, and Gostigo came in to bring bad news. There was protest, said Gostigo. The mariners had suffered enough. He had listened to their complaint. Many were against any further speculation and risk. They wanted to go home. Nothing else. Just to go home.

"How many?"

"I cannot give exact numbers, sir. But a large preponderance."

Gostigo's voice was soft and unprovocative, his eyes lowered. The Sultan's eyes widened with fury, but he too restrained his voice.

"I told you before, Mr Gostigo. If the mariners do not trust me, I would hear it from them."

"I remember, sir." He pointed at the door. "They are here."

"What, all? Have we space for this large preponderance?"

"I asked the marshal to choose spokesmen from the messes."

"Bring them in!"

Gostigo went to the door and five men were herded in by Smolkin, lined up before the desk, shouted to attention, stood at ease.

From the gunners, Cage. Dark-eyed and bony, but no snotty pantomime now. His hands safe behind his back. From the topmen, Rogers. He who had severed Jabbinoth's finger, still lean and self-sufficient. From the cookroom, Henrik, the feet astride, the massive calves bulging beneath the breeches, the shoulders sloping with muscle. From the archers, gaunt father Wotton, his eyes not responding when Tom's met them. From the carpenters, a youngster named Berrye whom Tom only knew as a cheerful face on rounds. He was not cheerful now.

The Sultan addressed Smolkin. "I understand, marshal, that these men wish to go home."

"So they tell me, sir." Square-shouldered Smolkin, rigid, impartial.

"How did you choose them?"

"They were named by their messmates."

"Was Mr Gostigo present when this selection was made?"

"Yes, sir."

"Was there any debate at that time?"

"No, sir."

"Why no maincourse men? No tiller crew? No party from the lateen? Not half the messes are here."

The marshal hesitated, and Gostigo said, "I thought a representation would suffice, sir."

Without glancing at him the Sultan lowered his hands wide apart towards the desk top, the fingers splayed out like carrots, and when the fingertips touched the wood the whole hand tremulous with the thrust.

"You are here on behalf of your messmates. I am going to ask each one of you whether you can truthfully claim to speak for the majority."

He stepped round the desk to the line of spokesmen. They had been stood at ease, but their posture was taut with defiance. Slowly he passed down the line, pausing before each man as he had paused to let them touch the ingot in the moonlight.

"Cage. Do you speak for many?"

"Sir!" Eyes steady, lips a thin crack in the black beard.

"Rogers?"

"Sir!" A sinewy hawk of a face, a pulse in the neck.

"Henrik? You understood what I said? You speak for the others?"

"I spik! All! All!" His huge fist thumping his heart.

"And you, Wotton?"

"Sir!" But something in the voice.

228

"And Berrye?"

"Sir!" A squeak. But no coward.

The Sultan turned to Smolkin.

"That is all. Go to each mess. Tell them to think well after their dinner. They shall have a decision before sundown. And ask Hesket to see me. I have carpentry for him."

The party went out, Gostigo last, but the Sultan called him back.

"Mr Gostigo." And when the door had closed: "You will not go to the messdecks or speak to the mariners on any subject other than their immediate duties."

"Does that mean—"

"It means that you will wait for your answer!"

The afternoon was sultry, a light wind on the beam. The ship was making a steady three knots, rolling very slowly in a hardly perceptible swell. Usually after dinner, with the main work done, there was the hum of talk. You could hear it rising from the gun deck. On the waist and forecastle men gathered in twos and threes. There were cards and dice. There was endless altercation in the seaman vocabulary, so violent, so limited. But today there was nothing above a murmur. Often the only men on the topyards were the lookouts. Now the upper rigging and yards were dotted with solitary figures like the sparrows who had sought refuge from scurvy in the treetops of their slum. Then there had been congestion and death. Now, with almost a hundred fewer souls aboard, the upward exodus was for a different reason.

There was suspense, the crisis of decision in one hundred and twenty heads.

Tom found father Wotton alone by the forecastle rail.

"May I ask you something, Wotton?"

"If you wish, sir."

The Dorset voice took Tom back to the afternoon of San Corda, but in the eyes there was a weariness.

"Why do you want to go home?"

"I have a wife. Our son is dead."

Wotton did not move, and Tom asked, "You do not believe in fortune any more?" And after no reply: "Have all the archers lost heart?"

"Would you blame them?"

229

"Then the Sultan cannot be trusted? Is that what they think?"

A long silence. Then Wotton looked away to the empty horizon, and shot out his hand as if he would point to an ocean of improbability, and cried with a passionate gasp that shook his body, "Two thousand miles to hit upon a single ship?"

Tom left him.

The sun was low astern but still well clear of the horizon when the ship's company were piped on deck for the second time. They assembled in the waist and again the Sultan and his officers faced them from the half deck. Behind the Sultan a canvas screen had been rigged with space at either end. At the starboard steps up to the half deck Marshal Smolkin stood beside a tray. On the tray a pile of wooden tablets the size of a man's palm.

The Sultan spoke.

"Some of you would dare no further. A few have offered to speak for all. That is not enough." He stepped to the rail. "Without me you will go home poor and defeated. Without you I cannot sail this ship. Let us make the decision. But let every man speak for himself and not for one another.

"Behind that screen you will find two barrels. One stands for venture, the other for submission. Each man will have his vote. But first you must hear the argument. Listen well, for your future depends on it.

"Let us hear from someone whose heart in all truth and honesty tells him to go home."

With an immeasurable irony of politeness he motioned to Gostigo, who glared back and said quietly, "I did not ask for this."

"Nor I. Since we differ, let us clear the matter. Tell them what you have been telling them since we sailed from Macaweo."

"It is a lie! I have listened to them! I know what they have suffered."

"Then let us all listen. Tell us why we should turn our backs on hope."

Gostigo went to the rail, stood for a few moments with his legs apart, his lips moving with thought. Then he threw his head back and spoke with clarity and aggression.

"Two hundred and fifteen men sailed from Lingmouth.

230

Ninety-five are dead. Sickness came upon us before ever we reached Panama. The gold we were to bring home is at the bottom of the sea. Since then men have gone to the sharks. The ship has been all but sunk. You see these occurrences as a sign of God's displeasure. You are right. We embarked in good faith, we believed that this mission would provide for our homes and help our Queen and country. We were wrong. We have been misled. At every point Almighty God has signified his vexation. The poor dead whale devoured by common gulls! The bird of ill omen blinded by its enemies, boiled and eaten on this ship! The scurvy, the flux! Think of your messmates! Remember how they died! When the gold vanished, you were promised merchantmen! There were none! Shall we retrace the passage of death, till on the whole of *Tigress* there is not one soul alive? Think of your loved ones! Think of yourselves! Have courage!" He clapped his palms to his temples, then, stabbing his finger at the Sultan, yelled to the faces below: "Have done with this madness! This monster!"

He stood back and the Sultan took his place. After Gostigo his firm voice was like a judge after the advocate.

"The gold was not taken by God. It was lost through the drunkenness of a single mariner. Our trials have been tests by God, not warnings. If He had wished to sink this ship or kill every man on board, He could have done so a hundred times over. You have been told to think of your loved ones and yourselves. Would those who love you be glad to see you without a groat in your hand? When *Tigress* drops anchor in Lingmouth bay, and the whole town is cheering, and you go ashore and they ask you what you have brought . . . will you be happy when all you can say is 'Nothing'? Is that what your comrades died for?" He paused and gazed at them. "My messmate is dead, like yours. But I have gained heart, not lost it. I am one of you. I wish your good as I wish my own. I believe in you as I believe in myself. You were told to have courage. I tell you now, with the conviction of all my life at sea, that this time the prize will be waiting for us to share."

He reached down, and Smolkin handed him a tablet from the tray, and he held it up to them and said, "Each one of you must put his vote into the barrel of his choice. No one shall observe you. Your destiny is in your own hands. One barrel is marked VINE—in blue. The other, in red—GOSTIGO. When the votes

231

are counted the decision will be absolute with no appeal. Let us make our choice, and God be with us."

He went behind the screen and appeared the other side. Viccars next, then Gostigo, and Robert Seaton, and Tom Dakyn. Slots had been cut in the lids, and Tom dropped his tablet and heard it fall, and was committed.

Every mariner followed in turn. Up the steps, eclipsed for his decision, seen again descending with the unfathomable self-satisfaction of a communicant returning from the wine and biscuit.

Smolkin was last, and the Sultan gave an order, and Hesket's men came up and removed the screen. The barrels were exposed side by side.

"Open the barrels, marshal!"

Smolkin took off the red lid and held the barrel high so that those in the waist could see, and upturned the barrel. A trickle of tablets fell on to the deck. A moment of dazed silence, then the blue barrel was held up, inverted, to disgorge an avalanche.

The Sultan bent, seized a tablet, raised it above his head, shouted, "For *Tigress* and—" but his words were lost in a rippling cheer. Men clustered forward, craning to see the scanty pile beside the red barrel, the other a decisive heap. Then hubbub, with relief ringing clear in the voices, as if each man had feared that he alone had found courage.

"No!"

Gostigo was on the half deck above them. His fists shook high. In a voice cracking with rage he yelled, "Never! Never! Never!"

He turned, stamped up the deck, was gone down the afterhatchway.

The cheering went on. The Sultan spread the small pile with his foot, called for silence, announced, "For defeat—nineteen! For victory—one hundred and one!"

A bellowing applause. Then voices from the rigging, "Nineteen cowards!"

"Put them overboard!"

"Let them swim home!"

And the Sultan's answering shout, "The vote was secret. Let it remain so. From this moment we have a single purpose. Let the few who doubted be thankful for the many who had faith." And with a final wave: "Enough! About your business!"

The mariners began to move away. Hesket's men collected the tablets into the blue barrel. The red barrel was heaved into the sea. Another delighted cheer.

And a sudden roar from Smolkin, "Avast!"

Tom swivelled, leaped forward, precipitated himself—as Smolkin precipitated himself from the other side. It was begun and finished in moments.

Gostigo was standing at the lip of the hatchway, brandishing a musket. Crying, "Devil! Devil!" in a wild trembling scream, and raising the musket. The Sultan for an instant was immobile. There was an ear-splitting "YAAAAAH!" from Smolkin. Gostigo's head jerked fractionally. The Sultan dropped to his knees. The explosion. Gostigo bowled to the deck, the musket dashed from his hands. The Sultan rising unharmed. Gostigo held by Smolkin and Tom, dragged stumbling like a sack with stuttering legs, brought to a standstill before the man he had tried to shoot.

The Sultan stared calmly at the bosun, then turned to the mariners who had halted transfixed. Others who had gone below were clambering up from the gun deck. He waited till the throng was collected in the waist. Then he said slowly, "As master of this ship, the *Tigress*, I charge this man now held before you on two counts. First, that he has, not once but continually, sought divers means to discredit our expedition and oppose our general purpose. That he has encouraged despondency and used whatever opportunities he found to challenge my command. Such conduct is mutinous, and as such I now ask you, as the jury in this case, to say how you find on the charge of mutiny. Aye—or No. Answer."

A resounding "Aye!"

"Second. In procuring a musket and aiming to shoot the master he has attempted murder. How say you? True or false?"

"True!"

"The penalty for either and both these charges is death. With the powers vested in me by the Lords of Admiralty, equivalent to a commission by the Queen of England, I am appointed to enact the penalty whensoever the jury shall pronounce the verdict of guilty. How say you? 'Guilty' or 'Not guilty'?"

The voice of *Tigress* erupted in a many-throated roar of: "Guilt-e-e-e!"

CHAPTER TWENTY-SIX

That night in the great cabin Gostigo talked.

When Tom came down for supper there were two gunners sitting outside the door. Inside sat Nils, Henrik's massive crony. Gostigo was alone at the table with a tankard and a jug of Macaweo wine already half empty. The table was set, and Gostigo grabbed Tom's tankard and filled it and handed it to him with a swaggering loop of the arm, exclaiming with fearful joviality, "Welcome, my friend. Now the party begins."

Tom took the tankard and just stopped himself saying, "Good health," and Gostigo smiled like a host, and sipped, and smacked his lips, and said, "Macaweo" in a loud voice, and began a blurred account of a long-ago visit to some equatorial encampment whose name he had forgotten. This was a Gostigo never seen before, vibrant, mouth and sunken cheeks mobile with emphasis, eyes pleading for attention below the heavy black caterpillar brows. Tom interjected politely now and then, but Gostigo rolled on as if he had made a wager against silence.

Viccars and Robert Seaton came in followed by a steward who served supper, a splendid meal from the salted delicacies of Macaweo. White cavally fillets as tender as halibut, quam breasts better than pheasant, juicy venison steaks from the red deer in the mountain forest. Most of the fresh fruit was gone, but pineapples and some prickly-pears had survived, and there was a mound of plantain and marsh potato, and much wine. An unforgettable meal, and everyone knew why, but no one commented till Gostigo, who had talked between every mouthful, pushed aside the last empty platter and said aggressively, "He sent Newcroft to me. I could choose my feast. I told Newcroft to do his best!"

Viccars said, "Bravo!" and everyone clapped, and the steward brought more wine, and the big Norwegian sat expressionless beside the door.

It was a long meal and Gostigo slid from topic to topic like an infant with toys, tiring quickly, snatching another. His childhood in Limehouse, Fernie his boyhood friend, companion on the voyages of youth, both younger than Joshua Vine whose foster-father Tebbige had sailed with the father of Gostigo. Vine himself he never met till *Tigress*. Questions of diet at sea prompted by a mouthful of quam, anecdotes of sail-making in the old days, inquiries of Robert Seaton about his training in surgery (the answers cut short), observations on mariners in general and a few in particular (the quartermaster who had caught the shark, the topman who gave his belt to a cannibal, the carpenter who had smuggled a woman aboard). No one listened very hard, but they all understood that if it was your last supper you would not want it to end.

When the table was cleared and the steward gone Gostigo began to have moments of silence, peering into his tankard. It was late, but no one went to his bunk. As they had kept vigil for Fernie before he died, so tonight was for the bosun, who now suddenly, when he appeared on the brink of sleep, demanded music.

Robert had not taken out his flute since Macaweo, and now the old tunes, "Leaves Green", "Nobody's Jig", "Dusty My Dear", brought memories of hot nights sailing westwards towards the gold. Robert played these and many others, all he knew except one. But when he reached for the flute case Gostigo tapped the table and said, "You think I would not want it? I want it more 'n all the rest," and Robert played Fernie's song, and Gostigo waved his tankard to the rocking lilt, and without warning began to warble in a high-pitched hiccuping voice:

> "She said 'Today's a shad time,
> 'Tomorrow'sh g-g-glad time;
> 'We shall love each other throooo
> 'Longishummer d-a-a-ay.'
> An' I'm waiting by the watersh o' Killala,
> An' the treesh are ba-a-a-re beshide Killala Bay."

He slumped forward at the table, dropping his head on to the crossed forearms. Stertorous breathing for a while, but when Viccars stood up and said, "I must get on watch. The Sultan will be wanting his supper," the bosun reared himself up and pointed an accusing finger upwards and shouted with surprising clearness, "Tell him! I regret nothing! Only the bad aim! Had I aimed well I would have done this ship a great service! I am lucky to die! He will take you all to hell! Tell him to send for

235

me, and be he the stubbornest man in the world I will show him his wickedness! Let him send for me!"

Viccars went out, and they waited, and Gostigo poured himself more wine, clumsily, not offering the jug. Robert lay on his bunk with an end-of-the-evening sigh. Tom said, "Time to turn in?" and Gostigo said, "I'm waiting. He will send for me." His voice was very tired. They waited, hardly talking, as long as it would take for the Sultan to have his supper. Much longer. But no summons came from the Sultan, and at last Gostigo kicked off his shoes and rolled on to his bunk, and Tom and Robert the same, too tired to undress.

Robert told Nils to put out the lamp, but Nils said, "No! No! Lamp stay!" As he was speaking a tall lateen crewman came in to take his place and Nils went out. There must be no darkness for the prisoner.

Tom turned his face to the bulkhead and thought he would not sleep because of the light. But he slept, and was woken by voices at the doorway. They had come for Gostigo. He was standing between Smolkin and the crewman, and when he asked if there would be breakfast Smolkin said no, and Gostigo without glancing back disappeared between the three guards with Smolkin following. The lamp was out and the pale light before sunrise grew at the portholes.

A steward brought washing water, and there was a pipe and the clatter of feet on ladders, and when Tom and Robert came on to the half deck the ship's company were lining the rails on both sides.

At the lower end, where the ballot boxes had stood, lay a heavy block of oak, gouged for the jowl so that the neck could lie firm. A shallow tray rested against the block. Beside it stood Hesket holding one of the big axes they had used for the rafts in Macaweo. He held it upright, reverently, his hands crossed at the top of the long handle, the blade on the deck. A square winding sheet of canvas was spread by the scuppers where a section of rail had been moved to let the burial shelf lie horizontal. A man stood with a needle and thread, and two others with mops and buckets.

Now the sun was rising in another glorious dawn.

They came down the quarterdeck. First the Sultan, then Gostigo with Smolkin and the guards. Gostigo was naked above the waist.

When they reached the block they halted. Gostigo was turned to face the Sultan, who looked at him steadily for some moments. Then said, "Would you have me read the scripture?"

"No."

"Will you pray?"

"Only to curse this ship and all who sail her."

"Do you wish the blindfold?"

"No."

The Sultan motioned, and Gostigo knelt on the deck and placed his hands apart and lowered his head on to the block. Between his shoulder blades the mat of black hair moved on the living muscle. The Sultan took the axe and positioned himself with his feet apart. He raised the axe in the sunlight. As the great blade fell it flashed like a diving kingfisher.

The severance was total.

The Sultan put down the axe and lifted the head in the tray.

Every man could see. No man spoke. Only a multi-gasp from the assembled throats, then a thud as Cage, the dour craggy man from Yarmouth, fainted.

The Sultan handed the tray to Smolkin, who gave an order, and the remains of Gostigo were placed on the winding sheet, and the sheet weighted with shot and sewn up, then laid on the shelf across the scuppers. The men with mops did their work quickly. The Sultan stood by the shelf, and looked up to the sky, and said:

"He lived with treachery and died with courage."

Then he stooped with Smolkin, and they tilted the shelf, and Gostigo, parcelled with his speechless head beside him, slid and dropped and vanished.

A dawn breeze caught the sails, and the new day poured a glittering expectancy across the water.

CHAPTER TWENTY-SEVEN

On some unpredictable day on the far side of the Atlantic would they find a ship worth capturing waiting to be captured? Could you hope, like a gambler with his last shilling on a thousand-to-one shot? Could you believe because you had been told to believe? Or was it because there was no alternative? Threadbare expectation was better than total failure. What would cheering

Lingmouth say to an empty *Tigress*? What would you say to yourself?

Sometimes at night Tom had such thoughts, but he never voiced them. In the great cabin there was no query or complaint. The ballot had been taken, and the only talk was about the events of the day and the plans for tomorrow. From the mess-decks Smolkin reported no trouble. As if a curtain had dropped on the misfortunes of the past, a chastened *Tigress* was moving towards her destiny.

There was a feeling of practical calm which stemmed, as everything stemmed, from the Sultan.

He explained to the officers in some detail, to the mariners in outline. The officers were shown the charts on the oak desk. They saw that on the morning of Gostigo's burial *Tigress* had lain on the thirtieth parallel, longitude inexact, but somewhere south of Bermuda. Far eastwards on this same parallel, off the coast of Africa, lay the Canary Isles. Between the Canaries and the Cape Verde Islands, eight hundred miles to the south, stretched the expanses of the Tropic of Cancer. Ships from India would call at one of the Cape Verde ports, Santa Antao as like as not, and then begin the last leg north. Spanish guard ships would be waiting in the Canaries, but in the ocean desert of Cancer the Indiamen were on their own.

So *Tigress* would cross close on the thirtieth parallel. The moment to turn south could only be decided by dead reckoning. And here the Sultan put his hand on Tom's shoulder and said, "We shall sniff it out together." An exaggeration, but it gave Tom a purpose.

To the ship's company the Sultan announced, "The madmen in Madrid are waiting for their hulking cargoes. So look to it. Practise your duties. Sharpen your skills. Every one of you has his own importance. When the time comes I want a hot ship."

So *Tigress* returned across the Atlantic, more slowly than she had come, for the winds were less favourable. Yet there was no violent opposition, as if the skies having tested her now relented.

No crowded messdecks, no worries that the victuals might not last. Cockroaches still revolting, but somehow more tolerable. No beer indeed, and half the wine gone in the storm, but water in plenty and the barrels of surgeon's medicine intact, pulpy juice from the big oranges of Macaweo that tasted like

238

lemon. Robert had insisted on those barrels and the mariners, remembering the scurvy, did not have to be ordered to take their tot.

A passage of busy days with hopes and fears left unspoken.

No absentees for St Chrysostom's morning prayer. The forenoons active with rehearsal. The Sultan drilling the sail parties and tiller crew in their managements, should the main canvases be furled for attack. Viccars sweating his gunners in every detail. No whale appeared for target, but markers were put out and the splashes checked and rechecked. With the same guns the distance varied, especially when the sakers were fired, and Viccars cursed the foundry for creating foul windage, and ordered the diameters of all shot to be measured. But it was an impossible task. Nor could the powder long-stowed in the heat be trusted to give uniform explosion. Viccars's cursing could be heard all over the ship, but the drills went on and there was confidence that no unsuspecting merchantmen, however well armed, would be trained like *Tigress*.

Long hot afternoons with dice and altercation, but no man's private optimism set against another's presentiment. It was better not to talk of what lay ahead. Gostigo had been everyone's catharsis.

Meals losing their variety with the fresh fruit run out and the fish and fowl all gone. Hog meat and venison, the best for salting, now taking the place of English beef on the outward journey. Meat in strips and cubes and slices, stewed or boiled, hardly disguised. Plantain and maize instantly recognizable. But no protest. After supper no rats to hunt, no brawling on the orlop, only the murmur of suspense. In the great cabin the Sultan joined his officers for supper and listened to their day, and most evenings Robert's flute gave a lullaby. One sweltering night Tom went on deck and heard the gentle cadences of "Killala Bay" rising like a theme song.

Thirty-seven days and nights on parallel thirty. Tom, with no archery in prospect, spent long hours casting the logline. Robert went through his manual, prepared his bandages and ointments, cleaned his instruments for surgery. The Sultan, with no Krauss to help him, spent all day on the upper decks, relieved for part of the night by Viccars, sometimes by Smolkin who had grown in authority. The archers returned to the duties they knew best, each mess benefiting by replacements for those who had died. The Sultan had asked for a hot ship, and that is what *Tigress* became, a fighting vehicle as efficient as practice could make her, the mariners alert, disciplined, savage.

On the morning of the thirty-eighth day she turned south, and now the sun was ahead at noon, and the lookouts were doubled, and spare men perched high in the rigging and on the topyards. At dusk next day six small merchantmen were sighted far to larboard and allowed to pass. On the third morning, as the hands came up from breakfast, there was a cry from the fore topyard:

"Sail ahead!"

At first the speck on the horizon, then the blob observed to be square-rigged, coming towards them. The ships were closing on reciprocal courses, each with the easterly breeze on her beam. In the next two hours, as *Tigress* watched, the vessel from the south grew moment by moment, and at last, when *Tigress*, flying no flag, had altered course to get to windward, the biggest carrack Tom had ever seen lay two miles to starboard.

As *Tigress* swung westwards the great bulk ahead loomed larger. She flew the flag of Spain, and as the gap closed she hoisted the interrogative pennant. *Tigress* answered by running up the flag of Dorset and firing a saker whose warning splash fell far short. No immediate response, but suddenly the Sultan at the mainmast shouted, "By God, they make a fight of it!" as the spritsail came in at the carrack's bows and her mainsails began to rise to their yards. From her midships a puff of smoke and the crack of a cannon, and a harmless splash.

A whistle blast from the Sultan, and *Tigress* began to furl for action, and he yelled down the hatch to Viccars below, "You know your aim. Save your fire till we get astern of her!"

That sentence spelt the beginning and end of the contest that was no contest, the unprepared against the prepared, the clumsy against the agile, the weak armament against the strong.

Tom watched the *Tigress*'s beam guns firing on the tall fat gaudy stern of her prey. First the demi-culverins from eight hundred yards and an answering bark from two small pieces mounted beneath the towering poop, bravado but no threat. Then the sakers and minions of *Tigress* at high angle, and the turn, and a second salvo from the other beam. *Tigress* sliding to

240

and fro, and the cumbrous ship spewing wild shots and twisting slowly to get more guns to bear, and *Tigress* keeping astern of her, pounding the shot where it would do most damage. But as yet no direct hit.

On the third leg, the distance now closed to a quarter of a mile, the culverins struck together and there was a wood-crunching thud across the water, and no more firing from the merchant guns. Now *Tigress* closed to a hundred and fifty paces, and found the mark with all sakers and minions, and turned again, and sank another total broadside into the painted castle whose only defence had been smashed. And a third time. The turn, the point-blank volley of iron.

It was enough.

The white pennant fluttered. The Sultan called, "Send your master." A boat was lowered from the carrack, then another. They came across, each rowed by four oarsmen. The first boat carried two figures with epaulettes on their jackets. The second had no passengers. A rope ladder spun down and the two officers were piped aboard.

The Sultan inquired, "Your ship? And your assignment?"

The answer from the taller man with barely an accent: "The *Salvaterra*. In the service of Portugal, loaned to the King of Spain. We bring merchandise from Calcutta and the coast of Malabar."

The boats laid off, and the Sultan took the officers to his cabin, calling for Viccars to join them.

In an hour they emerged. The surrender document had been signed. The Portuguese master and his mate would remain on *Tigress*. The Sultan sent for Robert Seaton and told him, "Your tools were not needed here, thank God. But they are needed on the *Salvaterra*. Take your party. Tend the wounded as you would tend our own." And to Tom: "Go with them."

The surgeon's friends, Nils and Henrik, four other seamen with equipment, Robert and Tom were ferried over in the second boat. It was an afternoon Tom never forgot. The *Salvaterra* had furled her sails to save them from general attack, but the sails had never been Viccars's aim. Instead his fire-power had been concentrated on the steerage in the lowest deck above waterline. Here was carnage. The long blood-spattered tiller where sixteen crouching men had received the first salvo, and ten been killed, and seven more who took their place, and

241

as many others scarred and mutilated. Minor wounds had been bandaged, but in the dim, reeking tiller-space the dead still lay huddled and two men groaned with injuries beyond repair. A crushed forearm and a leg dangling bloody and pulverized below the knee. Both needed immediate amputation.

There was no room beside the tiller, so Robert went for'ard, where the damage was less and the light better, and found a heavy chest that would serve as a table. Bowls of hot water were fetched and the man with the crushed forearm was brought in, a muscular Indian in patchy trousers, already beside himself with pain and fear. He was given a mug of brandy and a musket bullet to bite on, then laid on his back. Nils held the legs and Henrik thrust his weight on to the chest and two mariners held the bicep. Three *Salvaterra* seamen who had helped rig the space, two Portuguese and an Indian, flattened themselves against the bulkhead waiting for orders, terrified of what they would see. Tom, pressing on the man's forehead, saw more than he wished. The man was biting on the bullet but mewing through the clenched jaw. Robert worked fast, frowning, his eyes intent on the dripping elbow joint. He kept saying in a low steady voice, "Hold him! For God's sake keep him still!" The man was babbling like a cockatoo from another world, and Robert was reaching for the next instrument, and Tom's hands were slippery on the sweating forehead. Such pain! Such noise! But suddenly the noise stopped with a choking sigh, and Robert put the forearm on to the deck, and the man started sobbing with relief, and they bound his stump.

It was worse with the Portuguese whose shin had been mangled. He was stronger, harder to hold down, and there was so much more to hack through. Henrik was squatting on the thigh. Tom thought of Robert's words long ago under the stars—"*If ever I have to carve a limb from you.*" *Salvaterra* seamen had come in. There was a babble of encouragement and prayers, and the deep wordless groaning of the Portuguese, his teeth grinding on the bullet. Tom watched the knee joint opened up, but when Robert reached for the saw Tom shut his eyes. It seemed for ever. Then Robert called out sharply, "Not long now! Tell him! He's a brave man!" and they told him in chorus, and moments later the Portuguese spat out his bullet and gave a throat-shaking scream, and when Tom opened his eyes the leg was gone.

There were a dozen minor injuries, strappings and splints and slings. Then the ascent to the upper deck, climbing the wide ladders through what seemed a warehouse of enormous crates and bales, and on the waist the Sultan with the mate from *Salvaterra* and Smolkin and a crowd of *Tigress* seamen. The deck was milling with *Salvaterra* crewmen, and derricks were lowering barrels to waiting boats. The Sultan said the wounded were to be taken to *Tigress*. He went below with the mate, and the surgeon's party went down the long rope ladders, and the wounded were brought down in cradles, and when the Sultan joined the party they crossed to *Tigress* in three boats followed by four others full of barrels, the smooth water stained crimson by the setting sun.

Viccars was waiting, and when the wounded had been brought aboard the Sultan explained the plan.

The *Salvaterra* though damaged was seaworthy. Smolkin with his prize crew of forty armed men would be in charge. The *Salvaterra* mate would give advice on the way to the Azores. Their master would take passage in *Tigress* as an honoured hostage, a precaution hardly necessary. The Portuguese, unwilling servants of Spain, were in no humour to resist. At the Azores, where no Spanish warships patrolled, the *Salvaterra* crew would be put ashore with their master and their wounded.

So it happened.

Five days later they came to the main anchorage in Ponta Delgada, and the boats took the passengers ashore, not a man remaining, and *Tigress* with her prize astern rounded the western islands and set course north-east on the last thousand miles. Now the current favoured them and the skies blessed them with a loom gale from the south-west that swelled the canvases.

A passage of rising hope and belief hardened hour by hour. Of cooling air and jerkins and woolly caps as the two ships climbed the latitudes towards the fiftieth parallel. Of laughter at dinner when the last of the now-stringy Pecary hog was boiled in strips or cubes or slices (the limits for Newcroft's inventiveness with only hog to offer), the last of the weevil-filled Lingmouth biscuit pulped to a hot mash and washed down with the wine from *Salvaterra*. Of singing at night. Of no brawling. Of resonant voices at morning prayer. Of mariners never tired

243

of gazing astern at the monster vessel that followed, twice the width of *Tigress*, twice the length, four times the area of canvas, her sails triple-banked on the hundred-foot masts, yet hard put to keep pace because of the untold cargo nestling in her deep seven-decked belly.

Her master had taken the Sultan through the inventories. Two hundred and fifty tons of spice: pepper, mace, cinnamon and nutmeg. Fifty crates of drugs: Benjamin, galingale, aloes and camphire. Vast bales of silks: damask and taffeta, sarcenets and altobasses, the counterfeit cloth of gold, silks pure Chinese, silks sleaved, silks twisted. Calicos: the coarse, the brown, the white. Luxury of quilts from Burma and carpets from India. Quality dyes of every colour in the spectrum. Vats of perfume: musk and civet and ambergris. Two thousand elephant teeth and five hundred tusks. Porcelain from China to stock fifty palaces. Coconuts, hides, and two hundred bedsteads fashioned in ebony. In the master's cabin two five-foot iron-bound chests marked for personal delivery to the King of Spain. When the Sultan inquired, the master had smiled and said, "Not trinkets."

Accurate valuation impossible. But one night at supper in the great cabin the Sultan remarked to Viccars that every man on *Tigress* would surely receive ten times the annual emolument of a gunner first class in the Queen's navy, adding to steward Pulmar who was polishing a tankard with breath-holding indifference, "That is only a guess, Pulmar. Not to be repeated." So the ship was informed.

From dusk to dawn a shaded lantern was rigged on the stern of *Tigress* so that *Salvaterra* could keep station, and another on *Salvaterra*'s bows so that she could be seen to follow. Sometimes on cloudy nights when the pursuing shadow was hardly visible Tom stood on the poop and watched the light bobbing astern like a firefly drawn by some mysterious magnet.

When the loom gale dropped there was still a fresh wind, and on a sunny forenoon in late April they sighted the Lizard and turned along the familiar channel towards Start Point. Next evening they saw the outline of Devon and knew that two more dawns would bring them home.

No sunsights needed now. Tom standing with the Sultan at the compass plinth watched the coastline slide past, and felt the love unthaw in his heart.

He tried to picture Paxcombe. He imagined his parents and Alis Dewmark waiting on the jetty. They would have plenty of time. *Tigress* would be sighted three hours before arrival. What would he say to them? In his mind there was a strange shyness, he was like a child waking from a nightmare, not quite back in the real world.

Before Lingmouth there was a question he wanted to ask, but he was not sure how. The Sultan was not talkative. Over the whole ship lay the calm and privacy of homecoming.

On the final morning when the Dorset cliffs were a thread on the bow the Sultan said, "I told you it would be no cross-channel holiday. You have done well. Your father will be proud of you. Now you can set your home in order."

"Thanks to you."

"Not entirely. We were blown off course now and then, were we not?"

"But you found the way back."

"Did I? Or was it found for us? Eh, Sirius? Which was it?"

He threw a piece of biscuit and Sirius caught it in his mouth and sat down happily. The Sultan laughed and said, "The dog is wiser than us. He keeps his philosophy to himself. Yet I am in the mood for riddles. It is the coastline. Soon we shall all be ashore, talking too much and doing too little. So a riddle for you, Tom Dakyn—"

"Sir?"

"When the sea took you that day, the two of you, Krauss was kept and you were given back. Was it chance or was it the hand of God?"

"Who can say?"

"Therefore you had best believe. As the prophet said to his people—'The Lord your God hath dealt wondrously with you'—" he stabbed a finger at Tom—"And so He has with you!"

The Sultan was pleased with himself. He fondled his beard and took a deep lungful of the salty spring air.

Tom said, "May I ask you a question?"

"You may."

"The *Salvaterra*. You said you knew. You told us. Did you mean that?"

The Sultan did not answer at once. He called a helm order. Then with a look of self-amusement at the corners of those

245

confident amber eyes, "I knew that Francis Drake brought home the *San Felipe* last summer. I knew that the King of Spain had lost a fortune. I asked myself what I would do to replace that fortune, were I the king seeking to furnish an armada. There was only one answer. I would send another ship to bring home twice as much. I did not *know* it. Or when or where. But I took you to the place I thought most likely. And the *Salvaterra* was waiting. Do not ask me how. I trusted, and it was true. I told you—we have to trust."

When the ships came into Lingmouth harbour and turned into wind and dropped anchor *Tigress* flew the flag of Dorset at her mainmast, from her foremast the black pennant warning families that not all their menfolk had returned. But women with fear in their hearts were hugely out-numbered in the swarming, cheering crowds along the beaches and jetties.

CHAPTER TWENTY-EIGHT

Small sailing boats were bustling out from shore, headed by the barge flying the mayor's pennant. A ladder was dropped from *Tigress* and the mayor came aboard, a cosy man brimming with smiles. The Sultan greeted him and they went up to the poop where a table had been set with wine and the officers waited with the heads of messes. The mayor was introduced to each man and shook his hand with many compliments about heroes who returned with honour, to which the mariners responded with the polite silence that seamen reserve for effusive shoremen.

The mayor faced the Sultan and tapped the table and said, "We have a salute for you—from Lingmouth."

From under his tunic he drew a pistol ornamented like "Jonathan", and raised the barrel, and fired.

In answer from the skyline beside Rockways three puffs of smoke with three cannon blasts, and three more from the other claw of the harbour.

The Sultan smiled and said, "New ordnance, sir."

"Since you went away."

"And not entirely for our benefit?"

"We'll have no blank charges for the Spaniards.

The tankards were filled and drained. A buzz of pleasantries.

Now the small boats were circling both ships, flags hoisted on masts, there was the call of trumpets and the crack of hand guns. Cygnets frolicking round their parents. The whole bay was alive with welcome.

The Sultan pointed to the *Salvaterra*.

"Our prize! Did you ever see a better?"

"Never!" The mayor's round cheeks shook with affability. "And she took some finding, I dare say."

"There will be tales to tell."

"She is well laden by the looks of her."

"I doubt the registration officer will be disappointed," said the Sultan. "Let us hope he will not keep us waiting."

The mayor flushed. "We can inform him in due course. There is no hurry." Clearly the mayor had a pleasant surprise.

"How so?"

"We expected you before now. Lord Thomas Howard brought a message from Admiralty and the Queen. He said—"

"The Queen! Did she forgive us?"

"Forgive! Oh, you should have heard Lord Howard—her exact words—'Tell My Lordships that when Joshua Vine comes home with whatever prizes it may be he shall have time to examine his spoil, and when he is ready I shall send my agent to register and allocate such goods as Sir Joshua declares!' "

"You bear good tidings," murmured the Sultan. He filled the mayor's tankard. "We shall obey Her Majesty's command, and the spirit that prompted it."

He looked down the length of *Tigress*. The main canvases were already furled, the topsails rising. From the waist and rigging mariners were calling down to the circling boats. There was a flutter of waving hands.

The mayor said, "We saw the pennant. I told them that no one with a husband or son on *Tigress* should come out till the list is posted. It is a long list—for Lingmouth?"

"Thirty-one," said the Sultan.

"And the others?"

"Sixty-five. I shall come ashore with you."

Tom thought of those he knew. A third of the archers had been Lingmouth men. There was Pipkin and Dykes. And Latham from the tiller crew. Names and faces rushed through his mind. Some he could not recall. Who was that who cursed so dreadfully when he died? And now this welcome in the sunshine. The thing was done. He remembered what Alis Dewmark had said at the dockside, that *Tigress* would not sail in jest. Nor had she. But now she was home. The soft chalk cliffs, the voices from the boats, the lazy gulls overhead. One had perched on the lateen yard. A tern seeking scraps, no one-eyed barnacle goose crouching to die. Homecoming! Lingmouth with open arms! And he, Tom Dakyn? Wondrously dealt with, to be sure.

The mayor was saying something . . ."—bad tidings too. There is no way I can—"

"What tidings?" The Sultan stared.

"At Christmas." The mayor paused. His rosy cheeks seemed to contract and he looked round in anguish as if he expected someone to rescue him. There was no rescue. He said with official abruptness, "There was smallpox. It is over now. Forty-nine died. Some were parents or family of your ship's company. I have the list."

He handed a sheet of paper.

The Sultan glanced at it, flickered his eyes towards Tom, folded the paper, snapped, "We shall inform them. Let us go to my cabin."

"Sir Joshua!" said Tom.

"Come with us."

"If my name is on that list I would hear it now. If you please."

The Sultan looked at him gravely and said, "Tom. Your father is dead."

An icy shudder in Tom's chest. He heard an unfamiliar voice, his own, saying, "Is my m-mother—"

"She is waiting for you." said the mayor.

PART FIVE

The Enemy

CHAPTER TWENTY-NINE

In the barge Tom listened to the Sultan and the mayor talking. The *Salvaterra* would stay at anchor till the warehouse had been prepared. Then she would be moved to the deep-water jetty. *Tigress* would guard her in the bay. The casualty lists were posted at once, the mariners allowed ashore in relays, those from Lingmouth first. A civic reception would be held later. And Lingmouth had not been idle, said the mayor. She was ready for the Spaniards. Sir Joshua would see for himself. Not only the harbour cannon. New walls and bastions against invasion. Volunteers crowding in from the country to join the new militia. You could hear the musket practice up at the depot. No Spaniard was going to land at Lingmouth.

Tom heard but could hardly comprehend. It was unimportant. The barge was bounding on the tiny waves and the jetty was getting close. He looked for his mother in the crowd but could not see her.

At the jetty they had to force their way through a shouting mêlée of pats and handshakes, kisses on the cheeks from a blur of pretty faces. The Sultan went off with the mayor. Other boats were following with the first batch of mariners. Tom pushed his way through the crowd, looking for his mother. Someone touched his shoulder and a voice said, "Welcome home, sir," and there was Finch the groom, his face red with pleasure. He seized Tom's hand in both of his, "You're back, sir!" and Tom said, "Yes, I'm back!" and Finch said, "I brought the stallion for you, sir." As they moved through the crowd Tom asked, "Is my mother here?"

"No, sir. She's at Paxcombe. She'll be—"

His words were lost in a mighty cheer as the first boatload of seamen reached the jetty. Tom pushed on, with Finch cut off astern by jostling bodies. He caught up in a space near the sheds and Tom said, "Is she—well?"

"Oh yes, sir. God be thanked."

At that moment Tom saw the two women standing by the storeclerk's office.

They were fifty paces away but he knew who they were. When he came up to them he stopped. And laughed. Breathless.

Rose Dewmark was looking angular and prominent as she always did, dressed in something flowing that did not quite suit her.

Alis Dewmark wore a saffron dress trimmed in black with a green bonnet, her face a portrait on ivory.

"Alis!"

"Tom!"

"Rose!"

"Dear Tom!"

Embraces, greetings. Alis so poised and calm. What had he expected? That she would faint into his arms? Finch was grinning and wobbling his head like a guide from Macaweo. Rose said, "You know that Gertrude—"

"Yes, I know. She's at home."

"She has been living for this."

Tom said, "She is well? There is nothing wrong?"

"No, no, no. She has quite recovered—"

"Recovered?"

"Did they not tell you? She had the sickness, she and Lionel together. Do not worry. She is well now. But, Tom—be gentle with her. She has suffered so much."

He turned to Alis who said quickly, "You must go, Tom, at once. We shall meet soon, at the reception."

"When is it?"

"In two days, they said—"

"I shall be back tomorrow. The ship—"

"Yes, I know. But you go home now. That is the first thing." And to Finch, "Where are the horses?"

"At the Cockleshell."

"Let us not keep them waiting."

They made their way to the dock gates and round the cobbled street to the Cockleshell. Alis took his arm, but politely. She and Rose were chattering about the civic reception. Rose was on the committee. It had been planned weeks ago, so there should be no delay when *Tigress* returned. There had been arguments. One committee member, a caterer, had been told to resign.

Tom hardly listened. The streets were full. People with baskets stood at the corners. There was a queue with buckets at the water pump. Everyone seemed happy. A column of twenty men marched past, civilians with green armbands and carrying muskets tilted at various angles on their shoulders. A young officer was yelling at them to keep step. The sun was warm and balmy, not like the burning disc of Panama. If only Rose would stop talking.

In the Cockleshell yard the two horses stood tethered. Tom took Pola's bridle and loosened the rope, patting the neck muscle, speaking to him. Pola responded with snorts and stamps and head-tossing. Finch was already mounted and when Tom got into the saddle Alis smiled up at him and nodded.

"You will be at the reception?" he said.

"I shall be there. Everyone will be there."

Riding with Finch along the ridge towards Paxcombe Tom looked down at the farms and thought about his homecoming from San Corda when Panama was not even planned. They did not talk much. Tom asked if anyone else had died at Paxcombe and Finch said no. The Channel was flat and sunny, dotted with trawlers. Finch said he had never been to sea.

"I believe it is sometimes very rough, sir."

"Sometimes," said Tom.

The track dipped into a long shallow and rose over the brim, and there down the slope to the right lay the brown roofs of Paxcombe, and beyond it the faint grey margin of the English Channel. Two hares lolloped across the grassland. Tom felt a stinging behind his eyes.

They rode down to the courtyard where Ellen Rufoote was waiting, and Jackman the gardener, and Oschild, and all the servants and stable lads. Everyone who had prayed for him when he went away was here to greet him.

But no Gertrude.

He jumped down and gave the bridle to Finch and was surrounded with welcome. When he had touched every hand and answered every warm voice Ellen took him across the yard, holding his shoulder as she had when he was a child, through the open door and up the big staircase. On the landing his

251

mother's bow-fronted cupboard glowed red-brown in the sunlight. He stopped. Ellen turned back.

"What is the matter?" he said.

She did not answer. She was looking at him as she used to look when he had hurt himself.

"Ellen, you must tell me."

"She's so frightened—she's been up here all alone—she won't come down—I have to take all her meals—no one else is allowed—"

"Why?" he said. "Why must she be alone?"

Ellen hesitated, then said in a quiet defiant voice, the words rushing out, "It's her face after the smallpox. The doctor said if we hung red cloth in the window the marks would not come—he said it was the sunlight but we hung the cloth and the marks still came. She is still the same, she is well again, we all love her, I have told her many times—"

"You said she was afraid. What of?"

"That you would think she is not beautiful."

They walked on to the bedroom door and Ellen slipped inside. Tom heard the low voices and Ellen came out leaving the door open for him. He went in and the door closed and he was alone with his mother.

The room was dim, the curtains half drawn. She was standing at the window with her back to him.

"Here I am," he said.

"Tom!"

She stretched out her hand, still with her head turned away. He went to her quickly and when their fingers touched felt an enormous reunion. She swivelled round, putting her forehead on his chest so that he should not see. He smelt the thick fragrant red hair, put his hand under her chin and raised her face. She stiffened and said, "Tom, wait—" and he said, "I know, I understand, do not be afraid."

She put her head back and he saw her face. Her eyes were closed and he was glad because the sight of her taut, pitted cheeks had sent a shock through his whole body. He had never seen such wreckage so close. Had she looked then she must have witnessed his horror, but the moment's respite was enough and when she opened her eyes he was ready with a smile. She stood back holding both his hands and gazed at him.

"Tom! You are home! Thank God!" She paused, and then:

252

"Do not see me as I am now. See me as I was."

"You are beautiful," he said, "as you always have been. That is what I see."

And it was true. The mask was ravaged, but the big grey beautiful eyes, the real Gertrude, were shining with tears.

At first she refused to leave the room. Ellen brought them a frugal dinner on a tray and left them, and they sat at the window table in the half light, talking of Paxcombe and Lingmouth, not Panama. She and Lionel had caught the smallpox after a Christmas visit to the town. She had nursed him till she was too ill herself. He had called for Tom before he died. Ellen and Oschild had done all they could, but she could not bear to be seen by the others. From her window she had watched the gardens burst into spring flower. Lingmouth was full of soldiers. Lionel had said that England was a fortress from the Lizard to the Channel ports. Rose Dewmark had married her landlord. She was now Rose Spendlove, a happy augury perhaps. Tom said how Rose and Alis had met him at the quay, and Gertrude nodded thoughtfully and said, "You have known Alis since you were children." Tom was not sure why she had reminded him, but it was not the moment to ask. This was Gertrude's day.

As they talked she grew calmer. Once or twice she covered her face with her hands, and he drew her hands down and went on talking as if he had not noticed. They finished the plates of cold chicken and drank the bottle of white Burgundy and he said, "I have not tasted such wine for a long time," and Gertrude's pock-marked cheeks creased in her first smile and she said, "It was your father's favourite."

"I want to see where he is lying," Tom said.

"Oh, no! Not yet."

"I want you to show me."

"Tom, I can't—"

"Yes, you can. We'll go together."

In the corridor he took her arm. A maid appeared and Gertrude turned her face away and the maid hurried past and they went downstairs and out to the burial plot beside the chapel wall. The mound was covered with the velvet of new grass and laid with a wreath of fleur-de-lys, pale daffodils, rosemary and early honeysuckle. They stood in silence, then

253

went into the chapel and sat beside the brass plaque in the wall and prayed.

That evening Gertrude came down to supper wearing a tight-bodiced dress in oyster satin with a long full skirt trimmed with green lace. Her necklace and bracelet were chunks of amber. Two places had been laid at the end of the long table and the lamps moved so that they sat almost in shadow. Oschild served the dish of salmon fillets in pastry with a herb sauce and delicate spinach. As butlerish as ever, he poured the wine with a flourish of welcome. Claret and a fruit pudding, a Rufoote specialty. After the warm day there was a chill, and aromatic logs burned in the grate basket.

She told him how they had sent out from Lingmouth when the ships were sighted.

"So you brought home your prize," she said. "You found what you went for."

"In the end," said Tom.

"And now? You can do all the things you planned?"

"I can look after Paxcombe—and you."

"Lionel said you would. He knew. When he was dying I was afraid. But he said you would come."

She gave a little frown and shook her head.

When Oschild had gone and they sat by the smouldering fire she said, "Tom, I want to hear. But not too much, please. You were away so long. I know what the sea is like."

She did not want the death. It was hard to tell the story without death. He told her about the Cunas who believed they were descended from the river god. "They were good to us. They were our friends. But when we took the gold from the Spaniards the Cunas thought it was an ill omen, so they sank the rafts—"

But Gertrude was far away, staring into the fire. She did not ask how they had come home. And if she had asked, what would he say? There was a storm, and afterwards we sailed back to Africa and found the carrack? But Gertrude had hardly listened. She was fingering a disc of carved ivory that hung on a silk cord from her waist. He had thought it was an ornament, but now when she turned it over to show him he saw it was a mirror framed in tiny garnets.

"It came from Venice," she said. "Real Venetian glass!"

"It's exquisite!"

254

She showed him the back, a peacock with spread tail. "Lionel gave it me when you went away. He said if I was sad I could look in the glass and be happy."

She made as if to lift the mirror to her face, and Tom said "No!" and she dropped the disc on to her lap.

"Why not? So frightening?" Her face had gone slack. In the firelight the skin was like the rain-pocked water when Krauss had died.

"He said be happy. Not torture yourself with what is done and cannot be undone."

"You are like your father," said Gertrude. "You do not answer a question when it does not suit you."

"If I am like him, then you must do what I tell you."

"And what is that?"

"Help me with Paxcombe," said Tom.

That night in the round turret he could not sleep. After his bunk the bed was too soft. There were no snores. Through the open window the sky was pale with moonlight. He remembered his parents and Uncle Georges singing on the terrace below. Tomorrow he must see the gardens where the wreath had been picked. Spring flowers were Lionel's favourites. Clumps of early honeysuckle grew round the dovecote. No time for goodbyes on *Tigress*. But he would see them all at the reception. The *Tigress* story was not quite finished. What would she be doing when the Spaniards came? Joshua Vine would not be idle. And how would Gertrude be comforted? And where was Lionel? Surely, surely not under that mound of velvet grass? And what intentions had Alis Dewmark?

The new master of Paxcombe closed his eyes.

CHAPTER THIRTY

Tigress was already berthed but the *Salvaterra* still lay at anchor, all ladders inboard, deserted except for a military guard to stop any vessel approaching. The big dockside warehouse had been cleared and tomorrow she would be moved to the deep-water wharf and the unloading would begin. Tonight was feast night.

In the centre of the square an ox was roasting and round the perimeter whole pigs and sheep turned on the spits. Widgeon and poultry, geese and duck hung over the charcoal flames. In

255

the copper stewpans halibut and plaice, cod and sole, lobster, crayfish, crabs, oysters and mussels, winkles and prawns boiled in the herb-scented froth. Sweet puddings and tarts, syllabubs and flummeries for those who fancied them, but on the whole the mariners back from sea wanted meat and liquor in their simplest forms. On the trestles fresh-baked loaves were piled high and as darkness fell the wine vats and casks of Dorset ale were silhouetted against the cook fires. Long tables with benches were ready for anyone who could not find a seat inside. Sit where you please. Bring a friend, make a friend. Eat and drink and salute your heroes under the full moon.

At one corner, hoisted on scaffolding above the crowd, a twenty-foot outline of *Tigress* had been rigged out of spars and planks, showing the high poop and the three masts with their yards but no sails. Lanterns glowed from the mast-heads. Along the yards and rails hung lines of metal canisters and holders with a linkage of tar-soaked rope, the hastily constructed apparatus for discharging fireworks. A loving ostentation only awaiting a torch to initiate the unpredictable explosions and flames.

At the opposite corner a rostrum for the band who had fed early and now, clutching their shawms and lutes and sackbuts, were at the liquor counters preparing for the evening ahead.

Across the square from the Cockleshell the town hall was decorated with bunting and streamers. At one end there was a platform with a table for the mayor and his guests. The hall turned into a banquet room filled with tables for the crew of *Tigress* and their families and friends. Even their mourners. If you had lost a husband or a son it was better to come and hear him toasted and talked about than to stay at home with your grief. The room was packed and every mariner was a son of Lingmouth tonight. From East Anglia, from the reaches of the Thames, from Portsmouth and Plymouth and Bristol, this was their carnival, with girls at every table.

Beside the open door stood a trumpeter. At the table on the platform the mayor and his guests waited for Joshua Vine. The goblets were filled and eveyone was talking and smiling.

At one end the mayor. On his left, facing down the hall, Alis, then Tom, then two empty chairs. At her end was the mayoress, rotund and gracious, enclosed in brocade, beaming at the compliments from a resplendent Viccars arrayed in a chequered doublet, his beard short-trimmed, his back to the hall, a happier Viccars than had ever been seen on *Tigress*. Beside him was his daughter Jennie, an excited girl of seventeen with pale face and black hair. Then Robert Seaton, more than pleased to be next to Jennie Viccars. Then Rose Spendlove beside her new husband Valentine, a widower merchant fifteen years her senior, with a wart on his cheek. So back to the mayor.

They had met at the Cockleshell where Tom had booked his room for the night. The mayoress and the Spendloves had been solemn about the death of his father and the plight of his mother. But whatever sadness later there must be none now at the feast table. Lionel and Gertrude would have been the first to agree.

Sitting beside Alis he wished they were alone together. They had not had a moment alone since he saw her by the stores office. Alis was sitting in her long-sleeved peachy silk dress, joining in the cross-talk and banter, laughing at the smallest provocation. All the women were doing the same, they looked their best that way. He had a wild impulse to seize her and shake her and shout out, "It is done! I am home! Will you marry me?" but there was so much talk. He was drawn into it himself. Why had Viccars kept quiet about such a beautiful daughter? Where had she been while *Tigress* was away? With her aunt, said Jennie, but from her voice not much of an aunt. And Robert telling about the barnacle goose. Gasps from the mayoress! And Rose saying to her husband how Tom and Alis had been children together. Did Tom remember the nursery at Rockways when he came to visit? And Tom thought of the giantess Rose bringing them supper and the giant Michael Dewmark appearing with a bedtime story, and now Rose was not a giantess but a stout matron with jutting features married to this wealthy old widower with a wart on his shiny red face, and yet a cumbersome affection between the two as they glanced at one another.

What was Alis saying?

"Tom! I said what are you dreaming about?"

"You and me—when we were children."

"That was a long time ago." She smiled.

But there was something in her face, almost a shyness, as if she could not quite decide how to talk to him. It was absurd, yet

257

he felt the same himself. Desperately he said, "I want to hear all about you, everything—"

"Yes, we have a lot to talk about—"

"Do you remember what I said to you—before I went away—"

"Tom, not now. Later, when we are alone—"

At that moment the trumpeter by the door blew a fanfare and Joshua Vine came in piloting his sister Emme by the arm, he magnificent in purple doublet with breeches cross-gartered, she unobtrusive and small beside him. To cheers and foot-stamping they threaded through the tables and came on to the platform. The mayor met them and called for silence and began his oration—"Tonight it is my privilege on behalf of the citizens of Lingmouth to welcome home our great ship *Tigress* and those who sailed with her, and above all—" at which the cheering became an uproar, and Joshua raised his hand, and the mayor's speech was drowned, and the Vines took their place at the table, and Tom found himself next to the wizened figure he had last seen standing among the bull mastiffs at the door of Rockways. She looked as he remembered her. The long black skirt, the grey shawl, the face a puckered biscuit with black button eyes.

She had not spoken then and she did not speak now, but through all the introductions by her brother sat bobbing her small wispy head like a doll being waggled by its owner, the thin crack of the mouth expanding now and then, but whether in pleasure or anger it was impossible to guess. Not till the mayoress inquired in her best mayoral voice, "I expect you are glad to have your brother home?" did the words pop out as if from a gullet lined with sandpaper.

"He is home! He will not go away!"

"Surely not!" said Joshua, putting his hand on her shoulder.

"You promised me!"

"And I promise you again!"

The small head nodded, but the mouth still twitched with some cryptic misgiving.

Food trays piled with bowls and plates were arriving round the tables, and everyone was choosing, and the feast was under way. Food and ale and wine without stint. Voices rising. In the hall three hundred revellers and out in the square many hundreds more. The band was playing. Course followed course, and Tom ate and drank and stopped worrying and waited to be alone with Alis.

It was two hours before the mayor called for a final toast, and everyone clapped, and the hall began to empty. Waiting for the fireworks in the square the mayor's party split up, the mayor and his wife on a tour of courtesy, Emme at a vantage point with the Spendloves, and the *Tigress* officers taking the girls to meet some mariners.

The moon was away to the west and on the buildings big torches lit the perambulating crowd, their stomachs full, now ready for the dancing, singing and drinking. Some carried their tankards with them, some sat in clumps at the tables. The carcasses had gone but the fires still smouldered.

Tom took Alis's hand and they wandered through the crowd, stopping when a face from *Tigress* appeared, exchanging the greetings of shipmates ashore after the voyage, each thinking how different the other seemed. Warmth for Tom, admiration for Alis. Father Wotton looking like an old farmer with his arm round his wife. Smiles and handshakes from the archers, some a little drunk, some very. Viccars glimpsed uproarious with gunners Cage and Skelling, Jennie laughing alongside. Robert raising tankards with the two Norwegians. Joshua Vine in earnest agreement with the square-shouldered Smolkin. Robert and Jennie chatting with a carpenter whose name Tom could not recall.

At the end of a long table there was a free bench. They sat down and Alis asked about some of the mariners and Tom began to tell her. Suddenly he broke off and there was a silence, and he said, "Alis. What about us?"

She did not answer at once. The she patted the table, like a signal to herself, and looked at him and said, "When you went away you said something to me—"

"Yes?"

"You said—*If* you came back, and *if* you were rich, and *if* I was here—"

"I am rich. Or I will be. Were you worried?"

"Not that."

"Then what? I *have* come back, and you *are* here."

"There was one other thing. Do you remember?"

"Yes," said Tom. "*If* you were not married. You are not, are you?"

259

"No." She shook her head.

"Well then—"

"But I am going to be married."

He stared at her. His throat felt paralysed so that he could not speak.

Across the square a trumpet sounded. Had he gone mad? The next moment there was a loud bang and a great cheer as the firework of *Tigress* sprang to life in the sky. First a line of squibs bursting along the mainyard, then a snake of rope ablaze as it darted along the waist igniting canister after canister of flames, green and red and yellow. Then from the poop a series of *phuts* and *whooshes* and long hissing sounds and explosions bursting high overhead, some puny with white smoke, some brilliant with cascading stars.

"Who to? What is his name?"

"Edgar Lucas."

"Where is he? Why isn't he here? Alis!"

"He is not here because he lives in London."

"How did you meet him? Have you been—"

Bang! A single radiating *bumph* like a powder keg disintegrating on the forecastle with a mushroom of cloudy crimson. A bellow of approval from the crowd.

"Tom! I met him because he is a nephew of Valentine Spendlove. He was down here. Does it matter? Does it help you?"

"Spendlove! So he chose this husband for you."

"No, I chose him myself."

"How old is he?"

"A good deal older than you."

"And rich?"

"He is a jewel merchant."

"Of course! What else? Your mother must be delighted for you!"

"Tom!" A shout above the crackle of more squibs along the bowsprit. "I am marrying Edgar because I love him. I did not expect you to be pleased, but I hoped you would understand—"

"And so I do. He has money, and you will teach him to love. I remember that. But so will I have money. You might have waited. You might have given me the chance. Surely I had the right—"

260

"No! That is your mistake."

"Because I have loved you so long?"

"No! Because you have no right over me. It was in your fancy, as it always has been. You cannot put a mark on someone and brand them like a sheep and make them belong to you when they do not wish it. I have told you before. Whatever you may feel for me, I have only ever felt for you—whatever you may call it—but not love. Why are you so stupid? Why won't you understand?"

A man on a ladder was applying a torch to an object on the outline of the poop. Something had failed to go off. But the fixing must have slipped because the rocket screamed low over the square and burst against the roof of the hall. The crowd loved it.

"So this is the end," said Tom.

He was not trying for sympathy. She had never looked more beautiful, but he could feel the truth blazing out of her like a flame. Her truth. It was not pleasant, but it was very real.

"It may be the beginning," she said.

"For you."

"And for you too." She looked at him, and nodded. "Yes. You are different. A lot has happened to you. And to me. Now we have our futures, both of us. So let us wish each other well."

"Shall I see you?"

"No. It is better not."

"What future?" said Tom. "Where?"

"I can help you," she said. "I will show you how to begin. You must shut your eyes and say to yourself, 'I believe.' "

He knew what would happen, but he shut his eyes without saying anything to himself. When he opened them she was gone.

The band was still playing and there was singing and shouting and clapping from circles of dancers around the square. Along the *Tigress* topyards flares broke out. A voice like a herald bawled, "A broadside from *Tigress!*" and below the waist, from four frames denoting gun-ports, came four ear-shattering blasts in quick succession.

CHAPTER THIRTY-ONE

There was the *Salvaterra*. There was Paxcombe. Above all there was the prospect of invasion.

The unloading of the *Salvaterra* turned the huge warehouse into a cave of riches. Tom saw it empty, round the walls seven tiers of oak racks supported on pillars, the long roof windows shedding slits of light, the cranes and trolley ramps standing idle. Desolate as a room with no furniture and nothing on the shelves. Ten days later he saw it again. It seemed much narrower and shorter because every rack was loaded to the edge with bales and crates and packing cases, each section labelled in large letters, SPICE, PHARMACY, PERFUME, SILK, CALICO, HIDE, EBONY and a dozen other headings whose subdivisions appeared on the numbered tiers. The valuation, disposal and sale of such a bulk of fortune might take months of haggling by merchants, bankers and government authorities including Admiralty.

Regulations said that when a prize vessel was brought to harbour there should first be pillage, the sharing out among the mariners of the victims' personal goods not part of the cargo and no item exceeding forty shillings in value. Of the cargo itself, or its proceeds, the Queen was entitled to a personal five per cent, the Lord High Admiral to ten per cent, and of the remainder one third went to the Crown court for government expenditure, one third to the owners or backers, and one third to the victorious ship's company where the master and his officers could claim the sea chests of their opposite numbers, in some cases even a cannon or two, and thereafter the cargo to be distributed on a sliding-scale of shares from the master down to the youngest seaman according to their rank and skills.

A system open to interpretation and confusion.

Sometimes the Queen herself was a backer. She had once obtained seven hundred per cent return on her investment, and the whole court had enjoyed a week of sunshine. Sometimes there was no single owner and the backers quarrelled over claims. Sometimes the victuallers were shareholders and sometimes not. There were masters who cheated their crew. There were masters and crew together who broke bulk, landing the cargo for private sale, so cheating the customs, the backers and the Crown. There were corrupt agents who risked the gallows, not always successfully, to cheat the Crown and the owners.

This time the Queen, who knew the man she had knighted, cut through the fog of procedure and gave *carte blanche* to Joshua Vine. "When he is ready I will send my agent." In strict law there would have been delays. Vine the owner had been forbidden to commit piracy. In taking *Tigress* at all he had broken his promise. The Letter of Reprisal had been issued to Lionel Dakyn who had never set foot on *Tigress* and was now dead. The rights and claims of Tom Dakyn, who had no affidavit from his father, were legally debatable. But now the lawyers could only deal with "such goods as Sir Joshua declares". The result would be a bonanza for *Tigress* and a fortune for Elizabeth.

In the upper room at Rockways Tom watched Joshua Vine raise the lid of the larger chest addressed to the King of Spain. It was all silver, one half solid with bars, the other packed with dishes, goblets, candelabra and ornaments nestling in straw. Enough straw had been removed to reveal the staggering collection. Joshua lifted a pair of figurines on to the table, sinuous maidens bearing nut-dishes on their heads, delicately sculptured.

"From Benares," he said. "Their workmen are good."

"If the rest are like that—"

"They are." He stroked the silver maidens. "I am setting this chest aside for the families of those who died. For the Lingmouth men it will be easy. We shall have to look for the others, and we will."

The smaller chest contained nothing but four ivory caskets. These were placed on the table and as he opened them he said: "Pearl. Ruby. Emerald. Emerald."

The room had been pleasant in the morning sun. Now suddenly there was the milky sheen of pearl, the deep glow of ruby, and two dazzling green scintillations of emerald. The sparkle of wealth.

"I shall not declare them," said Joshua. "There are better uses. Ruby for the Queen. Emerald for you. Emerald for me. Pearl for *Tigress*."

Tom protested at being singled out, but Joshua said, "If your father had not obtained Reprisal we would not have sailed. He

263

risked his son to save his home. Be worthy of him."

"And Viccars and the surgeon and the mariners—"

"They will not suffer. There is still one third of the cargo of *Salvaterra*. They will all get more than they dream of."

Through the open window came a deep baying from below, and when they looked down on to the courtyard they could see the three mastiffs, Shem, Ham and Japheth, circling beside the raised terrace. On the terrace stood Emme Vine and a man servant with an apron holding the carcass of a red deer. Sirius was squatting back against the wall. The man threw the deer and the mastiffs closed in, one at the neck, the other two at the haunches on either side, an equilibrium of forces allowing the utmost wrenching power. The dogs' massive shoulder muscles tugging in three directions gave a hideous impression of violence. As the carcass began to part Tom turned away, and Joshua followed him over to the other window where down across the square they could see the harbour and the masts of *Tigress* now in dock for careening and the completion of the patch-up repairs at sea.

It was not yet known, said Joshua, what part *Tigress* would play when the armada came. He would find out when he went to London to take the Queen her rubies. First he would arrange an immediate payment to the ship's company. The consignment of perfume was easily marketable. The merchants would buy it and hold the money for the seamen, issuing notes of credit unless they demanded instant cash. They would be strongly advised not to take too much cash at once. Mariners could be fleeced in the shops and robbed in the taverns. Joshua would see to all this. The perfume would not be declared, and later when the Queen's agent came and the whole cargo was valued there would be a life-changing pay-out. Pillage was irrelevant. In any case the poor seamen of *Salvaterra* had taken their meagre belongings ashore at Ponta Delgada.

Tom thought of that other sunny morning when he had come with his father to pay their bill and they had heard about Panama. He remembered Joshua's phrase, "Your son shall be your premium." Now the debt was paid, but there was no Lionel. Instead, the man who had fathered them all would now ensure their future.

"I apologize for my sister," said Joshua.

"Why should you?"

"For her vehemence at the banquet. She does not understand great matters. She knows nothing of queens and kings and warfare. When I went away she thought I was forsaking her for ever. When I came back she made me swear I would never leave her again. I gave my promise. When the Spaniards come it will be a short affair, one way or the other. While I am away the dogs will look after her. They adore her."

"She knows the words of command?"

"Only *Quieto* and *Guarda*. Not the other, for her own sake. She has her sudden tempers. I do not wish to find some poor gardener torn to pieces."

"What *is* the Portuguese for kill?" said Tom.

"*Mata*! But do not ever say it in the presence of Ham, Shem and Japheth."

The merchants of Lingmouth shared vaults in a system based on the Bank of Relief of Common Necessity in Bristol, and here were brought the caskets of emerald and pearl for preliminary valuation. Tom was informed by the governor (who spoke in the passionless respectful voice reserved for the most important clients) that his credit now stood at one hundred and fifty thousand pounds on which interest at nine per cent would be paid, or credit notes issued for any amount within the total, or the sale of all or any part conducted on his behalf.

It was hard to comprehend. For such a sum he could have built the whole of Paxcombe four times over, or provided twenty ships equal to the finest in the Queen's navy.

In addition there would be his share of the allotment to the crew of *Tigress*, one third of the *Salvaterra* cargo after deductions. The Queen's agent would make decisions about the disposal and sale of the goods declared by Joshua Vine, but a merchant friend of Joshua had already inspected the warehouse and the inventories, and gave his estimate of the total value as something like seven hundred thousand pounds.

A realization of the dream with which he had sailed, but for the moment a dream that could still not be put into effect. The money was there but not the labour or materials. Every quarryman, bricklayer, plasterer and carpenter within reach was busy with the fortification of Lingmouth harbour. Stone and timber were unavailable for private works. It was annoying, but it did not matter. Paxcombe would not fall down. In those May mornings he got to know his home again, examined the roofs and walls and stables where money must be spent, rode round the farms where many workers had left to join the militia. The cattle and crops were maintained, but the wool was being stored because the wool trade was at a standstill. He spoke to the farmers and the town agents and the cry was always the same. "Let us beat the Spaniards first."

But all this was only postponement. Walking in the Paxcombe gardens, seeing the young lilies and apple blossom, praising Jackman for his terraced beds of blush pinks, he felt a surging exhilaration. Paxcombe had always been a wonderful home, but never with quite enough money for its full maintenance. Now he could feel the freedom coursing in his veins like quicksilver.

But why Alis? Why Lionel? Why Gertrude?

Were they the price of fortune?

With Alis the door had slammed in his face, but he would not search to open it. Her cry had been too real. If his love had been only fancy, let fancy be gone.

With Lionel it was not so easy. Morning after morning as Tom came downstairs he half expected to see his father at the breakfast table. Not to see him was bad enough, but in a strange way it was even worse not to hear his voice. Tom kept wanting to ask questions. Sometimes when he was alone he would ask out loud. The silence was baffling. He wanted to tell Lionel the *Tigress* story.

The worst was with Gertrude. She had been so pleased when he came home. For the first few days she had gone round the house with him room by room, and in the gardens looking up at the walls from every angle, and even up the ladder on to the roof, planning the new Paxcombe. She still hated to be seen, giving her household orders only through Ellen Rufoote and Oschild, but alone with Tom she seemed calmer, with less torture in her eyes.

Gradually this had changed, as if an experiment had failed. She stayed in her room for breakfast and seemed to have lost interest in the house. She would not go into the gardens when the staff were about. Only on walks through the fields did she take Tom's arm and talk to him. But the talk was nearly always about old times.

On the long grassy slope from the main gate down to the cliff edge there was a horseshoe of oaks planted a hundred years ago, the open end towards the sea. The rough turf was dotted with wild flowering shrubs, gorse, white hawthorn, fuchsia, myrtle and eglantine. In summer drifted a horde of butterflies, gentle, pastel cousins of the monsters in Panama. Rabbits and moles proliferated, checked only by the pair of buzzards who nested inaccessibly over the cliff.

Here Tom came with Gertrude, and they sat down, and Gertrude rested her elbows back on the warm grass. The May sky was all blue and the buzzards were looping very high overhead. For a long time she did not speak. Then she said, as if continuing a conversation, "I would like to be with him. I would like to wake up and find him beside me. I would like to go for a long walk and find him somewhere waiting for me."

"He is with you now," said Tom. "With both of us."

"Yes. You miss him too, I know that. But he and I belong together. From the very first moment I saw him I belonged to him. When that happens you do not have to ask questions or prove anything. Suddenly it is there, and it fills your life. And suddenly it is gone, and you cannot believe it."

That same May morning Joshua Vine took horse to London. He carried the casket of rubies for the Queen. Ten days later he returned bringing with him the Queen's agent, Sir Brian Harvye, a chief justice and personal friend of Elizabeth.

All Lingmouth was waiting for the news they brought. The merchants wanted to proceed with the disposal of the main bulk of the *Salvaterra* cargo. The sale of perfume had taken place, and the cash being released to the mariners was keeping the taverns busy night by night. Seamen who had joined *Tigress* from afar were waiting for all they could get before going home. Some stayed with Lingmouth messmates, the rest were in billets round the town. *Tigress* had become everyone's symbol. There were militiamen up at the depot. You could hear the musket practice and see the marching volunteers with their armbands. You could take the children to watch the earthworks being dug and the bastions being built. But Lingmouth was a community of the sea and *Tigress* her greatest achievement.

The news from London was twofold.

First, the preparations to meet the armada.

For some months there had been hesitation by the Queen,

arguments among her ministers, frustration among her admirals. The basic strategy of Spain was known. The Duke of Parma had a sizeable fleet off Dunkirk and several thousand troops waiting ashore to be brought across the Channel. At Lisbon was a much bigger fleet and an army of twenty thousand or more. The Lisbon fleet would cross Biscay and come up the Channel to join with Parma. Together they would invade.

Since the new year Francis Drake had been stationed at Plymouth with a force of cruisers and auxiliaries based round four great ships, *Hope*, *Nonpareil*, *Swiftsure* and his flagship *Revenge*. The rest of the Queen's navy was collected at the Channel ports under the command of the Lord High Admiral, Charles Howard of Effingham. For months Drake had pleaded that a greater fire-power was needed to meet the fleet from the south. Early in May he had gone in person to the Queen. She had responded at last. Lord Howard had left his nephew Lord Seymour with enough force to keep Parma's ships from leaving Dunkirk, and himself proceeded to Plymouth in his flagship *Ark Royal* together with seventeen other Crown ships supported by armed merchantmen and pinnaces from London.

It had been known in Lingmouth that Drake was at Plymouth, but the news that he had now been joined by Howard himself brought a heightened excitement. *Ark Royal*, completed only the previous year, was said to be the most beautiful and dangerous vessel ever built, eight hundred tons of destructiveness. Great events were approaching. If the battle did not come to Lingmouth, it would pass her doorstep.

Joshua Vine had received a royal welcome. Elizabeth had listened to the voyage of *Tigress* as she had listened long ago to the early life of Joshua Vine. But this time she believed every word. She was totally aware of the damage inflicted on the Spaniards by the capture of their mule train. She could not knight him again, but she accepted the rubies with what Sir Joshua reported as "the utmost grace". From the palace he went to the Admiralty, where he retold his adventure to Carey and Leveson and was met with an astonishing postscript. A report had just come in from a Dutch merchantman of how in Nombre de Dios the Spaniards were giving out that a fleet of eight English men-of-war had appeared outside the harbour and after valiant battle by Spanish protection vessels had sunk the ship that was setting out with the biggest bulk of gold bullion ever to leave the isthmus. No mention of corpses in the river bed or disappearing mules. An account clearly intended to avert the wrath of Madrid.

As to the future for *Tigress*, Admiralty had heard of her return but not the details. An instruction had been left for Sir Joshua by the Lord High Admiral. After so much sea-time *Tigress* must be brought to the first state of readiness. When Lord Howard was informed, *Tigress* would receive her orders.

Early in June Joshua brought Sir Brian Harvye back to Lingmouth. He would stay at the Cockleshell, a more convenient centre than Rockways for his discussions with the merchants and customs officers.

Tom, invited by Joshua to meet the Queen's agent over a bottle of wine, felt the authority of this calm handsome man of about Joshua's age, his dark hair and beard flecked with silver, his voice slow and precise, not accustomed to interruption, yet in the eyes a warm concern. "I have heard all about you, Tom Dakyn." When the two older men began to talk about the armada, and how slow the Queen had been to let the admirals act, and what Lord Howard had said to Sir George Carey in Sir Brian's presence, and the determined fury of Francis Drake, and the disposition of the Crown ships, Tom felt as if he were listening to Elizabeth herself and her most powerful advisers deciding the destiny of England.

And his own destiny?

Riding back to Paxcombe in the twilight he felt himself a small thread in a large tapestry not yet woven to its end.

CHAPTER THIRTY-TWO

His eyes were closed but he knew he was awake. He had been dreaming of his extremely clever remark which had made Gideon Jabbinoth roar with laughter, but now he could only remember Gideon laughing and not the remark. It was irritating. He tried to fall back into the dream but could not. Instead there was a sudden awareness that he was not alone in the room. He lay rigid, easing his fingers up till they grasped the edge of the coverlet. He opened his eyes. There was dim light. As he braced himself to leap up he felt lips on his forehead, and he twisted round and heard his mother cry "Oh" and saw her hand holding the lamp and her face as it drew back, the pallid cheeks a devastation of craters.

She gasped. "I'm sorry. I did not mean to wake you."

"What is it? Are you—"

"I could not sleep. I thought if I kissed you I could sleep."

"Sit down," he said. "Tell me. What is the matter?"

"Nothing. It was so hot. The room was like an oven."

She put the lamp on the bedside table and sat down on the coverlet. He saw she was wearing the house dress she had worn at supper. Her hair fell loose on her shoulders. She put out her hand and he held it and she said, "It was foolish of me. I was thinking of when you were a child and Lionel and I used to come and say goodnight."

"I could never sleep until you did."

"He was so proud of you. That first pony!"

"*Blossom*! I remember my first ride without being held!"

They talked of other firsts. His first bow and arrow, and when the dovecote was struck by lightning, and catching crabs in the rockpools under the cliff, and the birthday cake that got burnt. Her tight fingers went soft and in a few minutes she stood up and took the lamp, paused, looking down at him.

"Goodnight, Tom."

"You will go to bed now?"

"I will."

"No bad thoughts."

"No."

"Promise?"

"I promise."

But when she was gone he lay wide awake. There was no moon, no stars, the window an oblong of deeper black than the darkness of the room. With moonlight they could have sat by the stone lion or walked in the gardens. But it was better she slept. Now it was he who needed an opiate. He strained his ears for any sound from the terrace below, but there was none. He lay for what seemed hours. Would it be all night?

He woke suddenly with sun flooding the room, got up and dressed with inexplicable urgency. On the stairs he passed a maid with hot water. In the dining-room Oschild was laying the breakfast table.

"Is my mother down?"

"I have not seen her, sir."

270

Gertrude often walked in the gardens before the gardeners began their day. Tom went out. He could see over the low hedges. There was no Gertrude.

He ran back, up the stairs and along the corridor to her room. He knocked. No answer. He went in. The room was empty. Her nightgown lay unrumpled on the bed.

She must have waited for the dawn.

He called out, ran down shouting her name, found Ellen Rufoote in the hall, stopped a maid from the kitchen. Gertrude had not been seen.

In the courtyard the big northern gate was closed. She would not have gone that way. He could not imagine her walking alone up on to the track above the farms. But the horseshoe, he could picture her there. It was all he dared picture. He went down through the wicket gate by the stables. She was not in sight on the hummocky grassland towards the cliff. At the ring of oak trees he stopped and called again. There was no answer. Out into the loop of grass where dew was sparkling on the shrubs, white scuts of rabbits bobbed and disappeared. Nothing else moved.

A hundred yards away the cliff edge was sharp against the calm grey sea. He hurried on, saw the sun low and dazzling in the east, came to the cliff edge, found nothing.

Two hundred feet below the tide was in, almost covering the small black rocks. He could see nothing else. He looked again, fearfully. There was nothing.

A few yards to the left were the two iron posts marking the top of Paxcombe's private sea-path. The steep zigzag had been well cut with a thin guard rail on posts. He started down, watching his footholds, glancing below. At the bottom he stood on the narrow band of shingle, smelt the brown seaweed flapping on the rocks. There was only one place to look now. He walked along the shingle to the miniature cove where he had learned to swim. When the tide went out the swimming pool still remained. But now the tide was in, and on a smooth ledge he saw what she had left.

Her long house dress, her shoes, and beside the shoes the ivory mirror on the silk cord.

He gazed across the flat sea. A lawn without ripples stretching to the horizon. Empty.

He was not afraid to picture her now. When the light was just

271

beginning and there was no one to watch. Swimming with slow strokes, unhurried, out and out, to the place where Lionel would be waiting, the moment when her strength was utterly spent, her arm lifted for the last time, her wish come true.

Tom took up her clothes and climbed the cliff and rode to Lingmouth, found the coastguards, came back with them in the ketch, searched till dusk. But Gertrude was not to be disturbed.

CHAPTER THIRTY-THREE

With June came surprise for *Tigress*, uncertainty and rumour for Lingmouth, despair for Tom.

When the refit was finished (careening, a new foremast, all running rigging replaced, the decks oiled and tarred) a message was sent to Plymouth and the orders received. The *Tigress* would not be used to engage the enemy. Instead she was to be a carrier of culverin shot and powder for the great ships of the line. It made sense, said Joshua Vine. He called Viccars and Tom to Rockways to explain.

The fleet was at Plymouth. That was something. But because of the Queen's reluctance to act, the logistics had been badly neglected. Plymouth was not short of willing caterers, but the victualling needed expert management and this had hardly been attempted. It was doubtful if any Crown ship had more than three days' supply of food. The supply of gunshot and powder was even more alarming. Ships had been limited—one of Elizabeth's worst economies. *Ark Royal* herself could not expect to keep her main armament firing for more than a day and a half. *Revenge* and *Swiftsure* were the same. Now with the ban lifted there was a frantic activity ordered by the Lord High Admiral. Foundries were to treble their output, the shot assembled at arsenals spaced along the coast, ships to be loaded ready to replenish the fleet as it moved up-channel.

The English were planning to fight at long range, and the full culverin with its seventeen-pound shot would be their main weapon. So *Tigress* would be a carrier for ships with ten times her fire-power. Joshua was not pleased, but admitted the reason. *Tigress* would not sail without a quota for her own guns. He assured Viccars of that.

The crew would be streamlined to sail parties and gunners to handle the shot. A total of sixty would be enough, picked from volunteers who had been to Panama. There would be no lack. If any wished to take their prize money and go back to their home port, they were free to do so.

The citizens of Lingmouth knew little of fleet strategy and government decisions. The foundry on the hill beside the army depot was small and had not been in full operation since *Tigress* was preparing for Panama. Now they would do their utmost, with shifts night and day, but the stock of ore was low with no chance of any more.

They knew that Drake and Howard were at Plymouth with the great ships waiting to meet the Spaniards, but the real size and force of the armada and the troops it carried and how and where the battle was to be fought, all this was a vague image distorted by rumour. A hundred galleons were gathered at Lisbon. Some said five hundred, each with four tiers of guns twice as powerful as any English. Spanish cannon balls were red hot. They could set a town on fire. The troops on board, forty, fifty, eighty thousand, were the most savage in Europe. When they landed they had scourges, and every Protestant would be flailed to death, every child roasted. A trawler from Dartmouth had sighted the whole English fleet going south—returning a week later with torn sails in a gale from the south. What was happening? Was it true? A French merchantman had passed the armada off Portugal heading north, but next day the armada had vanished.

So June passed and early in July came another report, that once again the entire fleet had sailed to destroy the armada in its own ports, and once again a gale had driven them back. An omen? Did God Himself disapprove?

So Lingmouth worked and waited and was frightened for its children.

For Tom Dakyn it was a time of impatience and despair. *Tigress* was ready for sea. There would be no archers, but it was unthinkable that *Tigress* should sail without him. Joshua Vine agreed. Robert Seaton and Viccars would both be aboard. The crew were selected from twice the volunteers who could be taken. There would be no purser, but the old mate from San Corda, who had not come to Panama, was in charge of the stowage. He would combine the duties of mate and bosun. There was little for Tom to do. Joshua, thinking that he had

273

troubles enough at Paxcombe, had told him to come and go as it suited him.

But nothing suited him. Gertrude's death had crushed his heart for adventure. There was no labour for Paxcombe. He had lost interest in plans and dreams. He was wealthy. But what use? All that he and Lionel had hoped for that morning at Rockways had come true. But at what cost? No father, no mother, no Alis Dewmark. He met her in the street and she said she was to be married in August. She was going to London with her mother to choose the trousseau. He hoped she would be happy. She hoped he would be happy. They parted with a handshake.

The *Salvaterra* cargo was apportioned, the sale effected, the *Tigress* mariners enriched and protected as far as Joshua could achieve with credit and advice on not endangering themselves with too much cash. Those from distant ports who were not chosen for *Tigress* now went home taking bills of credit. Tom never inquired exactly how much they received. He did not care. He was told that Sir Brian Harvye had completed his work and had gone back to London. But, said Joshua, Sir Brian would return to Lingmouth to arrange the disposal of the *Salvaterra* herself. A syndicate in Cheapside were bidding, and Sir Brian would bring with him his son Roland who worked in the office of the Lord Treasurer.

Roland Harvye, said Joshua, was a very brilliant young man. He would probably be Lord Treasurer himself one day.

Tom was more than indifferent to the career of Roland Harvye. He gave no thought whatever to Sir Brian Harvye's son.

On the headland opposite Rockways they had built a bonfire, part of the chain from the Lizard which would blaze the news of the armada's arrival along the south of England. In the town hall was a square belfry. It had boomed the beginning of the *Tigress* banquet. It would boom again to summon the *Tigress* mariners from their lodgings and homes.

Tom longed to hear that bell. Every day the expectation grew. In July, with the second report of fleet movement, Joshua Vine asked Tom to come in to Lingmouth and sleep at the Cockleshell. Robert Seaton was coming to stay at the Viccars home. Tom forbade emotional farewells at Paxcombe, left Oschild and Ellen Rufoote in charge, and rode in with Finch who with tears in his eyes took Pola home.

Now *Tigress* was berthed alongside the wharf. For stability and access the shot was safer on the orlop than in the hold. Strong new racks had been fitted. They were full. The crew would sleep, if they slept at all, on the gun deck. Only the powder was carried in the hold, the big kegs as far below sea-level as possible.

July was half gone and at bedtime on the warm cloudless nights Cygnus hung overhead, and Tom looked up at the triangle of Deneb, Vega and Altair and thought of nights before *Tigress* had sailed for Panama. Uncle Georges had shown him Cygnus. Was it always eventful?

Sir Joshua had told him that Brian Harvye and his son would be at the Cockleshell that weekend. A meeting with the mayor had been arranged, which Tom might like to attend. It would be interesting to hear the expert Treasury view about the *Salvaterra*.

On the day of their arrival Tom spent the afternoon on *Tigress* helping Viccars with the gun deck messes. The prospect of an evening with some Treasury genius did not excite him. He was not needed at the meeting. He thought he would go to some tavern. Any would do. But first he wanted a bath and a clean shirt.

Coming down from his room he saw across the hall a couple sitting at the window table. The man, about his own age, was so good-looking that he could only be the brilliant Roland Harvye. There were no other visitors. The girl he was talking to brought Tom to an unbelieving standstill. He stared at her. The high rounded cheekbones, the wide-set eyes, the full half-open lips, the plentiful hair. It was Rakiocka the canoe girl with a pale cream skin, except that this new Rakiocka had her hair piled up into an extravagant bundle, not black but a rich dark auburn. She turned her head, saw him, stopped what she was saying, gave him a smile like sunrise, turned back to her escort.

It was too much. Brilliant Roland might just have been tolerable. It was not tolerable for him to have this extraordinary girl, especially when she smiled at strangers and then turned away.

Tom went towards the door, his heart thumping like a drum. He must get away from this cruelty. A voice behind him called his name. Sir Brian Harvye was coming downstairs. He crossed the hall with outstretched hand. "My dear Tom Dakyn! I have caught you. You must meet my son. He has been looking forward to it."

There was no escape. Never so unwillingly Tom followed him to the table. The young man stood up. The girl sat where she was. But again she looked at Tom as he had never been looked at in his life.

Sir Brian was saying ". . . my son Roland. Tom Dakyn."

They shook hands, and Sir Brian touched Tom's arm and said, "And my daughter Kate."

"Your *daughter*!" He had not meant to shout.

"My youngest daughter," smiled Sir Brian.

CHAPTER THIRTY-FOUR

At that moment Joshua Vine joined them. He asked if they were ready for the mayor's meeting, and Sir Brian said yes, and turning to Kate, "We may be late. I think the mayor is offering us supper. But they will look after you here. The food is excellent."

Tom said to Sir Joshua, "If you don't mind, I shall not be at the meeting."

"And miss the supper?"

"Please make my excuses to the mayor. But I must stay here."

"Must?"

"Because she cannot have supper alone. It would not be hospitable."

It was a good word and it worked perfectly. Joshua tugged his beard with a grunt and half a smile, Sir Brian nodded profoundly, Roland Harvye said, "Well done," and they went away.

"I couldn't help it," said Tom. "I had to."

"I'm glad you did. It is no pleasure to eat alone."

"It was your fault. You should not have smiled at me like that."

"Why not?" said Kate.

It was a low lazy voice from a warm curvy mouth. She stood quite still in front of him, as tall as he was, her wide eyes as blue as his own, her arms loose at her sides. She wore a grey dress flecked with green. There was something childlike in her immobility, as if to say "*What next?*"

"Have you seen the harbour?" he asked.

"Only from the window."

"It is better from the terrace."

He took her by the elbow into the dining-room, ordered wine, steered her through the bay window to a table where they could see the ships in harbour. *Tigress* was far away beside the wharf, but the *Salvaterra* lay at anchor, huge and empty after the unloading. There were some trawlers, and two French merchantmen together at mooring buoys, and a Dutch freighter, and a cluster of fishing boats near the estuary.

The wine and glasses were brought and the bottle left. He sat opposite across the small round table because he wanted to look at her. There was no difficulty or clever conversation or wondering what to say next. They said what came to mind, their questions and answers of no great import, common leaves blown to and fro, yet sparkling as if touched by some magic brush encrusted with delight. She told him about her home near London, the house on Richmond Hill with the shining snake of Thames far below, and the hedgehog, and her three brothers and two sisters, and the mulberry tree in the garden. He told her about Paxcombe, and as if to help him she said, "I know about your parents, Tom," so he spoke about Ellen Rufoote and his bow and arrow and Pola the stallion.

"Did you always ride when you were little?" she said.

"Yes. I had a pony called Blossom."

"I had a pony too, when I was four."

"Called what?"

"Apple."

They smiled together, not at the coincidence but because the spell was on them. He asked her how old she was, and when she said nineteen he thought he had never heard such music in a voice. Her hands rested on the table in front of her, the fingers plump yet very supple, white-skinned, twining together, making slow patterns of their own while she talked to him. The ships looked extraordinarily beautiful in the evening sun, and he described the *Salvaterra*, leaving out the amputations, and she said that her father had told her all London was talking about *Tigress* and Joshua Vine. "And you," she added.

"No, no," said Tom. "He was the one—for all of us."

They finished the wine and went in for supper and had another bottle with the spicy beef stew. The tavern would be full, but in the dining-room there were few people, none he knew. Again he could look at her across the table. He did not feel hungry, but Kate was munching away as if she had not eaten since breakfast, and in the image of his mind he was seated at another table, and although he could only see the bulge of her breasts beneath the dress he was sure that without the dress there would be a double-U on the line of the table and her hair now bunched up behind could reach her waist. She was a doe from the forest, her liquid eyes exquisite, not only from the savour of what she was chewing. That was the difference. This pale-skinned Rakiocka was an embodiment of the other who had been a hint and an assurance, though he had not guessed it at the time, and now he smiled at the beauty, as he had smiled then, and felt an inexpressible gratitude. Surely this was no accident? The mastication brought dimples in her cheeks, and her big eyes were now round with friendliness, now laughing slits of pleasure, and her closed soft lips made changing pouts of kisses.

After cheese and peaches they went back to the terrace. There were voices from the tavern at the end of the Cockleshell, but only a hum. Many citizens were preparing their weapons, fortifying their homes, loving their families. There was no wildness like the night they had celebrated *Tigress* in the square.

It was growing dark, and southwards in the moonless sky Vega hung playing her lyre, and beside Vega stood the arrogant Hercules, the skinny giant, his feet apart, his right forearm raised, his left dangling. What triumph was he boasting about? The slaughter of the Nemean lion?

"Do you know about the stars?" he said.

"No, darling. You tell me."

He told her a little, but he was thinking of the "*darling*", how what he had sought so long, with fancy and blunder and pretence and all the mistakes of loneliness, had now suddenly at this starlit table been found. He had no doubt, he knew it in his heart.

"They must be out there," came a voice from the dining-room, and Sir Brian and the brilliant Roland stepped on to the terrace.

Father and son did the talking. The mayor had been easy to handle. His wife wore a purple dress too tight for her. Sir Joshua had gone home to calm his sister who had become frantic with rumours of Spaniards. Some fool of a quarry worker had stolen a cow (not from the Dakyn farms). He had been caught roasting the carcass. Sir Brian thanked Tom for being hospitable. Roland, brotherlike, said, "She has had a good evening. Someone to listen to her for a change."

Sir Brian said, "Bedtime, I suppose."

Tom hardly heard what they were saying. The next thing he knew they were all on the upstairs landing, the others ahead down the corridor, and he was standing with Kate at her bedroom door. There were only moments. He lifted her hand and kissed it, like kissing a pale soft peach from the gardens of Arcadia. She raised her other hand and kissed her own fingers, stretched out, touched his nose, his cheeks, his lips, very softly, like someone blind longing to know a face. She whispered, "Goodnight, Tom."

"Goodnight, Kate."

She was gone.

Now he was alone in his room, at the window, looking across the bay. The ships moored and at anchor had lanterns, and *Tigress* over at the wharf had deck lights. The dream and the reality. Which was which? He still felt her fingers on his lips, the fire through his body, but he could not see her any more. She had disappeared. All he could see was the shining black harbour dotted with ship lights, and suspended above against an impenetrable background many dozens of lighted windows, the homes, and further up a line where the stars began, jewels spattered over the jet-black sky-lid, and a sensation of extreme preparedness and expectation, as if every living soul in Lingmouth was waiting for the enemy who must never, no matter at what cost, be allowed to land and despoil. And up over the knuckle of the cliffs there was Paxcombe.

Yesterday he had longed to hear the bell summoning her crew to *Tigress*, but now the longing was mingled with dread.

He still felt the fury of hate, but now also the tidal wave of hate's opposite. Could your brainpan contain two such elements without bursting? When would the Spaniards come? At dawn?

What time was there? What days were left for love?

CHAPTER THIRTY-FIVE

He woke when the dawn sunlight was flooding the room, got up and dressed and went downstairs because he could not bear to stay in bed. The Cockleshell was very quiet. He wanted to talk to someone, but the only people about were an old man sweeping the hall and a girl laying tables in the dining-room, and when he greeted them they made short, polite replies. He wanted more than that. Why didn't they say what a beautiful morning it was, how it did them good to see someone come downstairs looking so happy? Might they ask the secret of such an appearance? Indeed they might. He could tell them in one word. He wanted to talk about her, he did not care to whom or how slight the inquiry. But neither the old man nor the girl gave him an opportunity, and he went into the street and walked down across the estuary bridge and round the harbour where women were setting up the panniers and the scrubbed tables, waiting for the morning catch. When the boats came in there would be plenty of buyers, the fish being sold straight from the nets, but now it was too early and there were only the table-setters and the smell of seaweed and tar fresh in the nostrils. It reminded him of San Corda.

As he passed along a woman bending over a trestle straightened up and turned towards him. She was poorly dressed with untidy hair and a face like a crab apple in autumn. For a moment she looked surprised, as if not expecting a passer-by at this time in the morning. Then in her eyes, the windows in a worn face, he saw a terrible expression that struck some chord of memory he could not recognize. He gave her good morning, and she stared at him, as at an apparition, and said in a toneless voice, "You taught him to shoot," and without waiting for a reply: "Sir Joshua said he was drowned trying to save his friends."

"Forgive me," said Tom. "I do not know your name."

"Dykes," she said.

He felt stunned. This was what the Sultan *would* have told her, and no doubt the mariners had been instructed to say the same. The mother must be protected, must never know the horror of Elizabeth Bay. And suddenly he recognized the eyes he had not remembered. They were Gertrude's eyes from his childhood, when she cried that Uncle Georges had died "fighting for his faith," and now, as then, Tom hoped that this mother was only aware of the fact and not the details. He said to her, "Your son was a very brave man. He did not think of himself."

"His father says he will kill the first Spaniard who comes. We shall all kill them. I shall kill them too."

"I know you will."

He left the frail old woman and walked on to where he could see the bonfire on the headland waiting to be lit, climbed the steep path and found two men beside the tall plinth of faggots and brushwood strapped to a pole. The men waited in relays, looking westwards for the smoke to rise from the next beacon. When the Lingmouth fire was lit the big bell in the square would boom out for *Tigress*. He chatted to the men, walked slowly back to the Cockleshell hoping it was time for breakfast, and when he saw the harbour glittering in the early light he thought of the dawn when Gostigo had disappeared into the sea. What would they tell Fernie's sister of the two she had lost? Or Jabbinoth's mother? *They died for your sake. Be worthy of them.* But the whole story of *Tigress* and all who had sailed in her was too much to comprehend. He could only realize his own story, and that was not finished.

The Harvyé family were at breakfast, and Sir Brian called out for him to join them, and he sat beside Kate, not able to turn and look at her, but in wonderful proximity, their hands touching now and then. He was planning what to do with this day. Sir Brian and Roland were going to the *Salvaterra* warehouse over some minor problem of revaluation, and Tom offered to take Kate to the dry dock where he had first seen *Tigress* below the waterline.

"What's in there now?" asked Roland.

"I don't know," said Tom, and turning to Kate, "But I expect there is something that would interest you."

"I have never seen a dry dock," she said.

At that moment a figure appeared at the doorway. It was topman Rogers. He came across and stood to attention in shipshape manner and said, "Sir Joshua's compliments, sir, and will you please report at once?"

Whatever now? *Tigress*, with Smolkin and a skeleton crew

281

sleeping on board, had been ready for sea all week. Tom stood up and put his hand on Kate's shoulder and said, "I'm sorry," and Sir Brian said, "She can come with us. We shall see you for dinner, I hope."

And so they did, but only after the forenoon had slipped away. There had been a duplication of medical supplies, a second crate had been delivered, and the Sultan wanted Tom to help Robert Seaton arrange and stow the new phials and bandages for maximum accessibility. It was unlikely they would be needed. The duty of *Tigress* was to stay out of trouble, to deliver her precious powder and culverin shot when required. She must not expose herself to Spanish gun-fire. But nothing was certain, and the Sultan was leaving nothing to chance. He never took chances if he could help it, that was why *Tigress* had come home in triumph, not failure.

The checking and stowage took the whole forenoon, and the forenoon was one third of the day. Robert Seaton did not seem to mind. In the den, the only part of the orlop not occupied with racks of shot, Tom asked him how he was enjoying his stay in the Viccars house, and Robert said, "The food's good. Jennie Viccars knows how to cook."

"She's a fine girl."

"Aye, she's a bonnie lass." But it was said without significance, and Tom supposed that Robert, the careful Scot, was biding his time with the seventeen-year-old Jennie who had looked such a startling companion on the evening of the *Tigress* feast.

When the checking was done Tom went up to the waist and found the Sultan standing at the gangway.

"Thank you, Tom. It had to be done." He looked across the harbour. "There is a time for everything. A time for battle and a time for love."

"Yes, sir."

"The battle comes first. Then we shall all be free to love."

"I understand."

"So do I, Tom. I know a smitten man when I see one."

"Sir?"

The Sultan gave a little smile. There was a majestic calm in his whole posture, as he had appeared so often on the half deck at morning prayers. "The girl is yours, and you are hers. I have

282

never found it myself, but I can see it in others. She will make a wonderful mistress of Paxcombe."

"Yes! I felt that the moment I saw her."

"I know you did."

"Was it so apparent?"

"It was. So go back to her. I shall not require you again today. Show her Lingmouth, all that we are fighting for. But Tom . . . don't go past the depot. They caught a cattle thief yesterday."

At dinner, with Tom and Kate mostly silent, an aura of tolerance seemed to hang over the table, and the brilliant Roland made no brotherly remarks, and the way Sir Brian spoke to his daughter reminded Tom of Chucunaquiok, and when dinner was finished Sir Brian said, "Roland and I must get back to the warehouse. We shall see you two for supper, I hope. They say the band is giving a performance this evening."

There was warm sunshine, and no smoke from the beacon, and Tom held her hand as he took her round to the dry dock. There was a noticeable flux of people going up towards the depot, but Kate did not ask why, and he did not tell her. He knew what the Sultan had meant. For sheep thieves it was usually the gallows, but for this cattle thief it would be the massive falling blade, a more spectacular deterrent. It would not be too quick. One end of a rope would be attached to the lynch-pin and the other end to the withers of a heifer standing beside the block. When the thief was in position, prone, unable to move but with a view ahead, knowing the blade was poised high above his neck, the heifer would be led slowly forward. The rope would be a hundred yards long or more, and while the coils unfolded any citizen within reach was expected to walk beside the rope and help take the weight. It was not necessary to do much pulling, a moment or two was enough, but by touching the rope you showed that you were on the side of law and justice, and the thief as he watched the rope uncurling would have time to reflect that the pin would be drawn by an animal of the same kind as he had stolen. When Tom was fifteen Lionel had taken him to this ceremony and they had laid hands on the rope.

At the dry dock there were few onlookers, and he stood with Kate at the rail where he had stood with Alis Dewmark. Now it

283

was not *Tigress* with her swollen body, but a small pinnace, her careening complete, the props still visible as the tide rose. The dock gates were open, and soon the pinnace would float and the props would be removed and she would be taken out into the estuary. There were no workmen with their oaths and hammers, only a soft lapping of water.

They slid their arms round each other's waist, and Kate said, "I'd heard about you, but I didn't know what you'd be like."

"I'd never heard of you. Sir Joshua said your father was bringing his clever son with him, not a word about you."

"When you saw me with Roland, who did you think I was?"

"Some beautiful girl he had brought from London. I was mad with envy. If your father hadn't caught me I would have run away."

"When he told you I was his daughter, you shouted at him!"

"I'd never been so pleased in all my life."

"I very nearly stayed at home," she said. "I don't know what made me come."

"Because you had to. It happens like that sometimes."

"You believe that, don't you?"

"Yes."

"So do I," said Kate.

The sun was still warm, but it was getting towards the west, and they watched the pinnace being taken into the estuary, then walked round the harbour past the fishing nets on the beach. It was not time for the afternoon catch, and the tables were empty. The dawn brightness had gone and there was stickiness in the air and the harbour smells seemed heavier. Soon it would be evening, and they fell silent, both perhaps for the same reason.

On the way back they talked about what they saw, the gulls and the rowing boats and the shapes in the high white clouds, and when they passed the wharf where *Tigress* lay alongside they stopped, and he said, "Would you like to come aboard?" and she said, "Not now. When you come back," and he remembered another voice saying, "If you come back, and if I am here," but Alis Dewmark and all he had felt for her seemed an echo from childhood. Kate would be here, he knew that. But first, hardly credible, *Tigress* must sail out against the unseen, unimaginable host of ships and men now somewhere beyond the horizon, approaching.

It was a strange tense evening at the Cockleshell. Tom washed and dressed with clean linen and when he came down visitors were gathering before supper. The band was going to play in the square, and everyone was thankful for a way to spend the evening. He waited for Kate. Sir Brian and Roland came, and they ordered a bottle of wine on the terrace, and Roland said, "You'll have to wait, she's making herself pretty." When she did come Tom felt the same shock as when he had first set eyes on her. She wore a royal blue dress with a billowy skirt and tight sleeves and a silvery high-necked bodice. Her face was ivory pale with a blush of bright cherry on the cheekbones, her full lips a darker red precisely outlined, her eyebrows slim and pencilled. Her hair was coiled up elaborately behind, and on top near the front fringe nestled a new moon of emeralds and pearls, with earring globes to match.

She said, "I'm sorry to have been so long," and Tom said, "It was worth waiting."

There was a long supper. The dining-room was full, and the mayor and his wife waved to them. There was salmon and widgeon and ox tongue and a creamy gooseberry syllabub and good claret, and afterwards the band played and everyone strolled in the square, Tom and Kate hand in hand, meeting mariners from *Tigress*, sitting on a bench with Robert and Jennie, talking with a most courteous Joshua Vine, watching the sky growing dark but with few stars as clouds formed in the breeze, and with every moment that passed Tom was wishing all these faces and voices would disappear, that he and she could be alone together with no one else. The band finished and the square began to empty. As they went into the Cockleshell he felt breathless with exasperation. His heart was pounding. He said quickly, "I *must* see you before we go to sleep." She did not answer, but gave a soft gasp and slipped her hand up and gripped his arm with a sudden spasm that almost hurt him.

There were others on the stairs, and when they reached her room he whispered, "Later. When it's quiet."

CHAPTER THIRTY-SIX

He waited at the window in his room, but tonight the stars had all vanished and the blackness overhead was a suffocating shroud that seemed to bear down, as if Lingmouth had been granted frivolity enough, and the black harbour had no sheen, and because it was late there was hardly a lighted home in the pall across the bay.

Each time he thought the footsteps in the corridor had ceased another sounded, but at last the inn settled into final silence, and when he went back to her room the door was on the latch and she was standing by the window in her nightgown, her hair an auburn cascade in the glimmer of a single candle beside the bed.

She stretched out her hands, and he closed the door and went to her, and she put her arms round his neck and they stood against each other for a long moment before they kissed. Her soft lips seemed to melt the soul from his body, and he drew her very close and stood locked in an amazement of thankfulness. Was this how you passed into another world? Then she pushed him gently away, and he took off his clothes, and when he turned she was naked on the bed, reaching for the candle.

In the warm darkness her body was the most beautiful thing he had ever held and her skin spoke to him when he touched it. Her hair was a quilt beneath or a tent falling round his shoulders, silky and thrilling. Her lovemaking was simple and fierce and utterly generous. At the climax she gave a cry of pain, and he whispered, "My precious! My sweet!" but she clung to him and stopped his words with kisses.

With the wildness gone they floated, arms linked on a limitless ocean of sun-kissed waves, no sail in sight to the horizon, murmuring the nothings of content. At last they turned facing the same way, she with her back to him, and he felt her body against his from top to toe, and her heel tapping his instep was a delight he had never dreamed of, and he slid one arm under her so that he could hold both breasts in his hands, and when they bent their legs he was her chair, and she sat against him, her shape to his, and he drifted to sleep wondering how he had ever slept all these years with his hands empty.

They woke in the early morning and made love again, but there was no pain. Another dawn had come with no bell to arms. The sun had no vigour on the pale bedroom walls, so perhaps there was cloud or haze, but certainly not the breath-taking dawn of yesterday. He did not get up to see.

He said, "What shall we do today, my love? I can't take you to Paxcombe, it is too far. But I want something special."

"Anything will be special."

"Like catching a mole?"

"A mole?"

"When I was a child," said Tom, "my mother took me to the horseshoe on the cliff, and we found a mole. He had a soft black furry skin and pink feet, and I wanted to take him home and keep him in a cage, but my mother said we must put him back, and he crawled away into the heather, and my mother kissed me and cried, she shed tears."

"You loved her," said Kate, "didn't you?"

"Yes, I did. And my father. I wish they could have known you, both of them. They would have been so happy for me."

"Yes, darling?"

"Yes, darling!"

And suddenly:

Boom! BOOM! *BOOM!*

Slow sonorous reverberations across the square.

He seized her and they clung cheek to cheek, limb to limb, as if they could never part.

"You won't go away?" he said.

"I shall be here for you."

"Promise?"

"Of course I promise."

"For ever?"

"For ever and ever."

As he dressed, the summons an imperious gong in his ears, Kate sat on the bed, naked, cloaked in her hair, hands clasped round up-drawn knees, silent, the slow tears welling down her cheeks.

Through the window he could see black smoke from the bonfire on the hill, the fist of England shaking up into a windy sky.

CHAPTER THIRTY-SEVEN

The Rockways headland gave some protection but as they came into the open sea and turned to the south-west the wind was almost dead against and all forenoon *Tigress* tacked her way first to get well clear of the coast and then to take course down channel, a slow zigzag making less than three miles of progress for every five she sailed. There was a strange uncertainty, the horizon blank, the coast dwindling to starboard, a sensation of blindfoldness, knowing that sometime, suddenly, somewhere ahead the ships would appear, but whose and how many and in what order was not known. There were no detailed instructions, simply that *Tigress* with her powderkeg belly and culverin-shot-filled orlop must on no account get within enemy range, but wait till one of the Queen's big ships detached herself from action and came for replenishment.

All day the Sultan stood at the mainmast, no Sirius beside him this time. Whatever happened *Tigress* must not get trapped inshore. It was probable that the English fleet would work to windward of the Spaniards and therefore be astern of them coming up the Channel. So *Tigress* must loop southwards and link up when the enemy had passed. Now the coast was a bare thread and all day the ship crept on and the lookouts aloft were silent.

That night there was little sleep. Tom and Robert had no watchkeeping duties, but in the cabin they could only rest fitfully. On deck they saw the black water slip by. The Sultan and Viccars and the new mate kept watch between them, snatching an hour's sleep in turn. The mate, Morris Turner, had been at San Corda, but now he seemed almost a stranger.

This was Saturday the 20th July.

Sunday dawned clear but the wind was still strong. All day they moved on, waiting, straining their eyes, listening. It was near sunset when far ahead with nothing in sight came the echoing rumble of gunfire. At first toylike in the distance, then stronger, then with puffs of smoke on the horizon, and at last the sudden appearance of masts and hulls just visible against the sun disc. As *Tigress* approached the sun sank and was gone, and while the light lingered the gunfire stopped, and the high rectangle outlines of Spanish galleons showed in the last gleams before dusk. *Tigress* kept course, passing a mile or two to the south, and the Spanish outlines ended, and there was a gap, and other lower shapes appeared, and *Tigress* was level with the Queen's ships.

That night she hove to, and in the morning saw the battle fleet ranged in a loose semicircle with cruisers and pinnaces in attendance, and at the south end *Ark Royal* with her double tier of main armament and the two lateen sails astern. Five miles to the east lay the clusters of the Spanish.

Tom did not know what to expect. How did sea battles begin?

But on this Monday the 22nd July there was no battle. The wind had dropped to a gentle breeze and both fleets held to their station. Between them lay the casualties of the Sunday fighting, three Spanish galleons crippled, their ammunition gone. These were not great ships, and during the day pinnaces from Howard's fleet took them away towards Dartmouth without interference. In the afternoon a Crown ship which the Sultan said was *Revenge* was seen approaching from the south with a towering Spanish ship, the wrecked carcass of a galleon. The *Revenge* moved away. A pinnace from *Revenge* crossed to *Ark Royal*. A skiff from the *Ark* crossed to the galleon, figures went aboard, returned to the flagship. The galleon was left floating like the stricken whale, only her topsails intact, her yards shattered, her whole superstructure charred and torn.

The same skiff came to *Tigress*, took the Sultan away, brought him back two hours later. He was in fine spirits. The Lord High Admiral had welcomed him. The orders were clear. Today was for rest. Tomorrow, granted wind, there would be fighting, and when it was over *Ark Royal* would need every culverin shot that *Tigress* could provide.

That night a great calm spread over the sea, and next day the wind came at dawn.

At first from the north-east, putting the Spaniards to windward of the English. To recover the wind the English came south, aiming to work round the Spanish flank. The Spaniards replied by turning south to intercept them.

That was how it looked from *Tigress* hovering further south out of gun range. A distant silent pageant in the early light. To the west a fanning semicircle of English ships, to the east a looser formation of taller, bulkier Spanish ships, the two fleets

289

first sighted some six miles apart but coming south on converging courses. Lord Howard had told the Sultan that the Queen's ships numbered two dozen of the first class with another thirty cruisers and armed merchantmen. The Spanish had at least twice as many of both classes. As *Tigress* circled in retreat the two fleets came on, their sails whitening as the sun rose, still in silence as the range between them narrowed.

The gunfire broke out in a few stabbing blasts, turning to a cataract of explosion. At first the battle lines could be distinguished, left against right, a field of spray-stalks growing round the ships as cannon shot fell short of target or beyond, the hits too distant to observe, but soon the gun smoke rolled a pall of drifting obscurity across the arena and from then on, as ships singly or in groups engaged one another, the clear conflict of left against right changed to a fluid pattern of section against section, less or more visible as the wind lulled or blew.

But always the roll of gunfire, waxing and waning, continuous.

The Sultan, standing with his officers at the *Tigress* mainmast, said, "You are envious, Mr Viccars."

"So I am, sir."

"And I too. But the Spaniards will be beaten for lack of shot. That was what Lord Howard said to me. They cannot replenish. We can. If *Tigress* can keep the guns of *Ark Royal* firing we shall have done more than we ever could in battle. It is annoying, Mr Viccars, but it is true."

And still the roll of guns without pause. Tom thought of the *Salvaterra* and how three broadsides had brought submission. But these trained fighting ships could not be taken from astern. There was no submission to be seen now, no galleons being led away on either side, all visible ships firing all the time. It was two hours since dawn. The wind had shifted to the east and now the weaving and twisting of vessels half hidden by smoke made judgement impossible. What splintered sides? What holes torn? What messdeck blood? All through the forenoon the cannonade went on. The *Tigress* hands were piped to dinner, but they were soon back on deck and aloft to watch the battle. In the afternoon the wind was from the south and the sound of gunfire changed to an incessant thudding like the booms of the night storm at Macaweo.

And now a single ponderous hulk detached herself from the

290

smoky indiscrimination and moved eastwards and turned her bows to the south. Her guns were not firing. Slowly her canvases furled. In the distance her masts could hardly be seen. As she rested alone, square and still, the Sultan exclaimed, "Look! She wants it hand to hand! She begs for it! *Come and board me!* What fools do they think they deceive? Watch and you will see! Look!"

A line of five English ships had followed the Spaniard and were turning south.

"It's the *Ark!*" cried the Sultan. "Now we shall see what the Lord High Admiral does with poison bait!"

Slowly the line came on, but not to board. As they passed a culverin distance from the target each in turn poured out her broadside. Then the line swung about and passed again with five more broadsides from their starboard guns. Now other Spanish galleons were moving to the rescue, and the English turned back into the central commotion.

The Sultan said, "She was out of shot! She gambled! Her soldiers paid dear!"

The army! Tom had almost forgotten it. As the afternoon wore on and the wind came from the west and the firing began to die down he thought more and more of the army that had been carried from Spain in their thousands, now waiting in their thousands to be landed on English soil. Where would they land? How many? Could they be stopped? What would happen when invaders burst into your home? All England feared for their homes. And he for Paxcombe, the home of his ancestors, and now his own, to share with his love.

Since the moment he boarded *Tigress* he had been totally aware of Kate invisible beside him whatever he was doing, on the way down channel, through every hour of gunfire, but he had forced himself not to picture her too clearly, not to think of the Kate he had touched but of the girl he had seen at the table and would soon see again. *Suddenly it is there and it fills your life.*

He was startled by a hand on his shoulder. "They have had enough for one day," said the Sultan. "Tomorrow we shall replenish the *Ark*. And, if God wills, fire a salvo or two ourselves."

So ended Tuesday the 23rd, and on Wednesday when the fleets were off the Isle of Wight the calm returned and *Tigress* delivered her full cargo of powder and shot to *Ark Royal*. A piece of pure seamanship, delicate after the blustering chaos of the day before. Tom watched with Robert from the poop. *Tigress* reducing sail, losing way, sliding in a sweet curve, coming alongside gently on to the fenders, flinging check lines, reined to a standstill. Derricks rigged on the *Ark*'s waist. Slings and iron-bound crates on *Tigress*. The shot passed up by hand, the slings and crates loaded, hoisted, swung safely into the hatches. The powder kegs following, slings only required. The operation took the whole forenoon. The Sultan was summoned aboard by Lord Howard, was seen speaking to him and returned to *Tigress*. The lines were cast off. *Tigress* slid free. A wave from the Lord High Admiral. A cheer from the crew of *Ark Royal*.

It was the end of *Tigress*'s service against the Spaniards. She had taken all the powder and shot that Lingmouth could provide. The Solent had its own pinnaces and ferry craft to bring ammunition from shore.

But not quite the end.

When the Sultan came back he repeated what Lord Howard had told him. That in the smoke and confusion of yesterday the damage to English ships had been unbelievably light. Two cruisers holed above the waterline and a dozen men killed in one of the auxiliaries, but the big ships of the Queen, standing away from the enemy, having guns of longer range and better performance, had received no injury. The Spaniards on the other hand had taken enormous quantities of iron on to their soldier-crowded decks. That the battle was as good as won now. And when the Sultan had expressed polite surprise Lord Howard said that the opportunity of landing an army had come and gone, that the Spaniards were committed to force on to the straits of Dover, that once there they would never return, that if the wind stayed in the south and west their only destiny was to be driven into the North Sea, chased up into some Hebridean obscurity.

Months later Tom remembered that prophecy, so weirdly accurate.

That afternoon *Tigress* turned back against the wind, moved slowly west, and the Sultan, ordering double lookouts, stood at the compass saying repeatedly, "God give us a chance. One chance."

When the sun was low the chance came.

* * *

Past the Needles, found all by herself ten miles from shore, there was another stricken galleon. Not so big as the galleon off Portland, but a cumbrous monster all the same, her mainsail in tatters, her treble row of gun-ports gaping with barrels at every angle, her side holed a dozen times, her forecastle and poop deserted, a red canvas screen torn and shredded still stretched along the waist. From behind that screen were supposed to leap the boarding parties in close combat. Their boarding days were over.

The Sultan ordered a careful approach, fired a warning saker. A white flag was hoisted on the galleon's mainyard. Viccars was told to prepare the demi-culverins. There was not much ammunition, but enough for this beaten enemy.

The *Tigress* circled with short sail, came nearer, at last to within hailing distance. The figure of an officer appeared on the forecastle. The Sultan went out on to the *Tigress* bowsprit and called, "I accept your surrender!"

The answer came with heavy accent, "No shot. We cannot fight."

"Say 'I surrender to the Queen of England.' "

"We have our honour."

"In the name of the Queen I order you to follow me!"

The man did not answer. Instead he shouted something over his forecastle rail. From behind the red screen twenty men rose up in line. They held muskets.

It was not to happen. It could not happen. They raised their muskets. An instant of eternity. A crackling volley. The sight of the Sultan poised. Falling. Stretched on the Bosun's Roost. Motionless.

As *Tigress* swung away her sakers and minions spat out, and a moment later the demi-culverins. Seamen scrambled to the Roost. They lifted him on to the forecastle. Robert Seaton bent over him, rose in silence.

Tigress emptied every shot she had into the swollen ugly monster. Every shot but four. There were cries and bloodshed on her decks. She was left with her dead and dying and her helplessness.

On *Tigress* they carried him down to the waist, fetched a winding sheet, laid him with the brass-bound Bible at his side. The ship's company filed past to salute the man who had

293

planned for them, given them faith, brought them home with riches. Who trusting himself had blown two gaping holes in the coffers of Spain, who trusting others had lost his life. He lay crusaderwise, his arms folded, his feet crossed because he had died in battle, only his head and hands visible, none touched by shot. The rest of him a bundle of bloodstained clothes. His small strong hands rested calmly on his chest, his amber eyes were closed and his trim-bearded face had an amused expression as if he had just said something remarkable.

They sewed him up with four good shot to take him safely down and placed him on the shelf.

Viccars read out . . . "teach us to number our days".

Joshua Vine, the Sultan, slipped into the sea he loved so much and *Tigress* turned for home in silence, without her soul.

CHAPTER THIRTY-EIGHT

At the top of the Rockways path Tom stopped to get breath. There was no way of saying the unsayable.

He pulled the iron bell rod. A far-off clanging. A man servant opened the heavy, creaking door.

Tom stood in the dim hall. The man shut the door and went down the kitchen passage. Emme Vine came to the top of the stairs with Sirius at her heels. Sirius bounded down to greet Tom. The bull mastiffs, Ham, Shem and Japheth, appeared beside Emme. They came down together, slowly.

She stood on the last step, "Where is he?"

Tom said, "I have a message for you. I would like you to—"

"Where is Joshua?"

The mastiffs stiffened to a standstill. Tom paused. He said as calmly as he could, "I have some serious news. You must prepare yourself."

"No!" Like a wail of the damned.

"I can only tell you—he was very brave and greatly loved. He—"

"You killed him!"

"That is untrue—"

"You took him away! He promised me he would not go! You took him! Japheth!"

294

The massive animal turned its head towards her, uncertain, his shoulders rippling with steel muscle.

"Shem! Ham!" She daggered a wild finger at Tom. "Kill! *Kill!*"

What had Joshua said? "They might understand, even in English." *Might!* But the three beasts made no move. They stood, glaring at him.

He swallowed, said in a deep voice, as near Joshua's as he could, "*Quieto! Quieto!*"

He took a very slow step towards the door.

"*Guarda! Guarda!*" shouted Emme.

The one called Japheth stalked towards him, the mouth a crack open, saliva dripping from the jowl.

"*Quieto!* Japheth—*Quieto!*"

Now the other two were bristling, their red-flecked eyes steady, their jaws sagging open in a ferocious yawn.

Of all dangers, of everything that had imperilled him since he stood in the hot colonnade at San Corda—none had been more dangerous than this. He thought of the red deer dismembered.

Suddenly Sirius, who had squatted frightened by the commotion, raised his nose, opened his mouth, and gave a tremulous, long-drawn howl.

In that moment, as Emme clutched her head and shrieked, as the three mastiffs turned startled towards the howling mongrel, Tom seized the door handle, wrenched open the door, was outside, the door slammed, was down the zigzag path, was not followed, could hear muffled the high-pitched yowl of Sirius, the deep baying of the mastiffs and the screams of Emme Vine.

CHAPTER THIRTY-NINE

He lay propped against the bole of the oak tree, and Kate further down with her head back on his chest. This way they could both watch the rolling white clouds over the sea. She had loosened her bodice and with his left hand he could reach the soft muscle at the top of her arm. His right hand held hers, and they rubbed thumbs together and watched the clouds. Perhaps they need never talk. Was there anything of importance that could not be said by fingers on skin?

295

They had left the horses with Finch. There was no hurry. Later they would walk up the grass slope and he would show her their home. Everyone would be waiting and he could imagine the welcome. In the autumn there would be a wedding, the show piece, and then he would bring her back to Paxcombe, as Lionel had brought Gertrude, as Kate's first-born son would bring his bride. And one day a small boy would say, "Tell me about grandfather Tom," and someone would say, "He went to sea with a pirate and brought back treasure and found your grandmother Kate. She was very beautiful. He is said to have loved her very much."

A time for battle and a time for love. On *Tigress* during the Tuesday battle he had not dared to remember her lovemaking. They were making love now. The warm satin of her arm was his love. The battle had passed, and the enemy would not return. There would be rejoicing in the harbour streets, and mourning. Lingmouth would know how to salute her greatest son.

He had not spoken to Kate about the Sultan. That could wait. These moments were dewdrops on the grass before the day began.

The sea was a carpet of small grey waves, the sun hidden now in gentle cloud. Gulls floated at the cliff top. There was perfume from the bushes in the horseshoe.

The clouds kept changing shape, now an old man puffing his cheeks, now a dragon with a twisted tail.

There was a parting, not big, just enough to let through a handful of sunshine that moved towards them across the laughter of the waves.